HER
Greatest
MISTAKE

GREATEST LOVE SERIES BOOK 1

FROM THE LIBRARY OF

HANNAH COWAN

ISBN: 978-1-990804-11-3

Special Edition

Edited and Proofed by Sandra @oneloveediting

Cover Design by Booksandmoods @booksnmoods

Interior chapter designs by Jordan Burns @joburns.reads

Dedicated to all my curvy girls. Our self-worth is not dictated by a number on the scale. Here's to finding a man who would love you at a thousand pounds.

Playlist

Mary's Song (Oh My My My)— Taylor Swift ♥ 3:33

Leave A Light On — Tom Walker ♥ 3:06

F-150 — Robyn Ottolini ♥ 2:49

That Ain't Me No More — Matt Stell ♥ 3:12

Breakups — Seaforth ♥ 3:43

Thnks fr th Mmrs — Fall Out Boy ♥ 3:24

Grew Apart — Logan Mize, Donovan Woods ♥ 2:50

Totally — Madden, Jon Eyden ♥ 3:18

Hate You Like I Love You — Granger Smith ♥ 2:54

London — Filmore ♥ 2:44

Missing You — CHASE WRIGHT ♥ 2:48

Friends — Chase Atlantic ♥ 3:50

Wasted Summer — teamwork, Loote, John K ♥ 2:49

lights — elijah woods ♥ 2:55

back to you — Alexander Stewart ♥ 2:50

You're Still The One — Shania Twain ♥ 3:32

Nothing Hurts Like Goodbye — SLANDER, Kiiara ♥ 3:22

Livin' On A Prayer— Bon Jovi ♥ 4:09

Over You — Daughtry ♥ 3:25

Forget Me — Lewis Capaldi ♥ 3:23

This Love (Taylor's Version) — Taylor Swift ♥ 4:10

I Feel Like I'm Drowning — Two Feet ♥ 3:06

After You — Gryffin, Jason Ross, Calle Lehmann ♥ 3:45

Family Trees
CHARACTER ORIGINS

SWIFT HAT-TRICK TRILOGY

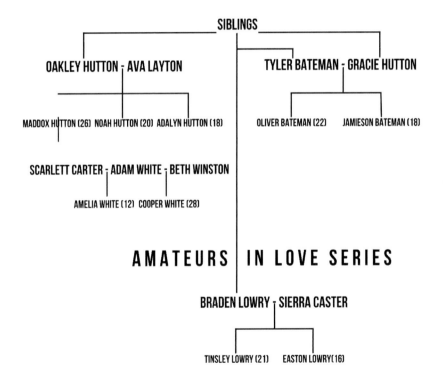

SIBLINGS

OAKLEY HUTTON ˥ AVA LAYTON   TYLER BATEMAN ˥ GRACIE HUTTON

MADDOX HUTTON (26) NOAH HUTTON (20) ADALYN HUTTON (18)   OLIVER BATEMAN (22)   JAMIESON BATEMAN (18)

SCARLETT CARTER ˥ ADAM WHITE ˥ BETH WINSTON

AMELIA WHITE (12) COOPER WHITE (28)

AMATEURS | IN LOVE SERIES

BRADEN LOWRY ˥ SIERRA CASTER

TINSLEY LOWRY (21)   EASTON LOWRY (16)

Authors Note

Hi, everyone! I wanted to make sure that before anyone jumps into this story that you know Her Greatest Mistake is the first installment in a second-generation series. This means that there will be a heavy helping of characters involved in this story, both new and from the previous stories. Keeping that in mind, I have written this as a standalone to the best of my ability.

In addition, this story and its plot revolves a lot around the inner workings of being a professional athlete. If sports romance novels that are heavily focused on said sport are not for you, I recommend not reading further.

If I am a new author to you and you are interested in reading the books prior to this one, I have included a recommended reading list. If not, I have also added a family tree.

For a list of content warnings, please see my website.

https://www.hannahcowanauthor.com/hergreatestmistake

Reading Order

Even though all of my books can be read on their own, they all exist in the same world—regardless of series—so for reader clarity, I have included a recommended reading order to give you the ultimate experience possible.

This is also a timeline-accurate list.

Lucky Hit (Oakley and Ava) Swift Hat-Trick trilogy #1

Between Periods (5 POV Novella) Swift Hat-Trick trilogy #1.5

Blissful Hook (Tyler and Gracie) Swift Hat-Trick trilogy #2

Craving the Player (Braden and Sierra) Amateurs in Love series #1

Taming the Player (Braden and Sierra) Amateurs in Love series #2

Vital Blindside (Adam and Scarlett) Swift Hat-Trick trilogy #3

PROLOGUE

Maddox

AGE SEVENTEEN

Soft, tight black curls tickle my throat, and the hard wooden planks beneath me have made my ass numb. Slivers from the unsanded, worn-to-shit wood bite into my exposed thighs, but Braxton's fruity perfume blows in the wind, helping mask the discomfort with something *so* damn good. Something that has my heart thumping hard inside my chest.

My best friend is curled into my side, sitting beside me against one of the walls of the tree house my dad and uncles built for my siblings and me when we were just kids. We've spent the past two hours pretending our curfews don't exist and praying for the rainstorm predicted on the weather radar to hit Vancouver and trap us in here.

I keep waiting for my mom to come running outside, yelling at me to drive Braxton back home before our parents ream both our asses, but it's been silent. I'm the only one in our friend group to have my license yet, and I've been known to use that to my advantage—conveniently "forgetting" to bring Brax back home on time just to wrangle a few more minutes with her.

Braxton never pushes me to bring her back, so I keep my mouth shut. Happily, at that.

"I can almost hear you thinking," she says, turning her face into my shoulder and heaving a sigh. I hold back a shiver.

"If you focus, I'm sure you could slip right inside my head."

She hums. "You would think so, but you're guarded up tight tonight. What are you thinking about?"

"You."

I don't know whether to laugh or cry when she doesn't seem surprised by my blunt reply. If anything, she seems comforted by it because her body shifts closer to mine. She grips my shirt in her fist, right over my heart.

With a swallow, I adjust my hold and slip my arm around her back, brushing the curve of her hip with my fingertips before resting my hand safely on her bent knee. My hockey jacket is splayed out beneath her, keeping her bare legs protected from the wood. We used to have blankets in here, back when our other best friend, Cooper, would hang out with us up here, but he graduated high school two years before us, and Mom has since cleaned up the tree house, thinking we would have gotten too old to hang out in here.

In a sense, she's right. We haven't played in this tree house since we were thirteen, but I'll continue to take Braxton up here every damn day for the rest of my life if it means we can be like this. It's easy to forget the rest of the world when we're within these walls, protected from the outside world.

"What about me are you thinking about?" she asks softly.

I drag my thumb over her knee. Back and forth, back and forth. What I want to say is too much, even if I think she already knows. Everyone does.

"Have you chosen a school yet?"

"No. There are too many."

"It's because you're brilliant. Every school wants you."

Her lips brush over where my neck and shoulder meet, and I

grind my teeth together to keep from groaning. Does she know she's doing these things? Or is it all subconscious?

"Thank you. I haven't chosen where I want to go yet."

"I always pictured you at some prestigious school in Ontario or Quebec, but you hate big cities, and your French sucks."

She pinches my chest. I laugh. "My French is better than yours."

"*Tais-toi.*"

"Funny. How long did you practice that one?"

I shrug. "Long enough to know I wasn't cut out to speak another language."

Her fingers release my shirt as she opens her hand and presses it against my sternum. "*Je ne veux pas te quitter,*" she mutters.

My brows drip. "I don't know what that means."

"The draft is coming up. Soon, you'll be gone regardless of where I choose to go to school." She changes the subject. My French is crap, but even I know that isn't what she said.

"So come with me. Find a school close to wherever I end up."

She shakes her head. "I can't chase you."

I shove a hand through my hair before removing my arm from around her and twisting my body so we're facing each other. My legs are long, and my muscles are too tight from my workout this morning, so I have to stretch them out along her sides, forcing her to sit with me wrapped all around her. Placing my hands on her bent knees, I lean close.

"Then let me chase you." I press my thumb to her bottom lip, feeling how soft and warm it is. How kissable her mouth must be . . . "I'll follow you anywhere. No matter what, I'll make it happen."

Her electric-blue eyes hold my stare with expertise, trapping me in her bubble. "I don't doubt that for a minute."

"Promise me something," I whisper, dropping my forehead to hers. Our noses brush ever so slightly. God, I'm breathless.

"Anything," she replies instantly.

I press my mouth to the corner of her soft lips and exhale. "Be my best friend forever. No matter what. Even when we fight or the distance between us grows. Promise you'll fight for us as hard as I will."

"I promise," she lies.

1

Maddox

PRESENT, AGE TWENTY-SIX

MY THIGHS BURN, THE MUSCLES TIGHT AND HEAVY WITH FATIGUE, but I don't slow down. If anything, the pain only pushes me to pick up my pace. In a blink, I'm shaking off the two Vegas Crowns players trying to tag team me and driving toward my target.

A smirk twists my mouth when I catch one of their defensemen by surprise and poke the puck out from right in front of him as he tries to clear it from their zone. Arrogance brightens my disposition as I bump his shoulder a bit harder than necessary and take off, leaving him spitting my name through his mouthguard. It's my second breakaway of the game. *Fuck yeah.*

Drops of sweat fall from my forehead and hang off my eyelashes as I close in on the goalie, his six-five frame doing a great job of blocking the net. Travis MacAvoy is one tough son of a bitch, but he's also weak on the glove hand. It's been a running joke with the team since we got on the plane and flew to Vegas yesterday. *Travis MacAvoy couldn't even stop a beachball.*

We've kicked Vegas ass tonight—leading by three with ten

minutes left to play. The rumours about good ol' Travis have held up, but with my sights set on that sweet spot of netting peeking out from behind his left shoulder, I ache to test the theory again.

I calm my breathing and flash a smile at the crowd before tightening my grip on my stick and snapping a shot off. It all happens so fast, just how I like it. The goal horn blares at the same time I quickly turn my skates to the side and come to a stop at the boards behind the net, snow flying.

The fans are silent, disappointment pungent in the air, and it only makes me smile wider. I wave a gloved hand at the ones sitting behind the boards, dripping in black and gold, their scowls etched deep. One bulky guy with a receding hairline and Vegas tattoos on his cheeks flips me the bird and boos loudly, encouraging the people close by to do the same. The sound spreads through the arena, and I soak it in, loving every second.

A body crashes into me from behind, and I laugh when my left winger and good friend, Bentley Daniels, claps the top of my helmet and jostles me around.

"Quickest shot in the league, baby!" he shouts in my ear.

There's nothing to do but grin and let the remaining Vancouver Warriors players on the ice join in on the celebration. The adrenaline in my blood cools as we break apart and I head to the bench, swinging my body over the boards. A water bottle is handed to me, and I grab it with a dip of my head before squirting the cold liquid all over my face and into my mouth.

The game clock ticks down as our second line works to keep the puck away from Vegas. The home team pulls their goalie with a minute left in the game, and Coach smacks me on the back as our lines switch again. I head back out to the ice and roll my shoulders as my linemates fall beside me and get into position, prepared to help our goalie secure his eleventh shutout of the season.

"Ready?" I ask them both as we set up for a faceoff.

On my left, Bentley grins wickedly while Logan Hart nods on

my right. I rest my stick across my thighs, pushing down on it as I bend at the waist, and then tap the heel of my skate on the ice three times.

I nod. "Bring it home, boys."

FRESHLY SHOWERED, I sit between Bentley and one of our best defensemen, Colt Warner, at a table in the media room with a microphone, a bottle of water, and a sea of reporters in front of me. The game ended half an hour ago, and like usual, we're the first players out of the dressing room.

The flashing lights make my skin itch, but after spending the past seven years in front of this level of media, it's become less terrifying. Everyone wants to talk to the captain, even when he would rather be anywhere else.

Bentley finishes answering a question about our next game and what we're hoping to accomplish—a win, obviously—when another reporter speaks up. He stands and introduces himself from one of the bigger sports reporting websites while I give him my attention.

"Maddox, can you describe how it feels to have another four-point game?"

Two goals and two assists. I clear my throat and rest my elbows on the table, leaning toward the mic. The reporter is familiar, like most of them are at this point. He wears an easygoing smile, and it helps settle the nerves I can't seem to get to piss off.

"It feels good. I have amazing teammates that help me get the job done," I answer.

He nods and glances down at his notes before meeting my stare again. "Any updates on your plans for next season?"

"Not any we're ready to share yet." I cover the slight bite in my words with a smile.

Again, he nods and sits back down. Another reporter is chosen, this time a woman with narrowed, calculating eyes. I straighten my posture.

"Rose Carpenter from Sports Weekly," she introduces herself, her tone sharp. I subtly lift my brow, feeling cautious. "Maddox, the fans are growing restless. Are you sure you don't want to say anything about your upcoming plans this off-season? Clear the air?"

I swallow down my discomfort. "The air doesn't need clearing yet. We still have a season to finish here. That's where my head is at."

Talks about my upcoming contract aren't the media's business, as far as I'm concerned. But I do understand the fans' curiosity. Vancouver is my home. Of course I want to stay here. My agent knows that. Everything else is beyond my control. There's still a lot more hockey to play this season, including the playoff spot we clinched a couple of weeks ago. The playoffs start in just over a week, and the team is ready. Hungry.

"Despite the rocky start to your career, I'm sure the other teams are frothing at the mouth for a chance to have you. Thank you for the time."

The woman sits down, and I grit my teeth. The dig was obvious, and I don't like it.

Despite that, I plaster on a smile and thank her before the pressure is finally shifted to the other guys. My skin is hot as frustration bubbles beneath the surface. When will the past stop haunting my present and future?

As far as I'm concerned, what happened after I was drafted is in my rearview. I don't dwell on it—I use it as motivation. As a reminder not to trust so easily.

Having it hinted at in front of my teammates and several media outlets isn't ideal. It's outright annoying. It doesn't matter how many hundred-point seasons I have or how many times I've nearly brought the Warriors to the Stanley Cup finals, I'll always be Maddox Hutton, the guy with the stick up his ass and his nose in the air.

The guy who passed on his draft team because he felt like he was "too good" for them. Assholes know nothing.

I suck in a breath when someone kicks my ankle bone beneath the table. Bentley is staring at me with a barely contained smile as I take in the emptying room.

His bleached blond hair has been freshly buzzed, and he's freshly shaven, like always. Personally, I think he just likes to show off his jawline because he knows it's his best feature, but while he might be vain sometimes, he's not vain enough to admit that out loud.

"Time to go," he says, patting my shoulder.

"Tell me I wasn't sitting here staring off for too long."

"Nah. You're good."

Thank fuck.

I push my chair back and walk beside him out the back door. Colt is waiting in the hallway, leaning against the wall with his arms crossed. He pushes off and settles on my other side.

"That chick was harsh," he notes, a slight Nashville twang brushing the words. It was only last season that he was traded to the VW from Nashville. He spent six years there.

Bentley grunts, "Must be new."

We walk into the dressing room and break apart to grab our shit. I throw my bag over my shoulder, swallowing a groan at the weight of it. "There's no reason to worry about where I'm going next season. The VW have been open about wanting to keep me."

"Why wouldn't they want you? You're in your prime." Bentley pulls his phone out of his bag and starts typing. "Wanna share an Uber back to the hotel? I'm fucking exhausted."

"Sure," I say. I'm running on goddamn fumes. A good long sleep sounds like heaven.

"You aren't coming out tonight?" Colt scoffs, bag in hand, when he joins us. "You're not taking an Uber. I'll take you back."

A few other players are still hanging around the room, but most of everyone is long done. This is our fourth away game in a row, and I know we're all ready to go home. My mom has been texting me about an overdue family dinner for the past few days, and I know I won't hear the end of it until I give her what she wants. Plus, I miss her food. Restaurants have nothing on Ma's baked potatoes and Dad's steak.

Bentley pushes the door open at the back entrance of the arena, holding it wide for us as we step into the underground parking garage designated for players only. Colt's rented Escalade is up a few yards, the windows dark, too dark to see into, and lifted just enough to appear big and beefy. I half expected to see an old truck in the Escalade's place.

"Hell no. All I want is a hefty serving of Chinese food and a good porno."

I throw my head back and laugh. "Fuck off."

Bentley shrugs. "What?"

"You're going to watch a porno instead of going out and getting laid?" Colt asks, bewildered.

"That still surprises you? We all know little Bentley here is shy when it comes to women," I tease.

Bentley deadpans, "Ha-ha. Hilarious."

Colt groans. "Whatever. Have fun spending your night with your hand and a pervy pizza delivery guy instead of free beer at a bar with your friend."

"Your taste in beer is revolting." I shudder for good measure.

Colt reaches out and tries to swat at my balls, but I quickly step out of reach, roaring a laugh. "Nuh-uh. Not the family jewe—fuck!"

I stumble forward when Bentley sticks his leg out behind me and presses his foot to the back of my knee. With my arms out to catch my fall, I hit the hood of Colt's SUV, and the alarm blares. I slant Bentley a withering glare over my shoulder as he howls in amusement, his hands on his knees. Tears make his blue eyes twinkle.

Colt is leaning on the driver's door of the SUV, his eyes squeezed shut as he wheezes and presses a button on his key fob that turns off the alarm. "Get in the . . . SUV . . . Maddox. I'll drop you both . . . off," he says between laughs.

I glower. "Fuck you."

"I need the security footage of that," Bentley says breathlessly. He shoots his hands up in the air and stares off dreamily while spreading them apart slowly. "*Maddox Hutton stumbling out of the arena after a win. Drunk or just unbalanced?* I can see it now."

Rolling my eyes, I push off the hood and walk around to the passenger seat of the Escalade before pulling it open. "Get in the car."

"Lighten up, sweetheart," Colt teases with extra twang in his voice. "You made my damn night. Thank you."

"Always aiming to please," I grumble, folding my large frame into the SUV. The dark interior is hot to the point of discomfort. "Hurry up. I'm going to pop like a popcorn kernel in a microwave if I sit here without A/C any longer."

Colt opens the driver's door and grins when he gets in, dropping his keys in the cup holder. He presses the engine start button, and I groan as the warm air starts to blow, trying to cool down.

"Good, princess?" he teases.

I tip my head back and close my eyes. "Yeah. Let's get out of here."

Bentley gets in the back seat, and we do just that.

2

Maddox

My head is groggy as I try to hide from the shrill sound blasting through my room. Burrowing my head into my pillow, I reach one lead arm out toward my nightstand and smack my hand around until I find my phone. Only a handful of people know my phone number, so if someone's calling in the middle of the night, it's important.

I answer the call and grumble a rough "Hey."

"Hi. I'm sorry, Dox. I know you just got home today, but it's Noah."

The fear in my little sister's voice has me pushing up in bed, sleep be damned. I blink to clear my vision and shove a hand through my hair. The sky is dark through the floor-to-ceiling windows that line my bedroom, and when I pull my phone from my ear and look at the time, I see it's just past 2:00 a.m. My stomach rolls.

"What happened?"

"He's at Ralph's." Adalyn sighs, the sound shaky. "You know he won't call Dad for help, and my car is in the shop. It has to be you."

I'm already out of bed and stepping into a pair of jeans by the time she finishes. In a few hurried steps, I'm walking through the penthouse, not bothering to turn on a light as I go. Ralph's isn't a place for Adalyn. It's a shithole bar for addicts and men I wouldn't want within viewing distance of my sister. The thought alone of her wandering around trying to find our brother is enough to have my blood boiling.

"When did he call you?"

"Only a couple of minutes ago. I called you once he hung up on me."

"Okay. It's good you called me. Go back to bed, Addie. I'm on my way."

"Thank you. Text me after."

"Will do." I grab my wallet and keys from the dish on the kitchen island.

She's silent for a beat too long. "Don't bring him back home tonight. Mom doesn't need to see it."

I close my eyes and pinch the bridge of my nose. "He shouldn't have called you. This isn't your mess. *Noah* isn't your mess."

"He's not anyone's mess. He's our *brother*, and I would rather him call me for help than stumble home and get hit by a car," she snips, and I can picture the sharp twist of her mouth as she scowls at the phone.

"He's barely twenty years old. It isn't okay for this to be happening. Mom and Dad need to take care of it. I'll pick him up tonight and bring him home with me, but I can't keep letting him piss his life away." A sniffle on the other side of the call has my steps faltering on my way into the private elevator. Guilt rips through me, and I soften my voice. "I'll handle it, yeah? I promise."

"He was excited when he called this afternoon. Said he was playing a gig tonight," she whispers.

I press the button on the wall for the main floor and exhale when the elevator starts moving.

Noah is a great musician. He has been since he was old enough to pick up his first instrument. It's just a shame he's wandered from that pretty path and ended up in a pit of quick-sand that keeps pulling him deeper and deeper every day. At this rate, it won't be long until he's sunk so far he won't be able to breathe. That's the day I fear the most.

"I'm sure he was. I'm leaving the penthouse now. I'll text you when we get back. Try not to make yourself sick worrying about us, okay?"

"I'll try. I love you."

"I love you too. Get some sleep," I order.

"Yeah, I'll try. Bye."

"Bye."

The elevator doors open as I shove my phone in my pocket and walk into the lobby. It's quiet, empty besides the security guard leaning against the front desk, scrolling through his phone. He looks up and gives me a nod as I walk past, and I return the gesture, albeit stiffly.

I step outside the building and just stand there, right in front of the glass doors, as the warm breeze runs over me. My head falls forward, and I release a tight breath.

"What have you done this time, Noah?"

RALPH'S IS a hole-in-the-wall bar in a part of town I wasn't familiar with until the first time I picked Noah up here. It's on a deserted road littered with closed businesses, all of which have boarded-up windows and Keep Out signs plastered to the doors. It's a place you don't go to unless your plan is to run away and hide from life. And when it comes to my brother, he wants to hide from everything. Not from fear like most assume, but because he just simply doesn't want to be around anyone.

There's only one person Noah has ever wanted to spend time with, and she lives across the country.

I lock my truck doors twice for good measure—even if it wouldn't be hard for someone to break into it if they wanted to badly enough—and start up the sidewalk. The drunks stumbling around outside of the brick building make my stomach churn as I brush past them. The air stinks like smoke and vomit, and needles are scattered across the concrete. If Dad knew I was here . . .

"Uh-oooh, the fun police is here!" one of the men slurs as I push past him. He's vaguely familiar, but not enough I can recall his name.

His bony fingers wrap around my wrist before I can create enough distance between us, and I slowly look down at where he's holding me before moving my eyes up to his. "What are ya gonna do? Arrest me? I remember you from last time."

"I doubt you remember what you ate for breakfast this morning."

I get a good view of him when he steps closer, shaking slightly. His pupils are black dots the size of one of the needles on the ground, and his lips are cracked and bloody. It's hard to keep my face neutral, but by some miracle, I do.

"Let go of me," I say calmly.

"Where's the please?"

I tense up when someone else moves to stand beside me, but a brief sideways glance is enough to know it's Noah. Still, I don't relax. I won't until we're far from this place.

"Let go of him," Noah orders gruffly. His voice is cold enough to make me shiver. He's detached, more so than normal.

"We're leaving." I rip my arm from the drunk and start to shove my brother down the sidewalk, away from that damned place. He doesn't fight me on it. He never does. "Where's your guitar? You don't have it."

"I smashed it."

"You smashed it?"

"Yep."

"Why?"

"I just did."

I halt on the sidewalk a few yards from the truck, my mind reeling. Noah notices I've stopped walking and turns to face me.

It's my first real look at him since he popped up beside me, and the distant look in his eyes makes my heart ache. His black hair is long, curling at the ends that brush the sides of his tattooed neck. It's pushed back and out of his face by a white checkered bandana. There's a slight flush to his cheeks, and his eyes are bloodshot.

"What are you on right now? Are you drunk?" I ask.

He stares at me, unblinking. "I never asked you to come here."

"Don't start, Noah. If you start this conversation right now, you won't like how it ends. Tell me what you took."

Finally, he blinks. "Our sister worries about me too much. She shouldn't have told you anything."

"She's eighteen, Noah. The last thing she should be worrying about is her brother getting fucking stabbed in some shithole bar because he's gotten high and picked a fight with the wrong person. What did you expect her to do when you called her for help at two in the morning?"

My pulse is racing, straining against my throat. This isn't normal. This isn't what should be happening to my brother. How did we even get here?

"I never asked her for help. I only called to tell her I was coming home. She texted me too many times tonight asking if I was okay, and I wanted to settle her."

"If that's the case, then you're an even bigger fucking idiot than I thought. She knew something was wrong the minute you called her. Now, get in the truck. We'll talk about this in the morning." I press the button on the key fob, and the truck's headlights flood the street.

"I smoked pot, and I'm a bit drunk. But I'm not an addict. The hard stuff doesn't appeal to me," he says. In a swift movement, he pulls a small baggie from his pocket and shakes it between us. A dark green, herby substance jumps around inside.

I shove my hands in the pockets of my jeans and lean back on my heels. He seems sincere, so damn sincere. I've never seen my brother take hard drugs, but hanging out in places like this and making risky choices . . . it makes it hard to believe him.

Noah has always been quiet and reserved. He wasn't a happy kid, and he only got worse when he hit puberty. I've seen him smile a handful of times in my entire life, and not one has been aimed at me.

"Put that away. And I'm trying to believe you, Noah, but fuck," I manage to say.

He puts the bag back in his pocket. "I was here for a gig."

"Addie told me."

He darts his eyes to the opposite side of the street. "It went fine. I hate it here, but it was a gig."

I nod. "Why did you smash your guitar?"

Suddenly, he's staring at me again, more focused than before. Fear flashes across his face when his eyes travel to the street behind me, and a feeling of desperation floods my system. I don't want him to close himself off from me right now.

He shakes his head, narrowing his eyes on something behind me. "Let's go."

"Tell me why you smashed your guitar. Please. Don't shut down now," I beg.

"Get in the truck, Dox. Now," he snaps.

Confused at his change in demeanour, I turn to follow his line of sight and curse under my breath.

There's a Hulk-sized man storming toward us, his snowshoe-sized hands balled into fists and long blond hair blowing in the breeze like a goddamn supermodel. One look at the fury on his face is enough to have me making a beeline for the driver's side of my truck.

"Noah Hutton!" the Hulk-man growls, his voice suddenly too close for my liking.

As soon as I spin back around to look for him, I find Noah shoved up against the hood of the truck, his shirt bunched in the man's fists.

"Get your hands off of me," Noah snarls.

I rush toward them, fear making me move faster than normally possible. I'm a big guy, but I'm nothing compared to the guy pulling my brother off the hood before slamming him back down again, harder this time.

"Not until you give me back the money." He reaches up with one hand and grabs a fistful of Noah's hair, pulling on it until his head flies back and the back of it smashes against the truck.

Suddenly, our size difference doesn't matter. Before Noah has a chance to collect his bearings from the impact, I'm kicking the back of the guy's knee and yanking him away from him by the back of his black T-shirt. I only manage to stun the Hulk-man for a few brief seconds because before I have a chance to move out of the way, a fist is flying at my face at the speed and force of a fucking semi-truck.

"The money is mine. I earned it," Noah says calmly.

Blood spurts from my nose, dripping down my front and staining my shirt and sweatpants. My eyes are unfocused, my face throbbing, but this isn't the first time I've been punched in the face, and it won't be my last.

Spreading my lips in a grin, I say, "I expected more from a guy your size."

The next hit comes at my gut, and the air whooshes out of me as his knuckles make impact, knocking me off-kilter. Still, I don't curl up and protect myself; instead, I ignore my instincts and spit a ball of blood and saliva into his face.

Noah's quick to interfere then. "Fuck. If you want the money that bad, then take it."

Something hits the ground beside my feet, but I don't take my eyes off the man in front of me. I hold his gaze, adrenaline making me reckless.

"You gonna get that, or should I?" I ask.

Tearing his eyes away from me, he glances at whatever fell beside us and, after a few seconds, gives me a final shove against the hood and lets me go to pick it up.

I catch a flash of white from down the street as a car door slams shut, closely followed by another. Footsteps pound the pavement.

Fuck. My. Life.

"Okay, big guy. Take your money and go," I say, trying to keep hold of the panic starting to swarm.

"If I see either of you here again, I'll kill you," he warns us.

Rage brews in Noah's dark eyes at the threat, and even if I know he would never hurt me, fear tries to spark anyway. He doesn't say anything to the guy, just stands in place and watches him like he's thinking of ways to make him disappear, never to be found again. Finally, the man turns and leaves, his hands still in fists.

My body hurts, but I ignore the pain as I push away from the hood and lift the neck of my T-shirt to wipe away some of the blood from my face. "We need to leave. Reporters are here."

"And they've already seen you," Noah says.

"Yep."

He puts his arm around my shoulders and pulls me up straight. "We need to get out of here. Now."

Nodding, I pull the keys from my pocket. "How did they know I was here?"

"You were getting your ass kicked by the bouncer. You're not a nobody here. Not in this city."

I want to scream when the footsteps get closer and closer and their voices start to break through our bubble. Noah's eyes are wild as he starts to lead me to the driver's side. His help only makes things look worse, but I'm not going to turn it away.

"What are you doing here, Maddox? Who was that man?"

"What happened here? Is this a drug deal gone bad?"

Lights flash in my eyes as the men rush forward, taking photos and trying to shove their recording devices in my face.

They move in closer as questions keep coming, but I ignore them all. I'm doing everything that I should be in this situation, but there's no reassurance in that.

I'm outside of a shithole bar, bloody and battered after getting my ass beat by some steroid-pumping bastard. The minute this story breaks, I'm in deep shit. The real story won't matter now. When it comes to the press, it rarely ever does.

Noah grunts at the reporter as he opens the truck door for me. My hands are shaky as I climb inside. He shuts the door before going around the back of the truck and climbing inside the passenger side.

I start the engine and grip the steering wheel tight. Lights continue to flash through the windshield as the reporters stand in front of us, blocking the way out.

"Honk at them. Make them move," Noah snaps, voice like a whip. The tattoos on his fingers strain with how tight he's squeezing his knees.

I do, and they jump out of the way, continuing to snap their pictures. Without hesitation, I pull away from the curb and onto the street.

"I'm in the middle of signing an extension with Vancouver," I rush out. "This is a nightmare."

"You'll be fine," he grunts.

I want to laugh and maybe even cry a little as I say, "No. I'm fucked."

3

Maddox

On Monday morning, my agent is silent at my side as we walk down the hallway toward the Vancouver Warriors owner's office. My stomach is doing somersaults, and I have to swallow profusely to keep the protein shake I chugged on the way to the arena from coming back up.

On the outside, I look cool and calm, but on the inside, I'm a nervous mess. We're headed right for shark-infested waters, and I'm bleeding buckets.

"Say something," I mutter, slanting a look at Dougie. The man has aged heavily in the time I've known him, but considering he was my father's agent and has been around our family for pretty much my entire life, it was bound to happen.

At fifty years old, Douglas Trelix is the best of the best. I'm lucky to have him on my side, even if he can be a real hard-ass when I need him to be anything but.

"That's one hell of a shiner you got there."

"You should see the bruise on my stomach."

Somehow, my nose isn't broken, but it's fucking ugly. My bruised right eye and sore abdomen made sleep last night nearly impossible. I think I lay in bed staring at the ceiling for a few hours before I finally managed to pass out just before the sun came up.

"Don't say anything when we get in there unless absolutely necessary. We both know how you can get," Dougie says.

"What's that supposed to mean?"

"You know damn well what it means. You can get real defensive, and now is not the time."

I blow out a harsh breath and come to a stop, turning to face him. My fingers curl before I shove my hands in the pockets of my slacks. "So, I'm not supposed to defend myself? I didn't do anything wrong last night. Even you can admit that."

"It doesn't matter what I think. You saw the articles this morning. Have you checked your Instagram? You've been trending since the first photo leaked. Nobody knows the real story but you, me, and your family. Everyone else sees the best player in the NHL spending a night out getting beat up in front of a dirty bar littered with used needles with his little brother. The same brother who they happened to catch throwing a wad of cash on the road and who was arrested for starting a brawl in that same bar a month ago."

"Noah doesn't need to be involved in this," I say sternly.

Dougie laughs humourlessly. "Too late. Now, get your ass in that office so we can get this figured out." He grabs my shoulder and squeezes as we start walking again, closing in on the office door. "Don't speak unless you have to. Let us handle this for you."

My brows pull together. "Us?" He ignores me, and my gut pinches. "Who is us, Dougie?"

Again, he ignores me, and I scowl as he knocks on the door, his knuckles hitting just below the gold plate declaring this Alexander Torello's office. Footsteps come from the opposite side, and I steel my spine. Whether I'm ready for this or not, I refuse to let anyone see me falter.

With a *goosh* of air, the door swings open, and Alexander himself greets us. His expressionless face cools the air, filling it with a thick tension that tries to rattle me. Harsh brown eyes meet mine as he takes me in, assessing in a way that makes my skin prickle.

"Maddox. Douglas. Come in," he commands after a brief moment.

"Nice to see you again, Alex, even under these circumstances," Dougie says smoothly, his confidence unwavering. He walks inside, and I follow, only stopping to nod and say a quick hello to the man holding my entire career in his hands. Pleasantries aren't on the table today, so there's no point in trying.

"Hello, sir."

He nods stiffly and shuts the door behind us. Only after he's moved out of the way do I look to the side of the office and narrow my eyes on the man resting against the arm of a leather sofa, looking as cool as a goddamn cucumber.

"Dad."

"Son," he replies.

Anger beats like a kick drum in my chest. My eyes say everything to him that I can't. *What are you doing here?*

Relax, his say.

Right. As if.

"Alex called me in this morning after the story broke," he explains out loud, but it falls on deaf ears.

Oakley Hutton is a Vancouver Warriors legend, and even though he retired fairly early on in his career, it was never because he was losing his skill. If anything, he was continuing to get better each season, his age be damned.

His relationship with the organization is tight-knit. The very angry owner watching our encounter at this very moment shared a handful of Saturday dinners with us while I was growing up, his late father being the previous owner during my father's career. Maybe that means I shouldn't be surprised to see my father here right now.

It doesn't even matter. This isn't my father's career, nor his business. It's mine, and I should have been notified before he was brought into the mix.

"Your dad dealt with his fair share of publicity nightmares over the course of his career, Maddox. And considering your brother is also involved in this, I wanted him here. Is that going to be a problem?" Alexander asks me.

Shoving back my annoyance, I shake my head. "No, sir."

"Good. Then let's get right into it. The press is swarming like flies on a cow's ass. This won't blow over easily. They have video footage of you getting your ass kicked by that guy outside of Ralph's. They have statements from a few of the people outside who said it was, in fact, a drug deal gone sideways, and the photos of Noah throwing the guy a wad of cash don't help your case. Now, we know that wasn't what happened, but I'm going to need you to take a drug test before you leave here today and another before the game Tuesday."

"Not a problem."

I've gone twenty-six years without touching drugs, and I'm not about to fuck that record up now.

"Then there's the other matter we need to discuss," he adds, and my stomach drops.

"What other matter?"

Dad steps up beside me, the air tense between us. "Roy Heights."

My blood runs cold as memories rattle the walls of the mental box I keep them locked inside. "What about him?"

"I got a call from him this morning. He tried to make it seem as if he were doing us a favour by letting us know beforehand, but we know that was just an attempt at a power play. He filmed a segment on Sports Weekly this morning to 'come clean' about what really happened between you two eight years ago. That dirty bastard has been waiting for something like last night to happen so he would have an opportunity to bury you," Dougie says, his voice tight, strained.

Dad places a sturdy hand on my upper back and moves it up

and down. "All he has is lies and a bitter soul. It won't work, son."

"This is why you're here. Not because of what happened last night," I note as everything starts to click into place. "What did he say on the show? What lies? Did he mention her?"

My boss steps into my line of sight and scowls. His eyes are dark. So dark. "First, we need a plan on how to clean this up fast. There's not much truth to what he's claiming, but there is some. We've done a good job of keeping it hidden, but there's only so much we can leave up to chance."

"What did he say?" I ask again, and even as Dad digs his fingers into my back in an attempt to silence me, I can't seem to stop talking. Not after I've heard Braxton's father's name for the first time since—

"He said that you fired him as your agent when you were eighteen because his daughter broke your heart and that because of your arrogance back then, he struggled to find any more clients. When he was asked about the events of last night, he also hinted at past drug use and violence as a reason why the relationship between you and his daughter never worked. He blames you for his terrible career and is proving that he isn't afraid of lying to get even," Dougie says.

It's all lies. Well, almost all of it. His daughter didn't just break my heart. She tossed it into a shredder and then took the pieces and stomped and spit on them. Still, that isn't why I fired Roy from his position as my agent all those years ago. That came after he ruined the first year of my career with his fake promises and my misplaced trust.

I draw in a slow breath to try and keep from throwing my fist into a wall. My composure is slipping quicker by the second, and as three sets of eyes watch me cautiously, I only get more wound up.

"When does it go live? What can we do?" I mutter.

"This afternoon. There's nothing we can do to stop it from

releasing. The only thing we can do now is try and deal with the aftermath of it," Dad says.

"There's nothing we can do? Seriously?" I look at Alexander when I ask the question, my stare incredulous. "You can't really be letting this get out."

His eyes narrow. "What is it you would like me to do? This is your mess, Maddox. You're lucky I'm not cutting my losses with you and letting you drown in this."

"He's right, kid. This story is going to come out whether we like it or not, and we need a way to cauterize the bleeding before your career has the chance to die," Dougie adds.

I grind my teeth together. "He's a dead man. He sold me lie after lie, and I believed every single one because of *her*, and it nearly cost me everything. Is that not enough for him?" Glancing at Alexander, I release a tight breath and focus on speaking calmly and letting my appreciation show. "You saved my career once, and I appreciate that you're willing to do it again."

He nods. "You're the best player in the league. Regardless of our personal relationship, I would have done the same thing for any member of my team in this position. You were young and naïve when you made those decisions. This side of the problem is not on you."

"We can't say the same about last night," Dad says, completely in parent mode now. "You should have called me as soon as your sister called you. Noah's life decisions are not your responsibility; they are mine."

I swallow my laugh. "We both know you're the last person Noah wants help from."

He tries and fails to hide a wince. "Regardless, this mess could have been dealt with better."

"We already have a few ideas on what to do next, but we want your opinion before we go forward," Dougie says.

I turn to him, catching his brief, encouraging smile. "What are you thinking?"

"We'll start with lifting your image from the gutter it's fallen in. Some charity work, fundraisers, an official statement denying Roy's claims and the accusations from last night, that sort of thing. You'll need to walk a straight fucking line, kid. If someone asks for a comment, your answer is that you don't have one. Avoid the press as much as you can. Keep up appearances, post on social media like normal. The goal is to make this look like one last-ditch effort from a bitter, washed-up agent to get revenge and a robbery gone wrong outside of that bar."

My stomach churns as nerves spark through me. "And if that doesn't work?"

It's Alexander who answers, his words clipped. "We'll cross that bridge if we get there."

4

Braxton

My veterinary clinic comes to life as I step inside and start flicking on the lights. As the room illuminates, I glance around with a weary smile. Squishy waiting chairs in a soft beige, stacks of magazines spread over the glass tables, animal-safe plants galore. The three kittens we have waiting to be adopted meow at me before running up the cat tree in front of the window. The runt of the litter—Rufus—stands on his hind legs and presses his front paws to the window as he lets out a low, long meow.

"No way, buddy. You only think you want to be out there because of the pretty colours, but trust me. It's not all it's cracked up to be," I tell him. He looks at me like he understands what I'm saying, which I definitely think he can, even if it's a bit unethical.

The clinic doesn't open for another hour, but it's only our third week in business with myself as owner, and the antsy feeling inside of me has yet to simmer down. We've done extremely well for only being open a few weeks, but I'm a self-diagnosed perfectionist and refuse to leave anything up to chance. So, I come in early and make sure everything is the way it should be before my staff and patients arrive.

My teal-blue Converse squeak on the tile as I head for my

office, fully intent on just checking the schedule and swapping my black cardigan for my white coat, but as soon as I spot the holes of missing dog food bags on the display wall, I change directions.

Before long, I'm dragging heavy bags of food out of the storage room and struggling to lift them onto the empty shelves. I may have gotten ahead of myself when I thought it was a good call to bring every missing bag out to the waiting room instead of taking them one by one, especially now that I realize I can't reach some of the higher shelves. My five-foot-five height makes me scowl.

I'm not short, but I'm not tall either. I'm stuck in the middle, neither here nor there. A place I've never liked to be.

The bell above the door jingles, and I blow stray curls out of my face as I look over my shoulder. I grin and drop the bag back to the floor.

"Thank God. I need your help to put these up on the shelves," I say.

Marco Creeve, the only other veterinarian I've hired to work at my clinic, gives me a beaming white smile as he shakes his head and quickly toes off his dirty shoes on the doormat. "There are employees whose sole purpose is to do these things for you, you know?"

With his pale green eyes twinkling, he meets me by the mess I've made and, with ease, lifts the ninety-pound bag of healthy-weight dog food I was just struggling with before setting it on the designated shelf and starting on the other bags.

I stand and brush the dust off my scrub pants. "I was already here. Figured I might as well get a head start. What are you doing here so early?"

"I have an early appointment. A golden retriever swallowed a teddy bear two days ago and hasn't eaten since."

"Crap."

"Nope. Hasn't done that either," he says, chuckling.

"Ha-ha. I'm going to clean myself up before we open."

"Sounds good. Micaela just pulled up outside. She'll get everything ready to go."

Micaela runs the front desk and pretty much everything else that needs to be taken care of in the front during the day. I don't know how I would do it without her.

With quick strides, I'm heading to my office for the second time this morning. The space is cozy, inviting, and I feel at home the second I step inside. With bookshelves lining the wall behind my desk and a desk chair I spent far too much on, it's my own version of paradise.

My coat is hanging off a hook on the wall beside my framed vet degree, and I take off my cardigan, exchanging it for the coat, and then brush my thumb over the stitched name like I do every morning.

Dr. Braxton Heights. Pride fills my chest.

I grab my stethoscope and loop it around my neck before sticking my hands in the pockets of my coat and heading back out. It took six years for me to finish school and another two to move back home, but this place . . . this *clinic* was a surprise. I'm proud of myself for everything I've accomplished in my life, and while I might have decided to take a risk as a business owner with hopes of impressing my father, I'm hoping that I'll grow to love it more and more each day.

It's the beginning of another journey. One I hope will turn out better than the one that pushed me to leave Vancouver eight years ago.

"I WANT to see Whiskey again in about three months for a follow-up shot, but for now, he's right as rain," I say, scratching behind the ear of a totally loveable chocolate Lab. From my crouched position, we're at eye level, and he doesn't hesitate to give me a slobbery kiss from my jaw to my eyebrow.

His tail wags excitedly and thumps against the wall as his owner, Cindy—an older woman with a silver bob and kind eyes—smiles at me and nods along.

"Whiskey, don't drown the poor doctor," she half-heartedly scolds.

"It's totally okay. I don't have a dog of my own yet, so I'm all for a bit of slobber." With one more ear scratch, I pat Whiskey's head and stand, my feet sore from the long day.

"You said you don't have a dog *yet*. Does that mean you're looking for a dog?"

"I would like to. I only moved back to Vancouver a few months ago and just haven't had the time yet," I tell her.

Cindy gifts me another genuine smile and hooks Whiskey's leash back to his collar. "Well, I wish you a great experience looking for your new best friend. Dogs are such amazing companions. I wouldn't know what to do without mine anymore."

"He looks like he would be a great cuddler. I'm sure he makes great company."

She laughs softly. "He's a bed hog, but it's just me, so I don't mind." Her happy tone dips ever so slightly, and I get the feeling she's been through tough times in her life. I want to reach out and hug her but decide against it. "I should let you get back to work, I suppose. I've let myself get chatty again. Thank you for the great checkup. We will be back in three months."

I reach around her and open the exam room door. The waiting room is empty, with Cindy and Whiskey being my last appointment of the day. The promise of a long, hot bath and a glass of wine has kept me pushing through the rest of the afternoon when the soles of my feet started to whimper.

"It was my pleasure," I say and lead the way to the front desk, where Micaela sits waiting. She grins when she sees us. "These two need an appointment for three months from now."

"Sounds good. Come on over and we can figure out when works best."

Cindy reaches for my hand and gives it a quick squeeze before leading Whiskey over to the desk. Micaela gets right to work figuring out the bill and when they should book the next appointment while I leave them and go to my office to start getting everything cleaned up and organized for tomorrow.

It's only just past five, but as soon as I sit in my chair and fire up my computer, my stomach grumbles loud enough I'm sure the people walking along the sidewalk outside could hear. That will teach me to skip lunch again.

"Hungry?"

I snap my head up and flush when I see Marco standing in the doorway, his paw-printed black scrubs fitting his body a little too nicely. He's a handsome man, with light blond hair the colour of hayfields in the summer cut short on the sides and just slightly longer on top. His eyes are a pretty shade of blue that I like to look at, but that's as far as my interest goes.

In all the years that I spent away at university, I'd only ever officially dated a couple of guys. Not a single one of those relationships was anything to write home about. I wasn't their type, and as soon as they realized that they weren't into chubby girls, I was last week's news.

"I'm starving. I worked through lunch."

"You work too hard. Take a break every once in a while. You deserve it," he says.

I collect my unruly curls in my hands and drape them over my back, wishing I had a hair tie handy. My smile is weak, exhaustion mixing with hunger. "I keep telling myself that too, but I never actually do it. Right now, all I want to do is eat one of those massive burgers from the diner down the street."

He taps his knuckles to the wall and stands up straighter. "Let's go, then. I'm on my way out, anyway. Let me buy you dinner."

I fumble my reply. "Like a co-worker dinner?"

"Sure." He shrugs. "Or not."

"Marco . . ." I start before my phone starts to ring from my desk drawer. It's a fight to keep the relief from showing on my face. I've always had expressive features—it's bitten me in the ass a few too many times. "Sorry. It could be important."

"No worries. I'll be by the front desk when you're done."

I nod stiffly and push away the unease that's crept up on me. Once he's gone, I pull out my phone and relax when I see the contact name on the screen.

"Hey, Mom."

"Hi, sweetie. Are you still at work?"

"I am. Nearly done for the day, though."

Knowing I'm not going to be able to concentrate on work anymore, I turn off my computer again and lean back in my chair.

"Perfect. I've made your favourite for dinner," Mom preens.

"Baked mac and cheese? Did you intend on bribing your way to a visit tonight?" I tease.

She laughs, and the sound is so bright it has me smiling big enough my cheeks hurt. "You know me too well. I made enough for you to take some home with you for lunches this week. Should I meet you at your house? I could help you hang up some of your photos in the living room that you've been putting off."

"Sounds good. I can leave right now, so give me maybe twenty minutes."

The sound of hands clapping floats through the call before she says, "I'll be waiting. Drive safe. Love you."

"Love you. See you soon."

I hang up and rush around the office, pulling off my stethoscope and ditching my coat before grabbing my cardigan and slipping it on. After flipping off the light and shutting the office door, I meet Marco by the front desk and give him my best apologetic smile.

"Dinner with my mom. I'm sorry," I tell him.

If he's too disappointed by the news, he hides it well, which I appreciate. It's best not to muddle our good work relationship with dinner dates.

"That's okay. Maybe another time. Let me walk you to your car at least. I sent Micaela home already."

"Sure. Thank you."

He hovers a respectful hand against the middle of my back, and we leave the clinic in silence. After I lock up, he walks me to my car and waits until I've driven off before getting into his own.

The radio plays softly as I smile and continue home. Another day down, and a great one at that. It might have taken a boatload of pep talks, but days like these are exactly why I came back home.

Nothing could ruin this for me.

5

Braxton

I GREW UP IN A COOKIE-CUTTER, WEALTHY NEIGHBOURHOOD. EVERY house was built sometime in the past twenty years and, as if forced by some sort of constructional law, given matching high peaks, dark stone and light siding, and tall windows.

Some houses have high fences to keep badgering eyes away or no fencing at all for the purpose of showcasing the intricately landscaped front yards. It's quiet, with no children playing basketball in the cul-de-sacs or doodling on the sidewalks with chalk. For as long as I can remember, it's been this way, and as I drive up my parents' looped driveway, a pang of sadness causes me to brake so suddenly my car lurches forward in front of the garage, the old brakes squealing.

I've only been over to my parents' house twice since I've been back in town: the night I moved into my new home, and right now, for an impromptu family meeting ordered by my dad over a phone call this afternoon. Every other time I've seen my mother and sister, they've come to my house, like for dinner last night, or we've gone out.

We're a close family for the most part—my mom, my sister, and me, that is—and the times I would fly home to visit them during the holidays were special moments for me. I expected to feel some sort of similar homecoming after I came back for good, but instead, I've felt like I'm missing something.

My move wasn't sudden by any means. I'm a planner. I like to know my schedule in advance so that I'm able to fit my life into the appropriate boxes, and I did all of that. So why do I feel so . . . wrong? Like I'm out of place?

It's probably stress. I'm so happy with the path I chose and how far I've come, but running a new business is hard. I knew it would be.

Yeah, it has to be the stress.

The evening sun shines on my bare arms as I skip knocking and walk right into the house. It smells like ginger and oranges, so Mom must have her essential oil diffuser puffing away somewhere close.

"Hello?" I call out, toeing off my flip-flops and padding barefoot across the deep brown walnut floors.

The main floor is one wide-open space with the living room on one side of the house and the kitchen on the other. The dining area is tucked in between, with a six-person glass table and a set of luxury, high-back fabric chairs with silver buttons down the front and back. The kitchen has dark cabinets that match the floor and bright marble countertops. All of the appliances are new, despite the reality that neither of my parents spends a lot of time in the kitchen.

I head up the stairs and scour the second level for my parents. Raised, muffled voices behind Dad's office door draw me in that direction. My stomach sours.

"You know how she was after, Roy. I can't believe that you would do this to her again," my mom scolds.

"She's an adult now. It's different."

What?

A feeling of uneasiness grows as I knock on the door and the voices quiet instantly.

Footsteps, and then the door is pulled open. Mom's cheeks are flushed as she attempts a smile and ushers me into the room.

She's a small woman, a bit shorter than me, but we share the same deep blue eyes.

"Hi, sweetheart. Sorry, we didn't hear you get in."

"I wouldn't expect you to over all that fighting," I reply.

Dad's words are stern. "Watch the attitude, Braxton."

I bite my tongue and paint on a fake smile. "Right. My apologies."

"It's okay, honey," Mom says.

Dad is leaning back against the front of his desk with his arms crossed and his legs outstretched, crossed at the ankles. He's a tall man, towering over both Mom and me, with a beefy build and a full head of dark curly hair. When I was a little girl, my sister and I used to pretend we were princesses and that our dad was our personal knight in shining armour, keeping the bad guys far, far away from our royal family.

That little girl would be heartbroken if she knew her dad would turn out to be the villain in her story.

Bitterness has me fighting back a frown. "What is this about? Why isn't Annalise here?"

"This doesn't involve your sister. Please, sit." Dad gestures to the long leather couch against the wall opposite his desk.

"So this is a family meeting but without Anna?" I scoff.

Mom touches my arm softly. "Please, just sit. I don't want to be in the middle of a fight between you two today."

"Fine."

For my mom and her alone, I sit on the cold couch in the tense, uncomfortable office. My father and I have been at odds for nearly a decade, and I know it wears on Mom. Unfortunately, that isn't enough of a reason for me to build a bridge over the past and walk across it.

Silently, she sits beside me, and the exhaustion radiating from her has me glaring at my dad.

He ignores my anger. "There's something coming to light this afternoon that might upset you, so I wanted to give you enough notice to prepare."

My breath skips. "What did you do?"

"Nothing that I shouldn't have done years ago."

Mom sets her hand on my knee, and I sneak a glance at her to find her chewing nervously on her bottom lip. I snap my spine straight and look back at my father.

"What did you do?" I ask again.

"I told them all about Maddox Hutton. He's going to pay for what he did to our family," he declares, chin tilted high.

I squeeze my eyes shut as a fierce pain rips through my chest. The sudden dryness in my mouth makes it hard to get my next words out. "The only thing he did to this family was trust us." Trust *me*.

"He ruined my career. He's the reason your mother has had to work herself to the bone at the hospital, picking up extra shifts and sleeping in the on-call room more often than in our bed. I haven't worked for another hockey player since he ruined me, and it was about time he got what was coming."

I grind my teeth. "You ruined your own career. We were all bystanders who were brought down with your sinking ship."

"Braxton, sweetheart," Mom cuts in, squeezing my knee in an attempt to calm me. I place my hand on hers but shake my head.

"No, Mom. If you guys brought me here to get my permission to do this, you don't have it. I knew I shouldn't have come here today, but I did anyway. Total mistake on my part. I'm not going to listen to this same bullshit from Dad. You can live with the guilt of knowing how much this hurts me. It's been eight years. You need to get over it, Dad. Madd—" I stumble over his name and swallow it back down. "He's happy. He's successful. Do what you told me to do when I moved away and get over it," I finish.

Dad pushes away from the desk and narrows his eyes on me. "He's a mess! Have you not seen the news? Maddox Hutton is a violent addict and a self-entitled snob. His contract hasn't been signed yet for next season, and hopefully, now it won't be. If Vancouver doesn't sign him, nobody else will."

I drop my eyes to the floor and laugh under my breath. For the first time in a long time, I force myself to say his name. "Maddox was born to play for Vancouver. Nothing—not even you and your stubborn idea of revenge—will be able to change that. He didn't deserve what happened. Neither of us did."

The reason my mom has to work herself to the bone is because her husband refuses to try and find another career path. He's so obsessed with the idea of revenge and redeeming himself in the hockey world that he's found himself lost at sea, too far from land to call for help.

"I stood by you back then when I shouldn't have, and I won't do it again."

With my words hanging in the air, I get up and leave, ignoring Mom's plea for me to stop as I exit the room.

I've forgiven her for not stopping what happened all those years ago, but I don't think I will ever forgive my father for what he did. It doesn't matter how much time passes, the guilt and regret weighs heavy on me.

They say time is supposed to heal all wounds, but I've begun to accept that this one will remain raw and vulnerable for the rest of my life.

6

Braxton

WEDNESDAY MORNING, I'M SITTING ON THE FLOOR OF HADES' kennel, giving him a good scratch under his chin when his thick, pink, slobbery tongue swipes across my cheek.

The two-year-old, eighty-pound American bulldog is as beefy as they come, but the only scary thing about this big boy is the amount of drool he produces. Hades is my favourite dog at the shelter and the one I spend the most time with. By far.

When I was first looking for potential locations for my clinic, I had wanted a blank slate. An empty building that screamed at me with potential. Of what could be with a bit of hard work. So, when my Realtor showed me what used to be Danver's Animal Clinic and shelter, I wasn't sold on the idea. Not only was it already a running business with old patients, but there was a full animal shelter attached to the back.

Running two businesses was never the plan—even one was stretching it—but as terrified as I was at the idea, one look at the adorable faces in the pens was all it took to have me signing the papers.

I've always loved animals. Even growing up without any pets—my sister is allergic to anything with fur—I always found a way to feed my obsession, whether that was spending my weekends in high school working at a horse ranch or staying too long after class cuddling the librarian's emotional support cat.

A career where I get to spend hours upon hours every single day with animals was a no-brainer. Having this small piece of heaven attached to my clinic is just a bonus.

"He almost got in the pool today," a soft voice says. I look up to find Sadie, the shelter manager, staring down at Hades and me from outside the kennel. Her brown eyes are warm as she takes in our position.

Sadie has been taking care of the shelter for as long as the place has been open, so when I bought it, I made sure she got to keep her job. Nobody knows these animals better than she does.

I move my hand behind Hades' ear and give him a kiss between the eyes. "That's a good boy, Hades."

"He'll get there eventually. I know he will."

"Has anyone shown any interest recently? I know we haven't had a chance to chat in a few days." Hope leaches from every word. Hope that he'll finally find a family who wants him and that one day the tortures of his past won't haunt him so deeply.

"No. Not yet. He's been through too much," she sighs.

My stomach rolls at the reminder of everything my boy has lived through in only two years of life. He was brought to the clinic on my second official day as owner by a teenage boy who said he found him broken and bleeding on the side of the road only a few streets over from what the police later found to be a dog fighting ring. The extent of his injuries had me struggling to keep my breakfast down as I got to work.

Despite the depth of his physical injuries, his trauma was almost worse. For the first few days after I fixed him up, he wouldn't move from the corner of his kennel and growled at the first sign of human life. Of course, that didn't stop me from personally bringing his meals in every morning and evening and trying like hell to prove that I wasn't going to hurt him. Finally, after a couple of weeks, he started to warm up to me. Each day is a new opportunity to prove my loyalty and show that he is safe here—something I put my everything into.

Unfortunately, even though he trusts and seems to care for me, it won't be easy to find a family that would be willing to put in the kind of work that I am. Even if beneath all of his battle wounds and big teeth, he's just a puppy who wants to be loved.

I try not to let myself dwell on that, though. When the time is right, Hades will find a family that will do *anything* to see his tail wag and those chops spread into his all-too-doggie grin. Instead, I focus on the small win of him considering jumping in the pool today.

He's not ready to play with the other dogs yet, and he might never be, but knowing that he's trying to overcome his fear of water makes me proud. We figure he was punished with water sometime in his life, which has led to his fear of it now, so we've never pushed. But gosh, he's thinking about trying. I'm grinning when he takes another swipe at my face, and his tongue slips into my mouth.

I crinkle my face in disgust and use the neck of my shirt to wipe at my face. "You're gross, Hades. And your breath stinks."

He cocks his head at me as Sadie laughs. "Feel free to try and give his teeth a brush. Sparkling white teeth will give a good first impression to the people coming by soon."

My brows pinch. "Who's coming? A potential family?"

"Did you check your email this morning?"

I smile sheepishly. "No. I had a crap weekend and dove right into work these past couple days. What did I miss?"

"You remember when I told you about the fundraisers and adoption day that we've always put on for the shelter every summer? To raise money and bring in some potential families?" she asks.

"Yes. The one in June." It's still two months away, but I've already made a note about it in my planner. "Do you need help with it? I was already planning on putting aside some time to help, but we can always hire a few people if you feel we need it. I'm really looking forward to this."

Sadie flushes a deep pink and takes her turn looking sheepish. "Actually, that's something I wanted to talk to you about later, but it's not what was in the email. What I wrote you this weekend was that we're getting help fr—"

Suddenly, Hades turns rigid, and his hackles rise. His pretty brown eyes focus on the door connecting the clinic to the shelter, and my body flushes cold. *Not good.* Softly, I place my palm to his side and hold it there.

Deep voices rattle from behind the door before it's pushed open and two men tumble inside. Hades shifts his body until he's standing between my stretched legs, his body hiding me and stopping my ability to see the newcomers. I pat his chest and press my cheek to his side, knowing that if I attempt to get up and create distance between us, he'll most likely revert back to some sort of aggression.

"Oh! You're early," Sadie says. Nerves vibrate in her words. "I'm the manager of the shelter, Sadie."

"Right. We talked on the phone," the first man says, sounding confident and sure of himself. It's too early to tell if that's a good or bad thing.

"I'm Bentley. It's nice to meet you, Sadie," the other voice says. This one is just as deep, but it's kinder.

"Likewise," she returns.

"Our third musketeer is just on the phone in the clinic. The woman at the desk said it was okay to come back here while we wait," Bentley says.

There's a third man? What is this about? It sounds like I'm going to spend the next few minutes drowning in testosterone. *Hard pass.*

"Who's killer and long legs over there?" the first man asks, and I'm immediately on the defense.

With a soft nudge, I move Hades out of the way just enough so that I can peek around his muscled shoulders and glance at the two men ruining my after-work cuddle.

"First of all, he's not a ki—" I start, only to have my throat seize around the rest of my sentence when my gaze falls on none other than Douglas Trelix.

A tsunami of emotions rushes at me as I plant my hands to the cold floor in a desperate attempt to remind myself that I'm on solid ground and not in fact being sucked up in a death wave.

I haven't heard his voice since I was eighteen, but even so, I should have recognized it.

"Braxton," he says, looking far from shocked at seeing me here. His lack of surprise is almost as concerning as him being here in the first place. "Is that your dog?"

It's now that I realize Hades has sensed my panic and is nudging my chin with his wet snout. I bury my fingers in his neck and take a deep breath.

"He's a shelter dog. But since the shelter is mine, yes, he's mine."

I move my attention to this Bentley person when he says, "He reminds me of a dog I had growing up. Protective as fuck."

Bentley is a massive man, with broad shoulders and tree trunks for thighs that could probably crush a watermelon with little effort. Just thinking about how many hours he must spend in the gym has my muscles aching.

He has dark skin, a sharp jaw, and a small silver hoop in his left earlobe. But despite his intimidating size, his smile is soft, almost calming. I take a liking to him immediately.

Looking away from him, I slant a curious look at Douglas. "What are you doing here?" Is *he* here? Is he the man on the phone?

I feel light-headed.

Douglas pushes a contemplating hand down his face and then tugs on his beard. "Do you intend to sit on the ground for this conversation?"

"Would you prefer Hades take a bite out of those expensive leather loafers of yours instead?"

"Fine. Have it your way," he mutters gruffly.

"Great. What are you doing here? I doubt either of you has ever stepped foot in an animal shelter, let alone one as small as ours."

Bentley clears his throat, earning a glare from everyone in the room. "Sorry, but how do you two know each other? I'm feeling very out of the loop right now, and I don't like being out of the loop. I like being in the loop, preferably dead smack in the centre of it."

I double blink at him. "I don't mean to be rude, but who exactly are you, Bentley?"

His lips part in surprise, and he stares at me intently, like he's trying to figure out if I'm playing him. "Serious?"

"Dead."

He's about to speak when the door opens, and the world stills around me. My pulse feels like a jackhammer in my skull as I stare with quickly blurring eyes at the bottom half of the new arrival. At a pair of tight blue jeans wrapped around thick, powerful thighs and clinched to narrow hips. I don't have to look up at the man to know who it is.

If the sudden change in the atmosphere wasn't enough, the throbbing in my chest is.

Like two pieces of the same whole that have been kept apart for too long, my half cries out for his, begging and pleading to be mended back together again.

His voice moves through me like a serrated blade. "Braxton?"

As if someone just punched me in the stomach, the air is pushed up and out of me, leaving me gasping. Gripping onto my last ounce of willpower, I ignore him and reach to the side to grab Hades' leash from the ground. I hook him up with shaking hands before pushing to my feet. Self-preservation tells me to get out of there while I still have my dignity, but his angry laugh makes me freeze.

"Running away again? I see not much has changed."

And just like that, I look up, and our eyes meet.

7

Maddox

THERE ARE A MILLION THINGS I WISH I COULD FORGET ABOUT Braxton Heights. Her obsession with '80s rock music and vinyls, the way the freckles on her right shoulder make the perfect shape of a star, her bouncy black curls, and her eyes. Those round, bright sapphire-blue eyes flecked with white and grey. There isn't another person on this earth whose eyes I've stared into more than the ones looking at me right now, for the first time in nearly a decade.

It's her eyes that I ached to forget more than anything. If I had, maybe I wouldn't have spent years keeping myself up at night because every time I closed my eyes, it was hers I saw.

I lied to her just now. She has changed—in ways that piss me the fuck off.

Gone is the teenage girl with permanently pink-stained cheeks and baggy clothes she wore to hide the body she hated. The woman in front of me now is just that. A *woman*. One who radiates confidence and poise, even now, as she tries to run from me. Again.

Even wearing the ugliest pair of scrubs I have ever seen, she's stunning. The teddy bear–printed pants hug the swell of her hips and thighs, and I can only imagine how perfectly they hug her ass. Each time I blink, I see the way her curved jaw tensed and those pouty pink lips twisted in distaste when she saw me walk into the room. Like my eyes had taken a damn picture of her and slid it into my memory.

Her pink-toned, pale skin is still covered in freckles, and I hate the part of me that wants to count them all to find out if any more have popped up since the last time we saw each other.

Despite the fact I know I shouldn't, I find it hard not to let my gaze stray from the hold her eyes have on me. I want to look her over again. Deeper this time.

Fuck. Not happening.

Instead, I flatten my lips and say, "You can't take off yet. It seems that we have things to talk about it."

The last statement is just as much for Dougie as it is for her. When the whole prospect of choosing an animal shelter as my, quote, unquote, "charity work" came to light, I figured it would be easy enough. Not that I think charity work should be easy— I've been taking part in this stuff since I was a kid and know how hard it is—it was just that spending time with animals was an appealing idea.

The last thing I expected was to come face to face with the only woman I've ever loved and have ever let break my heart since. This place has to be hers.

I'm a fucking idiot for not looking for a sign outside before walking blindly in here.

Helping animals and running her own clinic has been Braxton's dream since she was six. Dougie knew it was hers and sent me here anyway.

The wheels are always turning in that old guy's head, but it would seem as though they've picked up speed in the past twenty-four hours.

"We can't talk here. Hades doesn't like men," she says, her voice so damn smooth and the perfect mix between sultry and sweet. Goosebumps break out along my arms as I grind my jaw.

"Hades?"

She stares at the wall behind me as a flush creeps up her neck to her cheeks and ears. "Yes."

And just like that, I'm fourteen again.

Braxton gives me a white-toothed grin when she walks outside and spots me standing at my regular spot by the fire hydrant on the curb. My hands are in my pockets, but I'm quick to pull them out and wrap her up in my arms when she gets close enough.

Her usual scent of peaches and vanilla is tainted with the smell of wet dog, but I don't care. I pull her as close as possible and breathe her in.

"I missed you," I say after she pushes me away with a giggle.

"You saw me four hours ago."

"Exactly." I scoff.

She rolls her eyes playfully, and I softly move her to the inside of the sidewalk before tossing my arm over her shoulders. My dad taught me early on that the man should always walk on the side of the sidewalk closer to the road, and for some reason, it's always stuck. Maybe because I like knowing I'm protecting Braxton.

I've been bringing her to and from her summer job every day since she started last month. Yeah, it's a forty-minute walk from my house to the doggy daycare and another half hour from her house to mine, but I don't care. I take every minute of extra time I can have with her. Even if it means I have to endure sweaty balls in the summer heat.

"How was your day?" I ask.

She slides her arm around my back and leans into my side. "Amazing. If I didn't want to be a vet, I think I would want to run a doggy daycare. I can't get enough of all those cute smiles."

I don't have it in me to tell her that dogs can't smile. If anyone could actually make it possible, it would be my Braxton. All she'd have to do is flash one of her dimples and they'd be putty in her hands.

"Who was your favourite today?"

"Definitely Perry. He's perfected his shake a paw and can do both paws at once now," she exclaims.

"Have you thought of a career in dog training?"

She shakes her head. "I don't think that's for me. I prefer the end result rather than the journey getting there when it comes to training."

"That's fair." We hit the crosswalk just in time for the white stick man to start flashing, and we hurry across the road. "Your future dog is going to be the best-trained one in the world."

"Our dog, you mean," she corrects me.

I smile. "Yeah, my bad."

"Do you have any name ideas? You know how bad I am with names."

"Any name we pick now will probably change by then, Brax."

"Nuh-uh. Let's make a promise on it."

Glancing down at her, I take in the look of concentration on her face and stifle a laugh. "If it's that important to you, then fine. But this promise could compromise the integrity of all past and future promises if it's broken."

"Mmhmm. Now, tell me."

"Hades. I would name our dog Hades."

She looks up at me, her head craning back due to our height difference. Bright blue eyes glimmer with the promise of a future. God, I love that look.

"The king of the underworld. Scary and ferocious. It's a name for a big dog with dark fur."

I shrug, a rush of embarrassment flooding me for a brief moment. "It's just an idea, obviously. I don't know why I would choose that name. I guess I think it would be pretty badass."

Her fingers press into my side, and she moves closer. "No, I love it. Hades it is."

The memory leaves me breathless, and for a moment, I'm suspended in time, lost between past and present. It's not until an elbow digs into my side, the same spot young Braxton's fingertips were, that I come to.

"I'll wait for you outside, then," I snap before spinning around and shoving open the door.

My heart is racing faster than it does after a playoff game, and I hate it. Fucking detest it. The last person who should have this effect on me is Braxton Heights. I can't do this. I can't come back here again.

The waiting room is empty, besides the blonde watching me from the front desk. She gives me a timid smile, and I flash her a fake one in return before walking to the front window and staring out at the parking lot.

The door swings open behind me, and shoes slap the floor. Nobody speaks, and I don't turn around. Just knowing she's behind me is too much as pain continues to bubble in my chest.

"We need to get this over with now. I have another meeting in an hour," Dougie says. I ignore him.

"Maddox?"

I squeeze my eyes shut at the sound of my name. It falls from her mouth like it belongs there, and I clench my fingers.

A large hand clasps my shoulder, and one whiff of spicy cologne tells me it's Bentley. "Come on, man."

Pulling a breath between my lips, I straighten and walk to one of the beige chairs before sitting stiffly, keeping my eyes trained on the floor as everyone starts to follow suit.

I'm relieved when Dougie starts to speak first.

"If it's alright, we would appreciate if you sent your receptionist home, Braxton. This isn't a conversation we need getting out to the press."

I assume he's talking about the blonde.

"Yeah, okay. Give me a second."

Footsteps and muffled voices sound before the front door closes.

"Thank you. I know everyone is confused here, so I'll try to make this quick. Braxton, I'm sure you know about your father's latest tale as well as what repercussions would have followed suit. Clearly, this wasn't exactly your fault, but just hear us out."

She must nod because it's silent before he continues.

"How often do you keep up with hockey news?"

"I don't."

Dougie releases a tight breath. "Okay, well, Maddox was also recently involved in an altercation outside of a bar with his brother. This ultimately left the opening for your father to slither in with his lies and baseless claims. We're in rebuild mode, so to speak, and need your help. I wouldn't involve you if I didn't think it was our best chance, but alas, you just might be. I know you two haven't seen each other in a . . . long time—"

A rough laugh escapes me before I can swallow it. I feel eyes on me but still don't look up from the bleached spot of flooring in the centre of the room.

"What I was saying is that we have a plan for how to help his image, but beyond that . . . well, that's where you would really come in."

"You want to use the shelter? Fine. Sadie will be your girl for whatever you need," Braxton says.

"Yes, we want Maddox to take part in the fundraisers and adoption day you're set to put on in June. It will look good for him to help out with a local cause. But that's only part of it."

The slight tremble in his final words snatches my attention, and before I can stop myself, I'm looking at him, my eyes narrowed. He swallows thickly, and my stomach sours. *Don't do whatever it is you're planning, Dougie.*

"How close are you with your father?" Dougie asks cautiously. Careful isn't like him. He's unapologetic and confident. He doesn't get nervous.

"I don't speak to my dad unless I have no other choice. We aren't close."

"Then we have a proposition for you."

"Who is we?" she asks.

Bentley knocks my knee with his and shoots me a confused look. I shake my head, just as confused.

Paper crinkles, and I look back at my agent to see him pulling a stack of papers out of his briefcase. He flips through them quickly before handing them over to Braxton. Her hands shake as she grabs them and drops them in her lap.

I can't help but watch as her eyes start moving over the document, growing wider and wider the further down the page she gets. Worry has me leaning forward in my chair.

"An NDA? For what?" she asks slowly. Her nose scrunches in distaste.

Dougie copies my stance, bracing his elbows on his thighs as he watches her inquisitively. "Yes. We can't take any risks here, and what we're going to ask of you could very well be just as bad as what your father has done if word gets out."

"You don't trust me."

"Should we?" I ask, fighting back a wince when she flinches.

"No. I guess not. What am I signing an NDA for?"

Dougie taps his fingers on his thighs, looking more nervous than I was expecting. "We've gone over this with the PR management team, and we're certain this is both the quickest and most reliable way to help fix the damage Roy has caused. Of course, you're welcome to say no. Please just think about it before making your decision."

"Dougie, just come out with it," she sighs.

I nod in agreement. My stomach is in knots so tight a goddamn Boy Scout couldn't untie them.

"We want you to enter into a fake relationship. If Roy Heights' daughter is seen out with Maddox, it will bring doubt to some of his claims. Especially the one about you breaking his heart all those years ago."

He drops the bomb, and I burst out of my seat, my head shaking in bewilderment. I laugh, but the situation is anything but funny.

"No. Not happening."

Everyone looks at me, but it's Braxton's gaze that I focus on. Pain and rejection swirl in those blue eyes, and I push back the guilt that seeing those emotions on her makes me feel. I look at Dougie next.

"I should have been consulted about this. You should *not* have blindsided me here," I snap, shoving an angry hand through my hair.

"I'll do anything you need me to," Braxton murmurs.

I spin on her, my cheeks beating with the anger I'm trying to fight off. "No fucking way. I don't want your help."

Her eyes narrow slightly. "You don't have to want it. It looks like you need it."

"Yeah, because of your asshole of a father."

She drops her eyes to the floor, and her shoulders slouch. "I know. That's why I'm agreeing to help."

"We can find another way." *Can we?*

Dougie rises from his chair and inserts himself between us, facing my direction. The scowl on his face is one of pure frustration. "Knock it off. You don't need to like the idea, but it's the best one we've got. Don't take it out on her."

"Do you have a pen? I'll sign this today, and then you all need to leave. I want to go home," Braxton says.

Dougie cocks a brow as if to ask if I've gotten myself under control, and I dip my chin in confirmation. After staring at me for a few more seconds, he turns to Braxton and pulls a pen from the pocket of his black slacks.

In a blur, we watch as she signs the papers and hands them back to us, never once showing even a hint of regret. Her ability to be so accepting of this concerns me, but I keep my mouth shut.

This is my mess, and I'm grown enough to know when to pick my battles. Right now, I'm choosing to put my faith in the one person who doesn't deserve it.

I'm terrified.

8

Braxton

MADDOX HATES ME. HE HASN'T BOTHERED TO PRETEND OTHERWISE —not like I can blame him. I messed up, and time hasn't healed his wounds any more than it's healed mine.

Blindsided doesn't even begin to describe how I felt reading through the NDA Dougie handed me earlier. I've never seen such detail in a document before. This fake relationship has to seem anything but, and I don't know how to do that. Years ago, without a doubt. But now? With Maddox curling his lip at me every time I speak? It's going to be impossible.

I surprised myself by agreeing to help, but in that moment, all I could think about was that this could be my chance to make amends. To clear my conscience. I've been on the receiving end of Maddox's anger more than a handful of times over the course of my life, and I'm not about to back down from it now.

Of course, that's easier said than done when he's brooding beside me as we watch Dougie and Bentley take off in a Corvette whose price tag could rival that of my entire clinic.

"You don't have to stay," I mutter.

Sure, Dougie said he should stay back and spend some time with me, figuring out how exactly we're going to do this, but he's never been much of a rule follower. That combined with his distaste for being anywhere near me, I assumed he would have left.

"Where do you want to do this?" he grunts, not sparing me a glance.

I kick a rock with my foot and fight back an eye roll. "Don't sound so excited. We don't want you to burst."

He turns his head and looks at me at the same time I glance up at him. Our eyes meet, his deep and dark and brimming with annoyance. It almost makes me smile to see him so riled up.

"This isn't fun for me, Braxton. Honestly, this is the last thing I want to do today."

Ouch. "I don't want to do this any more than you do."

"Really? You sure didn't hesitate to hop at the chance."

"A nice person would have said thank you instead of harping at me for volunteering to help. I have to go against my family for this. You know that, right?"

His eyes narrow and crinkle at the corners. "Maybe you're not going against them at all."

"I signed your NDA."

"And I wouldn't put it past your family not to care about that."

He looks away, his jaw tight as I pull a long breath through my nose and blow it out. The tension in the air is thick, making it that much harder to stand here with him. Uncomfortable and uneasy are the two emotions I would use to explain this entire situation. Hurtful too, but I shove that one as far down as I can.

"If you're going to be a jackass, please just leave. We don't have to do this today," I grind out.

"My place," he says after a heavy pause.

"Your place?"

"We'll talk at my place. Not in a parking lot or back inside where I have a dog staring at me like an angry fucking bull."

I stifle a laugh. "Are you sure you want the enemy in your house? What if I were to take pictures of your underwear drawer and post them online?"

My attempt at a joke fails when he grumbles, "Wouldn't be the first time a woman has tried to sell my underwear for cash."

I open my mouth, then close it tight. What is the appropriate response to something like that? I'm sorry? Yeah, I don't think he would appreciate that right now.

Luckily, he doesn't wait for a reply. Instead, he pulls a set of keys from the pocket of his designer jeans and clicks the fob to unlock the doors to a tinted black truck I knew was his the moment we stepped outside.

Maddox's father had a truck just like it when we were growing up, and Maddox told me several times how he wanted one to match one day.

"Let me lock up, and we can go." I don't wait for his reply before turning around and doing just that, making sure to double-check the locks to appease my worry. When I finish, he's already leaning against the passenger door, scowling down at the tire and the fancy silver rim tucked inside.

I straighten my shoulders and lift my chin before I stride toward him, refusing to let him see how nervous I am. Of course, when he pulls open my door and grunts at me to get in, it becomes harder to hide the effect he has on me.

With one foot on the step bar, I pull myself into the truck and collapse in the seat with a huff.

A moment later and he's beside me, starting the engine and filling the cab with the familiar sound of "Livin' On A Prayer" by Bon Jovi. It's one of my favourite songs, and hearing it in this space has me fidgeting in my seat.

Besides the music—all of which seemed to be old rock—the ride is silent, and by the time we pull into an underground garage, I'm ready to be more than an arm's distance away from Maddox.

Being in his presence is far more intimidating than I remember, and it's more than just his anger and a mangled past. It's him—all of him.

His looks, his demeanour that borders on arrogance but

hasn't quite crossed over yet. This is a man that I used to know just as well as I knew myself but now seems so different that I feel actual physical pain at my inability to read him and understand his thoughts.

It's unfair to think this way, both to myself and to him, but I can't seem to stop.

The engine turns off, and I prepare myself for the gruff order to get out of the truck, but after a few silent moments, it doesn't come. I risk a glance across the cab and suck in a breath. Rich, vibrant green eyes are waiting for me, and I fluster at the intensity behind them. The air stills around us, and nobody moves. Nobody looks away. I think we're both afraid to.

The pull is still there. A part of me knew it would never disappear—not fully—but as if he's realizing the same thing, I watch as a guard falls back over his face, and he quickly snatches his wallet and keys from the console.

"We're here," he snaps, and then he's hopping out of the truck, leaving me to collect myself in his absence.

Yeah, we're somewhere alright. Somewhere we never should have ended up.

In the land of strangers.

"You live here?" I blurt out the minute we enter the penthouse. Yeah, that's right. *Penthouse.*

With black-and-white marble floors, lights that I didn't know could be so bright, and walls lined with floor-to-ceiling windows, I nearly trip over my feet in surprise as I try to keep up with him. The place is decorated sparsely, impersonally. Sure, the furniture is high-end, and it fills the massive open floor plan well, but nothing screams Maddox to me.

Where are all of the personal touches? His family photos? I

reach up and touch my lips only to find them in a frown. This place feels more like a hotel room than it does a home. But maybe this isn't a home. *No, I need to stop overanalyzing everything.*

"Yeah, I live here," he replies, pulling a beer and a bottle of flavoured water out of the fridge. My heart does this fluttering thing when he hands over the water before walking past me to the living area.

I quickly toe off my sneakers and follow, sitting on the opposite end of a long, white leather couch. The cold from the seat seeps through my scrub pants, and I shiver.

He notices. "Sorry, I like it cold."

"I know." I clear my throat and toy with the cool bottle in my hands. "So, how long have you lived here?"

"Two years."

Two years and it's still this . . . empty? My chest tightens.

"How is your family?"

"They're fine."

"Are you going to elaborate on that?"

"No," he grunts.

"The grunting is getting old. You're far from a caveman."

"I don't remember you being so pushy."

I fight back a wince and plaster on a smile. "I didn't expect you to remember me at all."

His laugh is so rough it sounds painful. "It seems you're impossible to forget. Trust me, I've tried."

This time, I don't try to hide how bad his words hurt. I swallow the knot in my throat and look away at the flat-screen mounted to the wall across the room and the electric fireplace below it. Anger tries to bubble to the surface when my eyes begin to sting, but before it gets the chance, I push it and the tears away.

I might deserve his distrust, but despite how angry he is with me over what happened in the past, I refuse to be treated like a doormat.

Twisting my upper body so I can properly face him, I say, "That's the last time you speak to me that way, Maddox. You're allowed to be hurt and angry with me, but you don't get to treat me with disrespect. You're not that guy, and I won't let you become that guy all because of my father. Don't give him that power over you."

"How do you know I'm not that guy? I'm a far cry from the boy you knew."

I shake my head. "No, I refuse to accept that your parents let you turn out to be a jackass. If Ava knew how you were speaking to me right now, she would have wrung you right out for everyone to see."

Finally, the hint of a smile pulls at his puffy pink lips. I want to say something else that would make him smile fully, not just show a tease of one, but his mouth returns to its flat line as he states, "You broke her heart when you left. Addie's too."

I press a hand to my chest. "Can you please tell me about your family? Just this once, then I won't ask again." My voice cracks, and I start to peel off the softening label on the dewy water bottle. "I've missed them."

"Dad runs a skating class in the summer twice a week for children under seven, and Mom helps my aunt with her dance studio whenever she gets bored at home. She retired two years ago, but Dad had been bugging her to long before that. They're your stereotypical snowbirds now."

The ice in my chest starts to thaw at the new information. Oakley and Ava Hutton were more than just my best friend's parents to me growing up. They were like a second set of my own, ones that were always home and present. I loved them—I still do.

"Does it really count as being a snowbird when you already live somewhere without much snow?" I laugh lightly.

Snowbirds are people who leave when the snow falls to go someplace sunny and warm and don't come back until the snow and cold is gone.

"That's what Addie said."

"How are your siblings?" I ask.

I don't miss the way he stiffens, but I put it down to everything that's happened with Noah recently. Clearly, it's a soft spot.

"Addie is good. She's graduating high school in June."

"Wow. That's exciting. What is she doing after?"

"She says she wants to travel the world. Dad is worried she won't come back after."

"Are you worried about that?"

Adalyn has always been the wild child. She loves adventure and taking risks. After she told me she wanted to jump out of a plane for her sixteenth birthday when she was only ten, I diagnosed her as an adrenaline junkie. It fit her personality in the best way, and I've always wondered if that stuck.

Maddox shrugs and takes a swig of his beer. My eyes become stuck on the column of his throat as it bobs with a swallow, but I force myself to look away before I get caught ogling him.

But oh boy, he has a strong throat—all thick and powerful with cords of muscles I itch to press my fingers into. Is it weird to talk about somebody's throat like this? Probably.

Yes.

"You can't keep my sister trapped in a bubble. She needs to go and experience life. But she'll come back when she's ready to," he says.

"I agree. Somehow, people always seem to find their way back to where there's supposed to be."

I think I believe that more now than I ever have before.

9

Maddox

HER WORDS HAVE MY GUT ALL TWISTED AND SORE. DIVING INTO THE past wasn't the plan, and if I don't move this conversation in a different direction, that's exactly where this one will lead us.

It's always been easy talking to Braxton; it's why we got along so well when we were kids. She would always lend an ear when I needed to vent, and I would have done just about anything to hear her problems in return. Fuck, I would have solved each and every one if it meant she was happy. But this is different. We're different.

The thought sparks a sharp pain in my chest. I shouldn't have brought her here, but my other options weren't great. Or at least, that's what I've been telling myself since I offered up my place.

It hurts having her here—in my living room, on my couch. Her perfume is a smell I never wanted to associate with my new home. It already lingers in my parents' house. I've never admitted it out loud before, but it's one of the reasons I refused to stay there after I was drafted. I found my own place instead, despite the fact I was only nineteen and it would have been undeniably easier to just stay with my parents.

I needed a fresh start. A new place where I wouldn't hear the sound of Braxton's laugh whenever it got too quiet or smell her fruity perfume each time I entered a room. If only I could have extracted her from my fucking soul as easily.

"How is Noah doing?" she asks, a tone of caution in her voice. My hackles rise at the topic change.

"You haven't gotten the rundown from your father?" I sneer.

"No. I didn't really give him the chance to tell me about that."

Interesting. "Noah is Noah. He's figuring his shit out."

"Dox. You don't have to pretend with me."

I actually flinch. Hearing the nickname on her lips again is like a slash through my insides. She sucks in a sharp breath at my reaction, no doubt, and I stare across the room, my jaw tight.

"Don't call me that."

"Okay."

She doesn't push further, and maybe that's what has me blurting out more about my brother than I have in years, to anyone.

"Noah is having a hard time. He's making stupid decisions and getting himself into dangerous situations. His relationship with Dad is in the shitter. He's broke off his ass, drunk or high on the daily. I don't know what else to do to help him."

"It sounds like he's lucky to have you on his team. Is all of this part of the reason why you were at my clinic today with a black eye and an NDA?"

"Part Noah, part my big mouth."

"How does it feel?" she asks, and I glance over at her, my brows lifted in question. "Your eye. It looks painful."

I shrug. "It's fine."

"Do you have ice? You should really keep the swelling down. Don't you play tomorrow?"

"Tonight, actually. I should have been at the rink for practice, but I've been let off today to get this figured out."

Before I have a chance to stop her, she's shooting out of her seat and rushing toward the kitchen. Craning my neck, I watch her from my place on the couch as she starts digging through the freezer and pulls out a bag of corn I didn't know was in there. After rifling through the drawers, she finds a dish towel and wraps it around the corn before bringing it to me. I stop breathing when she stops directly in front of me, so close our knees brush, and bends over my lap to press the towel-wrapped bag to my eye.

She's completely focused on her task, but I'm only focused on her and our close proximity. Fuck, my breaths turn shallow when she leans closer and drops an innocent hand on my thigh —just a finger length from my knee—for balance. I don't flinch when the cold fabric of the towel touches my swollen eye, not when I'm too busy watching her start to nibble on her thick bottom lip in concentration. My cock stirs as dirty thoughts flick through my head, like what would happen if I covered that hand with mine and dragged it up, up, up—

No. I know exactly what would happen if I did that. She would punch me in the balls and tell me to deal with all my shit on my own.

Hastily, I reach up and take the makeshift ice pack from her and release a tight breath when our fingers touch, and she jolts back, as if just coming back to her senses. Those round cheeks rosy up as she pushes a loose curl behind her ear and darts out of view. She's fussing around in the kitchen again, but this time, I don't look back. Instead, I take the time alone to gather myself.

I need to get my shit together. This is going to be a long few months if I can't even handle being in close proximity to her without popping a boner.

"We should make a plan. For the whole dating thing," she says a minute later, still working away in the kitchen.

"I'm not great at plans."

"You never were. But I am."

"This is going to look fucking weird no matter what we do. I don't date. Everyone in the league knows that. Some hard-core fans too. They won't believe that the first time I do, it's with the daughter of the asshole spouting off about me."

"Will it look weird because you don't date ever or because you don't date girls like me?" she asks, almost shyly.

Her question takes me by surprise in the worst way. "What is that supposed to mean?"

"I mean . . . I know I don't exactly have the figure of a hockey girlfriend. And that's fine—I just don't want to put you in an uncomfortable position."

My scowl is instant, and my response comes out growly. "No. That is not what I meant. At all. And there's nothing wrong with the way you look. *Nothing*, Braxton."

She's quiet for a few moments before she says, "Okay. Then we can make this relationship look however we want, can't we? We could have been dating in secret for years, or we could have something new."

Her feet pad along the hardwood before she comes around the side of the couch. She extends a steaming mug of what looks like tea to me, and I take it cautiously, not wanting the liquid to tip over the rim. Once I have the cup in a steady hold, she opens her fist and exposes two white pills resting on her palm.

"Drink that and take the pills," she orders when I continue to stare silently at the medicine. "It's just Ibuprofen."

I swipe them from her hand and toss them both back before gulping down the tea. The familiar taste of honey is like a soothing balm over the wounds that have reopened over the hellish past couple of days. Tea with honey has been a comfort drink for me since I was a child. I'm surprised she still remembers that.

Braxton sits on the opposite side of the couch and faces me, her lips twisted and legs tucked up beneath her. "Maybe I didn't want to be swept up in the crazy of your life when you were drafted, so we kept it a secret? Who are they to know?"

I chew on that for a moment. "I don't know if that will work. They'll dig into your background. Your schooling over the past few years, your social media presence. One bad tweet from when you were fifteen and you'll be the face of cancel culture."

"Actually, cancel culture doesn't really exist. I prefer looking at it as someone being held accountable for their past actions."

I heave a sigh and rest my head on the couch back. "Braxton."

"Right. Well, I don't have much other than my Instagram and Facebook pages, but both of those are as private as possible."

"What about while you were in university? Did you do or say anything that could come back to bite you?" *Any bitter boyfriends?* I leave that last part out, not sure I want to hear the answer.

Braxton's eyes narrow on me for a brief moment before relaxing. "I went to a few parties and kissed a few boys, but that's really it. I was too busy with my classes to make stupid decisions."

I tighten my jaw. A few boys? "Great."

"What about you? Anything I need to be concerned about?"

"You mean other than the fact I'm a heavy partier and an arrogant son of a bitch? No, I can't think of anything else."

She giggles, and the sound makes my heart skip. "Right. So, we haven't been dating in secret. It's new, then? A rekindled love?" She swallows as I stiffen.

"Yeah. Good enough for me," I mutter, feeling uncomfortably awkward.

Braxton nods. "What do you need me to do as your fake girlfriend? Is it just going to be games and stuff? Because I can do that easily enough, although I haven't been to a hockey game in years."

"We're about to enter the playoffs, so I'm assuming you'll need to be there for most of the games. The award ceremony is coming up in June, and I'm up for a couple of them. You'll probably need to be there for that too."

She nods. "Okay."

"How are you going to tell your family about this?" I ask, worry starting to fester.

"I don't know. They won't believe me if I tell them we're suddenly dating, not after everything that's just happened, but I can't tell them the truth either. Dad can't find out it's fake."

"Fuck," I mutter.

"I'll avoid it for as long as I can. At least until we're seen together for the first time."

"When is that going to happen, anyway? Dougie, that fucking asshole, didn't tell me anything about what we're supposed to do."

"I think we've talked about enough tonight. You and Dougie clearly need to chat before we do anything else. I don't want to mess anything up with this."

"It wouldn't be you that messes this up, Braxton."

Her expression turns quizzical. "You won't mess it up either. Sure, we might not be friends anymore, but we're both adults. I agreed to do this, and I'm not going to go back on that. We'll get this cleaned up, and then we can both get back to our lives."

"Right. You're right," I agree.

Yet for some reason, that sounds all wrong.

10

Braxton

AGE SIXTEEN

With a cup of tea warming my palms, I walk into Maddox's room and softly shut the door behind me. I stifle a laugh when I find him curled in the fetal position, just like he was when I left a few minutes ago. Tucked beneath a thick black duvet, he's nothing but a large blob on the bed. A mess of chestnut-brown curls peeks out from beneath the blanket, though, splayed out on a matching black pillow.

The sixteen-year-old baby came down with a stomach bug last night and called me just after six this morning, begging me to bring him back to health. With his family on a weekend trip to Toronto to see friends, he's home alone. There was supposed to be a hockey tournament starting tomorrow, but at this rate, he's going to be spending the weekend in bed instead.

I don't mind taking care of him. Actually, I kind of like it. But I've never minded doing anything when it comes to Maddox. Any time together is worth taking.

A slow, pained groan comes from beneath the blanket as I set the steaming mug on his bedside table and ease onto the bed beside him. I pinch the edge of the blanket and start to slowly peel it back, exposing a very, very shirtless and muscled Dox with his eyes shut and his lips parted on a breath.

He groans again, this time sounding more uncomfortable than in pain. The sudden exposure to the cool air is probably responsible for that.

"I brought you tea," I murmur.

One tired green eye peeks open. "What kind?" he rumbles.

"Lemon with honey."

"Thank you, Curly Fry." He slips an arm out from beneath the blanket and pulls on one of my tight curls for good measure. The other eye opens as he grins, flashing me two rows of gleaming white teeth.

I swat at his hand. "Enough of that name."

"I like it."

"You like referring to me as a kind of deep-fried potato?"

He rolls his eyes before circling my wrist with his long fingers and pulling on me until I move closer. A flash of self-consciousness has me adjusting my loose T-shirt back over my stomach when I feel it start to ride up. My leggings are a size too small, and the band keeps rolling down when I sit, leaving me feeling too exposed. I meant to throw these away the last time I did laundry, but I was in such a rush to get here that I must not have noticed the pinching of the material in my hips or the lack of stretch across my butt.

Maddox has seen my body change more than a handful of times over the course of our friendship. I've gone from skinny to overweight and then back again more times than I can count, but this time, I seem to be stuck on the heavier side. It's just how I am—how my body is. I've always gained weight easily and had to work my ass off—literally—to get back to where I was.

I eat when I'm stressed, and when I eat, I gain weight that brings feelings of resentment toward myself, which in turn makes me eat more. It's an evil cycle of mental torture that I can't seem to put an end to.

Fingers intertwine with mine. "Hey, what's wrong? What happened?"

My cheeks thump with embarrassment. "Nothing, sorry. I must have spaced out for a second."

"Is that what we're going with?"

I stare at our joined hands, and my heart flutters. Just like it always does. But I also ignore it—like always. "Do you think I'm pretty? Like, in a woman way, not a best friend type of way."

His brows tug in, creating a crease between them that I want to smooth out. There's almost an angry glow in his eyes, but that can't be right. Why would he be angry with me?

"No. I don't think you're pretty," he replies tightly.

My face burns with rejection. A bucket of ice water crashes over me, and I bite my tongue hard in an attempt to distract myself from the burning behind my eyes.

"Thank you for being honest," I whisper while trying to pull my hand free.

He squeezes my fingers, refusing to let go. "You're not simply pretty, Braxton. That would be a goddamn insult. You're the most beautiful girl I've ever seen. Cut that shit out right now," he growls.

Before I have a chance to let his words fully sink in, he's reaching behind him and grabbing something from the other side table. When he finds what he's looking for, he drops it in my lap.

"Who's in that picture frame?" he asks.

I slide my finger along the edge of the black frame and stare down at the photo inside. Tears blur my vision. How have I never noticed this there before?

"Me," I answer.

"Yeah. You."

"Why do you have this?"

He rakes his eyes over me, huffing a breath. "Why do I have a photo of you riding a horse, wearing a pair of boots that were probably covered in shit and a hideous helmet hiding your curls on my nightstand?"

"Yes," I whisper.

"So that I can look at you before I go to bed every fucking night, Braxton. You're not simply pretty. You're the most beautiful girl in the world. Never think otherwise."

The compliment is so honest. So raw. "You look at this every night?"

A rumble grows in his chest as he snatches the frame back and sets it back on the table. In one lightning-quick move, he has my back pinned to the headboard and himself settled between my knees. Our hands are still linked, and our close proximity screams trouble. We don't get this close to one another—not on purpose.

I fight to keep my expression casual, unbothered. His eyes flare. "It's the picture, or I piss off your father and force you to live in this house with me so I can have the real thing instead."

A shiver racks through me, and he must notice because he smirks, the sight of it way too damn attractive.

His voice drops, becoming a deep rasp. "I know which I would prefer, but I'm nothing if not respectful."

Holding eye contact with Maddox is easy, but looking away is a mission I always fail. There's something about the pure possession and control in his gaze that turns you spineless. I don't fight the transfer of power. I hand myself over to him with my hands out and don't regret a damn thing.

"You look like you're feeling better," I squeak.

He drops his chin and laughs deeply. Giving my hand a final squeeze, he slides his fingers free. "Let's watch a movie."

"A movie?"

"Yes, sweetheart. A movie."

Another one of his damn pet names. Everyone knows I'm nowhere close to sweet.

"Get back under the covers, and I'll get it ready," I say.

"You got it, boss." He flops over onto his back and shoves his legs under the blanket before pulling it up and over him.

I scurry off the bed and take my time grabbing the TV remote from his dresser. Maddox is my best friend, but everyone seems to think he wants to be more than that. I don't even remember a time when he wasn't flirting with me or scaring off any guy who showed even the slightest bit of interest in me. But that's just how Maddox is. He's protective and flirty. He wants the best for me, and I trust him completely when it comes to making sure I don't wind up with someone who doesn't treat me how I deserve.

Regardless of the feelings I have for him, I won't risk our friendship on a silly crush. We wouldn't work in a romantic setting, anyway. He's Maddox Hutton, and I'm just me.

Whatever schoolgirl crush I have on him will eventually wash away as easily as a drawing in the sand on a seashore.

But our friendship? That's going to last until the end of time.

11

Braxton

PRESENT

I SHOOT UP IN BED AND RUN TREMBLING HANDS OVER MY HAIR AND face. My fingertips touch the drool on my chin and swipe it away. The late-afternoon sun shines through the open window as a warm breeze makes the sheer curtains dance. A car horn blares somewhere in the distance, and I grab onto the noise, using it to ground me.

It was a memory. It wasn't real. I'm twenty-six, not sixteen. My blankets are white, not black. I'm alone. He's not here.

The reminder isn't comforting. No, instead, it makes me feel . . . empty? I sigh, pressing my palms into my eyes and rubbing the sleep away.

It's been over a week since I was at Maddox's penthouse, and in that time, all I've managed to think about is how far in over my head I really am.

We've texted a couple of times, mostly after his conversation with Dougie, where they discussed what our next move should be and how we were to act at our first public appearance, but other than that, it's been silence. It would be too easy to simply move on from the past and start fresh, so awkward tension is what we're left with.

Today the Vancouver Warriors play Colorado on home ice, and I get to make my official debut as Maddox Hutton's girlfriend. To add even more pressure to the situation, my seat tonight is right beside his family.

Talk about jumping in with both feet.

Nerves flutter beneath my skin as I push out of bed and head to my closet to get dressed. I left work early today after spending hours unable to concentrate on anything but the ulcer I was growing in my stomach. I came right home to shower the smell of animal off me and then take a nap. From the time on my alarm clock, I woke up earlier than I planned to.

My walk-in closet is incredibly underwhelming. With one half filled with nothing but matching scrub pants and tops and a mostly empty other half with dressier outfits and jeans, it's obvious how often I actually leave my house for anything other than work.

I grab one of my nicer pairs of jeans from their hanger, along with a thin sweater, and turn to leave, but a flash of green from inside a half-open box makes me pause. That specific box should have been in the basement. It's labelled *basement* for a reason. One the moving company clearly didn't care about.

My feet carry me toward it despite my annoyance, and I crouch, staring at the box like it might grow arms and take a swing at me. Carefully, I peel back the flaps and suck in a sharp breath. The white stitched name across the back of the old Warriors home jersey has my stomach doing backflips.

I still remember the day I bought this jersey, a month after Maddox was signed by the VW. The shop owner had hardly set the new Hutton jerseys out when I came in and bought one. It was almost nostalgic buying it. I was just so proud of him that the reality of our broken friendship wasn't enough to keep me from grabbing this last piece of him.

Not once have I so much as tried it on, but if there were ever a time to give it a whirl . . . it would be tonight. Suddenly, my head is full of pain-in-the-butt questions and insecurities.

What if he doesn't like it? What if it doesn't fit after all these years? Will it make me look desperate?

The sound of my phone ringing in my room is an unexpected but grateful distraction. I leave the jersey where it's been tucked away and rush to answer the call.

"Hello?"

"Hey. Am I interrupting something? You sound out of breath." Cooper, one of Maddox's and my closest friends since childhood, laughs into the speaker.

"Nope, not interrupting. I just ran to catch your call. You know how I am with running." I walk over to my vanity and frown at the new pimple on my chin. *Perfect timing for a breakout.*

"I think you would like it if you really gave it a shot. It's good for the mind."

"My mind is just fine, thank you, Dr. Cooper."

He chuckles. "You're the only doctor here."

"Technically, we're both doctors. Your doctorate is just way cooler than mine."

"You think a doctorate in art is cooler than you being a veterinarian? Nah, Braxton. Maybe your mind isn't as solid as you think it is."

A smile cracks through the stiff muscles in my face. "Did you call for a reason other than to make fun of me?"

"You see, I did, but you just make it too easy to rile you up."

"You're an ass."

"That would actually be you. Considering you didn't seem to be planning on telling me about your new boyfriend before it went public," he scolds me.

"Who told you about that?" I groan.

"Who do you think?"

"Oh," I mutter.

Maddox, Cooper, and I used to be thick as thieves growing up. Sure, Maddox and I were closer, but I think that had more to do with our two-year age gap with Cooper. At least, it did in the beginning.

After everything that went down with the two of us, I kept in contact with Cooper but never had the guts to ask about Maddox, and he knew better than to bring him up. I'm sure he and Maddox had the same agreement regarding me. Coop was the perfect Switzerland, and for that, I'm beyond grateful.

"Yeah, oh."

"I'm sorry. I was going to tell you, but I wanted to wrap my head around this first before dragging you into it."

"I understand that. I just expected you to be the one to tell me, that's all. We've always been more open about that stuff than Dox and I are."

"Are you saying that I'm your favourite?"

"Don't try and change the subject. What's up with this fake dating stuff?"

"It just sort of happened, Coop."

"Just sort of happened?" he echoes. "You signed an NDA."

"Geez, did he just crack right open and spill everything?" I grumble.

"You could say that."

"Great," I huff.

"This is a terrible idea, love. Are you sure you're making the right move?"

"No."

A pause, and then a long exhale. "Promise me that you're going to protect yourself. I can't see you like that again."

"A zombie, you mean."

"Sad," he corrects me.

"It was my fault, Coop. I've accepted that, and my life is better for it. This could be my chance to right my wrongs. To earn his forgiveness and finally close that chapter of my life."

He's not the only one afraid of what could happen and how it could drag me back down into the hole it took me far too long to crawl out of, but I refuse to miss out on this opportunity. It's now or never. Whatever comes . . . I have to be ready for it.

"He's nervous too, you know? The guy could barely get a breath in through his rant."

That does little to settle me, but I keep that to myself. "I found his jersey in my closet."

"Are you going to wear it today?"

"He told you about today?" I ask while walking into the closet and staring at the box again.

"Yes."

"Do you think I should wear it?" *Say no.*

"I think if you're trying to get over what happened, that yes, you should. It's a step forward."

I frown. "You suck."

The laugh that follows my insult is pure Cooper—sunshine and rainbows. "Addie is picking you up, right?"

"That's what Maddox said."

I haven't seen Adalyn since she was ten. Besides Noah, she's the one I'm most nervous to see again. Does she hate me as much as her oldest brother does?

"It's a good move. Addie is the more open one of the entire Hutton family. I don't think she holds a grudge against you, just your father," Cooper says.

I nod even though he can't see me and close the gap between me and the damn box. "Okay, yeah. I can work with that."

"Yeah, you can. You've got this."

"Thank you, Coop. I love you."

"I love you too. Talk later, B. Have fun."

"I'll try. Bye."

We say goodbye, and I set my phone on a shelf.

With a new sense of determination, I crouch back down in front of the box and peel back the top, brushing my fingers over the jersey before pinching it and holding it up in front of me.

Nodding, I suck back a deep breath and stand before pulling the jersey on and tugging it as far down my torso as it will go. I hold my arms out in front of me and start to relax when the sleeves are a good length. When my eyes fall to my stomach, I smile.

It's a perfect fit.

And half an hour later, I'm done up properly. Foundation, mascara, a peachy lipstick, and a quick touch-up to my hair is all it takes for me to feel like a new woman. After a couple of spritzes of perfume, I'm grabbing my purse and starting to put my phone inside when it chimes with a text.

Unknown: I think I'm here.

Just like that, I'm ready to throw up. The grilled cheese I made for dinner churns in my stomach as my nerves come racing back.

Me: On my way out!

I've already switched all the lights off and locked the back door, but after spending eight years in Toronto for school, I double-check the lock before slipping on a pair of white sneakers and stepping out onto the front porch.

My new home is a two-bedroom, two-bathroom new-construction townhouse with high peaks and a big front window that makes the living space appear bigger than it is. Being the third unit in the long row of homes, I share two walls with neighbours. It isn't always ideal to be sandwiched between two households, but I've been lucky enough to have respectful ones on both sides. It helps that I'm usually gone early in the morning and home in the later part of the evening, so I doubt I would see or hear much of anything regardless.

When I spin around on the porch, I spot a deep red Jeep waiting on the curb a few feet ahead of where I live. The windows are heavily tinted, and there looks to be a social media handle on the back one. I straighten my shoulders and stride toward the beefy vehicle, my curls bouncing with each overen-thusiastic step.

My courage starts to falter the closer I get, and the moment I come up on the passenger side and catch a glance at the driver, I stumble. I slam a hand to the front door to catch myself as my cheeks flare with embarrassment.

The window rolls down as a drop-dead gorgeous blonde leans out and stares at me with wide eyes and lips parted.

"Braxton?"

"Adalyn?"

12

Braxton

It takes me a full minute to gather my wits and slide into the Jeep to take a proper look at the youngest Hutton sibling.

Her baby face and innocent blue eyes are no more. Instead, her features are sharp, and her eyes are wild and spark with crazy stories that I ache to hear all about. The loose waves that hang over her shoulders are a platinum-blonde colour with hot pink and teal highlights throughout in true Adalyn fashion. A healthy flush softens the sharp lines of her jaw and cheekbones, and her glossy lips break out in a grin, revealing straight white teeth.

"You're gorgeous," she says before surprising me by throwing herself over the centre console and pulling me into her arms. "I missed you."

"Me? You're stunning." I ease my arms around her petite frame and squeeze her tight. "And I missed you too. So much."

We hug for longer than probably necessary, but it still isn't long enough. When we pull back, I can't seem to stop smiling. Addie falls back in her seat but keeps her body turned toward me. Her eyes hold mine, and I reach out to grab her hand.

"I still can't believe that you're back. When Dox told me you were, I kicked him in the shin and told him not to lie to me about you," she says.

I laugh at the image before smashing my lips together. Guilt swirls. "I should have called. I guess I was too scared of what you would say when you picked up."

She nods thoughtfully. "I'm mad at you, but I'm more hurt than angry. Now I understand why you left, but back then? God, I thought you were such a bitch."

"I don't blame you for that."

She squeezes my fingers. "We can't change anything now, and you're helping my brother when he needs all of us rallied around him. That's all that matters right now."

"I need you to know how sorry I am, though. You didn't deserve to be left with questions. The last thing I wanted to do was hurt anyone. I just . . ."

"You couldn't stay. I know. I get it."

I blow out a breath. "Yeah."

"We forgave you a long time ago, Brax."

"Everyone but him." I force myself to keep from rubbing at the growing ache in my chest.

"You know why he hasn't," she says softly. "Give it time. After everything is said and done with this mess he's found himself in, I'm sure the past will be left in the past, and you can both move on."

I give her a grateful smile. "Thank you, Addie. But I want to hear all about you. Tell me everything."

"That's a dangerous thing to say, babe. I'm a talker."

"Don't care. Give me the full rundown. Don't miss anything."

We release each other's hands, and she adjusts herself in the driver's seat before pulling the Jeep onto the road. The sun is setting in front of us, casting a beautiful glow over the horizon. With the sunroof open, the radio playing a country song, and the comforting company of an old friend, I feel good. I tuck the memory of this feeling away for later tonight when I'm sure I'll need it.

"Well, I signed up to be a Girl Scout about two months after you left and only managed to last three weeks before I was kicked out for refusing to listen to the leaders on a camping trip. Then I joined a few school sports teams, but nothing really stuck."

"I can't picture you as a Girl Scout or on a sports team."

She laughs, the sound so pure and carefree. "Me following a stern set of rules and a schedule? I was setting myself up for failure."

"You've always been a wild child. Everyone else should have known better," I tease.

"That's what I said! Anyway, Cooper and Dox taught me to skateboard when I was fourteen, and I broke my ankle a month later and then my wrist a few weeks after that. Dad hid my board for a while so that I couldn't hurt myself again, but after I got my first job at that adorable little cupcake shop on Clover Street, I bought a new one. Surprisingly, that hobby has stuck around over the years. Have you ever skateboarded?"

"No way. My balance is awful to start with."

"You should try it anyway. I can teach you sometime."

I glance at her and smile. "I would like that."

"It's a date." She changes lanes and steps heavily on the gas. I jerk in my seat while she taps her hands excitedly on the steering wheel. "Do you remember when I said I wanted to skydive?"

"Of course I do. You scared the crap out of me when you told me that."

"Well, I did it! You should have been there, Brax. There's nothing like it. *Nothing*."

My jaw hangs open. "You actually did it? Your *dad* let you jump out of a plane?"

"After he knew how happy it would make me, of course he did." She winks. "It helped that Cooper volunteered to join me.

I'm sure Maddox would have, but you know how terrified he is of heights."

"Cooper jumped out of a plane?" I sputter.

"It was him or Noah, and Noah wasn't in the right space to be doing anything like that."

My heart warms. "Cooper did it for the both of you." God, I love that guy.

Addie's neck and ears are pink when she says, "What about you? Besides slaving away at school, what have you been doing?"

"Well, I definitely wasn't doing anything as exciting as jumping out of a plane. I spent most of my time rushing between school and work, but after I graduated, I did take a trip to Spain with a few friends. It was probably one of the best weeks of my life."

My college dormmate spent two days convincing me to come with her and a few of her friends on a trip to Madrid, and while we were all dirt poor and had been living off ramen noodles for the past couple of years, she managed to get me to come. I still don't know how she managed to do it, but I don't regret my decision. Not even a little.

Besides my decision to pack up my life and go to school across the country, it was the most impulsive I'd ever been.

"Oh, my God! Where did you stay? Barcelona is on my list of places I'm going to travel to next year."

"Right. Your big trip, right? We stayed in a hostel in Madrid. If you don't mind rooming with strangers and having to share a bathroom, it's not a bad option."

She shudders. "Sharing a bathroom?"

I laugh. "Maybe budget to stay in hotels."

"I've been saving money for this trip since my sixteenth birthday. Everyone thinks I'll change my mind about leaving, but it won't happen."

"Do you have anyone to go with you? I think you going alone is what's freaking everyone out."

"Yeah, right. Maddox will be in the middle of the hockey season, Noah would rather chew off his own finger than travel with me, and Cooper is too damn old now to be any fun. Unless you're going to volunteer, I'm shit out of luck."

I frown. "If I could, I would. Your brothers are out of the question, but Cooper would pout so hard if he heard you call him 'too damn old.' He's only two years older than me, for the record."

"Two years is a long time in old man years."

A laugh slips out before I can stop it. "Fine. What about your friends? I'm sure there are a bucketload of teenage girls wanting to go scout out sexy European men."

"The people who pretend to be my friends are social climbers. They're not interested in a real friendship." She twists her mouth and glances at me. "Have you really not kept up with any of us? Not even on social media?"

"No. I should have, but I knew once I went there once, I would have fallen down that rabbit hole and ended up doing something stupid like drunk call your brother."

She fights back a smile. "Right. Well, I have a decent following on social media, so most of my friends from school or online are either after me for a quick jump in their follower count or to get close to one of my brothers. So, yeah. That's a no on bringing any of my friends with me."

I double blink. "Oh. How many followers? I thought that was an Instagram handle on your back window, but I wasn't sure."

"A couple million. Honestly, the self-promo was Maddox's idea. He's the one who kind of got my career up and running."

"Your career? A couple *million*? Gosh, Addie. You haven't even graduated high school yet."

She shrugs. "I just do some modelling and small things like that. Really, I use my page to show off all of the crazy things I do. It started out as me just posting the footage from my skydive and a few tricks on my board, but things kind of spiralled from there. When you have a famous dad and brother, a large following kind of just falls in your lap."

I can't tell if she's happy about that. The last thing a young girl needs to worry about is social media and everything that comes with it. I'm not sure whether to be angry at Maddox for encouraging this or proud that he's trying to help her out.

It's not any of my business, I remind myself.

"Oh no, I know that look. Trust me, I'm happy doing what I'm doing," she adds.

I stay silent and watch her for a few moments as she turns down a road behind the arena and finger waves at the security guard standing at the entrance to an underground parking garage. He waves back and ushers us inside, and a second later, Addie parks. There's no hint of a lie in her open expression, so I decide to believe her. Adalyn Hutton isn't the type of girl to settle. If she were unhappy with what she was doing, she simply wouldn't do it.

Her courage is one of the most special things about her. Would it be weird to say I look up to someone so much younger than me?

"Okay. I believe you."

She grins. "Do I say thank you?"

"No. Definitely not." I snort a laugh.

I take a look out the window and blow out a long breath as the current situation comes racing back. We're here, and there's no turning back now.

"You look like you could hurl," Addie notes, a twinge of sympathy in her voice.

"I'm nervous to see everyone," I admit.

"Don't be. They're excited to see you. Well, Mom and Dad are. They forced Noah to come tonight, so just ignore him. He's in a bad place."

Great. "Okay. I can do that."

"Oh!" She reaches into the back seat and pulls a huge pink purse onto her lap. Rifling through it, she clicks her tongue. "We have to take a photo and post it before we go in. My brother's orders."

"Seriously?"

She pulls her phone out of the bag and swipes the screen, pulling up the camera. "I know it seems over-the-top. But they want to spark the rumours, and this is the fastest way."

"Fine," I relent.

"You can give Dox shit later. I actually encourage it."

I shake my head, smiling. "Just take the photo."

Not needing to be told twice, she leans toward me as I do the same, and we both pose for the photo. She snaps it quickly and starts typing furiously before shoving the phone back into her bag.

"There. Now we can go."

Addie turns the car off and hops out, but as I go to follow her, my phone pings. I slide it out of my jeans pocket, and my eyes widen at the message.

> Maddox: Breathe. You've got this.

> Me: Thank you. Good luck.

I breathe deeply and, with newfound confidence, join Addie outside.

13

Maddox

BENTLEY SHOVES MY SHOULDER BEFORE FLOPPING DOWN BESIDE ME. The dressing room is ripe with both nerves and the always lingering smell of sweat. There are ten minutes until we hit the ice for warm-ups, and with Coach delivering his pre-game speech just minutes ago, we're all giving ourselves pep talks before it's time. It's game three of the first round, and if we win tonight, we'll be up by three and one step closer to the second round—opponent still to be determined.

This is my seventh season with the VW, and we're still without a cup. I feel the pressure to bring this team to the title like a fucking dumbbell on my chest. That's what I'm here for, yet I've failed every year.

I'm Oakley Hutton's son—the face of the Vancouver Warriors. And despite what Alexander and all the suits upstairs promise me, it doesn't stop the suffocating feeling of failure each loss brings.

You don't pay a franchise player ten million dollars not to take you to the cup final game, and you sure as shit don't renew his contract when he hasn't done his part.

I won't feel confident in my future until my lips are on the Stanley Cup.

"Your eye looks better," Bentley notes, bending over to tie his skate.

"Feels better."

"I've been waiting patiently for the scoop on that chick from the vet place, but I'm getting antsy. I'm about to be real offended if you weren't planning on explaining."

I roll my shoulders and pull at the neck of my jersey. It's hot as fuck in all this gear. "Not here, man."

"Why not? They're all going to know about her real quick anyway."

My stomach tumbles. Sweat breaks out on the back of my neck, and I swipe it away with a firm hand. I haven't been this nervous before a game since I was a teenager, and despite my feelings about my looming contract, this nauseated feeling is all courtesy of Braxton.

Seeing her in the stands watching me play and cheering me on used to electrify me. It made me believe that while I was on that ice, I was invincible. Untouchable.

But now? Now I worry I could be taken out at any moment. Her presence is a weakness that I can't afford but can't refuse either.

"She was my best friend for most of my life. Since we were five. The last time I saw her was before I re-entered the draft."

"That's a long time with no contact. Seven years? Eight?"

"Eight. I was eighteen when I entered the first time and nineteen when I re-entered."

"Are you going to elaborate, or are you going to make me use force?"

I roll my eyes. "Braxton's father was my agent, despite my dad's protests. Braxton was my best friend, and I didn't think much of her dad, but I trusted him because I figured he wouldn't do anything to piss off his daughter. It was obvious how attached to each other we were."

"You loved her," Bentley interrupts.

I look at him, my eyes narrowing. My guard is so high even I'm having trouble seeing over it. "What?"

"Nah, you can't hide that shit from me. I saw it the minute you two got in the same room together. You loved her back then and probably still do now."

"You don't know what you're talking about. Yeah, I loved her when we were kids, but that was a *long* fucking time ago." I block out the voice in my head that tells me I'm a goddamn idiot and push on without letting Bentley respond.

"Roy Heights wanted an easy payday and thought I could make more money if I went with a team other than the one that drafted me. But he messed up and could have cost us both of our careers. Luckily for me, he was the only one of us who lost everything. If I hadn't had my family name in my back corner, I wouldn't even be here on this team right now."

"What did Braxton have to do with it? That sounds like a whole lot of drama, but none of it explains why you two cut contact."

My laugh is bitter and burns the whole way up. "Who do you think convinced me—"

"Game time! Get your asses out there and bring us this win!" Coach roars from the doorway. The team breaks out in hoots and hollers, and my words drift off to a place I hope they never come back from.

It's game time. Nothing else matters. Especially my past with a woman who risked our entire friendship over the fear of losing me.

Braxton

"Row three," Addie says from in front of me. The steps down to the seats nearly at ice level are steep, and she is flying down them. I'm struggling to keep pace with her.

Conversations drawl on around us as the intensity inside the building grows and grows with each minute that passes. It's a sea of green tonight, and it makes me feel a bit less awkward wearing Maddox's jersey.

When we first arrived, I started counting the number of Hutton jerseys I saw, but I lost track somewhere along the way. Maddox and his father wear different numbers, and yes, maybe I was keeping track of how many Hutton jerseys were decorated with a number eleven for his dad and number twenty-one for Maddox.

It made my heart swell to see more twenty-ones.

Adalyn turns into our row, and my pulse picks up as she shuffles past several pairs of feet. The moment I see the familiar faces of Ava and Oakley Hutton, everything I planned to say slips away. Ava's green eyes soften when they land on me, and she's pushing out of her seat and closing the distance between us before I have a chance to prepare myself.

"Oh, Braxton," she whispers before collecting me in a warm embrace. I sag in her hold and hug her back as tears fill my eyes. "Look at you."

She smells just how I remember. Like freshly brewed coffee and oranges. If she notices me smelling her, she doesn't say anything. Our hug lasts for what feels like a lifetime, but with her rubbing her hand up and down my back and just simply holding me, I don't rush to back away.

"Mom. Sit down, please," a deep, rough voice says. Ava jolts away like she's just remembered where we are, and I fight back the urge to glare at the man who dared interrupt our reunion.

I find him over Ava's shoulder, sitting between Oakley and Adalyn. He's already looking at me with tar pits for eyes and a scowl that would have me running for the hills had I not known this man since he was in diapers. His aura screams fuck off, and I choose to smile at him instead of glare. When he curls his lip at me, I take that as a win.

"It's good to see you, Noah," I say.

"Wish I could say the same," he sneers.

Ava sucks in a sharp breath. "Noah."

"Don't be an asshole," Addie scolds.

Noah ignores them all and turns back to face the ice, dismissing me. It's easy to brush off his attitude because I know I deserve it.

"We're glad you're here tonight," Oakley says, his piercing green eyes digging deep into the blue of mine.

The protective papa bear has arrived, and he's assessing the potential danger I could bring his family. I've always loved this side of Oakley. He would do anything to keep the people he loves safe. I just hate that right now he's eyeing me like I'm the potential threat.

"Me too."

I give him a smile as I take a mental step back. Feeling like a burden has got to be one of the worst feelings, and I hate that that's how being here makes me feel. Maddox's family can paint a pretty picture of how happy they are to see me again, but it won't change how *I* see this situation.

I've gotten their son into this mess, and now tonight, when they should be having a blast cheering him on at a playoff game, they're stuck babysitting me. The girl who broke everyone's heart and then ran away while they stood bleeding.

Ava, as if sensing the change in me, grabs my fingers and sits on one of the black fold-down seats. Her eyes are warm as she looks up at me and pulls ever so slightly on my hand. I sit beside her and cross my ankles beneath the seat.

Addie is sitting too far away for my liking, but I'm not about to call her over and ask everyone to shift down a seat so I can use her as a human-sized comfort pillow.

"I'm sorry about Noah. He just . . . doesn't like these things," Ava says softly.

"Hockey games?"

"It's not so much the game but the crowd that comes with it."

"You don't have to apologize for him."

I remember she's still holding my hand when she squeezes once before releasing it. With a tight release of breath, I pull it back and clasp my fingers together on my lap.

"This must be so nerve-racking for you. Of course I have to apologize for him. We want this to go well."

"Well, I appreciate it. Thank you."

My spine snaps straight when players from both teams start flooding out from the dressing room and push onto the ice. The Colorado players take one end while the VW take the other. Like magnets, my eyes are drawn to Maddox as he skates a few quick laps around half-ice and then comes to a dead stop by the blue line.

My heart clunks around in my chest when our eyes collide, locking together in a heavy embrace. With a quick shake of his head, his shoulders drop, and the end of his stick pushes backward, nearly tripping one of his teammates as they skate behind him. White noise bubbles in my ears when he adjusts the stick and tucks it beneath his right arm before pulling off his left glove.

I shake my head woodenly at him a single time, but he acts as if he doesn't see it. *This wasn't part of the plan.* We hadn't planned on doing anything yet besides having me here tonight. Ava gasps, and I know she wasn't told about this beforehand either.

As if in slow motion, I watch as he drops the glove and then covers his heart with his fist before pulling it away to point at me. A swell of emotion builds and builds inside of me as I push myself to press two shaking fingers to my lips and kiss them before pointing right back. Just like I used to.

The moment shatters like a broken mirror. Hurt and anger flash across his face seconds before he's spinning around and quickly grabbing his glove off the ice. Shock and disbelief have me in a chokehold, but it's the searing pain of our beautiful past being tainted by our broken present that does the most damage.

Girls giggle a few seats away when Maddox pulls his helmet off and squirts water from a Gatorade bottle over his head before shaking out his wet curls. He's only been on the bench for a minute, but he's already leaning over the boards, ready to get back out there. It's only a junior game, but that doesn't matter to him. Every game is as important as an NHL game.

His features are tight with determination, but his eyes are light when they find me in the stands. He grins at me, and I wave back. "You got this," I mouth.

He glances at his coach before looking back at me and mouthing, "For you."

Then in one quick motion, he has his glove left off and pounds his chest with his fist before pointing across the rink at me. My laugh is pure and raw as I kiss two fingers and point back.

Ava's hand on my knee has me jolting back to the present just in time to see the teams clearing off the ice, preparing for their big entrance that comes ten minutes later.

I spend the entire time sitting in silence, and nobody tries to get me to speak.

14

Maddox

"Hutton! Hang back a sec," Coach orders once the dressing room has started to clear after the game. I'm usually one of the last ones out, but that's how I've always been. The first guy there and usually the last one out.

Colt and a couple of other players tip their chins at me as they leave, but Bentley lingers, his eyes full of concern.

"All good, man. Go home," I say.

He doesn't look convinced. "You sure?"

My relationship with Coach has never been great. He thinks I'm a spoiled kid with a famous last name and a chip on my shoulder. But I never chose my last name, and the chip on my shoulder is what pushes me to be the best player on that fucking ice. He only seems to mind it when we lose.

"Positive." I nod.

"Text me later. Good game tonight."

It was a three-to-one game, with two of those goals being mine and the other his. I grin. "You too, sweetheart."

And then he's gone, a low chuckle following him out the door. I finish buttoning up my shirt—opting the leave the top two buttons undone and the tie I wore earlier stuffed in my bag

—before slipping on my black leather shoes and heading to Coach's office.

I find Coach Pelant sitting on the soft brown sofa at the far side of his office with his head leaned back and legs spread wide. He looks about ten years younger with his eyes closed and the stress lines between his thick eyebrows relaxed. I almost don't want to interrupt his small break, but he's already noticed me.

"You played good out there. I was worried you would be too distracted to focus on the game tonight," he says lowly, sleepily.

I lean in the doorway and push a hand through my still-damp hair. The quick shower I took after the game was solely for Braxton's benefit. Usually, I prefer to shower at home, but I doubt she would have appreciated having to take a ride home with a guy who smelled like a homeless man's sock in the summer.

A pinch in my chest has me moving on with this conversation. I don't want to think about her right now. Not how devastated she looked when I pointed at her on the ice and definitely not how fucking awful it made me feel watching her purse those lips and kiss her fingers, knowing that the first time I get to feel those plump lips against mine, it won't be real. It will all be an act.

Fuck. *Enough.* We haven't even talked about that yet. That's a topic for tonight.

"Hockey is always top priority to me," I answer.

"I like that about you, Maddox. I can rely on you. It makes my life easier."

I tense. "You're welcome."

He answers by pushing up into a proper sitting position and leaning forward with his elbows on his thighs. Turning his head, he looks at me. *Really* looks at me.

"I talked to Alex and your father last night. It seems I was the last to know about your new project, but I'm here if you need anything."

My jaw tenses when he refers to Braxton as a project, but I

bite my tongue. "I appreciate the support. If that's all, I have to say hi to my family before they leave."

"Yeah, that's all. Let me know if you need anything. Try not to miss any more practices. The team can't see you getting special treatment."

This time, I let my tongue run free. "Special treatment? You think me taking care of my family and getting myself into shit with the press is special treatment? Alexander did for me what he would have done for any of his players at my skill level. I've worked my ass off to earn his respect."

His thin upper lip curls the slightest bit, and I prepare myself for a comeback I know I won't like, but a set of footsteps behind me cuts the conversation short. I turn around and startle at the sight of Braxton in the dressing room, frowning at me.

"Sorry, your mom asked me to come find you because it's taken you longer than usual to meet them, and security let me back here with this pass I got from your dad—" She lifts a laminated card hung around her neck by a lanyard. "I knocked on the door first, but nobody answered, so I came in and then heard you talking—"

"Braxton." I cut her off, the corner of my mouth trying to lift. "It's fine. I'm done here anyway."

In my peripheral, I catch Coach moving toward me and quickly step into the doorway, blocking his view of her. I don't know why I feel the need to protect her from him, but I don't have it in me right now to question it.

"I'll see you tomorrow," I tell him before turning my back on him and closing the gap between me and Braxton. She looks fucking amazing in green, but I swallow the compliment that has inched its way up my throat.

I'm as stiff as a board, but she doesn't say anything as I press my palm softly to her lower back and lead her out of the dressing room, leaving my bag behind. Her perfume tickles my nose, and the sparks attacking my palm become impossible to ignore. She shifts closer, and I don't push her away. Not right now.

"I'm sorry for interrupting," she sighs.

I move her in front of me as we leave the dressing room, and my eyes zero in on the name and number on her back. It looks perfect, like it was meant to be there. My dick hardens instantly, and I quickly adjust it before she notices.

"It was good timing, actually," I mutter once we reach the player-only hallway. My family should be waiting by the garage entrance. I would love to see a security guard try to tell Dad he can't park there anymore.

"Your coach seems like an asshole."

"He doesn't think I deserve what I have. Acts like my dad has gotten me where I am in this league. Everything that's happened recently is only reinforcing his belief," I tell her, opening up in a way that surprises me.

"He's an idiot and an asshole, then. You've worked for this. For all of it."

"I know. He can't convince me otherwise. It's just shitty that he can't be in my corner while we figure this out."

"He's just one person. You have the support of so many others."

"You're right."

I glance down at her and pull in a long inhale. She's let her curls run free tonight, and they bounce and bob with each step we take. Long lashes flutter over her eyes and sweep the skin beneath. There's a natural flush to her cheeks that pushes through the makeup on her skin, and I ache to feel how warm they are against my fingertips.

She's so beautiful it hurts.

"You've probably heard it a lot tonight, but you played really well out there. I haven't watched a game in a long time, and I forgot how much I actually enjoy it."

"Why did you stop watching hockey?" I ask.

She hesitates before saying, "It reminded me of you."

I drop my hand from her back and shove it in my pants pocket. With a strangled cough, I clear my throat. "Right."

"We need to clear the air, Maddox. Sooner rather than later if we want this to work. I can't do this with you if I constantly feel like you hate me. It's only going to get harder from here. Your sister posted a picture of us earlier, and your page is already overrun with questions."

She sounds exhausted, and I won't pretend I don't feel the same way. It's time to get everything out in the open, even if that doesn't bring the forgiveness she's hoping it will. I need this fake relationship to work, and if we react to each other the way we did before the game tonight, nobody is going to buy it.

There is only a month and a half until the adoption day. We can handle each other for that long. Right?

"You're right. It's time we cleared the air."

Braxton

MADDOX'S CHEST is nearly pressed to my back as we stand on my front porch, and I unlock the door. Thankfully, it's late enough that I won't have to worry about my neighbours seeing him here. Especially not Ralph, the hockey fanatic.

I'm relieved Maddox didn't fight me on my offer to come to my place instead of his again. If we're going to do this, I need to be somewhere comfortable, and his stone-cold penthouse is not that place.

I push the door open, and he mutters, "Cute."

It is cute. It's bright and smells like the strawberry-scented wall plug-in in the living room. My furniture is mostly handed down and repurposed besides the fluffy white, faux-fur rug tucked in front of a velvet, teal couch and cozy black armchair. I was going through one of my aesthetic moods when I stumbled upon it, and I folded like a lawn chair in the wind at the image of it inside my home surrounded by vibrant colours.

"Thanks. Living room okay?"

He grunts a reply, and I take that as a yes, leading us through an archway that he has to duck his head under. I stifle a laugh and flip on the light.

"You live in a hobbit home," he grumbles, sitting on the couch. Surprisingly, he doesn't have any complaints about it. He just stretches out his legs and drops his head to the couch back and stares at the popcorn ceiling.

"I don't. You're just massive." With a slight turn of his head, he cocks a brow at me. My eyes go wide as my body heats. "Screw you."

The corner of his mouth twitches slightly, but he doesn't smile. "Who's starting? You or me?"

"You make it sound like this is a simple business transaction."

"I'm just tired, Braxton."

I chew on the inside of my cheek. "Tired of tonight or all of this?"

"I'm tired of everything at this point."

"I'm sorry."

He looks back at the ceiling, his jaw tensing. "Just tell me why you did what you did and then took off. You ruined everything and then left us all behind. I've racked my brain for years trying to figure out why your first instinct was to run from me after everything we've been through, but I still can't figure it out."

"Would you have forgiven me if I had stayed?"

Silence. Another jaw tick.

"Exactly. I didn't *want* to leave. I had to."

"Bullshit. You didn't have to go anywhere. I would have forgiven you. I loved you."

Scolded, my eyes fall to my lap as they begin to well with tears that I quickly blink back. "I couldn't even look at you after what happened."

"Yeah, well, you were the only one I wanted to see."

I flinch. "I was young and couldn't bear the thought of losing you. I thought I was doing the right thing for me. *Now* I know I was wrong, but I made a mistake. There's nothing else I can say in my defense. I've paid for my actions every single day for eight years."

"A mistake?" he echoes, shooting forward on the couch. His eyes are wild and angry when they meet mine. "You told me you thought your father's idea for me to reject my draft offer was the right one for me. You knew the risks that came with that choice, but you let him talk me into it and then helped convince me it was the right move when you knew it wasn't!"

"I was scared! It's not a good explanation, but it's the only one I have. I was young and selfish and in love with you, and you were moving to Florida!"

We're so close now, and I blink, confused how we got here so quickly. Our knees are touching, and the hand I have pressed flush to the cushion is only inches from the tip of his pointer finger. I look back up from our hands and gulp at the fire in his waiting stare.

I want to touch him so badly, just to remind myself he's really here. Despite the anger and broken hearts, I miss him deeply. Just one brush of my thumb along his stubbled jaw or across his puffed bottom lip—or better yet, his arms around me. Something so simple would heal me more than any number of words.

"If you had loved me the way I loved you, you wouldn't have lied to me. And you would have stayed and fought for me when I nearly lost everything."

"Maddox," I whisper brokenly.

He tears his eyes away and sits back, creating space between us that I immediately want to take away. Instead, I tuck my hands beneath my thighs.

"I'm so sorry. I should have stayed. I should have fought for your forgiveness, even if I never got it. You deserved better. Everyone did."

His tongue darts out to lick his lips before he asks, "Do you know what the worst part of all of this is?"

"What?" My skin clams up.

"That after everything, I still can't find it in myself to hate you."

15

Maddox

PAIN FILLS HER EYES AS A TEAR FALLS. THEN ANOTHER. AND another.

She's crying right in front of me, and fuck it all to hell, but I can't stop myself from reaching for her. I slide one arm around her back and another across her front in order to wrap her up and pull her into a tight hold. My chest tightens when a sob racks through her, and she tries to pull away from me. She swats at my arms and shakes her head, sending her tears flying. The second one hits my neck, I'm done.

"Enough, Braxton. Stop fighting me."

"Let me cry! Just let me hate myself for this a bit longer, and then I'll stop," she pleads.

I would if I could. Instead, I clasp my hands at her back and pull her all the way across the couch until she's settled on my lap. She sniffles and buries her face in the skin where my shoulder and neck meet before going lax. Slowly, I unclasp my hands and cautiously place them on her back. I should move them up and down in a rubbing motion or something, but I stay frozen like a fucking loser.

"I'm so sorry," she whispers, repeating the words I've waited to hear for so long. The same words I promised myself I wouldn't accept when and if I did hear them.

The smell of her fruity shampoo is so overwhelming in this position that I have to tilt my head back and rest it on the back of the couch to get away from it. I refuse to give in to the voice in my head telling me to bury my face in the tight black curls and take a whiff of it straight from the source. But I'm not as strong as I thought I was because while I don't give in to the one urge, I do another.

I shut my eyes and drag my hand up her spine and along the bare skin of her neck until my fingers slip through those curls and spread wide over the base of her skull. Fuck. Me. She shivers against me, and I grit my teeth at the rush of pleasure that follows. Soft and warm and fitted goddamn perfectly against me.

"I can't forgive you," I say roughly, the words scraping my throat on the way up. "Not right now. Not yet."

A soft, choked cry, and then she nods so slightly I barely feel the movement. "Okay."

"But we still need to do this. I still need your help, so I'll try to focus more on the present and not the past. That's the best I can do."

"I'll do everything I can to help you. I promise."

My fingers tighten their hold on her hair before I relax them, not wanting to hurt her. "Our next game is at home again in two days, and if we win, we'll enter the second round. Whenever our first game is, you'll need to be there. I know you don't like to fly, but you should come to a few away games too. I can get it arranged so you can fly on the team plane."

"You don't have to do that. I can fly on my own."

My mind is already made up, so I move on. "We need to figure out public appearances outside of just games. The adoption day is a given, but until then, we need to be seen together."

"Do you go out after games? To bars?"

"Not really. Sometimes."

"I think we should start there. Adalyn mentioned posting pictures of each other online too."

Right. Like the one she took and tagged me in during my game. I had to silence my phone after that, but it was Alexander's idea, and what he says goes. "That works."

Slowly, she lifts her head from my shoulder and looks away before wiping at her face. A sniffle cuts through the silence just as easily as it does my chest before she's looking back at me with a timid smile.

"Sorry about that. I'm just going to . . ." She frantically climbs off my lap and drops to the cushion beside me. Her cheeks are flaming red, and while younger Maddox would have teased her about being embarrassed over something so small, the older version does not. "Thank you for . . . that."

I shrug and pick an invisible lint off my chest. The movement has a burst of her perfume flying from my shirt, and I decide right now that I'm tossing it out as soon as I get home.

"I'll text you tomorrow, and we can go from there."

She nods. "Okay."

An awkward silence falls over us, and I take that as my sign to get the hell out of here. Standing, I push my hands into my pockets and nip at my bottom lip. Do I just say bye? Fuck, I hate awkwardness.

"I'll walk you out," she says, sensing my discomfort. I release a breath and follow her back through the small portion of her house she showed me to the front entry.

I slip my shoes on, and she opens the door for me. My muscles are tight and bunched as I walk outside and stiffly turn to face her.

"So . . . I'll text you, then," I say.

Her lips twitch. "You said that already."

"Right."

"Drive safe."

I tip my head. "Yeah. Lock up after me."

And with that, I'm practically jumping down the porch steps

and taking off down the sidewalk. After checking that she's shut the door behind me, I get in my truck, start it up, and then peel onto the street, feeling more rattled than the last time I got my ass thrown into the boards.

I'VE BARELY SUNKEN into bed and pulled my blanket over my chest later that night when my phone buzzes on my bedside. I debate leaving it, but something has me scrolling through the messages, spotting one I should ignore at this hour but don't.

> Braxton: What about kissing?

> Me: Not unless absolutely necessary.

Especially if the annoying pang of excitement that just ricocheted through me is anything to go by.

> Braxton: Should we make some sort of agreement?

> Me: Like in that stupid movie with Noah Centipede?

> Braxton: To All The Boys? That's rude and so not his name.

> Braxton: Wait . . . did Addie make you watch that, or are you into teen romance now?

> Me: Addie.

I get roped into every kind of movie when it comes to my sister. I've been forced to watch the entire *Twilight* saga enough to hit fangirl status.

Braxton: Is that a no to the agreement? I can do one up tonight.

Me: Do you think we really need one? Just don't kiss me and we'll be good.

Braxton: That's it? So, everything else is on the table, then?

Me: Are you planning on doing something I won't like? What's with the 20 questions?

Braxton: Just want to make sure we're on the same page.

I drag a hand down my face and heave a sigh. It's a fair enough reason, but there's something bugging me about it. Maybe it's that I don't want to plan this entire thing out with a list of do's and don'ts. It will be more believable to just go with the flow.

That's what I'm going with, anyway.

Me: Let go of the planner, Braxton. When it comes down to it, we need to be believable. That means we should do whatever is necessary to ensure it is.

Braxton: Okay. Yeah.

Me: You good now?

Braxton: Yes. Thank you.

Me: All good. Goodnight.

Braxton: Night. Don't let the bed bugs bite.

They don't, and two days later, I park my truck in front of Dad's and step out into the afternoon sunshine.

My parents' house is the same as it's been since I was a baby

—large and in charge but somehow warm and homey at the same time. A wraparound porch with flower baskets hung along the entire length of it, a looped stone driveway, big windows, and a balcony that comes off my parents' bedroom and looks out to the trees at the back of the property.

Today, there are pink and white balloons and streamers joining the flower baskets on the porch, and I chuckle at the Happy Birthday banner hung above the door.

The driveway is full of vehicles that I weave around before coming up to the front door and pushing my way inside. The pile of shoes spread around the foyer isn't the least bit surprising. My family is massive, and even in this big house, it can get a bit crowded.

"Where's the birthday girl?" I shout after I've added my shoes to the pile.

"Is that what I am? And here I thought I was just an old woman now," Mom teases, coming toward me with her arms open.

I step into her hug and squeeze her tight. "Happy late birthday, Ma."

"Thank you, baby."

After a moment, we pull back, and I toss my arm over her shoulder as she leads us through the house toward the backyard, where I assume everyone else is.

"Your gift is in my truck. I know how much you hate crying in front of people, and my present is a guaranteed eye gusher," I gloat, feeling smug.

She pinches my stomach, and I bark a laugh. "You're a little shit. I thought you already gave me my gift."

"That was only the first one." I give her a soft squeeze. "You know if I could have made this party work earlier, I would have, but—"

"No apologies. You're here now. I know how hockey season is, especially right before playoffs."

If anyone would know and understand the life of a hockey

player, it would be the woman who married Oakley Hutton, but the guilt is still there.

I wish I had more time off around her birthday so that we didn't have to celebrate it with the entire family well over a month later. But at least I was able to see her on the actual day, and I think that meant more to her than a big party.

"Dad spoiled you, yeah?"

She giggles. "Of course he did. You know him better than that."

"I told him to buy you a yacht, and he laughed at me, so I doubt his gift could have been that good."

"*You* could have gotten me a yacht," she points out.

"You got me there."

"He booked us a trip to Greece because I've been wanting to go since your uncle went years ago. I think he did *just* fine."

"Oh, swoon," I sigh dramatically, and she pinches me again before laughing.

"You tease, but one day, you'll do the same things for someone."

"Don't hold your breath, Ma. Your hair might turn grey before then."

She scowls up at me and scoffs, "We both know I'll never go grey."

"Are you sure? I think I see . . ." I pinch a piece of hair between my fingers and hold it up in front of my face.

"You do not!" She swats at my hand, and I drop the hair.

I snort a laugh. "Look at that. A false alarm."

We stop in front of the patio door, and she says, "Go say hi to everyone. They're antsy."

"Yes, ma'am," I say. Then, I pull the door open and shout, "Your favourite person has finally arrived!"

"Cooper's here?" my cousin Jamieson yells, looking around the backyard, bypassing me entirely.

I narrow my eyes. "Aye, asshole. Don't you have a football to catch or something? Are you sure you're okay to use that axe? We wouldn't want you to get a callus on those precious hands."

The wide receiver drops his head back and bellows a deep laugh. His grip on the axe Dad keeps by the woodshed loosens as he drops it on the grass and then crouches to slip a stack of chopped logs into his massive arms before carrying and dropping them in front of the blazing fire. It's a bit out of control, but if I had to guess, someone probably started it with gasoline.

Something I'm sure Jamie's firefighter older brother, Oliver, wasn't entirely thrilled about.

"These hands see more hard work than yours, pretty boy," Jamie teases me after brushing off the wood chips from his arms.

"When's the last time you did anything even remotely labour-related, son?" My uncle Tyler grins at his youngest son.

"Probably around the same time you did," Jamie returns.

Shaking my head, I take in the familiar scene of our big family spread throughout the yard. Behind Jamie, Oliver and my uncle Ty are chatting with themselves, keeping watchful eyes on the fire while sitting on low-rise wooden patio chairs with beers in hand. Adalyn attempts to toast a marshmallow on the blazing flames, her face twisted with concentration.

Tyler's wife—my aunt Gracie—is busying herself with a long white table piled with food and presents. That's the direction Mom takes off in, and a second later, Dad is behind her, wrapping his arms around her middle and pulling her back into him.

My heart warms at their affection. It's the same type of love I've seen them show throughout my entire life. Suddenly, I frown. There is only one face missing from the crowd, and it's one that has to hurt Mom the most.

"Where is Noah?" I grind out, facing Addie now.

Addie looks at me over the flames. "Toronto."

"Toronto?"

"Look, before you blow a gasket, he didn't go for no reason."

"We're celebrating Mom's birthday, Addie. There's nothing more important than that."

She cocks a brow. "Really? You're being a hypocrite right now."

She's right, but I don't admit that out loud. "He went to see Tiny, didn't he?"

"Of course he did, Dox. But he was here on Mom's actual birthday, so just let him go see his best friend without the judgment. You should know how he's feeling better than anyone."

Slowly, I lower myself to the grass and pull my knees up, draping my arms over them. I don't like him leaving like this, but my opinion means shit to my brother, anyway.

Tinsley Lowry—or better known to all of us as Tiny—is my uncle Tyler's half-brother's daughter. While a goddamn mouthful, there's no blood relation to me or my siblings as Tyler married into the family. And thank fuck for that because Noah has been in love with her from the moment he laid eyes on her.

Dad always told us that Huttons are like penguins. We mate for life. And while I didn't buy it when I was younger . . . I think he might not have been as out to lunch as I thought.

Hopefully, the tradition skips Adalyn because I'm *so* not ready for that yet.

Noah is different with Tinsley . . . warmer, kinder. She's the only one who has ever been able to get through to him, and while that's great and all, she lives in Toronto with her family, and, well, Noah is here. At least with him there for a while, I won't have to worry about him getting into trouble.

"What did you get Mom for her birthday?" I change the subject, and Addie's face immediately lights up.

"O-M-G! I got her a new luggage set for their trip to Greece. You know how Mom is when it comes to buying herself new things. I swear she's had her old luggage since she was my age."

I nod along with her. Mom spoiled us rotten when we were kids, but she hardly spent anything on herself. Dad made up for it, though.

"That's great, Addie. She'll love it."

"Yeah, she will." She flicks her gaze behind me briefly before looking back and batting her eyelashes. "So . . . theoretically, how mad would you be if Mom and me invited Braxton to the party today?"

I narrow my eyes. "Why?"

"'Cause, cousin. Little Braxton Heights is walking over here as we speak," Jamie notes, and as I quickly get off the ground, I find him staring toward the back door.

"Adalyn," I grumble, following Jamie's line of sight to find Braxton stepping outside.

My lungs pinch as I take her in. A flowy yellow sundress with short sleeves and white lace flows down her body, hitting her mid-calf and cinching at her waist, showing off her curves and the swell of her tits. A pair of white trainers and a twinkling diamond necklace that hangs just above the crease between her breasts in the shape of a heart finish the look.

Half of her hair is pulled back and secured with a clip, keeping it out of her face. My fingers twitch, wanting to remove that clip so her curls fall free.

"When did that happen?" Oliver mutters behind us, and I don't know if he's talking about our reunion or the fact she's grown into a woman, but I get annoyed regardless.

"She's not for you," I snap.

"So, she's yours?" he asks.

"It's not your bus—"

"Women don't belong to men, Oliver, but yes. Braxton is here *with* Maddox," Addie answers for me.

I look over at her with questions in my eyes, and she mouths, "Go with it."

Unease swirls, but against my better judgment, I listen to her. With three strides, I'm leaving them behind and am in front of Braxton, using my six-three frame to block her from view of anyone else.

One smile is all it takes to have me all twisted up inside. I try to grapple for self-control, but having her here, at my family home again, fuck.

"You look like the sun," I blurt out. My eyes widen. "I mean, the dress. It's yellow like the sun . . . sunshine. It's bright. Yeah."

The blue in her eyes is so clear I can't look away. She blinks at me once, twice, and then asks, "Do you want to borrow some sunglasses?"

16

Braxton

THE GROUND GROWS UNSTEADY BENEATH MY FEET WHEN MADDOX'S lips part on a smile. Gleaming teeth and a dimple sunken deep in the apple of his right cheek. I want to reach into the pocket of my dress—convenient, right?—and grab my phone to snap a photo of him.

The smile is beautiful and real, so real that I can't help but smile back. And oh boy, does it feel amazing to smile with him again, even if it's a once-off.

"Do you happen to have an extra pair? I forgot mine in the truck," he deadpans.

I shove both hands in the pockets at my hips before pulling the inner fabric inside out. "No room."

"Shame."

A pop of blonde peeks out from behind Maddox a second before Adalyn joins us. She pushes in front of her brother and grins at me, her lips and cheeks a matching shade of bright pink.

"You look so beautiful, B," she starts in a tone that has me immediately nervous. "And I'm begging you not to kill me here, but other than Mom, Dad, and me, nobody else here knows about the whole fake dating thing. That means it's showtime," she says, far too happily for my liking.

She planned this—it's obvious. The conniving, youngest Hutton sibling has asked for hell from her brother, and as much as I want to be upset with her, I don't think I ever could be.

Maddox scowls. "What? I'm not lying to our family."

She rolls her eyes and pops a hip. "Auntie Gracie can't keep a secret to save her life, and neither can Jamie. You let them know the truth about this, and it will get out within the day. Now, it's either do this here where you can deal with everyone's reactions in person or over social media when you'll have to deal with countless calls and texts. I'm surprised they've left you alone after I posted that photo of us."

"Not everyone is as addicted to their phone as you are, Addie," he grumbles, levelling her with a stern look. "You should have warned me about this. We aren't prepared to do this yet."

"I feel bad lying to everyone. Your parents are okay with this?" I ask, worrying my lip.

"Totally. And I've already told Cooper to keep his mouth shut when he gets here too."

Maddox blows out a long, deep breath and watches me over his sister's shoulder. He arches a brow, and I shrug, leaving the ball in his court. This is his family, so what we do next should be his decision.

"Fuck. Fine," he relents, and Addie claps excitedly.

"I'll leave you to it, then. Remember, make it believable, or it will have been for nothing." She tosses me a wink before slipping out from between us and rushing—no, more like skipping —off.

"Is it really necessary to convince my family? Whether they believe it or not, it won't change how the public sees me."

I swallow the ball in my throat and take a step toward him. With the distance between us shrunk in half, I don't feel nearly as confident as I did walking in here.

His looming, strong frame makes me seem tiny in comparison, and I almost laugh. Tiny is not a term I've ever used to describe myself, yet in the presence of the world's hottest man, I can't think of a better description.

"Are you scared you can't pull it off?" I ask. "Say the word and I can fake a stomach ache and leave. But just so you know, everyone is watching us right now. They're expecting to see something."

His eyes tighten at the corners, and suddenly, he's *right* in front of me. I'm poking the bear, but I feel the furthest thing from scared.

Tilting my head back, I slowly track my gaze up his front before finding his waiting eyes. The heat behind them has me on the brink of paralyzed, and when he lifts one hand to cup my cheek and jaw, I think my knees shake. His palm is so hot against my skin, yet I shiver like it's ice-cold.

"I can pull it off. Can you?" he counters, and the next second, he's swiping his thumb across my bottom lip and sucking in a pained breath. "Lean up for me, Curly."

I do without hesitation, obeying his command. Planting my hands on his chest for balance, I swallow a moan at the feeling of hard, toned muscles. My fingers move on their own, taking advantage of the moment by exploring the planes of his chest one ab at a time. He shudders when I drag my hands up, up, up and use them to grab his neck and pull him down toward me.

Voices wrap around us, hints of curiosity and surprise only adding to the heightened emotion inside of me. Everyone is watching, and it only fuels me to take this further. All the way.

The moment our lips are a hair apart, I bump my nose to his and whisper, "Make it believable, Dox. Kiss me like you love me."

His other hand cups the opposite side of my face before he leans me back and follows the curve of my body forward, bringing our mouths together. Like sticking a fork in an electrical socket, my body bursts with sparks, starting from my lips and spreading outward until I'm burning from the inside out.

I twist my fingers in his T-shirt and fall into the kiss. Our first kiss. Our fake kiss.

Fake.

The word repeats in my mind, but I ignore it. Shove it away into a box and lock it up tight. This feels anything but fake, and when Maddox's chest rumbles with a deep groan, I release a whimper into his mouth. He swallows it eagerly before parting my lips with his tongue and delving deep.

Our mouths move at a quick pace, and the kiss turns dirty, desperate. Years of anger, frustration, and betrayal battle with childhood love and longing, turning what should have been a quick show of fake affection into something meant for quiet, private nights tangled in bedsheets.

I nearly tip over when he rips his mouth away, and hot, angry puffs of air hit my face. A flush works its way up my throat to my cheeks and ears as he glares down at me, his pupils blown.

"Are you okay?" I ask softly, cautiously. The fingers clenched in the material of his shirt relax as I pull them away and drop my hands to my sides.

"No."

A hand on my back makes me jump, and Maddox's eyes leave mine to glare over my shoulder. I try to collect myself, but I'm all over the place, my mind in shambles.

"Get it together, guys. You're going to blow it." It's Cooper.

"You're late," Maddox grunts, stepping back from me, running a hand down his front over the wrinkles in his shirt that I created.

The hand on my back rubs up and down once before dropping. "Got here at the perfect time, it seems. Drop the broken expressions, and go deal with the questions. Maybe smile. Look in love."

Maddox snorts. "Yes, Dad."

I face Cooper and smile, hoping he can read the thank you in

my stare. He smiles back before sweeping me up in a hug. It's an
I missed you hug, and I soak it up.

"Happy you're here, Brax," he says.

Cooper isn't as tall as Maddox, but it's still a task to look up
at him from this position, so I don't bother trying. I bury my face
into his chest instead before pulling back and patting him on the
stomach.

"Right back 'atcha, Cooperoni."

"Do you need some more time to chat, or are you ready to
say hi to everyone, Braxton?" Maddox snarks. I scowl.

"Right. My bad for wanting to say hi to my friend."

"You'll have plenty of time to gossip later."

"Gossip? Don't be an asshole. Not—"

"Not what?" he interrupts.

"Not after that."

"That what? Kiss?" He shakes his head, laughing in a way
that has my stomach twisting painfully. "We were pretending.
You need to focus on what we need to do next. They're going to
swarm us. Our story is weak at best."

"Okay, chill out. Get it together, Dox, or you're going to be
the only one responsible for your downfall," Cooper says in a
no-bullshit tone.

"Are you going to take the heat from us, then? Or are you just
here to be the angel on my shoulder?"

Cooper thins his lips and cocks a brow. He looks like a dad
prepared to scold his kid for being smart-mouthed, even though
he's only two years older than us. His maturity can be jarring for
those who don't know him well. Personally, I love it.

"Watch it. I'm not here to be anything but a friend. You don't
need anybody to take the heat from you. Just make your plan
believable. You saw each other again and decided to give it a shot."

"*That's* believable?" Maddox asks incredulously.

"Why not? It's been eight years. They don't know the whole
story between you two, anyway. Just parts of it."

"Cooper's right," I say. Maddox's intense stare does little to make me waver. "But the longer we stay here whispering, the more questions they're going to have."

Finally, with a harsh laugh and a shake of his head, he relents. "Fine. Okay. But if this fails—"

"It won't," I reassure both him and myself.

Cooper flashes me a half smile before patting Maddox on the bicep and brushing past us. Addie shouts his name from somewhere in the yard, but the nerves buzzing under my skin, distract me from listening to what she's saying.

This is Maddox's family. At one time, I considered every single person here mine as well. They deserve the truth, but this isn't about what I feel and think. It's about helping Maddox. If keeping the truth a secret will ensure that happens, then I'll do it.

"Ready?" I ask.

"As ready as I'll ever be." My fingers tingle when he links them through his and squeezes my hand. "They'll get over it. You don't have to feel guilty about lying," he adds, reading my mind.

I drop my eyes to our clasped hands. His is calloused and burning hot, and it swallows mine, making it look so delicate.

I straighten my shoulders and pull on a smile. Then, I wait for him to turn around and face the crowd before stepping up beside him and tightening my grip on his fingers. He returns the squeeze.

A slow clap starts from the left side of the yard, and I find an older and much buffer-looking Jamieson Bateman watching us with a shit-eating grin. Beside him, his dad and brother look more shocked than anything. Not that I can blame them.

"You know what? I called it. Didn't I, Dad? I told you they would get together one day. You owe me a hundred bucks," Jamie gloats.

The corner of my mouth twitches. "When did you place that bet? Before or after you asked me out in the tenth grade and I turned you down?"

His bright blue eyes twinkle with humour, and the look almost grounds me. Jamie has always been a joker, and I love that even after all this time, he hasn't lost that quality.

"After. I had to shoot my shot before wishing you off to another man."

"We all told him it was a long shot. You and Maddox have been meant to be since you were children," Maddox's aunt joins in, her voice watery as she and Ava close in on our position. I stare at Gracie and swallow down a wave of guilt at the pure joy in her expression. "You're so grown up!"

I laugh weakly, fumbling with something to say, but Maddox beats me to it.

"You're telling me. When I saw her for the first time, I nearly fell to my knees. She's always been beautiful, but shit. She's the most gorgeous woman I've ever seen."

His blunt words have my pulse thumping. His thumb draws a path of fire across the top of my hand. My lungs are so constricted I fear I might pass out as I gaze up at him. At the sharp line of his jaw and side profile worthy of a magazine cover.

"Dox," I breathe.

He ignores me, pushing on. "It's true. One look was all it took to decide I wanted her back."

"That's so romantic," Gracie says dreamily. "And your parents knew about this and didn't tell me?"

Maddox shifts me in front of his body and moves our connected hands to rest against my soft stomach. The weight of his arm wrapped around me relaxes me. It feels so natural to be like this, and warning bells blare at that epiphany.

He presses his face to my hair, and I hear him inhale. *Is he smelling me?*

"We asked them to keep it to themselves until we were ready to announce it to the world. You know how it is," he answers his aunt.

"Good call. The press can be ruthless," Tyler adds.

Gracie turns to Ava and takes hold of her arm, pulling her close. "This is just so exciting. Maddox's missing piece is back."

Ava's eyes find mine, and I blink back the burn behind my eyes. Her smile is real and raw and reassuring, but it's her son's words from beside me that have me struggling to keep my balance.

Three words and I'm struck down at the knees.

"Yeah, she is."

17

Maddox

AGE SEVENTEEN

I'M SURROUNDED BY MY TEAMMATES, BUT MY EYES ARE ON HER.
Always her.

Braxton is curled up on a beanbag chair in the corner of the smoky room. Her legs are pulled up and tucked beneath her as she presses her cheek to her shoulder and smiles sweetly at one of my teammates. He grins back and says something that has her laugh ringing in my ears and wrapping around my chest.

Brody punches my arm. "You listening to me, bro?"

I tighten my grip on the dewy beer bottle in my palm. "No."

"Fuck you, man," he roars, words slurred.

It's his birthday today, and here we are, drinking and watching his guests smoke up, knowing that not a single player on my team is touching that shit. Brody's dad is our coach, and while a hard-ass most days, I know he approved this party.

I invited Braxton because Friday nights are ours, plus the thought of being here alone for hours without her seemed like a goddamn punishment. Maybe I wouldn't have bothered showing up in the first place had I known one of my teammates was going to move in on her while I was wishing Brody a happy birthday.

They know the rules when it comes to Braxton. What happens next is on Collins.

I only manage to take one step toward them before Brody pushes himself in front of me and leans in close enough I can smell his beer breath before singing, "Nope. Not happening."

"Oh, it's happening." I step to the side, but he follows me. A harsh exhale parts my lips. "Get out of my way." I sweeten my tone. "Please."

He laughs. "Nah. You need to chill. It's one girl. There are at least ten of them here that would love a trip around the sun with Maddox Hutton."

I wince. "No thanks."

As far as my team and everyone else knows, I'm far from a virgin, and I plan to keep it that way. They would never let me live it down if they knew the truth.

Tossing his hands up, he jostles the liquid in his red cup, and it spills over the lip and onto his shoes. He groans. "Look what you made me do, Madman. This is a sign from God himself. Don't go over there."

"I'm going over there," I declare before extending my arm and pushing my beer against his chest. He grabs it from me.

"Want me to save this for you, or . . .?"

"Drink it, dump it. I don't care."

He shrugs and lifts it to his lips before tipping it back. I pat him on the back and leave him there as the movement has him choking on the warming froth and coughing a couple of times.

My pace is hurried, and my blood burns hotter and hotter the closer I get to the two of them. Sure, Collins is sitting on his own beanbag, but if he's in talking distance, he's still too fucking close to her.

"I actually have an Australian shepherd. She's a big cuddler. I think she would love you," Collins says, all easy confidence. Jackass.

My jaw is so clenched I'm waiting to hear the telltale crack of broken bones.

"Awe, how old? Shepherds are my favourite breed of working dog," Braxton replies, grinning.

"I don't know about working, but Collins is quite the dog," I inter-rupt. "You should hear his locker room talk."

Braxton's eyes fly up to meet mine as she quirks a brow. Collins, on the other hand, glares at me like he wishes I would fuck right off. The feeling is mutual, so I only grin in response.

"Got room on that thing for me, Curly Fry?" I ask Braxton, but I'm already on my way over and squishing myself beside her on the beanbag before she can reply. It's clear there is not enough room for both of us like this, but there's an easy solution to that.

With one arm around her back, I slip my hand beneath the thigh pressed to mine and lift her onto my lap. She stiffens briefly, but I kiss the back of her head, and she relaxes. I adjust my arm around her so I can lay my hand on her thigh as I stare at Collins with a possessive look that I'm not the least bit ashamed of.

"That's better," I murmur.

He rolls his eyes and folds his arms across his chest but doesn't say anything. If he did, it wouldn't end well.

First day on the team, I warned them away from my girl—my best friend—and told them what would happen if they went around me and tried something. He's lucky having Braxton in my arms has made it impossible to follow through with the repercussions.

Later.

I curl the hand on her thigh into a fist to keep from stroking it with my fingers and softly bump her cheek with mine.

"I'm sorry I was gone for so long. Brody is a needy birthday boy," I mumble.

She laughs softly. "It's fine. Collins was good company. Don't be a jerk to him."

"I wasn't a jerk."

"You were."

"He knows better," I whisper against the back of her ear.

Fuck. I think she just shivered. No, she definitely did.

"Knew better than to what? Converse with your best friend? Protective much?" she asks, voice strained.

"I wear the four P's proud, baby girl."

"Four P's?" Collins chokes.

I lean my head back against the beanbag and meet his stare with cold eyes. "Yeah. Protective, possessive, proud, and packing."

"Jesus Christ," he mutters.

Braxton pinches my thigh and looks over her shoulder at me. My lips spread in a grin at her scolding frown.

"You're going to get yourself punched in the face one day," she says.

"Been there, done that a few dozen times. As long as you'll be here to patch me up after, it'll be worth it every time."

My words are sincere, and when her cheeks fill with colour, I know she knows that too. I'm being overly flirty with her tonight despite the fact I know I should be toning it down.

We're best friends. She doesn't want a boyfriend, and I don't want to risk ruining our friendship over my feelings. Yet for some reason, it's getting harder each day to remind myself of all that. Especially when I see her with another guy.

Now isn't the right time. Next year, I'll be playing in the NHL, and she'll be in vet school. Our next few years don't line up how I want them to, and that kills me. I've debated holding off on entering the draft, but it would only earn me another year with her, and who knows what could happen in that time. I would only be denying the inevitable.

No, the only thing left to do is hope that she can find a school close to me—wherever I end up. If not . . .

Stop. I don't want to think about that yet.

"Where did Brody go?" Collins asks, his voice like a blowhorn in my ear.

I bury my face in Braxton's hair and close my eyes, savouring the moment before she takes it upon herself to find my drunken teammate. She can be too kind-hearted for her own good.

"Probably upstairs. I don't know," I mutter.

"We should help," she says, and I hold back my groan.

"I was thinking we could leave and stop at Lucy's diner before we go home. Maybe see if that cat is still hanging around out back."

Braxton perks up, her eyes now lit with a healthy sense of adven-

ture that makes my heart beat faster. One day, I hope to wake up to this feeling every morning and fall asleep to it every night.

"Yes! Let's do that. Now? Can we go now?" she rushes out, looking as if she's holding back a squeal as she starts to squirm.

I smile at her so wide my cheeks burn as I nod and quickly press my lips to her cheek.

Braxton Heights will be my girl one day, and when she is, there's no way I will ever let her go.

We'll be forever.

18

Maddox

I'm watching Braxton laugh with all the important women in my life behind the safety of the kitchen window when Dad finds me. We haven't seen each other since we were together in Alexander's office, and I've been avoiding his calls. I won't feel sorry about it either. Not when he orchestrated this entire thing behind my back.

"How long have you known that Braxton was back in town?" I ask him, not bothering to look at him.

He moves up beside me and follows my stare to the back-yard. "The moment she got a Realtor and started looking for a building for her clinic. I don't think she knew that she chose the same one who helped Adam find his hockey arena and your aunt her dance studio."

"So, Adam told you?"

Cooper's dad and my mom's closest friend since university isn't much of a gossip, but by the raw surprise on my aunt Gracie's face when she saw Braxton, it's safe to rule her out.

"He was out for lunch when Dexter—the Realtor—got Braxton's call. There wasn't anything malicious about it, just two friends talking. The guy didn't realize Adam would know the girl and come tell me."

"You knew she was here for weeks."

"I did."

"And you didn't tell me." The words sound as bitter as they taste.

"I didn't."

I turn my body and face him, the betrayal I feel seeping from my every pore. He looks at me and frowns but stays strong, not apologizing or telling me that he knows it was wrong.

"Why not? I should have been told, Dad."

"So you could do what? You haven't even let us say her name since she left. Why would I tell you that she was back when I didn't think it would matter?" he asks.

"Because she's Braxton. She'll always be my business," I snap, pushing an angry hand over the top of my head. "I don't know whether to be pissed at you or fucking cry. You blindsided me, and now she's here, and I can't turn and run. Instead, I have to hug her and fucking kiss her, as if the past is forgotten and—"

Suddenly, I'm sandwiched between two tattooed arms and pulled into a tight hug. A ball forms in my throat. Dad has always been an open, emotional man, but hugging isn't something we do often. This, right now, I accept this moment without a second thought.

"You've never had a serious girlfriend, Maddox. You're twenty-six, and it's obvious that you've been holding out for that girl since you were five. Your mother and I . . . we worry about you. As soon as I heard Braxton was back, I thought it was a sign or something. I knew you wouldn't go to her on your own, and if I had told you when I found out, you would have shut down and forced all of us never to speak about it again."

"So, you tried to force it instead?"

He sighs. "I thought I was doing the right thing by not telling you, but I was wrong. I'm sorry I hurt you. If you want me to go to Alex and tell him the plan's off, I'll do it. We'll void the NDA and figure something else out."

I swallow, stiffly shaking my head. "No. We're already in it."

Plus, the thought of never seeing her again now . . . dammit. *She's gotten to me.* She's started to sink her nails back into the holes she left behind. The ones that never seemed to close up.

We can't go back now. *I* can't.

"I made a mistake. I'll wear it."

Nodding, I pull back, rolling my shoulders in an attempt to loosen the tight muscles. "Mom and Addie wrangled everyone else into this mess too."

"Your mom has her hopes up about this. Maybe that's my fault too."

"She thinks it'll become real, doesn't she?"

Dad smiles sheepishly. "You know how she is. Your sister too. They're two peas in one matchmaking pod."

"They're going to be disappointed when the charade ends." And I'm going to feel like shit breaking their hearts when Braxton and I go our separate ways.

"They'll get over it."

He sounds as unsure as I feel. If after eight years they haven't gotten over the possibility of me and Braxton, will they ever? It seems unlikely.

Movement in the yard has me looking out the window again, and like a flick of a switch inside of me, I'm suddenly brimming with anger. The sight of Jamie with his hand on Braxton's forearm as she grabs a glass of lemonade from the table has me heading for the door.

"No fists," Dad calls knowingly, chuckling behind me.

I flex my fingers and say, "It's Jamie. If he gets hit, it's because he deserved it," before pushing my large frame out the door and stepping outside.

"HAVE you shrunk since the last time I saw you? I swear you used to be taller," Jamie teases her. I want to rip his smile off his face and stomp on it.

"I think it's more plausible that you got taller. You're one of the tallest wide receivers in the NCAA, right?" she asks.

My steps falter on the way to where she stands. Her question is like a blow to my pride—knowing that she didn't keep up with my career but did my cousins. Jealousy pricks at me as I clench my jaw and continue on my warpath.

"Keeping tabs on me, sweetheart?"

I let my shoulder crash into his, relishing in the groan he releases as he drops his hand from her arm. *Good, I hope it hurt.* Sweetheart my fucking ass.

Braxton looks up at me, meeting my harsh stare with one of her own. "That was rude," she states.

I slowly lift my eyebrow. "Rude?"

"You got some linebacker in you, Madman," Jamie jokes.

"Is there a reason you came storming over here like an angry bull?" Braxton asks me, ignoring Jamie. My inner caveman likes that a lot.

"You're here with me," I remind her before glaring at my cousin. "Don't touch her again."

"Yeah, I'm aware of who I'm here with. I'm also aware that he's being a jackass right now," Braxton says tightly, and when I look back at her, I find her scowling at me, one hand on her hip.

Pretending I don't wish it was my hand on her hip, I scowl right back. "When I'm with a girl, she's mine to touch. If anyone else had touched you the way he did, I would have beat him into the fucking ground."

"Lucky me, then, I guess," Jamie grumbles before he walks

away. Or at least I think he does. I don't spare him a glance to check.

I nearly beat at my chest when Braxton doesn't either. Even when the muscles in her face tighten and she takes an angry step toward me, I have to fight back a grin of victory.

"You're a lot more possessive than you were before," she informs me, as if I don't already know that.

She has her chin lifted to look at me, and I pinch it gently between my thumb and pointer finger, holding it in place. The soft gasp that falls from her lips has me throbbing in my jeans.

"Possessive? Oh, baby. You haven't seen possessive yet."

"So, what was that just now? Jealousy, then?"

I take a step closer, sliding my hand across her jaw and then cupping her cheek in my palm. The way she's looking at me right now, like I'm the only person she sees, not Jamie or anyone else around, it does something to me. Something that should scare me enough to have me backing up and calling it a day. Instead, I take that one final step left between us and close the gap, hoping that she can't feel the erratic beating of my heart pressed against her.

I'm aware that we're supposed to be pretending, and maybe that's what gives me the confidence to keep doing these things. To keep touching her and flirting with her. If it's all under the pretense of a fake relationship . . . it can't mean anything. Right?

I drop my head until our breaths intertwine and lower my voice. "And if it was jealousy? What then?"

"I would say you're just as blind now as you were when we were teenagers," she whispers before stepping back, forcing my hand to fall from her face.

My mouth fills with bitter disappointment as she rushes past me, back into the house. I watch her pull open the patio door and walk inside, feeling confused. So fucking confused.

"Are you even going to make it two months?" Cooper asks, his words judgment-free as he moves in beside me. Eavesdropping asshole.

Emotionally exhausted, I just shrug. "I don't know if I'll make it two *weeks*, let alone months."

"Looks like you don't have much of a choice."

"Thanks for that."

He looks toward the house and exhales tightly. "What will it take for you to forgive her? You know just as well as I do that you're more upset with her for leaving than anything that happened with her father. You've admitted that to me more than once. Hell, for the longest time, I was convinced that even if you had never played hockey again, you would have been happy as long as you had her beside you."

"What does it matter now?"

He shoots me a look that says, *are you serious?* "Don't you ever think about how great things would be if the past was left where it belongs and we could move on and make new memories? We could be the three musketeers again. Don't you want that?"

I twist my mouth in frustration. "I don't know what I want."

"Come on," he pushes.

"Look, I know that I just look like a stubborn ass, and maybe that's exactly what I am. Or maybe I'm just a guy with a good sense of self-preservation. I love you, man, but you don't understand what I'm feeling."

He doesn't look as if he buys what I'm selling, and I internally groan. "I don't? Huh. That's funny because I remember losing a lot that day too. I just didn't let her get away from me the same way you did."

"What are you saying?" I ask through gritted teeth.

Cooper rubs a rough hand over his mouth—a tell that he's trying to rein in his frustration. Not driven by emotion, he's always the most level-headed person in the room. I don't know whether to take it as a compliment or not that I have the ability to push his buttons so easily.

"I'm saying that maybe you're pushing the resentment you

hold toward yourself for letting her leave onto her, and it's keeping you both from moving on."

I bark a laugh, the realness in his statement startling me. "Thank God you didn't go into psychology," I force out.

His smile is sympathetic, and I fucking hate it. "Yeah, maybe I'm just talking crazy right now."

"Wouldn't be the first time," I say lightly in a weak attempt to lighten the mood.

He lays a hand on my shoulder, and his smile becomes more relaxed. "You know I'm here if you really want to talk. Always. Think of me as Switzerland. I'll always be neutral ground."

"I appreciate that."

"Cooper! Come here for a second!" Adalyn calls from her place on a high-backed wicker chair. I glance in her direction and see she's waving her phone in the air, eyes on us.

I look at Cooper and snort. "Have fun with that."

"She probably wants me to give her more advice for her trip."

"I don't suppose you're going to tell her not to go?"

He laughs. "You know that wouldn't work."

"Worth a shot."

"Loosen the reins a bit, man. She has a good head on her shoulders. Even if it might be full of crazy thoughts and ideas."

Loosening the reins isn't an easy task for me when it comes to Addie, but I don't argue with what he said. He might not be family, but he's been around long enough to know her just as well as I do.

"Appreciate the advice. And thank you for coming today. It means the world to Ma."

"Just your mom? Come out and say you're happy I was here to give you such stellar advice, Mad dog. I promise I won't spread it around that you're the grateful type," he teases, grinning wide.

Rolling my eyes, I roughly pat his cheek. "Get the fuck out of my face before I smack you."

He belts out a laugh and steps back, tossing his hands up. "You're welcome. I'm here whenever you need me."

I tip my head at the promise and watch as he releases an exaggerated sigh and heads toward my sister. As soon as he's gone, that's when the last few minutes come crashing back in.

Is what he said true? Do I hate myself for what happened more than I tried to convince myself I hated *her*?

19

Braxton

Two days later, I'm celebrating the Vancouver Warriors' first-round sweep in a sweaty VIP section of a club I've never heard of. It's a mess of flashing lights, dirty dancing, and deep male laughter, and while I would rather be at home, I've learned that when Alexander Torello orders you to do something, you do it without question. Especially when you have an agreement and a selfish father hanging over your head.

I haven't gone out to a club since university, and even then, I never really had the time to enjoy myself. Between the sickening amount of coursework, exams, and time spent at the small animal clinic that took me on for my work experience hours, fun wasn't really a priority. But even when I did make the time, I can't say that I was ever invited to hang out with professional players in the VIP section of a club while they complain about their rankings on the newest NHL video game.

This is entirely new territory to me, and I'm not above admitting that I feel a bit out of place.

"Hutton is the only one who didn't get fucked by the ratings this year. I mean, they have me as an eighty overall? There's no way!" one of the players shouts, outraged on the far end of the couch. He's a bit rugged-looking, with a thick, bushy beard that looks like it would feel scratchy and deep bluey-purple eyes.

Maddox shakes beside me with a low laugh. His bicep flexes against the side of my bare neck, where he has it slung over my shoulder. The tight-sleeved, black T-shirt he wore tonight fits him a little *too* well and leaves all the roped muscles of his arms on full display.

I nearly swallowed my tongue when he picked me up earlier, and that just won't do. Not even a second after I slid into the passenger side of his truck, I promised myself that I wouldn't embarrass myself tonight by drooling over him. Our kiss at his parents' house left me in shambles—wounds torn open that I couldn't seem to stitch shut again. It's obvious we're both ignoring our rule break and the obvious tension it left between us. If I thought I could have gotten away with it, I would have said no to coming out tonight.

"They rated me an eighty-seven," Bentley, one of the team-mates Maddox seems closest to, chimes in proudly.

Out of all Maddox's friends, I think I like Bentley the most. He's outgoing, but not in the type of way that can get on your nerves. He doesn't need to be the centre of attention but doesn't mind when the spotlight finds him. Maddox really likes him too, and I trust his judge of character.

"See? Now I know they fucked up," the first guy replies, scowling at the bottle of Don Julio on the table in front of us.

Tequila is my drink of choice, but I haven't reached for the bottle once. Neither has Maddox. It's not that I don't trust these guys . . . actually, I don't. But that's only because I don't know them.

"What's your rating?" I ask Maddox, my voice low.

His arm flexes as he tilts his head toward me to reply just as quietly, "Ninety-two."

"That's high."

He keeps our heads close, and I can smell mint on his breath. "Highest there is."

"Who's after you?"

"Elias Svensson. A rookie."

"He's that good?" I ask.

He hums. "Better than I was at his age."

"I doubt that," I mutter.

Just because I didn't exactly follow his career after I skipped town doesn't mean that I've forgotten how amazing he was, even as a teenager.

Crossing my left leg over my right, I grate my teeth when my leather skirt digs into the outside of my thigh. The heeled boots I chose to wear aren't high by any means, but they still make the soles of my feet ache, and the relief that rushes through me when I lift my foot and let it dangle over my leg is enough to have me stifling a moan.

My black top is tight, with long sleeves and a deep, plunged neckline that makes my boobs spill out a bit. Five years ago, I wouldn't have known how a good bra can make all the difference for big-chested women like myself, but now? Now I'm not afraid to slip on a bustier beneath a low-cut dress to show off one of my best assets.

I think that I look sexy tonight, but I was hoping that once we got here, I would feel a bit more confident. Maybe it's the other women sitting around our little section of the club that are making me doubt myself, with their popping collarbones and toned legs that look like they go on for miles and miles, or maybe it's not. I've spent years learning to stop comparing myself to the women who don't share my shape, but everybody has low moments. Moments of self-doubt and that stupid voice that reminds you that you're either trying too hard or not enough.

It's easier to say you're better than that, but it's a hell of a lot harder to believe it.

Maddox draws my attention back in as he pushes out a rough, raspy exhale. I risk a glance at him and find him staring at where the bottom hem of my skirt cuts into my thigh, making it bulge from the pressure. My lungs pinch as I watch him, not able to tell why his eyes narrow, his jaw jumping as he continues to stare at my leg.

I gasp when he removes his arm from my shoulders and drops a hand to that same thigh, his thumb drawing a line along the hem of the skirt. His palm is warm, so, so warm as it rests there, not moving, just squeezing ever-so-slightly.

"What—what are you doing?" I sputter, swallowing thickly.

His eyes are dark as they find mine, snaring them. "You're supposed to be my girl, right?"

"Yes."

"There isn't a chance in hell that I wouldn't be all over my girlfriend if she looked as good as you, Braxton," he says, voice deep and growly.

His hand moves then, and the thumb he had brushing the hem of the skirt slips just beneath it. The rough pad of his thumb glides along the tightly pulled material, toward the inner part of my thigh, where the pressure releases and the skirt is no longer biting into my skin.

The compliment makes my core clench, and I want to rub my thighs together, but he's taken that option away from me.

"Thank you," I breathe, unsure of the correct response here.

He laughs, but it's bitter. "Anytime."

"Do you know any of the women up here?" It slips before I can stop myself, and I regret asking instantly when he flinches, his hand stilling where it lies on my thigh.

Did that sound as jealous as I think it did?

"Not really," he replies, too casually.

"What does that mean?"

"It means that I don't really know them. They're just women the guys have picked from the club to sit up here with us."

I fight to keep my lip from curling. "That sounds . . ."

"Skeevy? Yeah, I guess it does. But that's just how it goes. They're happy to be here regardless. It sounds worse than it actually is. Nobody forces them to join us."

Relief races through me when his thumb starts to stroke my leg again. I flit my gaze to the women in the VIP section and, for the first time since being here, take in the genuine enjoyment on their faces. Can I really judge them for that? It seems like a no-brainer to want to be chosen to join a bunch of sexy, successful men for a night of free drinks and good company. It sounds like a college Braxton's dream.

Hell, with Maddox here, it sounds like an adult Braxton's dream too.

"Everyone looks like they're having a good time. I didn't mean to sound judgmental," I admit sheepishly.

He draws a line of fire across my thigh with his index fingernail and mutters, "This is new to you. Even after so many years in the league, I still find most things hard to grasp. It's just . . . different."

I roll my lips. "Well, you look like you have it all figured out."

"That's the point." He laughs softly, and I'm left confused.

"What are you two whispering about?" Bentley asks, leaning over the two players between him and Maddox, sparkling eyes fixed on us.

I stiffen my spine and drop my hand over Maddox's, subtly trying to push his off my leg. He only tightens his grip.

"They're probably talkin' about all your turnovers tonight," Colt Warner slurs.

"My turnovers? What about your dive in the third, Cowboy? Two minutes for embellishment," Bentley returns with a roll of his eyes.

Maddox ignores them both, that damn thumb of his stroking my thigh again. Back and forth, back and forth, but never attempting to drift any higher. Even as I shiver, slipping further into his hold, he keeps his touch respectful.

"What's embellishment?" one of the women asks from the lap of that bushy-faced player with the near-purple eyes. She has a beautiful heart-shaped face framed with wavy, dirty-blonde hair.

"It's what Liam here did when he told you how good he is in bed," Maddox says.

Burly man—Liam—sends him a withering glare and tightens the arm he has wrapped around the woman in his lap. "If you're not getting any, Hutton, just say so. Your girl couldn't be farther away from you if she tried."

"I don't need to have my girl humping my leg to know she's mine," Maddox tosses back confidently.

"Is that it? Or is she just not that into you?"

I tense slightly, but it's enough for Maddox to notice. He dips his head, and a soft pair of lips brush the tip of my ear. A zap of electricity shoots down my side.

"Liam is a shithead. Ignore him," he murmurs.

Some of my unease slips away, but not all of it. "He isn't really wrong, though."

His breath hits my ear in a huff. "About what?"

I gulp. "We look a little . . ."

"Tense?"

"Yes," I breathe. We couldn't look further from a cozy couple if we tried.

A beat of silence, and then he says, "Are you okay with getting closer?"

Am I? "Yes."

I don't dare move a muscle as he grazes the tip of my ear with his teeth and smooths a hand down my leg, stopping at the inside of my knee.

"How much closer?"

"Get on my lap, Braxton," he orders softly.

I might not have had anything to drink tonight, but I'm drunk on something. There's no other explanation for why I follow his command and move to stand in front of him.

For a rare moment, I watch him from above, taking in the full image of him. The slightly spread legs, wide chest, and thick arms. *His confidence.* It would be damn near suffocating had I not spent most of my life acclimating to it.

"My lap," he repeats, hands smoothing down his thighs in a silent invitation.

I swallow hard, staring at his fingers, lust making my thoughts drift. *Yes, sir. Anything you want.*

Next thing I know, there's a pair of thick thighs beneath mine and a hard chest against my back. Maddox wastes no time before touching me again, resting one hand back on my thigh while the other dances over my hip.

His touch nearly undoes me, each one cautious but sure. Like he knows I won't reject him but isn't sure if *he* can handle more.

"Jesus, Liam. Don't you have a hotel room you can go to?" Bentley barks, drawing everyone's attention.

Darting my eyes to Liam and the girl on his lap, I flush at their new position. It's not embarrassment that has me turning red, but the look of pleasure on her face as her hips swirl in his lap, his face buried in her neck.

A rumble builds in the chest at my back as Maddox follows my line of sight and presses his forehead to the side of my head.

"Do they make you uncomfortable?" His voice is gravel.

"No," I reply, shocking myself.

He shifts in his seat, that ghost of a touch on my waist becoming a firm one. "Fuck."

"Does it make *you* uncomfortable?" I ask nervously, unsure of how to read his discomfort.

He pulls his head away and drops it back against the couch, eyes to the ceiling. "They're not what has me feeling this way, Braxton."

My mouth dries up. "Oh."

This time, his laugh isn't bitter. It's genuine, and it settles some twisted-up part inside of me. "Thank you for coming tonight."

I twist to knock his shoulder with mine, but the move has my ass brushing something hard and thick. *So thick.* Oh, my God.

He hisses a breath and stills me with his grip on my hip.

"You're welcome. I agreed to help you, and even if I hate places like this, I won't go back on my word," I rush out, attempting to hide the fact I now know that his cock is just as big as I thought it would be. And that he's hard. *For me.*

"This won't be a regular thing. I don't plan on going out much more this season. This is just for Alex."

"I know. But still."

He nods. "Thanks."

Suddenly feeling Liam's eyes on us, I blurt out just loud enough for Maddox to hear, "We should kiss."

"I thought we said no kissing."

"We broke that rule already. Plus, Liam obviously doesn't believe us. Do any of your teammates?"

I'm too scared to look around and see if the other sets of eyes are as sceptical as Liam's.

"I don't know. I haven't asked," he admits.

I exhale slowly. "So kiss me."

"Braxton, I don't give a shit about what these guys do and don't believe."

"I do."

"Are you sure?" he asks, and I meet his stare, my heart catching at how open his eyes are.

"Yes," I say instantly. "Please."

His eyes drift across my face before he's moving. Big, strong hands grip my cheeks as he takes my face in his hands and dips his head, bringing our mouths a breath apart.

"Relax," he whispers, and I force my tensing muscles to relax, not realizing I had tensed them in the first place.

I swallow, and as I dart my tongue out to wet my lips, he's kissing me, stroking the tip of my tongue with his. Fingers tangle in my hair, pulling me closer, and I whimper into his mouth, flames flaring to life beneath my skin.

On a moan, I lift my hand to rest on his jaw, letting the scruff tickle my palm as his cheek warms my fingertips. The kiss is quick and hard and full of something that makes my chest ache. Like magic, the music and the lights and the dozen sets of scrutinizing eyes on us fade to nothing. Suddenly, it's just us. Maddox and me.

God, how I wish we could stay right here forever.

"Fuck yeah!" Colt shouts, and I barely register the words.

If it weren't for Maddox pulling away, I would have stayed in his embrace for hours. The realization is nothing short of terrifying.

The openness in Maddox's eyes is gone as he looks away and sits back, leaving me heaving in breaths, feeling like a complete idiot for letting this happen again. He's put distance between us with a simple twist of his body, and I'm not above admitting that I hate it.

But it's when he keeps that distance throughout the rest of the night, even as he walks me up to my door only an hour after such an explosive, toe-curling kiss and offers me a forced goodnight, that it becomes obvious hate is not a strong enough word.

I'm left watching him walk away from me through the tiny hole in my door, a promise of another fake date lingering and a cold fist clenched around my heart.

20

Braxton

It's been a long few days of silence.

Other than the couple of texts exchanged with Maddox confirming our date for tonight, neither of us has mentioned the kiss at the club nor the way it's furthered the rift between us.

I've put everything into work, hoping that it would help, but I should have known better. After eight years of doing everything I could to forget about Maddox, not once did it work.

He's a thorn in my side. One that I can't seem to find the strength to yank out.

Maybe I'm a masochist. When it comes to him, I very well could be.

That would explain why regardless of how much I thought I would be dreading dinner tonight, I found my best dress and shoved it into my work bag this morning. A tiny—okay, maybe huge—part of me wants to blow him away. Make him completely weak in the knees when he sees me.

But now that I'm thinking about it . . . I don't remember taking the dress out and hanging it up. *Wrinkles.* So many wrinkles.

"Shit," I breathe, snapping out of my thoughts and handing Dex the Doberman back over to his owner—a gentle yet sharp-tongued brunette named Cherry—and getting them situated with Micaela at the front desk. I throw my hand up in a quick wave to Cherry and rush off to my office.

My sneakers squeak on the waxed floor with each hurried step, and I nearly fall into my office in search of my bag. I find it beneath my desk, in one of the little cubbies I like to store my lunch bag and water bottle that I never seem to actually drink from, and rifle through the contents before gripping onto the velvet material of the dress and pulling it out. Hanging it up in front of me, it's just as I suspected.

It resembles the skin of a hairless cat.

Groaning, I drop my arms and curl my fingers in the velvet. It's too close to when Maddox told me he would be here to go home and swap dresses, but there's no way I'm going out to whichever fancy restaurant he chose in this.

I'm about to pull my phone out and send out a very embarrassing text asking him to push dinner by an hour when there's a knock behind me. Spinning around, I force a smile in Marco's direction.

"I know, I know. I said I would be leaving early, and I'm still here looking far from ready to leave," I huff.

The scrubs he's wearing today are covered in mini Mickey Mouses wearing sunhats and swim shorts, but despite how much I might want to, I don't ask where he got them. One thing we both bonded over when we first met was our love for different patterned scrubs. As far as I'm concerned, if I have the option to wear scrubs without a lame, bland colour, I'm going to. Holiday prints are my favourite, but—

"You look frustrated. What's up?" Marco asks, coming into my office with his hands in his pockets and a furrow between his brows.

I hold the dress up. "Velvet wrinkles easy, and I kept it shoved in a ball in my bag all day."

"Oh, that's an easy fix. I have a travel steamer in my office."

"You do?" Surprise is thick in my tone, and my cheeks flush.

"I mean, that's great. I don't, but maybe I should think of getting one."

He flashes me a grin and nods to his office across the hall. "I go out a lot after work to meet my parents for dinner. They're the fancy type. Dress shirt and slacks without a wrinkle in sight."

I follow him out to the hall and into his office, taking in the identical layout and similar furniture. It's clear he's taken more time to get situated than I have over these past few weeks. With picture frames and a jar full of Werther's candies on his desk and even a couple of throw pillows on the small brown loveseat, he's gotten comfortable. I've only just managed to hang my credentials on the walls.

Marco shifts behind his desk and pulls out a small handheld clothes steamer and a fabric hanger. Impressed and relieved, I smile.

"You're a lifesaver," I say.

He winks. "I'll take that title any day. Now, hand me that dress."

I do, and he slides it over the hanger before walking toward the window and hanging the dress off the curtain rod. It takes him a few minutes to get the wrinkles out of the dress, and by the time he's done, I'm antsy.

Glancing at my watch again, I inwardly curse when I see I should have been out front waiting for Maddox five minutes ago.

"Here you go. Wrinkle-free," Marco sings, handing it over.

The deep green velvet material is what drew me to it in the first place, and no, that's not because I know Maddox's favourite colour is green. Or maybe it is. At this point, I don't know if I trust myself as much as I should.

The dress is form-fitting, with a deep V between my breasts and the material tight over my hips and ass. There's a slit up the left leg, from hem to just above my knee, and it shows just enough skin to be both sexy yet elegant. Paired with black heels, the outfit will look perfect.

I trail my index finger over the thin gold decalled straps—another selling point. "Thank you, Marco. I appreciate this so much."

"Anytime. Feel free to use my steamer anytime you want."

"Braxton," a deep voice says, my name sounding growly and far too sexy.

A shiver travels up my spine as I slowly look up and over at my date for the night. I stare at Maddox and the crisp, black suit pants and matching long-sleeve dress shirt that are wrapped around his tall, muscled frame.

Thick thighs stretch the material of his slacks, and I wonder how tight his pants must pull across his ass, knowing exactly just how nice of an ass it is. The black pants also cinch tight at his waist under an expensive-looking leather belt with a silver buckle that gleams in the dull office light. He has the top button of his shirt undone, exposing a sliver of the black ink that must be scrawled across his chest, and he's rolled the sleeves up once, or maybe twice, leaving his roped forearms open to greedy eyes like mine.

I gulp, and it's louder than I anticipated, but even the prospect of embarrassment isn't enough to tear my eyes away from this man. A pulse grows between my legs when our eyes meet, and his nostrils flare, an almost angry look crossing his face. But it's not angry. It's something dirty and intense, something that isn't appropriate for work and definitely not when my co-worker is right here, watching like he has no idea what's happening.

So, why haven't I looked away and excused myself to get ready?

Why do I continue to stare across the room at him as if he might come storming toward me and take me in his arms?

I blink. Once, twice, and a third time as I finally break eye contact and take a physical and mental step backward.

"I don't think we've met. I'm Marco. I work with Braxton," Marco says, words directed at Maddox.

"Yeah, great," Maddox replies bluntly. I feel his eyes beating into my warm face. "We need to leave soon, or we'll miss our reservation, baby."

Parting my lips in surprise at the pet name, I find him watching me with an unwavering stare. He lifts his hand toward me, and with two slow steps toward him, I let it wrap around mine, hiding the zap that singes my skin when we touch.

Baby sounds so good coming from his mouth that I want to command he say it again. Fuck the consequences. But Marco doesn't seem to want to let us leave without talking to the scowling giant beside me.

"Actually, I think I know you. You play hockey, right? The Warriors?"

Maddox tenses. "Yeah."

"Maddox Hutton!" Marco shouts, eyes lighting up. "I saw your playoff highlights on TV last night!"

I squeeze the long fingers threaded through mine with a punishing grip when he takes a few seconds too long to reply. I'm not even sure if he was planning on saying anything in the first place.

"That's me," he mutters. "Do you want an autograph?"

"That would be great! Thanks." Marco rushes to his desk and, after searching a couple of drawers, pulls out a pen and a pad of paper. "I don't watch much hockey, but I think the Warriors made it to the second round, right?"

"Yeah. First game against Arizona is on their turf this Friday night," Maddox says, and I file that information away for later.

He grabs the pen and paper from him and scrawls something that resembles an MH with a number 21 looped through it and then hands it back.

"Thanks again. I didn't know you and Braxton knew each other."

I smile slightly. "We grew up together but just recently reconnected."

Suddenly, Maddox has his arm over my shoulder and is

tucking me into his side. His cologne is familiar, and I breathe it in while sliding my arms around him, one pressed to his stomach and the other his back. He stares at Marco while I look up at him.

"Look, Marco. Braxton is my girl, yeah? She's precious to me. Can I trust you to take care of her when I'm not here?" He sounds too serious. Too real.

My eyes fall to the ground as an ache rips through my chest. *Fake.*

"Of course," Marco says.

"Thank you. I appreciate that. So, Braxton will see you tomorrow, then."

"Yeah. See you in the morning, Brax. Have a good night."

I quickly look up and smile at Marco. He looks beyond uncomfortable, and I inwardly wince. This isn't exactly the kind of situation I would have chosen for us all to fall into.

"You too. Goodnight," I rush out, snatching my dress from the curtain rod before waving quickly and letting Maddox pull us from the office.

When we reach my office, he shuts the door behind us. Warm breath hits the top of my head, and I look down to avoid his eyes. There's a spotless white sneaker touching the side of my dirty one. A barely there smile toys with my lips. "Why are you smiling?" he asks softly.

"Your shoes. You still wear sneakers with your dress clothes," I whisper.

His chest moves with a laugh. "When I can get away with it. Tell me you're wearing yours with this dress." He toys with the gold strap, slipping his finger beneath it and rubbing the fabric hanger.

Good God. I'm jealous of a hanger.

"They won't match," I choke.

"They'll match me, though, right?"

"Yes."

"Then leave the Nikes on."

I go to pull away from him, but he tightens his grip, keeping me in place. With a completely dramatic scowl, I say, "Heels it is. Please let go of me so I can get dressed. I don't want to miss our reservation."

"You hate heels," he pushes.

"Oh, let it go."

"If you wear heels, I'll end up needing to carry you out of the restaurant by the end of the night because your feet will hurt."

I step out of his embrace, not letting him keep hold of me this time. Then, I turn to glare at him, holding the dress that should have already been on against my front.

"I've gotten used to heels over the past eight years."

He arches a brow, a playful aura about him now. "Really? Should we make a bet, then?"

"Depends what the stakes are."

"You don't want to know what we're betting on first?"

"You don't think I can last an entire dinner with heels on, and I think I can. Am I missing anything?"

His smirk starts slow, growing and spreading across his face at a turtle's pace. "Nope."

I pop a hip. "You're lying. Spill it."

"Nope. Name your stakes, baby girl."

"I'm not a fan of that nickname."

He scratches at his facial hair, but I think he's trying to hide his smile. For some reason, that has pinwheels spinning in my tummy.

"Baby is okay, but baby girl isn't?"

"I never said baby was okay."

"I took your blush and subtle smile as approval, but maybe I was wrong."

"It doesn't matter. It was for show, and it helped ensure Marco bought into the façade. I feel bad about lying to him, by the way. We didn't need to bring him into this."

"No? I think he needed to know you have a boyfriend. The guy looked at you too intently. I don't like it."

"Too intently?" I start to laugh, but he looks far from entertained. That only makes me laugh harder. "Come on. He's a co-worker and a damn good vet. He's been a great help."

He nods stiffly. "Right. Well, that's that, then."

"Nope. Now you're going to tell me the stakes of this bet and then leave me to get dressed. At this rate, I'm going to end up going in what I'm wearing."

"Go for it. I don't need you to wear a dress," he says, shrugging.

I roll my eyes. "Right. I can see the Twitter posts already. Hurry and leave me be."

"Fine. If I win, you have to wear my jersey every single day for the remainder of the Warriors' playoff run."

I scoff. "No way. I'll have to wash it constantly. Especially if I have to wear it to work."

"Sorry, but I'm not budging."

"Okay, you know what? Fine. But if I win, you have to wear a pair of my scrubs out to dinner in Arizona."

He roars a laugh that tingles my toes. "Your scrubs? No fucking way. Do you see what you're wearing right now? Not to mention there's no way they'll fit me."

I glance down at my scrub top and then back up at him. "What's wrong with my scrubs?"

"They have clouds with smiley faces on them."

"Exactly."

"Are you pussying out on me, Maddox? Is the big bad hockey player too scared of a pair of printed scrubs to make a bet?"

His deep green eyes soften at the same time he whispers, "There she is."

"What do you mean?"

He smiles weakly before dropping his head forward and shaking it. "Nothing. It's nothing. I take the bet."

When he looks at me again, it's with a sadness that I feel down to my bones. Without the right words to say, I feel like a failure. The light mood we just created has been snuffed out by that damn darkness. But instead of grappling for it like a helpless fool, I let it go with the plan of finding it again tonight.

"I'm going to get dressed. Give me ten minutes?"

"Sure. I'll be in the waiting room."

I offer him a smile, and he returns it with a weak one before leaving me alone in the room, a dress in my hands and a yearning for him that I can't soothe.

21

Maddox

HIDING A BONER IN THE MIDDLE OF A BUSY WAITING ROOM ISN'T exactly my idea of a good time.

Braxton has me hard enough I fucking ache, and all from some harmless banter. I blow air out my nose and spread my legs as far as they'll go in the chair I'm sitting on and lean forward, covering the mountain in my pants with my forearms.

Several sets of curious eyes fall on me before quickly flicking away, and I do my best to smile pleasantly at a few people. After a few minutes of awkward silence and forced smiles, my leg starts to tap, and I check my watch again.

Five minutes feels like fifty.

Pushing out of the seat, I walk around the front desk and down the hallway back to Braxton's office. The door is still shut, so I lean against the wall to wait. A dim, quiet hallway is better than out there, being watched like an animal in a zoo.

I fiddle with the buttons on my shirt, undoing one just to do it back up again. The tattoos that paint my chest flash each time I undo the button, and I stare down at the corner of the one I do my best to keep hidden. From everyone, myself included. I cautiously circle the tip of it with my thumb and close my eyes tight at the pain that grows with each second I focus on the design. On the memory forever etched on my skin.

The sound of the door clicking has me quickly doing up the button, tucking the design away again.

As I look up, my lungs pull in tight, painfully. I swallow, but my throat is dry.

"Is it too much? Not enough? Be honest."

Braxton runs frantic hands down her body, and I follow their tracks eagerly. My fingers twitch, wanting to take over for hers and touch her all over. Beautiful feels like an insult. It's not enough.

Barely tamed curls, shiny pink lips, fluttering black lashes. The deep green dress hugs her body like it was made for her, and for the first time in my life, I'm jealous of a piece of clothing. All the way down to the pair of dirty, well-worn sneakers, she's a vision. And she's mine.

For tonight, she's mine.

It hurts to breathe, like my chest is too tight to expand for a full breath. I rub at my mouth, at the start of a playoff beard, and mutter a quiet "Fuck me."

Her brows furrow, and she twists her mouth. "That bad? Crap. I didn't bring a backup outfit."

I push off the wall, take a step toward her, then abruptly stop. Huffing out a breath, I stare at her puffy lips as they untwist.

"No. You're perfect," I say roughly.

Colour fills her cheeks as her teeth sink into her bottom lip. My cock throbs, and I reach down to adjust it in my pants, not thinking twice about it. She watches me do it, eyes hot with desire, and fuck if that doesn't make me even harder.

"We need to go," I rasp.

She nods slowly, distractedly, until finally, her eyes travel up my body and find mine again. "We do."

Fuck it all to hell, but I want her right here, right now. No amount of inner scolding or self-preservation can convince me otherwise. Time changed so much between us, but it didn't touch how desperately I want her. If anything, it's only made it worse, that much more intense.

I feel like I could drown in her presence. Like I can't breathe unless she says I can.

I've been holding back for days, and this feeling right here, it's shaking the ground beneath me, threatening to send my walls toppling over.

I'm aware of all of this, but I can't find it in me to run. Not from her. Not again. Not right now.

"Come here, Curly," I beg.

Her throat bobs with a swallow. "No. You come here."

I was right earlier. It only took a few days, but my Braxton is back. The quick-tongued, fiery girl who never took my shit and could give it back just as good as I gave it.

Before she has a chance to prepare herself, I'm moving, leading her back into the office with my confident steps and kicking the door shut behind us. I don't stop moving until her ass hits the desk, and she gasps, staring up at me with wild eyes.

In one quick movement, I grip the backs of her thighs and lift her onto the smooth wood, setting her down as gently as possible. I place my hands on the desk and move in close, selfishly filling her space with my presence. A small part of me expected her to fight me on it and maybe push me away, but instead, she shifts, and I glance down to find her legs spreading just enough that I can move my body between them. Finding her eyes again, I lick my bottom lip and exhale a long breath.

"There will be reporters watching us tonight, making sure we're really together. We should practice so everything looks believable," I breathe, nudging her nose with mine.

It's a copout. An excuse to kiss her. And it's obvious.

We've already practiced. I've already felt her against me, tasted her mouth and ached for more. But I need more. I need it right now.

I press my mouth to her cheek and fight off a shudder. The feel of her against me has me losing my mind. Our closeness is almost too much but also not nearly enough. I kiss her cheek and then trail my lips across her skin to her jaw, kissing her there too.

She grabs at my sides and breathes out shakily, digging her fingers in. "Practice how? We already kissed. Twice."

I shake my head and bury my face in her neck. She smells so fucking good. "Those were different circumstances. This is big time. Their attention will be solely on us. Those kisses won't cut it this time."

"Okay." She shudders against me, and I move one hand from the desk to her back, bringing her to my body. "So, what will?"

I drag my nose up the column of her throat, breathing her in one last time. When our eyes meet again, they lock and hold as tension makes the air crackle around us.

"It has to be real. Passionate. Sexy. Reporters can smell a fake relationship from a mile away." My lids fall to half-mast as I hover my mouth over hers and slip my hand from her back to her waist. "Tell me you want me to show you."

I watch her lips as she says, "I want you to show me." And then her mouth is mine.

A rough, strangled groan escapes me the moment our lips touch, and she leans up, offering herself to me. I tighten my grip on her waist and grab the back of her neck with my other hand, threading her hair through my fingers and using the silky strands to pull her head back, giving me easier access.

She pushes her chest out and tries to move closer, seeking my body, and I ache to give her what we both want, but her dress stops me. The way it's pulled tight at her thighs keeps me from pressing us together, and without thinking, I'm splaying my hands on her thighs and curling my fingers in the velvet.

A barely audible whimper hits my mouth as she pulls back just enough to look down between us, at my fingers that are pushing the bottom of her dress up her thighs, inch by fucking inch.

"It's staying on, baby. It's just in my way," I murmur, breathless. This is the most intimate we've ever been, and my chest feels crowded, like my heart has grown five sizes.

Her nails dig into my side. "It's okay. Keep going."

We both watch as it climbs higher and higher, exposing more of her bare thighs and making it harder to keep from dropping to my knees and kissing the soft, creamy skin over and over until she pushes me away.

Once it's no longer in my way, I leave it so that it still hides her panties and drift my hands back down her legs, stopping just above her knees. Then, I step closer, parting her legs further and finally pressing us together.

Her gaze flies up at the brief feel of my cock against her centre, and then she's capturing my mouth again, this time slipping her tongue between my already parted lips. A rumble grows in my chest when she covers one of my hands with hers and starts to move it to her inner thigh, holding it in place.

I squeeze it but keep it right where it is. Caution has me stumbling around in my mind, unsure of what to do next. Suddenly, my confidence is gone, and I'm breaking the kiss and rearing back, breathing heavily.

"I think that's good," I wheeze, staring behind her at a blank wall. "Good job."

"I shouldn't have done that," she rambles, her voice quivering with hurt.

"No, I shouldn't have. I don't know what's wrong with me. This wasn't right."

Angry with myself, I drop my forehead to her shoulder and tense my jaw. I want to keep her close but also run as far as possible. Expecting to feel guilt and regret for what just happened, I wait for it to hit me, but it doesn't. I don't know if that makes me feel relieved or even more confused.

Silence, and then she mumbles, "I wouldn't go that far."

"I didn't mean it like that . . . I just—"

"No, I got it. It won't happen again," she says, softly pushing at my chest to get me to back up. I do, and she slides off the desk, quickly adjusting her dress. "We've already missed our reservation. I hope you have a backup."

The next few moments happen in slow motion. Braxton collects her purse, flattens her hair, and then brushes past me on her way out of the office, not even checking if I'm behind her. It's not until she's saying goodbye to her co-workers that I make it back to her side, grabbing her hand and refusing to let her get away. She lets me lead her outside in silence, but I only make it to my truck before breaking.

"I have no idea what I'm doing here," I admit.

Sighing, she turns to face me. "What do you mean?"

"This." I wave between us. "You and me. God damn, Braxton. It's been eight years, and I still can't keep myself in check when I'm around you. What happened back there was a prime example of that. I mean, come on. Look at you. You look fucking amazing, and I just needed . . . I needed to touch you, feel you. You drive me utterly insane. And when I said the kiss wasn't right, it wasn't because it didn't feel like it. I said it because that's not what we should be doing right now. Kissing like that? That's a disaster waiting to happen."

She leans her back to the passenger door and stares at the concrete. I want her eyes on me, and frustration bubbles when she refuses to look up. Still, I listen to her next words intently, trying to dissect each one as it comes.

"I feel like we just keep going in circles. Hot and cold. Yes and no. You haven't forgiven me for everything in the past, and that's something I just have to accept, but I can't turn it off as easily as you can. I thought I would be able to handle seeing you and being with you like this, but I feel like a teenager all over again. I don't want to be the girl who falls for the guy who won't give her what she wants again. And I'm wise enough now to know I've stumbled down that same path. I have to turn around before I get lost, and that means we need boundaries. Clear-cut ones."

I fist my hands in my pockets and frown. "What are you

talking about? I wanted to give you *everything*. You're the one who didn't want that. You never gave me any clear idea that you wanted what I wanted until suddenly, everything was going to shit, and you were begging me not to tell the world about your father. I thought I was pretty damn obvious with my feelings."

"If you wanted me as much as you think you did, then why didn't you make a move? I loved you so much back then, and all I wanted was to be yours. Not just Maddox Hutton's best friend. But after years of friendship, I assumed that maybe I was misreading you."

"Misread me? Braxton, I have a tatt—"

She shakes her head and interrupts me. "Please, let me finish."

I close my mouth and nod stiffly.

"When you got drafted to Florida, I panicked. Then my father brought up the idea of you not signing with them, and I made a rash decision. The wrong one. I thought that maybe if you just stayed a bit longer that you would finally tell me how you felt, and then after you got redrafted, we would be a couple, and I could just find a school wherever you wound up.

"When we were seventeen, I told you that I couldn't chase you, but my idea of my future changed so quickly I couldn't keep up. And then suddenly, I was eighteen and rash and desperate. Definitely a bit toxic. If I could go back, I would do everything differently. I wouldn't have sided with my dad, and I would have made the first move. But that's not what happened, and I need you to forgive me and move forward, or I don't know if I can do this."

She lifts her head and finds my waiting eyes. "I've lived with a mountain of guilt and pain for nearly a decade. Please don't make me carry it any longer. I can't take seeing that hate in your eyes every single day for the next few months. If you can't put it all behind us, then we need to make peace with going our own ways for real this time."

22

Maddox

AGE EIGHTEEN

Braxton opens her front door and lets me inside before pulling me in for a hug. I accept the affection eagerly, and when she pulls away, I kiss her cheek and slip my shoes off.

She has her glasses on today—a thick-rimmed, rounded pair she wears for reading—and her hair is pulled up into some messy-ass ball on the top of her head. I poke her nose and grin.

Even in a pair of baggy sweatpants and one of my sweatshirts, she manages to take my breath away.

"You look cute," I say.

She swats my hand away from her face and rolls her eyes. "I was filling out university applications, not dressing to impress."

Braxton's sudden decision to wait a year after graduation to go to university instead of going this fall was a big one, and while she tries to deny it, I know it was because she was waiting to see where I ended up being drafted first. I did everything I could to convince her not to risk her future for me, but she was dead set on it, and one can only fight for something so hard before giving in, especially when the idea of her wanting to wait for me is selfishly everything I've ever wanted to hear.

"Who said you didn't impress me?" I tease.

"Well, did I, then?" She spins in a circle, her arms flailing at her sides. When she comes to a stop, she cocks a brow at me.

"Always, Curly Fry."

"Good answer. Now, come see my dad before he storms down here and gives us crap for getting distracted."

I nod, but nerves swirl. Being summoned to your agent's office at 5:00 p.m. on a Sunday isn't really the best sign. The entire way here, I was trying to rack my brain for anything that I've done or said in the past few days to get me in shit, but nothing has stood out.

I've been a good boy, so to speak.

"Do you know what this is about?" I ask Braxton when we start toward the staircase. She moves up in front of me, suddenly way too tense. "Brax?"

"No. We haven't talked much since you guys got back from the draft."

That was a month ago. Knowing that the Heights usually have family dinners every Tuesday and Saturday night, I'm not sure whether I completely believe that. But this is my best friend. We don't keep secrets.

"He hasn't been happy? I've felt like I'm on cloud nine since we got back. I'm not so sure about the heat in Florida, but I'm nothing if not willing to try new things."

That makes her laugh, albeit a bit forcefully. "You? Willing to try new things?"

We reach the second floor, and my stomach tumbles the closer we get to her father's office. "Your sarcasm is so hurtful."

"I'm not the one who refuses to try strawberry milk because chocolate is good enough or goes green at the idea of buying a pair of Adidas sneakers instead of Nikes."

I scoff. "All I'm saying is why change a good thing? I love chocolate milk and Nikes. Why mess that up?"

"It's just milk and shoes. It's not like shaving your head or waxing your eyebrows."

"I actually think I could be down for waxing my eyebrows. They're a bit bushy these days."

She giggles and stops in front of a closed door, looking over her shoulder at me. I memorize the sight of her timid grin and rosy cheeks.

"Your eyebrows are fine," she says.

I kiss the side of her head. "Flattery will get you everywhere, sweetheart. Come on, let's get this over with and then go get some ice cream. I've had a craving for a strawberry-cheesecake Blizzard from Dairy Queen since I woke up."

She laughs softly, knocking on the door. "Dairy Queen it is, then."

"Come in," Roy orders, and I gulp as Braxton opens the door and we step inside the office. Her dad is sitting behind his desk, his usual scowl pulling at his mouth. "Please, sit."

I collapse on the sofa and watch him cautiously. Braxton sits beside me, too far for my liking, but I know that's all because of her dad. He's never liked seeing us too close together. It's always bugged me, but considering he's fingers-deep in my NHL career, I've kept my mouth shut.

"Braxton, you don't have to be here. I'm sure your mother would like some help with watering all those flowers of hers out back," he says.

Suspicion blares, and my hackles rise. Clearing my throat, I say, "I would prefer her here, actually."

"I can go, Maddox. It's okay." Braxton starts to rise from the couch, but I lightly grab her wrist, stopping her.

"Stay. Please."

She sits back down.

"Very well," her dad grinds out. His hands are clasped and resting on his desk, and my eyes are drawn to the lack of wedding band on his left hand.

My parents have been married for nearly twenty years, and I've never seen either of them without their wedding rings. Their marriage has been happy—more than, really—but Braxton's parents have not had the same type of relationship. They're married on paper, nothing more.

"I want to discuss something with you, Maddox. Something that I think will be beneficial to your career in the long run, not just the

present," Roy starts. *I nod once.* "Florida isn't where you belong. I think you know that just as well as I do."

"I never pictured myself in Florida, but it's not like I would be stuck there forever," *I say.*

"Right. But in that time, who's to say you don't get injured? Your father was injured early in his career."

I sit up straighter at the mention of Dad. "My dad played for his dream team and gave a thousand percent of himself every single game for years. What happened to him was unlucky. The odds of that happening to me are low."

His jaw pulses, and I sink back into the couch. "What I'm trying to get at is that the future is unpredictable. You were the number one pick. I'm sure you've heard the rumours about the toxic locker room energy in Florida. Not to mention the coach is a blubbering idiot."

Everyone has heard about the team energy in Florida. Dad has already had this talk with me to help prepare me for what I could be walking into, but at the end of the day, I would only be there for three years until my entry contract is up.

"It wouldn't be forever," *I say, holding firm.*

He exhales slowly, like he's trying to keep his calm. "Florida doesn't need you, Maddox. They have two solid top lines, and you'll be lucky to see more than five minutes of ice time a game as the team stands right now. I don't say this to take a crap on you here, but you'll be forgotten if you sign with Florida. By the time your entry-level contract is up, you'll be lucky to get traded to a top team. That means a much lower offer on your next contract."

I swallow, my unease growing and growing and growing. This isn't going at all how I thought it would today. Dad would lose his shit if he knew what was happening.

"Roy, if we're serious about this, I need my dad here. What you're talking about doing is something my old man has instilled in me never to do. I can't just agree on the spot."

He scowls so deep he looks downright pissed off. "Look, kid. I have Florida's contract on my desk right now. If you want to sign it, we will right now. But I'm telling you as both your agent and your best friend's father that you will regret it," he says, voice firm, almost angry.

I look at Braxton beside me, quickly taking in her tight posture and the way she's watching me with guarded blue eyes. My worry is instant.

Flicking my eyes back to her dad, I ask, "So, what exactly are you suggesting I do? Turn down Florida and take my chances at getting picked up by another team before the season starts, or re-enter the draft next year?"

Neither of those options is ideal. Not in the slightest. In reality, they can be career killers.

"I think we can find you a much better team before the season starts. Vancouver is an option. Their interest is blaring. It has been since you were fifteen. I think if given the right chance, they'll jump at you."

A small spark of hope grows inside of me. "And if they don't? Then I have to go through this entire process again? What if I end up right back in this situation? The risk is too much."

"I think it would be worth it," he states confidently.

Overwhelmed, I focus on Braxton again. The girl I love is right here beside me, and this is going to be her future just as much as it will be mine. Her opinion means everything to me.

"What do you think about this? Is this the right move, Curly? Because you know I can't do the wrong thing here," I mutter softly, reaching for the hand she has on her thigh, taking it in mine.

Her lips part slowly, and her answer surprises me enough I have to do a double take.

"I think my dad is right. Florida isn't for you."

"Yo—you're sure?" I stutter. Fucking stutter.

She nods. "You deserve better. You deserve the best."

"I could have the best later on. I don't need it right away."

"But if you could have it, why wouldn't you just take the chance?" she whispers.

My chest is tight. The room feels suffocating despite the large size of it. My gut tells me to call my dad to get his perspective. He would *know what to do better than anyone, but at the same time, this is my career. My future. It should be up to me and the girl I hope is there for all of it.*

"You're sure?" I ask her.

Her eyes fall to our hands, and she mutters a shaky "Yes."

I squeeze her fingers and meet Roy's stare.

"Okay. Get it done."

23

Maddox

PRESENT

SHE'S GIVING ME AN OUT. AN EASY ONE AT THAT.

We could chalk this up to a bad call on Dougie's part, and they could find me someone different to play this game with— someone I have no connection to, someone free of the ghosts of our pasts—or I could just figure something else out on my own.

I've never wanted to be that guy. The one who rebelled against the help of people who really did know what the fuck they were talking about because he's too damn stubborn to listen, but this entire time . . . I've been fighting the process. All because I haven't given myself the chance to move on and forgive the rash decisions of a teenage girl.

The broken heart and self-pity that I've carried when it comes to Braxton has blurred my judgment, and it's abundantly clear to me now as I watch her face crumple and her eyes well with tears that I've hurt her along the way.

I've never wanted to hurt Braxton. The thought alone used to tear me up inside, and eight years later, it still does. You don't spend thirteen years with someone and not still hold a light to them somewhere inside of you.

This is a woman who I planned to spend my entire life with. Who I knew inside and out and, in turn, knew me the exact same. Love like that might dull after what we went through, but it didn't fade. Not with distance or time or the trail of broken pieces left behind.

I was a fucking idiot to think I could keep her from peeling back the covers and revealing those feelings again. And for her to think she misread me all those years ago? Fuck. That.

I'd been planning my proposal since I was twelve. Her thinking she wasn't my entire universe for the better part of my life is just offensive. To both her and me.

The realization strikes deep, and I have to focus on not passing out on the pavement at the intrusion of it.

"Nobody is going their own way. You're not leaving me again." My tone is sharp, focused.

Braxton blinks slowly, clearly confused with my sudden change in demeanour. I don't blame her.

"Then what? All of a sudden, you're ready to move forward? I'm not in the mood for pity, if that's what this is."

"It's not pity. It's me hating the way your eyes don't shimmer with happiness as you stare at me right now but with tears *I'm* responsible for. It's me accepting that I've been a surly fucking dickhead since I saw you in your clinic and wanting to do better. It's me telling you that you're a goddamn idiot if you think for one second that you were misreading me. That if I knew you would have said yes and that both of our families wouldn't have killed me, I would have gotten down on one knee and asked you to marry me when we were teenagers. I might not ever forget what happened, and it might take me a little while to fully forgive you, but I want to move on. With you.

"That's real. That's raw. That's the furthest thing from pity. We're going to do this damn thing, and I'm going to get my best friend back in the process. There's nowhere for you to run that I won't find you this time. You got that?"

My chest is heaving, but I don't let that stop me from

storming toward her and trapping her against the truck door between my arms like back in her office. It's not arrogance that has me noticing the rapid rise and fall of her chest as I dip my head and look into the blue depths of her eyes but simply my inability to focus on anything else. When she's close, she's the only fucking thing I see.

"Say something," I breathe, nerves alive in the words.

She rolls her lips and swallows, and like a horny idiot, I follow the curve of her throat to watch it bob, pulling tight before relaxing.

"You've stunned me to silence. Some would say you're a lucky man."

My jaw ticks. "Lucky? I want as many words from you as possible. Tell me the name of the person who told you it was lucky to have you be silent, Curly."

"I don't need you to vanquish my enemies," she whispers.

"I want to. Every single one of them." It's blunt. Honest. Real.

Gentle fingers prod my side, searching for something that I don't care how long it takes her to find. Her touch seeps into my bones, and I press our foreheads together, finding it hard to breathe with our closeness but not ready to back away quite yet.

"Do you really think you can do this?" she asks, breath hot on my jaw.

"Yes." I don't hesitate. "But only if you don't chicken out of this bet because I'm starving, and I can't wait to see you in my jersey again." Smirking, I drop a quick kiss to her forehead and step back, offering her my arm. "Shall we?"

Her laugh is more of a harsh snort, and her cheeks redden as I laugh with her.

"Aren't we taking the truck?" she asks after a moment, suspicion growing in her eyes.

"That wasn't in the rules. It's such a beautiful night that I thought we could walk there." My smile is pure evil.

Her eyes bulge. "That's most definitely cheating."

"Cheating or using the lack of rules to my advantage?"

"Both."

"Nah, you're just a sore loser."

"I haven't lost anything yet." She lifts her chin stubbornly.

"Then, by all means. Let's go." I shake my arm and flick my eyes down to it before returning them to her just in time to catch her half-hearted glare. "You know what, just because I'm so nice, I'll even take care of your brutalized feet afterward. How does that sound?"

"Like you deserve a smack across the head."

"Harsh, baby girl."

She takes my arm, digging her nails into it just enough to have me hissing a rough laugh.

"There's that name again," she scolds.

"I'm as stubborn as a mule."

She shakes her head as I take her hand, softly lacing our fingers before we start down the street. We veer out of the small, quiet business complex where the clinic is located and onto the busy sidewalk. It's all hustle and bustle as bodies swarm the streets, and suddenly, I wish I had grabbed a hat or something on my way over.

"Do you even know what time it is?" she asks.

"They'll find us another table if we've lost ours when we get there. Don't worry about the reservation."

She nods. "The perks of being famous. How could I forget?"

I look down at her and smile. Her snark is welcomed. I missed it.

"It comes with its disadvantages," I say.

She hums. "Right. Like the underwear bandit who posted pictures of your intimates on social media?"

"That's right. It was a few years ago, though. I don't let people I don't know into my space anymore."

A dramatic gasp. "But then how do you meet women? I doubt you're on Tinder."

"Easy. I don't."

"What do you mean you don't? Come on, don't lie to me."

I shrug. "No, really. There isn't anyone that's going to cause any problems with the plan, if that's why you're asking. I don't date. I haven't in a long time."

Of course, I don't plan on telling her why I haven't dated since the disaster with Rory three years ago, but she has other plans.

"Why not? I thought that once you were in the league, you would try to make up for lost time. You never dated anyone before you were drafted."

We come to a stop behind a crowd of people waiting at a crosswalk, and I step up behind her, so close I can smell her coconut shampoo. Pulling our joined hands behind her, I press them to her back and lean in, lowering my voice.

"It's hard to date when the only woman you want, you can't have."

She sucks in a sharp breath as the stick man blinks across the street. I move back to her side and pull her across my body, taking the outside of the sidewalk while smiling at a few people who are looking at me as if they know who I am.

It's almost comical how stunned I've made her over the past half an hour. Her mind has to be spinning like a mouse on a wheel at this point.

"Hockey has been my focus, anyway. It's life consuming. Especially right now with playoffs. I dated one girl a few years back, but I was an awful boyfriend. Didn't give her the time or attention she needed."

"That's sad but also understandable. I remember how busy you were when we were just teenagers. I can't imagine your schedule now," she says.

"It keeps me on my toes, but I think I just didn't want to put the effort into the relationship either. Couldn't see myself with her long term. I don't think I would have a problem giving my all to someone if I could see a future, you know?" *Like I do with you.*

She looks up at me and smiles sheepishly. "Yeah, I know. I dated in university, but it wasn't anything life changing either."

I hear a record scratch in my ears as my mind halts, snagged on the words *I dated*. Who did she date? And why does the thought of her in another man's arms have my blood starting to simmer?

"Oh. Who did you date?" My words are scratchy, like I swallowed a handful of glass shards in the past five seconds.

Her body shakes with the smallest of laughs, and I scowl. "I'm not telling you that."

"Rory Tellerman. That's the woman I dated," I blurt out.

"Okay . . ." She trails off.

"Now it's your turn."

She makes that snorting laugh sound again. "You're relentless."

"What if one of them decided to come back and try to win you back? I have to know who to prepare myself for. You know, as your fake boyfriend." *Yeah, that makes sense.*

"Hunter King and Logan Parker. And I doubt either of them so much as remember me, let alone want to try winning me back."

I furrow my brows, frowning. "Why do you say it like that?"

"Like what?"

"Like the idea of them wanting you back is at all unrealistic."

The wooden sign with cursive letters spelling out the name of our restaurant peeks out above a long row of shops, and I start to slow my steps, not wanting to cut this conversation short.

Braxton is taking too long to answer me, so I give her hand a squeeze, hoping to reassure her enough to speak whatever she's thinking.

"You know I'm not skinny, Maddox. It's hard to miss. I'm not everyone's type, and I've accepted that. Hell, I've even grown to appreciate the honesty I get from the men who tell me that straight to my face, even if it's a blow to my pride every time. I would rather the honesty than be used as some experiment for men who have never been with a chubby girl before. That's all I was to those guys. A naïve girl who thought that a guy was into me, even though he really only wanted to know if he was attracted to bigger girls."

Rage. Red, blinding rage roars deep inside of me. Words evade me. All I can think is how badly I want to hurt those guys for hurting her. For tainting how she thinks of herself and how much she's worth in a relationship.

All it takes is one pull on her hand and she's following after me, trying to keep up, her heels clicking at a fast pace on the sidewalk. I pull us into a break in the buildings and grip her hips, pulling her in close to my body. The soft flesh beneath my fingers is the furthest thing from a turnoff. I rumble a groan at how easily this woman turns me all the way on.

There are questions in her eyes, along with far too much doubt. One look at her has me willing to fall to my knees and beg for forgiveness on behalf of every single man who has stopped her from feeling like she's the most beautiful woman to exist.

"First of all, if you refer to yourself as chubby again as if it's a big bad thing, I will spank your ass so hard you won't be able to sit for a week. And second, I want to kill those men. You . . ." I drop my head and shake it. My tongue feels tangled, but I force myself to keep going.

"You are everything, Braxton. And you deserve to feel like it. There is not a single part of you that I don't love. That I don't want to touch and kiss and memorize. Those guys, they were boys. Small-dick, insecure pricks. They wouldn't know a good thing if it smacked them in the face. And you? You're the *best* fucking thing. Okay?"

A subtle nod as a tear leaks from her eye. A tear I gently wipe away with the pad of my thumb before pressing my lips to her forehead and holding them there for what feels like hours but is really only a few seconds.

"You're perfect," I breathe against her skin before inching

back and wrapping my finger in one of her curls. My knuckle brushes her cheek, feeling how warm it is. "I'm proud to have you as my fake girlfriend. There is nobody better. No one."

She surprises me by stepping up on her tiptoes and kissing my jaw, hovering her mouth over it as she says, "Thank you."

"There's no thank you needed. Just have dinner with me and eat until we're so full we have to waddle home. Can you do that?"

I pull her into my arms and hold her tight, loving the feel of her cheek against my chest, right over my heart as it thumps quick and hard. She lets out a long breath, and it warms my skin beneath my shirt.

"I can do that."

There's more I could say. Maybe more than I should have said. But I hope that what I did say made a difference. If it takes me the rest of time, I'll help erase the damage those assholes caused. That's a promise that I make to myself right here, right now.

No matter what happens in the coming months, I will be here to remind her just how amazing she is.

24

Braxton

Our waiter returns to our table, quietly setting a tequila sunrise in front of me and a glass of Diet Coke in front of Maddox. We both thank him before he shuffles off, having taken our dinner order a handful of minutes ago.

I lean forward and close my lips around the straw in my drink before taking a sip and glancing around the restaurant. It's a beautiful place, maybe even somewhere I would come again. Quiet with dark, cool tones that I would expect to make it feel more like a club than a high-end place to eat, it's actually quite romantic. Not uncomfortable at all.

Our table is tucked in the furthest corner from the front, and I don't know if that was the original placement because, just as I thought, we missed our reservation. But just like Maddox said, the hostess was quick to find us another place to sit. A private table, which I'm grateful for.

The words he said to me outside are still fresh in my mind, wreaking havoc on my heart and soul. I've never had anyone tell me those things before—let alone a man—and I'm at a loss for what to do with myself. Is it too much to throw myself across the table and plant myself in his lap? Yeah . . . probably.

Today has been an absolute whirlwind of emotions, and I

feel more exhausted than I did during finals in my last year of vet school. If I were with anyone else tonight, I would have opted to go home and curl up in bed instead of going out to dinner, but I'm with Dox, and that's worth feeling dead on my feet.

We're starting fresh. Well, as fresh as we can, considering our history. It feels like a weight off my chest knowing we can move forward together and hopefully find ourselves back to where we were before everything bad happened—or close enough to it.

I don't think I could ever silently pine after a man again the way I did Maddox, and after today . . . I'm positive that I'm about to fall in love with my childhood best friend all over again. It should terrify me, but it's weird because for the first time in a long time, I feel completely at peace with the idea.

Maybe it's because I now know how he felt when we were younger. How he pined for me as hard as I pined for him and that all the nights I lay awake in my bed convincing myself that he loved me back weren't ill wasted after all.

It might sound arrogant, but I think he's found himself in the exact same position. The fake couple façade is only going to act as an accelerant to our resurfacing feelings, and if I were a gambler, I'd put money down on us falling harder and quicker than we maybe would have otherwise.

I'm damn near positive about it.

And I'm ready for it.

I just hope he is too.

"How are your feet feeling?" Maddox asks, humour thick in his voice.

Pulling out of my thoughts, I release my straw and smile sweetly. "Perfect. Like they're cozy in a pair of fuzzy slippers."

"Really?"

"Really." *Not.* There are blisters on my heels that have to be the size of loonies. As soon as we sat down, I slipped my shoes off beneath the table.

"You're probably not nervous about the walk back to the

truck after this, then." He's watching me coyly, trying to keep from smiling, but his twitching lips are giving him away.

"Nope." I pop the *p*. He hums low, and I startle when the toe of his sneaker touches the tip of my big toe. His eyebrow jumps, a smirk spreading across his perfect features. "What? I have sweaty feet."

"Come on, Curly Fry. Just admit defeat."

"Not happening."

"Fine." He shrugs and wraps long fingers around his dewy glass before bringing it to his lips and letting the cool drink slide down his throat.

It should be a crime to look so good drinking Coke.

Setting the glass back down, he slowly swipes away the wetness on his lips with his thumb, his sly gaze unwavering. Christ, that shouldn't turn me on, but here I am, squeezing my thighs together beneath the table and struggling to breathe.

"Do you not drink alcohol?" I blurt out, snaking a hand behind my neck to wipe away the perspiration.

He leans back in his chair and taps his fingers to the white tablecloth. "Not usually. Definitely not during playoffs. We have practice tomorrow, and alcohol slows me down."

"Does it bother you that I'm drinking? I could have ordered something else."

"Fuck no. I'm a grown man, baby girl. I can handle a bit of a tease."

Oh. "You know that the equivalent of baby girl is baby boy, right? Unless you want me to start calling you that, stop with the baby girl."

He drops his head back and laughs, the sound so beautiful that I can't help but watch him, soaking up how good it feels to hear that sound again. It has my heart all turned in on itself.

"What's so funny, baby boy?" I ask through a giggle.

"Fucking hell, I missed you," he replies, shaking his head as he falls forward, elbows planted on the table now. "But you win. Please no more baby boy. It hurts my ego."

"Oh, poor Maddox." I pout. He just grins at me, looking as if he loves my teasing. Maybe he really does.

Our conversation comes to a halt when our waiter appears and starts to set our food down in front of us. The teenager avoids eye contact with both of us, and I can only assume that he's a Maddox fan who's been warned not to make a big deal out of serving us. It's adorable the way he nervously fiddles with everything on the table, organizing the silverware and setting new salt and pepper shakers down before scurrying away.

"Thank you!" I say before he gets too far away. He turns to give me a quick smile before turning into what might be the kitchen. "He's adorably nervous."

Maddox looks away from his plate of steak and potatoes and surprises me with how warm his eyes are. "He's serving a beautiful woman. Of course he is."

Heat spreads from my chest upward, and I don't even want to know how splotchy I look. "I think it might have more to do with the NHL player across from me, but thank you for the compliment. You're being ultra-sweet tonight."

"Making up for lost time."

When my heart kerplunks in my chest, I know I have to move this conversation along before I end up in cardiac arrest in the middle of this restaurant. The press would eat that up, though, I'm sure.

"Have you seen any reporters? If they're not here by now, I doubt they're coming. I guess it is just dinner. Are they actually interested in seeing that stuff?" I ask, finally taking in the meal in front of me.

Baked mac and cheese and a thick slice of garlic bread. Clearly, I'm as fancy of a girl as they come.

"Oh, they've been here since we walked in, sweetheart," Maddox states before popping a piece of steak in his mouth.

I freeze. "What?"

"Relax. And don't look around for them like a crazy woman. We want everything to seem as real as possible, and that's exactly what we've been doing. I didn't tell you because I didn't want you to act any differently."

It makes sense, but I shiver with nerves anyway. Then there's a hand covering mine and fingers slipping across my palm. My eyes fall to the back of Maddox's hand as he holds mine so delicately, like he's scared it'll crumble if he's too rough with it. I release a tense breath, pressure suddenly building in my chest.

"It's different talking about it and actually doing it. It never gets easier either. Having so many people watching your every move. If you're feeling uncomfortable, we can leave right now," he says, his tone so calm and reassuring that I fall headfirst into it, letting his words do exactly as he intended them to.

I give my head a small shake. "We came here for a purpose."

"And we've done it. Tomorrow will be a lot for you. They'll post their photos on every sports page in the morning, and your social media will blow up with questions, maybe even some things I would rather die than have you read." He frowns deeply, and I squeeze his hand. "I should have prepared you better for this. I'm sorry."

"I wouldn't have agreed to this if I didn't know what would happen after. I'm not a weak little girl anymore. I'm ready for it."

"You were never weak," he murmurs.

"I tried not to be. And I've only gotten stronger since. I got this. I promise."

He stares at my mouth—at the smile I've placed there for his benefit—and nods. I flip our hands and start to trace the lines on his palm, one by one. Goosebumps crop up on his forearms, and my smile grows.

"If you need me tomorrow, call me. Don't just text me. Call. Okay?" he asks.

"Okay," I agree. "I can do that."

And as easy as that, we go back to eating our dinner, the watching eyes fading back out of thought, leaving just him and me.

"I TOLD YOU SO!" Maddox shouts into the night, his body shaking with laughter beneath me.

He has my purse over his shoulder and me on his back, starting to carry me down the sidewalk toward the clinic like we both knew would eventually happen. In my defense, I did stick it out for the first half of the walk, but as soon as blister number one popped right open and ruined my shoes with bloodstains, I was down for the count.

The cold breeze rushes up the back of my dress, where I hope I'm not flashing my lace panties to each car that passes. His fingers are sunk deep in my inner thighs, and it's taking everything in me not to beg him to move them higher, to the spot between my legs that's absolutely soaked by this point in the night.

We can't be even five minutes from our destination, and despite my hiked sense of arousal, I haven't stopped laughing the entire walk home. It feels better than words.

He adjusts his hold on me for the briefest second as he presses the button for the crosswalk, and I'm reminded once again how easy it seems for him to hold my weight. It's doing wonders for my self-confidence, but I keep that to myself.

"Well, a bet is a bet. So, I hope you're ready to have a stinky fake girlfriend at all your games," I tease. I'm actually looking forward to wearing his jersey every day, even if I'll have to do laundry far more often.

"Stinky or not, I can't fucking wait, Curly Fry," he says as we start across the road.

I lean my cheek to the side of his head and intertwine my fingers at the base of his throat. A whiff of his cologne blows up at me from his front, and it finally hits me why I'm so familiar with it.

"I bought you this cologne when we were seventeen," I say, inhaling the scent.

"You did," he confirms.

"And you still wear it?"

If I remember correctly, it's cheap. Definitely not what I would expect the NHL's top player to be wearing.

"Do we have to talk about this?" he asks quickly, and I swallow back a surprised giggle.

"Oh my God! Are you embarrassed?"

He pinches my thigh, making me squeal as he blows out a long breath. "Yes. Of course I am."

"You're adorable. Don't be embarrassed. I'm actually kinda flattered. Have you been buying it all these years?"

"No, I've been using the same bottle for nine years," he says, sarcasm heavy in the words. I roll my eyes. "Yes, I've been buying it. I have to order it online now because it's not popular enough to be in store."

I drop my face to the crook of his neck and laugh into his shirt.

"You laughing at me isn't exactly helping with the embarrassment, you know?" he grumbles.

My heart skips when I ask, "Did you really miss me that much?"

When he suddenly crouches and releases my thighs, I take the hint and drop to my feet, staring up at him, confused. It's now that I realize we're in the parking lot of my clinic. The *empty* parking lot. His truck is only a few feet away, and the street lamps are on, casting the faintest glow on the pavement.

Maddox turns and meets my gaze with dark eyes. There's no hint of the lighthearted energy that was just buzzing around us. Instead, the air is buzzing for an entirely different reason.

"I missed you more than I've ever missed *anything*. You took a piece of me that day, and I've been searching for something, anything, to mould into the hole left behind, but it was impossible. Now you're here, and that hole? It's gone. So yes, sweetheart. I missed you. And wearing the cologne you got me made me feel like I didn't lose you entirely while you were away. I've worn it every single day."

"Dox," I breathe, blinking back tears. His vulnerability today has shaken me, and I know it's my turn.

Without speaking, I reach toward him and slide my purse from his shoulder. I unzip it and reach inside, rooting around until I feel what I'm looking for. The thin elastic band and square beads make my fingers tingle as I grip the bracelet tight and pull it out, holding it up in front of me.

His eyes fall to the bracelet, and he sucks in a breath.

Maddox's Girl.

Along the length of the elastic, eleven tiny square beads that he slid on one by one when we were seven shine under the street lamp. A single double knot keeps it all held together.

"I'm not as good with my words are you are. But I've kept this with me every single day. So, please don't be embarrassed about the cologne. I missed you just as much as you missed me. If not more."

"I want to kiss you," he croaks, and I notice a sheen to his eyes that makes my knees shake.

The corner of my mouth lifts. "Then kiss me."

There's nobody around to see, but one time without the pretense of practice won't hurt. At this point, I don't care if it does.

He clasps his hand over the one I have holding the bracelet, and our fingers curl around it as his other hand comes up to hold the back of my head and he pulls me close, kissing me hard.

The kiss is hard but soft. Urgent but patient. Confusing but all too clear at the same time.

In other words, it's entirely real.

25

Braxton

> Maddox: What are you doing today? Would I be considered needy if I asked to see you?

THE TEXT MESSAGE IS THE LAST THING I SEE BEFORE SLIPPING INTO A cab and rambling off the address to my favourite brunch place in the city to the driver. With a giddy smile, I set my purse on my lap and start to type a reply. Before sending it off, I snap a quick photo of myself wearing one of his jerseys and attach it.

Me: *Day 1 of my punishment. And I'm working. But on an extended lunch break right now as I have brunch plans.*

Me: *And you're a bit needy . . . but it's ok. I don't mind *wink emoji**

Maybe I'm teasing him a little, but what's the harm? I need the sliver of joy it brings when those said plans include a tense conversation with my family over a plate of strawberries and cream crepes.

The offer—or more like summons—for a brunch meeting came last night, not long after Maddox tucked me back in my car and sent me home, my lips swollen and already missing the feel of his. I fell quick and hard from my high the instant the text came through.

It was Mom who made contact, but I'm not naïve enough to believe it wasn't ordered by my father. Choosing my favourite spot to eat reeks of one of his plans. A place with nowhere to park on a Wednesday during peak brunch time. If I have to take a cab, I can't run off as easily as if I had driven myself.

I'm almost offended he thinks I would fall for it. That he could make me feel comfortable and naïve to his plans and then blindside me.

I can't say I didn't see this coming. Honestly, it took longer than I thought it would for him to find out about what I've done.

My phone vibrates, and one look at the message has butterflies flapping in my stomach.

> Maddox: Good jersey choice. And who are you having brunch with?

> Me: I've been craving crepes for so long. I can almost taste them already.

> Maddox: Who?

> Me: My stomach is grumbling.

> Maddox: Fine. Have it your way.

I nip at the inside of my cheek.

> Me: That doesn't sound comforting. What does that mean?

Three minutes go by without a reply, but as soon as I see the word Read appear with no sign of him typing . . .

> Me: Don't you ghost me right now Maddox Jamieson Hutton.

Read.

> Me: This is my least favourite game ever.

> Maddox: Have fun at brunch, baby girl.

I blink at the message before tossing my head back and laughing. The cab driver looks at me oddly in the rear-view mirror, but I just keep laughing. As much as I want to be annoyed with Maddox, I can't. Instead, he's unknowingly helped me relax.

A handful of minutes later, the driver drops me off outside of Tina's Brunch and Tea House, and I fiddle with my hair, stalling going inside. I peer inside the big windows, searching for my parents in the midst of all the full, pretty pink tables.

They're in my favourite booth. The one right beside the long, pastel-clothed pastry table and mimosa fountain. My parents might be sitting with their backs to the window, but I would recognize them anywhere. Front or back.

I grind my teeth. Is it worth it to call in to work for the rest of the day so I can get drunk off champagne and orange juice?

"Are you planning on standing outside or going in to have those crepes you're so horny for?"

I look for the owner of the voice, feeling more terrified than excited to see him. My eyes are bulging when they land on Maddox. He's closer than I expected and a total freaking vision in thigh-hugging dark jeans and a thin, deep green T-shirt the exact shade of his eyes in the early afternoon sun. The backward cap on his head has me swallowing a groan. I'm a sucker for the backward hat.

"What are you doing here?" I rush out, anxiously fiddling with the hem of the jersey that lands just above my hips after I tied the front to avoid looking like I'm wearing a potato sack.

His eyes travel appreciatively down my body, and I fight back a blush as he flashes me a Cheshire cat smile. *Must focus.*

"Those aren't the words I was hoping for, but I'll take them. You never did like surprises," he says, coming to a stop only a foot in from me. In one quick swoop of his head, he's kissing my cheek and collecting my hand in his. "Hey."

I lean into his lips but arch a brow when he pulls away. "Hi back. How did you know I would be here? I thought I was perfectly vague."

He narrows his eyes, scowling. "Yeah, wasn't a fan of that. I had to come here and make sure you weren't meeting another fake boyfriend. I don't share. And really? You said crepes, and unless they're from Tina's, you won't eat them. It was easy to piece it together."

And if I remember correctly, he only lives a few blocks over.

"It's worse than another fake boyfriend, Dox. My parents are inside."

My anxiety must be obvious because he starts to rub my arm while bringing our joined hands to his lips and kissing my knuckles.

"I'm glad I'm here, then. You're not dealing with this by yourself."

I shake my head, looking back into the window. There's another person at the table now, and when a head of flaming-red hair catches my eye, I blow out a small breath of relief.

"My sister is with them. I won't be alone."

"Little Annalise Heights is inside? It's been too long. I can't wait to catch up." Maddox tosses me a wink. When I still don't relax, he sighs and cups my cheek, drawing circles on my tense jaw with his thumb. "Your father doesn't scare me, Curly. I'm just doing what a good boyfriend would, right?"

I nuzzle into his palm, staring up at him, looking for even the slightest bit of hesitation, but he's all confidence.

"If you're sure. My father isn't known for being subtle. He's going to be livid to see you with me. It isn't going to be pretty," I warn.

Dox's grin is pure arrogance. "Then I can't wait."

"Okay," I breathe, nodding one too many times. "Let's go in, then."

He wraps his body around my back and holds my hand tight as we walk to the door. Extending an arm around my head, he pulls it open for me, the bell chiming as we enter.

My stomach falls between my knees when my dad whips around and finds the two of us. Sharp as daggers, his blue eyes cut deep.

Maddox immediately flanks my side and slips his free hand around my waist, pulling me tight to his body. His hot breath warms the top of my head before he kisses me there and whispers, "We leave when you want to."

I nod stiffly, and then we're at the table.

"Braxton!" Annalise squeals, jumping out of the booth and ripping me away from Maddox before pulling me in her arms. I smile into her pin-straight hair and hug her back.

While my little sister may be four years younger than me, she's always been mature for her age. It's one of the reasons we became so close so young. My opposite in every physical way, she looks more like Mom than Dad.

"It's only been a few weeks, you know?" I tease, pulling back.

"Oh, I know. You used me for free labour when you moved into your new house, and then I was chopped liver." Her glare is weak and wavers when she moves it to the man still glued to my side. "Maddox Hutton. I see you've gotten quite massive over the years."

A loud laugh rips out of me before I can suck it back. My sister lacks a filter. No matter who she's around, she can't seem to ever find one. It's one of the things I love most about her.

Luckily, I don't have to worry about Maddox having a problem with it. He only lets out a deep laugh of his own and gives her a genuine smile.

"It's nice to see you again, Anna."

My sister flashes a grin. "You two sit. I'll pull up a chair, and then maybe you can both tell me why I had to find out about this relationship on social media and not in person."

She lifts a brow at me and then walks away in search of an open chair in the busy restaurant. I face my parents, choosing to focus on my mom and her tired eyes as I slide into the booth opposite them. Maddox follows, but he doesn't wait for either one of my parents to get the first word.

"Mrs. Heights, it's nice to see you," he says, slinging his arm over my shoulder, keeping me close.

I risk a glance at my father and find his lip curled, his focus on Maddox. Hate, disgust, rage. It's all there on his face. He's not bothering to hide it, and that's a terrifying realization.

"Hello, Maddox. We didn't know you were coming, or we would have ordered you a beverage when the waitress was here," Mom says apologetically.

Dad scoffs, taking a break from trying to make Maddox disappear into a cloud of smoke with his eyes to glance at me.

"I raised you better than to show up with uninvited guests. And what are you wearing?"

"Do you not like it? I figured I would show some team spirit. I'm sure you know how well our hometown is playing in the playoffs this season."

Rage lights his eyes. "If dressing like this and bringing him here with you is some sort of act of rebellion—"

"I'm far too old to rebel, Dad. And if we're going to talk about my new boyfriend, he should at least be here. Don't you think?" I counter.

"Stop this charade, Braxton. We all know you're not together."

Maddox drops his head to the dip of my shoulder and chuckles lightly, almost dangerously. Lips part on the side of my neck, over the heavy thump of my pulse, and lightly suck. My skin lifts with goosebumps as he starts to draw shapes on my bicep. Every few seconds, he slips them higher up my arm until they're tucking beneath my shirt sleeve.

"It's embarrassing that after this long, you still don't believe how in love I am with your daughter. She's been mine since the day we met, Roy. It would be smart to start believing just how much she means to me."

The sheer possession in his tone has me fighting back a shudder. My core clenches, the feeling of his touch on my arm and his thigh pressed to mine almost too much. It should feel wrong to be thinking about all the ways I want him to prove those words to me while we're in public, but I can't help it.

Sexual tension has always been a problem between Maddox and me. Since I was old enough to recognize the feeling of sexual want, I've been dreaming of having him that way. I thought that back then it was crazy how badly I wanted him, but now? I wasn't prepared for how downright consuming it would be. I feel it through every thread of my being.

"You're not right for Braxton. You never have been. I don't know how you convinced her to go along with this scheme, but if it doesn't come to an end, you won't be the only one not welcome near my family," Dad snaps.

At that, my heart cracks up the middle. I numbly register the screeching sound of a chair scraping the floor and my sister's voice, but I don't look away from my father.

"Sorry, guys. It's packed in here, so they had to get me an extra chair from the back."

Maddox is tensed up tight beside me, holding me like I'm the only thing keeping him from climbing over the table and wrapping his hands around my dad's neck. I don't dare look at my mother.

"What is that supposed to mean?" I ask, calling upon every ounce of my courage.

Dad's stare is pure fire, but his words burn far worse. "It was your mother's idea to do this here so that you didn't make a big scene and embarrass all of us further, but if you don't put an end to this little game and come out with a statement saying that this was all one big misunderstanding, you will not be welcome in this family anymore. If this is a cry for attention, congratulations, you've got it. But I will not let you make a fool of us because you're feeling unloved."

The blood drains from my face. That small crack spreads.

"What the fuck did you say?" Maddox snarls.

"Braxton, baby. That's not why I insisted we come here. I didn't know this was going to ha—" Mom starts before Dad cuts her off.

"Don't, Larissa. For God's sake, can you just let me do something without needing to be the good guy?"

He's leaning forward, his fingers white from pressing down on the table so hard. The vein that always pops out when he gets angry is throbbing in his forehead. I'm surprised it hasn't burst.

Mom, on the other hand, stiffens and closes her mouth. Any hope I had that she would finally have enough of Dad's shit and tell him off for once poofs into thin air.

"So, it's not just your daughter you treat like shit, then? It's everyone? What a keeper. And I wonder why the league won't touch you with a ten-fucking-foot pole," Maddox says, not even a twinge of fear in his voice.

"You want to talk about why the league won't work with me? That would be your daddy, right? The great Oakley Hutton who couldn't stand that someone other than himself had an idea of what your future should look like," Dad throws back.

Maddox goes deathly still. "Keep my dad's name out of your mouth before I ruin Braxton's love for this place with the memory of me decorating it with your front teeth."

"And here we are again. Back to my daughter. I'm always painted as the sole reason for you needing to re-enter the draft, but she played a part in that decision too, didn't she? Some would argue she is more to blame than I am."

I startle at how easy it is for my father to throw me under the bus. Like I'm an easy casualty. Yet, it doesn't hurt as much as I thought. Maybe because he's already done enough damage to our relationship. Maybe when it comes to my love for him, I don't have anything left for him to break.

It's a sad thing to accept, but our relationship ended the day I left Vancouver. Maybe it even had before then. Roy Heights is the man whose blood runs in my veins, but he's never been much of a dad. This fallout was always coming, and I'm glad I wasn't alone when it happened.

I lift my arm and cover Maddox's hand with mine where it clutches my arm, giving it a squeeze that's meant to comfort the both of us. I'm so grateful to have him here with me.

"You're really going to blame an eighteen-year-old girl for your mistakes? For your greed? You never wanted to help me. You thought if I skipped out on Florida, that because of who my father is, Vancouver would have picked me up and in turn would have been able to offer me a heavier contract. It was never about the team or the coach. It was always about you and how thick you could line your pockets.

"I don't know how you have anyone left at this point. You burn every bridge you build. The only reason the full truth never came out about you was because of Braxton. It would be a hell of a lot worse for you had she not begged me to keep out the details. You owe her a thank you. But at this point, we all know it would fall on deaf ears."

Maddox is eerily calm as he finishes speaking and looks at me, his lips forming just the hint of a smile.

When he speaks, he doesn't look away. "I don't really care what you think about our relationship. Believe it or don't. You can shit on my name to everyone who will listen because the best thing you've ever done for me is bring Braxton back into my life. It's the only thing I will never hate you for."

26

Maddox

THE SILENCE FOLLOWING MY STATEMENT IS SO, SO LOUD.

Braxton's eyes on me have it impossible to look away. They're so blue. So beautiful. They remind me of the deepest parts of the ocean where the bright blue becomes a dark navy, as if someone added a million cans of black paint to deepen the colour.

But while I fear the ocean, I don't fear her.

I move my arm from around Braxton's shoulder and drop my hand into her lap instead. With my thumbs running over her knuckles, I finally look away, turning to her dad even if that's the last thing I want to do.

"If you continue to spew lies about me, I'll take you to court for slander. That's a promise," I say.

Feeling calmer than I expected, I look at my girl again. She hasn't turned away from me, and that makes me feel like the luckiest son of a bitch in the entire world. Her lips part with a smile—just a small, reassuring one—but it does the job and then some.

"You have no idea what you're doing," Roy says, shaking his head at me as if he genuinely can't believe what I'm saying.

"No, you see. That's the difference between this conversation and the one in your office eight years ago. I didn't know what I was doing with you then, but I sure as shit know what I'm doing now."

"I don't know what I was expecting from this meeting today, but for the first time in years, I can say you surprised me, Dad. Who knew you would be so willing to throw me in front of a bus to save yourself," Braxton says sharply, grabbing her purse strap and dropping the heavy thing onto the wooden table.

"Honey, please stay and finish your breakfast with us. At least let me drive you home so we can. Don't go back to work and ignore this," Mrs. Heights begs her daughter, a quiver in her voice.

"Are you serious, Mom? You just want her to sit here and listen to this?" Annalise guffaws. "Let her go. Actually, let us all go. I'm with Brax on this."

"Quit being dramatic, Annalise. This isn't your business," Roy grunts.

"No? Then why was I invited to this lame excuse of a brunch? Can we even call it that when we haven't eaten? Did you pay the waitress to avoid our table while you did this?"

"I was hoping your presence would help keep your sister calm enough that we could have a grown-up discussion about this. The waitress isn't needed yet. This isn't a conversation I want interrupted," Roy snaps.

"Well, that just proves how little you know about the women in this family because we get vicious when we're hungry. And I'm damn near ravished," Anna growls.

Braxton laughs under her breath, and I flash her a grin, laughing right there with her. Annalise whips her head toward us, and as soon as she sees us laughing, her anger starts to lift.

"You're telling me you decided to have this conversation in public when you wanted privacy?" Braxton asks, as dumbstruck as the rest of us, minus her dad.

Roy narrows his eyes on her, and my smile drops as I glare back.

"I knew you wouldn't come to the house," he says.

"You mean after the last time you asked me to come over only to blindside me with your plan to sabotage Maddox? Wow, imagine that."

My interest spikes at those words, and a wave of frustration starts to build before I push it away. *What was she supposed to do, you big idiot? Stalk me on social media and send me a message warning me?* Even if she had, I probably wouldn't have believed her.

"Your sarcasm is unbecoming."

"I beg to differ. Nothing is unbecoming on Braxton," I chime in.

"Stop it. That's adorable," Annalise swoons despite the seriousness around us. I wink at her.

A noise of frustration comes from across the table before Roy pulls out his phone and starts typing furiously at the screen. I don't know whether we're being dismissed or if he just has something he thinks is more important than this to deal with right now.

Either way, it's rude. My grandpa would have this asshole's phone out of his hand and in the middle of traffic if he were here. My mom's father is a total hard-ass, but in the most ooey-gooey-centre kind of way.

Braxton snorts. "Well, don't let us disturb your business. We're leaving."

"Not yet. Look at this first," Roy orders. I wait, expecting him to hand the phone to Braxton, but he holds it in front of my face instead. "Go ahead. I want you both to see what you've done by carrying out this whole act. Read those comments and tell me if you still think you're doing the right thing."

I rip the phone from his grip and bring it close, taking in what's happening on the screen.

It's a few pictures of me and Braxton from last night on one of the bigger sports pages with the caption *"Maddox Hutton off the market? Swipe to meet his new girlfriend—Braxton Heights, the daughter of Hutton's former hockey agent, Roy Heights. Is this a shot at daddy or is Roy out to lunch?"*

The caption doesn't bother me. We expected this reaction when the news broke. But shit. I can't look away from the photos themselves.

Braxton on my back, my hands tight on her thighs, her purse strung over my shoulder, and wide, blissful grins lighting our faces. I want the pictures for myself, preferably so I can blow them up and hang them on my living room walls.

"Is this supposed to piss me off?" I ask.

"Scroll down."

I do, and my stomach folds further into itself with each comment I read. There are over two thousand comments on this post, and while the majority are just curious hockey fans, some of them make me want to puke. I swallow the boulder in my throat and tilt the phone out of Braxton's view when she tries to lean over my body to see what they say.

"They're fantastic photos. If you know who the photographer is, please let me know so I can get a copy of the originals," I say, hoping nobody can hear the struggle behind the words.

Roy's anger is so evident I feel it across the table. "You're going to let my daughter be called those horrific names and not do anything? This is precisely why I don't believe this relationship is real."

"Dad, I really don't care about what people on the internet say about me. I already knew this would happen." Braxton sighs.

"Braxton doesn't need me to protect her by monitoring everything she sees, but I *will* still protect her. Don't take my lack of visible reaction as calmness. The last thing I ever want is for her to face any sort of negativity in her life."

Braxton has always been strong enough to look out for herself, but while I meant what I said about not monitoring what she sees, I still lock the phone and toss it onto the table in front of Roy without letting her see the comments. If she finds herself looking later on, that's her business, and I'll be there if she wants me. But her first encounter with internet trolls is not going to be in a crowded restaurant in front of her father.

"Sounds like a copout to me," Roy mutters under his breath.

I shrug. "It would. You have no idea what it means to truly protect someone. You don't know how to give someone the kind of protection they both need *and* want because you don't bother learning that much about them. You're really going to preach to me about protection when not even ten minutes ago, you were throwing your eldest daughter under the bus to cover your ass? Right."

"Dox, I really just want to leave," Braxton murmurs.

I smile softly. "Sounds good to me. But we're not leaving here without your crepes."

Appreciation shines in her eyes as she nods. "Go. I'll be fine. There are some things I want to say before we go."

"Be right back," I whisper before lifting her chin with my pointer finger and kissing her, not giving a single fuck that her dad is glaring daggers at us.

I kiss her softly, slowly, taking my time, and once I've sated my need enough to leave her alone with her parents, I bump her nose with mine and pull away.

I don't like leaving her here alone with them, but if it's what she wants, then that's that.

After stealing another quick kiss, I slip out of the booth and place an order at the counter for crepes, pancakes, and every sort of meat they have at this place, all while sneaking glances at the table.

My chest puffs out as I watch Braxton lay into her parents, her little sister joining in every few seconds. The more I watch, the more curious I become about the relationship the two sisters have. They used to be close, and I'm glad to see that still seems to be the case.

There are so many questions I want to ask Braxton. So many conversations I want to have about every little thing she's done these last eight years and what she wants for the rest of her life. We've barely been back in each other's lives for three weeks, but I feel like I should know more.

Maybe that's my worry talking. Worry that she'll disappear on me again before I get the chance to find an answer to all my questions. I don't want to rush, but the idea of taking things slow with her doesn't seem to be an option anymore.

We tried that once, and I ended up losing her. Maybe not for that exact reason, but I can't help but wonder if I hadn't waited and I had just kissed her and told her I loved her when we were younger if that would have kept her from leaving.

It's all what-ifs. I have to remind myself of that. We can't go back. There's only now and what we do next.

And right now, I want to carry her out of here, take her back to my place, and force her to tell me everything. I want to tell her all about me and my family and see if she's as proud of me for my career as I am of hers. I want to tell her about every win this season and show her every highlight reel that's been made for me. And then . . . then I want to bring her to my bedroom and do every single dirty, unhinged thing I've ever imagined.

I want to completely lose myself in the feeling of being with her in such a vulnerable way. I want to hear every sound she makes when she feels pleasure and how they change and grow when she's about to come.

I want to ravish her.

Fuck. I want it all. Every. Last. Thing.

"Here you go! That'll be fifty-four dollars and ten cents," the woman at the counter says.

I tear my eyes from the table and smile at her, noting the stack of Styrofoam containers she's putting inside a brown paper bag. After paying, I carry it over to the table.

Whatever they were talking about comes to an abrupt stop when I reach them and grin at Braxton.

"Ready?" I tuck the bag in my elbow and hold it against my chest as I offer her my hand and help her up.

"Ready," she breathes out.

I'm surprised to see Annalise standing beside us, purse in hand. She notices my confusion and asks, "Did you think I was going to sit here and eat after all of this?"

I roll my lips to hide my smile. "Of course not."

Placing my palm to Braxton's lower back, I follow Annalise outside, not a single one of us looking back at the table before we're on the sidewalk. I'm sure the lack of attention burns Roy deeper than any goodbye.

"It was great to see you again, Maddox. The three of us will have to have dinner together or something soon," Annalise says, reaching over to give my wrist a squeeze once we stop just a few steps away from the restaurant.

"The Warriors play our first second-round home game on Tuesday. You should come with Braxton," I offer.

In all honesty, I'm asking for both Braxton and myself. Fans are crazy on a normal day, but when you throw in the buzz of the playoffs and the recent news of our relationship, I'm worried about having her out in the stands all alone.

"I would love that!" she squeals.

Braxton's smile tells me I made the right call.

"Great. I'll send Curly the tickets, and she can send you all the information."

"Can't wait. Text me when you get home, 'kay? We need to coordinate our outfits or whatever girls do when they're dating someone famous," Annalise tells her sister.

I stifle a laugh.

Braxton rolls her eyes and pulls her in for a quick hug. "There won't be any outfit planning. I have to wear Dox's jersey."

"Every single day," I add.

Anna looks between Braxton and me with heavy suspicion. "This sounds like a story I want to hear. I thought you just wore Maddox's jersey today to piss off Dad."

"Killed two birds with one stone, I guess. I'll tell you all about the bet tomorrow. I have to get back to the office before Marco gets overrun," Braxton says.

My scowl is immediate. "How well do you know this Marco guy?"

Anna giggles and pats Braxton on the back. "Good luck with that. I'm going. Love you lots." Then her eyes are on me, slightly more narrowed now. "Take care of her."

"Always," I promise immediately. She nods.

"Bye, Anna. Love you," Braxton says, waving when her sister starts to head off in the opposite direction as us.

When she slips through the crowds of people and we lose sight of her, Braxton steps in front of me and wraps her arms around me, resting her cheek to my chest.

Surprised but not stupid, I return the embrace, keeping her pressed to me, not giving a shit that she can probably hear how fast my heart beats for her. I contemplate dropping the bag of food so that I can put both of my arms around her, but I'm starving, and I need to eat before practice, even if breakfast food isn't what my trainer would approve for pre-practice body fuel.

"Thank you," she whispers, blowing out a content breath and pressing even closer, like she's trying to burrow herself into my chest.

She wouldn't have any complaints from me if that were the case.

"For what?"

Vivid blue eyes pierce my green ones when she tips her head back and smiles.

"For coming back to me."

27

Braxton

THE DOORBELL RINGS THREE TIMES AS I'M SLIPPING A PAIR OF SOCKS over my freshly painted and dried toenails. The forest-green polish disappears beneath the white fabric as a flash of embarrassment washes over me.

Did I really paint my toenails the colour of Maddox's eyes when he won't even see them? Yeah, I did. I also painted my fingernails to match, dug out my nicest lingerie—tags still on—and slipped it on beneath my clothes because as much as I can try to pretend otherwise, there's a small part of me that's hoping tonight, maybe he'll get to see it.

"Some would call you a dreamer," I mutter under my breath, getting up from the edge of my bed and heading to my front door, a thong string riding further up my butt cheeks with each step.

I blame Maddox for putting these ideas of lingerie and nail polish in my head. If it weren't for his text earlier asking if I wanted to go to his place after the game, I probably wouldn't have even started thinking this way. At least not already.

The past few days without him have been . . . lonely. With him in Arizona, I've felt his absence like a cold fist in my chest.

Our reconnecting has only brought everything I've tried to keep shoved deep, deep down right back to the surface. It's obvious that I'm struggling with it all. Both mentally and physically.

We've been running around each other for years, the sexual tension building and building until now I'm left feeling like a ticking time bomb. Only much hornier.

Something has to give, and while I can admire his seemingly magical grasp on control, I want him to be the one to snap. To finally put an end to this game of foreplay we've been playing so I can satiate this suffocating need I have for him.

Clearly, I'm a mess.

With flushed skin, I give my head a shake and open the front door, expecting to see my sister but finding no one. Instead, a big brown box with a bulging top is parked on my porch.

I blink at it before carefully touching the side with my toes. When nothing beeps or blows up, I figure it's safe enough and drop to my haunches to pick it up, surprised by the weight of it.

Stepping back inside, I drop the box on the countertop. Curiosity at full capacity, I grab a pair of scissors from the knife block and cut the tape. The box flaps jump open, the tape being the only thing keeping the overstuffed thing closed.

My jaw slacks as I stare down at what's inside and slowly pinch the card on top between my fingers, lifting it to read the messy scrawl.

With you by my side, we're going all the way to the cup, and that means you need more than one jersey. Take your pick, there's every style of VW jersey I've ever worn in here. And yes, I signed each one and I'm writing this note with a very sore wrist. Kiss it better later? Can't wait to see you.

Love, Dox

My heart swells to twice its size. I try to remind myself that it's only been just shy of a month, and falling in love with someone in that time isn't logical. But how can I convince myself of that when I'm already so close? When I'm on the cusp and the furthest thing from afraid?

I was in love with this man for half my life, and while time apart and bad decisions created a rift in my feelings, I think I could happily spend the last half of my life the same way.

The doorbell rings again, snapping me from my thoughts. I run my finger over the last two words written on the card, feeling the indents left behind from the hard press of a pen, before slipping the thick paper into the back pocket of my jeans and going to answer the door.

This time, it is my sister on the other side, and after I quickly gather my things, she whisks me out the door and into her car before heading to the arena.

The energy in the arena is electric. I'm positive my voice is going to be gone tomorrow from how loud I've been screaming.

I've been to too many of Maddox's games to count, but the two NHL games I've come to have been so different in comparison. The VW fans are intense and downright crazy, but that's what makes these games so amazing. Their love of the sport is beautiful in the most chaotic way possible.

Then there are the players themselves. There's a reason they play in the NHL. Their talent is unmatched, and as I watch

Maddox slip through two Arizona players while poking the puck from the stick of another, it's made abundantly clear to every single person in the building that he was born to do this.

He's quick, even with his size, and incredibly agile. Moving fluidly, he evades two big players as they prepare to try and check him and enters the Arizona zone. The closest player is still too far away to keep him from lining up a shot in front of the goaltender, and as Dox snaps the puck, I hold my breath, watching it cut through the air.

The goalie lifts his left glove too late, and the puck skims his shoulder before sinking into the netting. Red lamp flashing, the goal horn blares through the arena. Maddox skates away from the net, his arm lifted and glove pointed directly at me.

His grin is blinding as he stops at the boards directly in front of Anna and me and shouts, "For you!"

My cheeks warm as I blow him a kiss and listen to the giggles behind me. Anna lifts a hand to her forehead and drops her head back, sighing dramatically. I bite my lip, watching him skate off again, wondering how all that endurance pays off in the bedroom.

Crossing my legs, I push my hair behind my ears and will my temperature to fall back to a safe range.

"So, when are you two going to bone?" Anna asks far too loudly, and I whip my head around to glare at her when the girls behind us gasp.

I noticed them as soon as the warm-ups started and they started fawning over the guys, specifically Bentley, who "accidentally" lifted his jersey up and flashed our entire section a whole rack of abs.

I'm pretty sure nobody was complaining about the free show. Especially not Annalise, who looked him dead in the eye and made a *call me* motion.

"First of all, don't use the term 'bone.' Especially not in public. And second, that's so not something I'm going to discuss."

She scoffs. "Don't be shy. If I had to be around that guy and not ride his face on the daily, I would be strung just about as tight as you are right now."

"Annalise," I groan, desperately trying to focus on the faceoff happening at centre ice.

"Braxton."

"You do know where we are, right?"

"Of course I do."

"So you know this isn't the time or the place."

She shrugs. "According to you. I think this is the perfect time and place. There's nowhere for you to escape."

I huff, staring at the ice and the rush toward the Arizona zone. With my voice low, I ask, "How do you even know we haven't?"

"Is that a serious question?"

"Yes."

She shakes her head at me and pats the hand I have resting on the connected armrest.

"The way I see it is that either the sex is so good that you can't look at him without replaying it in your mind or that you haven't slept together yet, which is why you're eye fucking each other whenever possible. I don't doubt the sex with that guy isn't anything less than mind-blowing and toe-curling, but there's no way you would be this against talking about it if it was actually happening. You've never been sticky when it comes to sharing anything with me before." She's quieter now, keeping the words for just us.

Guilt slashes me down to the bone. She should know that this isn't a real relationship. I should tell her everything. It's not fair to keep this from her.

I'll ask Maddox about it tonight.

"Maybe I want to keep this to myself. Maybe it's just special to me," I blurt out.

Her eyes soften, lips tugging into a soft smile. "Is that it? Because that would be really adorable."

I deflate. "No. We haven't gone there yet."

"Why?" Her tone is judgment-free. Just curious. So curious.

"It just hasn't happened. Things are different now . . ." I rack my brain for the answer to her question, and when I find it, it just flows out of me. "We haven't even talked about what were really doing here."

She nods along, her lips pursed as she takes in all I'm saying.

"Is that all?"

"What do you mean?"

"I mean, is there anything else? I don't think it will be long before you both break and finally talk about whatever is going on between you, but I don't think that's the only thing you're in your head about."

My stomach pinches. It's right there on my tongue, but it almost feels too embarrassing to admit.

"Braxton, I won't judge you. You know that," she adds, finding my hand and squeezing my fingers.

"I don't know about him, but I . . . I'm nervous, I guess. Nervous that he won't like what he sees when and if we get there. We might have known each other for forever, but there's a lot of me that he hasn't seen." It all comes out on one heavy breath, and I blink back a sudden burn in my own eyes. "I want to go there with him. I want to so badly that sometimes it's all I can think about. But I don't know how I will react when we do get there. What if I just freeze or freak out on him? Or worse, what if he's the one to freak out?"

This time, it's me squeezing her hand. I hold it so tight she couldn't pull it away if she wanted to.

"Maddox Hutton has loved every single piece of you since you were both too young to even know what love was. Your fear is normal. Everyone gets nervous before being intimate with another person. That's just part of being human. But you shouldn't let it keep you from taking that step. If you're both ready, it'll happen naturally. You're the strongest woman I know. You got this," she says softly, words quiet, gentle.

I smile at her, nodding. Her words sink deep and help fight back some of my self-doubt and worry. The rest is up to me.

"I appreciate you. You know that, right?"

She winks. "I know. And I've always got your back. I'm sorry I didn't do more to help at brunch."

"Don't apologize. Dad was out of line, and Mom shouldn't have played into his games again," I mutter.

"I don't even know why they're still married. They can't stand each other." She pauses, biting at the inside of her cheek. "Do you ever worry about your own marriage after watching theirs? Like, do you ever think, what if mine turns out the same? What if my husband becomes another version of our father and I lose my backbone like our mom?"

I contemplate that. "Yeah, sometimes. I had Maddox's parents' marriage to look at growing up, though. Maybe that's why I'm not completely against the idea. I think I still want to get married someday."

"I don't know if I ever want to. The idea of giving the man I marry the same power over me that Dad has over Mom seems like torture," she admits.

That makes me frown. My sister is too young to be so fearful of love.

"A real marriage isn't about giving your partner power over you, Anna. It's about sharing it. Giving and taking in equal parts. I know it's hard to understand that when you've only seen it one way for so long. But there are happy marriages. Amazing ones that last for lifetimes."

"But what happens—"

The goal horn rings out again, and suddenly, we're thrown into a rush of screaming fans and raining VW merchandise. Annalise jumps out of her seat, clapping and screaming as our home team takes the first win of the second round by a score of three to one.

I hate that we're leaving such a heavy conversation incomplete, but I'm also aware that my sister isn't one to love heavy topics and that she won't go there again with me right now. I just have to hope that she was really listening to what I said and that it resonated somewhere inside of her.

Joining in the celebrations, I replay her reassuring words to me and pray that they can help calm my nerves come tonight.

God knows I need all the help I can get.

28

Maddox

"How does it feel to grab your second straight win?" the reporter asks Bentley, his recorder lifted. With his eyes wide and lips parted with excitement, it's like he's on the edge of his seat to receive the same answer we always give these guys when they ask stupid questions.

Bentley gives the guy a tired smile. "Feels great. It's what we came out to do tonight."

We're all exhausted and antsy to get the fuck out of here. Most of the guys are going out to celebrate, but I have other plans. Much more important ones.

Our press manager, Penny, gives the go-ahead to another reporter, and I swallow back a curse when I see a familiar woman stand. I've already forgotten her name, and I curse myself out for that too. I should have looked her up or something after last time.

Alexander was clear that when it came to the press, I wasn't to sit in on the post-game interviews until Braxton and I had made progress with our fake relationship, so this is the first time I've been back since before Roy's story broke. With the chatter focused more on my new relationship, we hope that it will take the attention away from all of his other claims.

"Rose Carpenter from Sports Weekly," she says before holding out a long, skinny arm, recorder in hand. "Maddox, do you have an update on your contract?"

Annoyance bubbles in my blood. I roll out a long breath and stare at her, my gaze intense with the hope of making her squirm. I lick the back of my teeth before I speak.

"No. Not at the moment."

"You have fans nervous. Do you not have anything to give them? At all?" Her return is quick, like she was expecting me not to have an answer for her.

"The fans know I love Vancouver and that I love them."

"Right. So, you have nothing, then? I'm sure you know that suspicions are growing."

I thin my eyes, leaning forward with my elbows on the table. With a rough swipe of my hand over my beard-covered jaw, I say, "Rumours. Not suspicions. We'll be ready to share before next season starts. That's all I can say."

"What about the rumours about you and Roy Heights' daughter? Do you have anything to say? Can you confirm or deny the speculations that you're in a relationship?"

"Her name is Braxton. And yes, we are together."

Rose's eyes flare with something I immediately don't like at the confirmation. It's the look of someone who's desperate for a story.

"And her father's allegations? Is it true you have anger issues? Do you take drugs?"

Like a fucking dog with a scent, this one.

"Next question. And keep it on topic. This isn't a damn gossip circle," Penny snaps, and I release a breath when another reporter stands, asking Bentley about his three assists tonight.

My eyes wander to the door as I debate making a run for it, knowing Braxton is on the other side of it, waiting for me to take her home. To my home.

The next few minutes drag as my excitement to get her out of here builds and builds, leaving my anger at this Rose Carpenter to sizzle out. I've made a mental note to research the hell out of her as soon as possible, and hopefully, I can find something that I can use to get her banned from further interviews.

As soon as the interviews come to an end, I'm out of my seat, a fire under my ass. I give Bentley a grin as I pass him, and the wink he sends me says he knows exactly where I'm going and why I'm in such a rush. We haven't really had time to chat about everything that's happened recently, and I want to fix that as soon as possible. He's been a really good friend to me over the past few years, and I know guys like him don't come around often enough.

The crowd moves slowly out the doors, and as soon as I break through, I'm searching for Braxton in the hallway. With a harsh exhale, I find her waiting by one of the big windows that look out to the street behind the arena. She has her hands tapping her outer thighs as she rocks forward on her tiptoes and then falls back to her heels. Every time she falls back, I watch her perfect, peach-shaped ass bounce, wishing I had it gripped in my hands.

She has no idea how sexy she is, and that is a fucking crime.

"I've never wanted to be out of this arena as badly as I do right now," I say, stepping up behind her and dropping my arms over her shoulders.

She melts into me, rolling her head to the side and looking up at me through thick black lashes. My heart thumps in my chest, probably right against her cheek.

"Are you tired? You played amazing out there."

I dip my head and lift her chin with a gentle touch of my finger before pressing our lips together. It's a soft caress of our mouths, a tease of what I hope tonight brings. I graze her bottom lip with my teeth before forcing myself to pull back.

"Thank you, baby. And no, I'm not tired at all. Wide awake, actually," I rumble.

Her lips tug at the corners. "Well then, take me to your place. I'm feeling very snoopy and want to see everything you didn't want to show me the first time I was over. Underwear drawer included."

She attempts a wink, and it might just be the most adorable thing I have ever seen. The way both of her eyes close, one just a beat behind the other one, has my stomach in my throat.

"Let's go, then, Snoopy," I croak, spinning her in my arms so we're face to face, chest to chest.

"The happy couple! Would you mind answering a few questions for Sports Weekly?"

Rose Carpenter's voice has my entire body tensing. I keep my eyes on Braxton and watch as her brows furrow, and she shifts and looks behind me.

"I'm assuming she's talking to us?" she asks.

I nod. "That reporter has a set of balls on her."

"What do you want to do? She's walking over here right now."

"She has questions about us and your father. Just don't answer unless you absolutely want to. She can't make you say anything. They're not supposed to do this here," I mutter.

I wait for her to give me some sort of acknowledgment, and when she nods, I spin around, keeping her behind me. But when she shifts to my side, I know it was a long shot keeping her out of this.

Rose wears determination like a fucking second skin, but it's the furthest thing from admirable. The more I'm seeing this woman, the more of a problem she's becoming. Outside of the press room, we're off limits. It's an unwritten rule that the press follows, and I'm not impressed in the slightest that this new girl seems to lack the respect it takes to follow it.

"I don't have anything else to say. If you want to ask more questions, come to our game in Arizona on Saturday," I bark.

She doesn't falter beneath my harsh tone. If anything, it seems to excite her. "Braxton Heights, I'm Rose Carpenter. I know your father."

And there it is.

"Hi. Sports Weekly, right?"

"Yes. It's a pleasure to meet you." Rose offers Braxton her hand, but Braxton reaches for my hand and links our fingers instead.

"You work for the site that published my father's story, correct?"

"Yes. It was a big story for us," Rose confirms.

"I see. Now, do you always publish such bogus stories, or did he simply make you an offer you couldn't refuse? If it was money, I wonder how many zeros it took for you to write something so bold with no proof to back you up."

I choke on air, staring at her with flashing hearts in my eyes.

"And coming up to players after they already spent forty minutes giving post-game interviews isn't that admirable. I don't spend much time around these types of things, but even I know that isn't protocol," she finishes, all sass and confidence.

My cock swells in my track pants, and I'm about thirty seconds away from being rock hard in the middle of this hall-way, where damn near anybody could see. Suddenly desperate to get the hell out of here, I tug on Braxton's hand and shift her to my front, letting her feel exactly what her words have done to me. Her sharp inhale is barely audible, but I catch it.

And when she pushes back against me ever so slightly, I bite my tongue to keep a groan from escaping.

"We're leaving. I hope you got what you came here for," I blurt out.

Then with rushed steps, we leave Rose standing there, neither of us looking back.

I PARK the truck and release the breath I've been holding for the past ten minutes.

My grip on Braxton's thigh is tight, way too tight, but the heat against my pinky has me on the edge of losing control, and the handful of flesh is the only thing keeping me grounded. I don't know how my hand travelled so high or how I've managed to spend most of the drive with my pinky tracing the seam of her jeans right over her goddamn pussy, but I am, and I can't seem to pull back.

Neither of us spoke a single word on the way home, but we didn't need to. The crackling tension around us spoke volumes.

There is no doubt in my mind that we're thinking about the exact same thing. The thin fabric of my track pants does little to hide my throbbing cock, and I would have to be a blind man not to have caught her wandering eyes more than once during the drive.

Her breaths are as shaky as mine. As uneven and stressed. The flush on her neck and cheeks and even her ears has me wondering how pink and warm she is everywhere else.

Fuck.

I release my grip on the steering wheel and reach over to turn off the truck, still not removing my other hand from her thigh.

"You ready to go in?" My voice so fucking strained it sounds garbled.

She shivers, and it's almost my undoing.

"Yeah."

"Okay. I need you to get out first."

"What?" The word is so quiet I almost don't hear it.

I glance at her and curse at how dark those blue eyes are as they watch me.

"Baby. I need you to open your door and step outside before I fuck you in the cab of this truck."

Her lips part on a low moan, and I toss my head back, slipping my hand further up her thigh, my pinky climbing and climbing until it brushes something cold.

The button of her jeans.

"Braxton," I warn, rolling my head to the side to watch her.

My palm is between her legs now, cupping her pussy through her jeans.

"Maddox," she whimpers.

My name has never sounded better. Not fucking once.

"Undo the button for me." It's an order, and she takes it as such. She fiddles with the button until it pops and the zipper slides down. "Good girl."

A soft noise pushes past her lips at the term, and I make note of that reaction as I drag my hand up her mound and over the open flap of her jeans. My fingers brush an elastic band before finding soft lace beneath it.

I curl my fingers in the lace and pull, her following gasp music to my ears when the fabric wedges between her pussy lips.

"I want to see you, Braxton. I want to see how these panties look cutting your pussy in half and how ruined they are when I pull them off because of how wet you made them. The first time I touch you, I need to see you. I've been imagining this for too long not to have it all."

She nods, eyes brimming with desire. "Take me upstairs. Please."

29

Maddox

I'M ON HER THE SECOND WE STEP INSIDE THE PENTHOUSE. I SWALLOW her gasp as I back her up against the wall and kiss those perfect fucking pink lips.

My tongue slips inside her mouth, and I push her legs apart with my knee, stepping between them, fitting our bodies together because I'm too desperate for her to not have every inch of me pressed against every inch of her. Her moan makes my lips tingle before it shakes its way down my body, bringing forward a sound of my own, one far more wild, carnal.

I'm a mess of greedy, desperate touches, but so is she. My hands are in her hair, palming her throat as the pulse batters beneath it, and then on that fucking ass—gripping and squeezing and pulling until another cry fills my mouth.

Braxton claws at my biceps and tugs at my hair, giving just as much as I'm taking. Her fingers are like personal shock devices. Every touch feels like electricity zapping beneath my skin, and I fall into a deeper haze with each sting.

We've finally smashing down the wall that has kept us from tearing each other's clothes off with our teeth and letting go, accepting that this was inevitable from the start.

Now we're desperate. Out of control. Making up for so much lost time.

"You need to be sure, baby. Fucking positive." I drag my lips from her lips to her jaw and down to her pulse, giving it a hard suck. "Because once won't be enough for me. This isn't a one and done."

Her whole body shudders. "Yes."

I shake my head, my beard scraping her skin, turning it red. My chest grows tight at the idea of her wearing my beard burn all over her body.

"Yes what? Need to hear you say it."

"I'm positive. Not a one and done. Not us," she whispers.

I nip at her throat, over the blossoming purple mark that beats in time with her heartbeat, and dig my fingers into her thighs before lifting and wrapping them around my hips.

She releases a surprised noise, and her thighs grip me tight. Those sparkling blue eyes fill with uncertainty as I lead us further into the dark penthouse, her in my arms where she fucking belongs.

"What's that look for?" I ask softly, brushing my nose along hers.

"You don't have to carry me. I can walk."

"In every single one of my dreams, this is how I'm bringing you into my bedroom for the first time. Let me make it a reality."

She rolls her swollen lips before wetting them with her tongue. My underwear grows sticky as I leak precum like a loose tap.

"In your dreams, I'm probably not this heavy." She says it so timidly I barely catch it. But I do. And my frown is instant.

"Did you forget who I am in the past five minutes? I could bench-press you in my sleep. You're fucking perfect."

To my disappointment, my words haven't done shit. My lungs pinch at the shame keeping her lips from tipping into my favourite smile. Those men in her past have done so much damage to how she sees herself in intimate situations, and I battle off a blistering rage.

I look over her shoulder just in time to turn into my bedroom, and a beat later, I'm setting her on the edge of my bed and turning the bedside lamp on. The soft light filters through the room, illuminating Braxton and her stiff body. I open the nightstand drawer and pull out a picture frame.

Two steps and I'm in front of her, dropping to my haunches and letting the frame hang between my legs. I look at her and hope that she can see just how happy I am to have her here, in my bed. In my goddamn life.

She meets my gaze head-on, and a flare of pride fills me.

"Do you remember the photo I kept of you in my nightstand? The one of you riding that massive black horse named Kit-Kat?"

Her cheeks flush. "I do."

I swallow a sudden ball of nerves before setting the picture frame on her thighs, face up. "The first time I showed you this, it was because you asked me if I thought you were pretty, and I remember being so stupefied at the question because I thought it was obvious."

"You remember that?"

Her bottom lip wobbles as she traces the edge of the frame with a trembling finger. I set my hands on her knees and slip my thumb back and forth over her jeans.

"I remember everything," I admit, pressing my lips to her knee before pulling back. "You have never been just pretty to me. Not when I was a boy, not when I was a zit-faced teenager, and definitely not now that I'm a man. All I want is for you to feel confident with me. No matter when or where, I want you to know that I believe everything about you was custom-made just for me and that I love every single inch of your beautiful body."

There's a crack in my voice when I finish and carefully pick the frame back up and set it to the side.

"I have loved you at a hundred pounds, and I would love

you at a thousand. Let me show you how much I love you right now."

Surprise and a bit of disbelief flash across her face before being replaced with a look that shakes the ground beneath me.

Suddenly, she's reaching for me and taking my face in her hands. Pressing my bottom lip with her thumb, she leans in and whispers, "I have never stopped loving you. Not once. I don't think I know how."

The world shifts. All of my broken pieces heal, and my jagged edges smooth out. Every hollow part of me fills with something warm and reassuring. A sense of home hits me like a brick to the balls. A feeling of rightness.

I push to my feet, and with a firm grip around her thighs, I lift Braxton and toss her up the bed. Her giggle floats around the room, sinking into the walls and making the big, cold penthouse feel warm and homey.

"I'm going to devour you, baby girl." I reach behind my head and pull my shirt off, tossing it somewhere in the room before lowering my hands to the band around my hips.

"Is that a threat or a promise?" she taunts, pushing up on her elbows to watch.

But then suddenly, her entire demeanour changes to one of pure shock. I would have missed what caused her to look so devastatingly surprised had her eyes not been locked on the tattoo on my chest, the one she's never seen before, and I feel my nerves skyrocket.

Her lips part, throat bobbing heavily. "Is that . . .?"

I brush my thumb over the ink-drawn heart and the B + M that fill the centre. It sits directly between my pecs, over the organ that beats only for her.

"Yeah. The heart we engraved in the trunk of the tree beneath our tree house when we were fourteen."

"When did you get that tattooed?" she whispers.

I swallow. "My eighteenth birthday."

"Maddox . . ." Vulnerability tugs at her features. I ache to make it go away.

"I've never once regretted it. Not after you left, and definitely not now that you're back. Whether we found each other again or not, you were always going to be with me. Right here." I stroke the tattoo a final time before dropping my hand.

"Maddox." It's a soft, beautiful sound.

"Yeah, baby?"

"It's beautiful. I love it. And you. God, do I ever love you," she sighs.

"I love you, Curly Fry. Now and for the rest of my goddamn life."

Heat flares in her eyes as she pulls her bottom lip into her mouth and sits, toying with the hem of her jersey. My muscles freeze when she slowly pulls it up her torso, revealing inch after inch of freckled, peach-toned skin. My gulp is audible when the heavy fabric hits the floor.

"Fuck. Me," I groan.

Thin black lace cups her heavy breasts. Splattered with freckles, they rise and fall rapidly with her quick breaths. Erect, pale pink nipples poke at the lace, begging to be freed, and they get their wish when she slips a hand around her back and tugs on the hooks. The straps fall from her shoulders, taking the bra with them, and I hiss a breath when it hits the bed.

"Pants next." The command scrapes my throat on the way up.

"You first."

I manage a rough laugh. "Deal."

Hooking my fingers beneath two waistbands, I shove both my pants and underwear off in one go, stepping out of them a second later.

"Holy shit," she breathes, eyes focused on my cock.

I grab it at the base and squeeze, fighting my eyes from rolling back. I'm so fucking hard that my balls are tugged up tight, desperate for release. One slow stroke from base to slick tip is all I gift myself.

"Pants, Braxton."

Blinking, she quickly pops the button and shimmies them down her legs. I reach out and pull them the rest of the way off, one foot at a time, before discarding them on the floor.

When she fingers the band of her panties, I give my head a rough shake.

"Leave those on."

Her eyes snap up, finding mine. "Okay."

I sink my knees into the mattress and move toward her, stopping at the small opening between her legs. My palm meets her shin as I slide it up her leg, up to her knee, cupping it softly. Her skin is so warm and smooth, so perfect. I want to feel it all. I want to explore every single beauty mark and freckle with my tongue. But that's all for another time. Once we've burned off some energy and I'm not questioning whether or not I'm going to turn out to be a four-pump chump.

With her knee in my hand, I push it toward her, opening her up for me. I repeat the move with the other leg and groan at the image of her spread out for me, those black panties wet in the centre, just like I knew they would be.

"Do you remember what I said in the truck?" I ask, reaching between her legs and gripping the soft lace in a fist. Glancing up, I meet her stare.

"Yes," she whispers, legs clenching with anticipation.

"Tell me."

Colour burns her cheeks. "You're bossy in bed."

I bite the inside of my cheek to keep from smiling, then drop my thumb to that wet patch in her panties, brushing the small little bump beneath them.

She jolts, thrusting her hips against my hand. Her face twists in the most delicious way, so I do it again, this time moving it in a slow circle.

"Dox," she whimpers.

"Tell me what I said in the truck," I repeat, taking my thumb away from her clit.

"You said you wanted to see how my panties looked cutting my pussy in half." She pushes out the words with the same desperation I feel deep in my chest. Her hips twirl, seeking out my touch, but I ignore her silent plea.

I pull the wet lace up toward her instead and watch as they dig between her pussy lips, creating such a pretty fucking picture. Dipping my head, I kiss the line of her panties, right at the centre, and then drag my tongue up each puffy lip.

Her taste has my cock leaking into the sheets as I press the flat of my tongue right over where her entrance hides and then release my grip on her panties. I dig my teeth under the fabric tucked tight in her pussy and pull it out, sucking at the wet patch.

"Happy?" she coos, tightening her eyes to glare at me as if she's not burning up with pleasure.

In one quick move, I have her panties torn in half and a red line on her hip where they used to sit.

"Fucking ecstatic," I murmur before pressing my lips to her bare sex and slipping my tongue around her weeping entrance, teasing her inner walls with soft strokes. "What about you? Are you happy?" I pull her clit into my mouth and suck.

"So, so happy," she sighs, fingers scraping down my scalp and curling in my hair.

I release her clit and flick it with my tongue. "You taste fucking perfect. Just like I knew you would."

"Mm, and what exactly do I taste like?"

I slide a finger inside her pussy and grit my jaw at the lack of protest. She's so wet it slides right in. I add a second finger and curl them until I feel that soft spot that makes her back curl and eyes fall shut.

"Mine, Braxton. You taste like mine."

30

Braxton

FIRE RIPS THROUGH MY VEINS. MY CHEST IS PINCHED SO TIGHT IT hurts to breathe, but it doesn't matter. None of it does. Everything falls to black the minute Maddox puts his mouth on me.

One stroke of his tongue up my pussy has me writhing in the sheets, clawing and clutching at them like I might fly away if I don't find something to hold on to.

The vulnerability that clogged my mind just minutes ago is gone, replaced with a thick sense of comfort, even as I lie bare, completely exposed to this beautiful man. His eyes are lit with a raging inferno as he blinks up at me from beneath heavy lashes. A mix of desire, lust, and love. Such an obvious, fierce type of love. The kind you read about in fairy tales.

The kind I've dreamed of sharing with Maddox since I was a little girl.

I loosen my grip on the bedsheets and reach for him, desperately slipping my fingers in his soft curls and exhaling a shaky breath.

He draws a lazy circle around my clit with his tongue, fingers moving inside of me in ways that make my toes curl as I gasp, "If I taste like I'm yours, does that mean you taste like you're mine?"

"Do I taste like I'm yours?" he echoes, pulling his fingers out and using them to spread me open. I shiver, hips bucking in an attempt to have him fill me again. His lips tilt in a sly grin. "Baby girl, I more than taste like I'm yours. I fucking am yours."

He lowers his mouth to my entrance, and I cry out when his tongue enters me. A moan vibrates up my core, pinching at my clit and making my legs shake. I tighten my grip on his hair, pulling and pulling at it until he reaches up and grabs my breast, squeezing and pinching at my beaded nipple.

He groans against me, face buried deep in my pussy, not daring to come up for a breath. My teeth tear at my bottom lip as I arch into him, fighting off a scream at the heat growing in my belly.

"Are you going to come, Braxton? Do you want to fill my mouth with your cum? Hmm?" he asks, the words sinking into my warm walls.

"Yes," I croak, nodding over and over again. But then he stops. With a wet smacking noise, he's pulling back and releasing my breast to pull my fingers from his hair. "Maddox," I protest, my mouth damn near hanging open.

"The first time you come for me, it's going to be around my cock," he states as he moves up my body, hot skin dragging along hot skin.

His hands find my chest again, and he takes a nipple into his mouth, sucking and nipping at it as my thighs clench and my pussy aches.

"And the first time I come for you, it's going to be wrapped up tight in your pretty little pussy. The first and only one I've ever been inside."

The tip of his cock slides between my lips, rubbing back and forth, my arousal mixing with his. I mewl at the feeling, wrapping my fingers around the back of his neck and using the hold to pull him away from my chest until we're face to face.

It's not until he nudges my head to the side and starts to kiss and suck on my neck that his previous statement penetrates through my desire-fogged mind.

"What do you mean? The first and only one?" I pull him away from my neck, my eyes wide.

A soft, lazy smile spreads his lips. He drops his forehead to mine, and the head of his cock notches at my entrance, holding there for a brief moment before slipping through my wetness again. I exhale slowly, fighting to keep my thoughts together.

"It's always been you, Curly," he whispers, staring down at me with such open affection it steals my breath. "I guess it was just a subconscious thought. I have never wanted to be like this with anyone else. Not once."

My eyes water, a burn growing in my nose. "Dox. Oh my God."

Concern twists his features. "What's wrong? Should I not have said anything?"

"I didn't wait," I breathe out, lifting my other hand to cup his jaw. Regret fills me from the bottom up, making my stomach swirl. "I should have. I wanted to. But I just thought . . ."

"You thought we wouldn't see each other again and that if we did, I wouldn't want you," he finishes for me.

I swallow, nodding stiffly. "But you waited. You waited eight years."

"I've waited my entire life to have you like this, and I would wait another lifetime, regardless of what you decided to do. Just because you didn't wait doesn't mean you love me any less than I love you. It just means I hurt you as deep as you hurt me. I don't blame you for moving on. But what we did and didn't do doesn't matter now. What matters is that I'm the last one to have you like this."

A hot tear tracks down my cheeks before it's covered with Maddox's lips. He kisses my tears as they fall, and I let him, knowing that in a way, these tears symbolize a turning of a page. The start of a new journey. A new chapter to our story that isn't filled with past mistakes and broken hearts.

"We wasted so much time," I whisper.

"But we have so much time left."

He's right.

I lift my chin and kiss him, a blanket of acceptance falling over me. My heart is a thumping mess in my chest as he returns my kiss and runs a hot palm along my body before gripping my thigh and hitching my leg over his hip. The move opens me up to him, and the second the wet head of his cock slips inside my entrance, I'm crying his name.

"More," I whine, wiggling my hips and digging my heel into his ass cheek, but he doesn't move.

He's frozen, eyes locked on my face, jaw tight, clenching over and over. His bicep is bunched and strained as he holds himself above me. "Condom. Do you want me to use a condom?"

I blink, bewildered. "A little late now, cowboy. But no. I don't want you to use a condom. Only if you want to. I have an IUD."

"Fuck no. Just trying to be gentlemanly. I want you bare," he grunts.

Wrapping my other leg around his hip, I pull him further into my body, stars bursting behind my eyes at the stretch that follows. Having him like this feels like coming home, and a warbled sound escapes me as I seek his body.

He blows out a harsh breath against my lips. "Jesus fuck, baby. Stop tightening around me, or I swear to fuck I'm going to be a two-minute man."

"I'm not." I stifle a giggle. "It's just been a long time."

"A long time?" he rasps, pushing the rest of the way in. I nod, and when he pulls back out, he drops his head to my shoulder and stares down my body to where we connect. "Your cream is all over my cock, baby. Just for me."

"Just for you," I whimper.

He thrusts in harder this time, his eyes flying up to watch my lips part at the burst of pleasure. "I spent so many nights fucking my fist to the thought of you beneath me, puffy pink lips parted just like they are now. My dreams pale in comparison to the real thing. I knew they would."

"Harder, Maddox. Please. Don't be gentle with me," I plead, not above begging. Not with him.

I'm already so close, being edged making my desperation that much worse. Each stroke of his cock is sending me higher and higher, and for the first time in my life, I'm certain I'm going to come without needing my clit stimulated. I should have known it would be this way with him. As if it could have been anything less than perfect.

With a carnal noise ripping up his throat, Maddox thrusts hard, so hard I let loose a scream of pleasure, curving my neck and pinching my eyes shut. I move my hips in time with his pumps, my patience non-existent.

A sudden warmth around my throat has my eyes flying open again. They fall to a thick wrist and then the fingers pressed to my pulse as they tighten just enough my breaths thin, and that high I was climbing toward picks me up and tosses me right off the edge.

"I'm coming," I gasp, lost to the world as I reach ecstasy.

It hits like an electric charge and rips through my body without warning. My legs tighten around his narrow hips, and I buck against him, squeezing and fluttering around the cock buried deep, keeping it snug inside.

"Oh, *fuck*. That's my girl. I can feel you squeezing me," he groans, staring down at me as I come, his face twisted in a look of sheer pleasure and a possession that would make me preen if I wasn't still in the clouds, refusing to fall back to earth just yet. "Wanna fill you up, baby. But I need to hear you say it's okay."

I'm trembling, digging my nails into his back as he fucks me into the mattress like a man who knows exactly what he's doing despite his lack of experience.

But maybe that's just because we were made for each other. Maybe this is just another example of why I believe that so deeply, with everything in me.

His hair is stuck to his forehead, sweat beading on the flushed skin before I push it out of his face and press our mouths together, falling back to earth and breathing out, "Yes. Yes, *please*, do it. Make me yours."

He parts my lips with his and sucks on my tongue before rolling his forehead over mine, pushing down the slightest bit harder on my throat. I watch with rapt attention as his face twists, and his perfect white teeth clamp down on his lower lip before a guttural growl crawls up his throat.

It's a sound that makes my core clench, wanting more, despite the slight soreness that's blooming there. I nip at his jaw, and his back muscles ripple as his thrusts falter. Warmth floods me, and I moan at the feeling, nuzzling my face into his throat, against the rapid fluttering beneath his warm skin.

"You are already mine, Braxton. Been mine for two decades, and you'll be mine for the rest of time, I promise you that," he murmurs, growing still with his cock seated deep inside me.

Despite how hard I try to fight the sudden wave of emotion, my eyes swim with tears again. His words sink deep, down to my very core, and then etch themselves there in permanent ink. A promise tattooed on my soul.

"Is that a pinky promise?" I whisper, meeting his warm stare.

He drops from his shaky bicep to his forearm and starts to press feather-light kisses all over the side of my face. I smile when he grabs my hand from its place on his back, bringing it between us and resting it between my breasts.

"That's a pinky promise." He loops our pinkies together and then places them to his lips. Once he's kissed them, he moves them to my mouth, and I do the same.

Then, he shifts and starts to pull out, pushing back to his knees. I inhale a sharp breath at the movement, and his brows tug with concern before I shake my head and smile.

"I'm okay."

His throat bobs with a swallow as he nods and looks between my legs at what I assume to be the cum I can feel leaking from my entrance. I have no doubt I look as well and truly fucked as I feel, but I can't tell what he's thinking. For the first time tonight, he looks guarded.

"Was I too rough with you?" he asks, his voice sounding pained.

"No. God, no."

"Did I hurt you when I grabbed your throat? I should have asked if that was okay."

"I loved it. Couldn't you tell?"

I push up on my forearms, about to reach out for him when he shifts and two cautious fingers slowly slide through my swollen flesh. A shudder works through me when he scoops a puddle of his cum that's leaked down my pussy and pushes it back inside of me.

His pupils flare as he works it in, and I clench around his fingers, a stupid, silly grin growing on my face when he groans.

"Braxton," he warns, flicking his eyes up.

"Yes?" I bat my eyelashes.

"I'm not going to fuck you again yet. You're sore."

"Who said anything about fucking?"

He narrows his eyes, scratching at his jaw before crawling back up my body and sliding his fingers into my mouth. The same ones he just had inside of me.

I wrap my tongue around them before sucking, tasting our mixed flavour, holding eye contact. As soon as I see his cock starting to harden again, a strong sense of pride takes hold of me.

"You want me to fill your mouth with something bigger, baby?"

I bite down gently on his fingers and nod.

He taps my nose with his thumb. "You want to suck my cock?"

I bite harder.

"Bite me again and I'm going to flip you over and take you from behind, sore or not."

Liar.

I grin, and he pulls his fingers out. "What if I like both those options?" I ask.

"Mm, I guess I'll have to choose for you." He pinches my chin with his thumb and forefinger and pulls me toward him as he leans back. "Hands and knees, baby. Suck your cock."

31

Maddox

THE TEAM FLIGHT ATTENDANT ASKS IF I WOULD LIKE A DRINK, AND I decline, choosing to sit and brew in my seat with a growly-ass attitude instead. I'm actually really fucking thirsty, but I don't call her back, not trusting myself not to snap at the poor woman more than I already have on this flight.

We lost tonight, and I'm in a terrible mood. Game five of the second round, and we got our asses handed to us. Turnover after turnover, and most of them came from me.

I scrub a hand over my face and scratch at the thick playoff beard. I've never liked growing a beard, but playoffs are my exception. Braxton hasn't said whether she likes it or not, and maybe I should ask.

Fuck. *Braxton.*

She should have been sitting beside me right now, head on my shoulder and legs tossed over mine as she slept beneath the dim aisle lights. She should have been in the arena cheering for me. My good-luck charm was missing tonight, and I felt it. That woman is as much a part of me as my right arm, and I played about as well as I would have if someone had chopped it right off.

I exhale a long breath and unlock my phone, our last texts still open on the screen.

> Me: I missed you last night.

> My Girl: Just last night?

My chest shakes with a laugh. That's an understatement. I've missed her from the moment she left my penthouse yesterday morning. Her job is almost as needy as mine, and as proud of her as I am to see how successful she's become, I'm still feeling like a scowly asshole when it comes to sharing her.

I kept her with me as much as I could over the past few days, either holding her hostage in my bed or showing up at the clinic whenever I got the chance, even if I had to sit in the waiting room and be gawked at while she was with patients. She was supposed to fly to Arizona with me yesterday but had an emergency with one of her patients that couldn't wait. Now I'm antsy to get home and spend the next two days in bed with her.

> Me: No. But you knew that already.

> My Girl: For a fake boyfriend, you're sure needy.

> Me: Say it again, baby.

> My Girl: Say what again?

> Me: We've never been fake. Remove the word from your vocabulary.

> My Girl: *Gasp* Really?

> Me: I'll be in Van in three hours. Stay up for me.

> My Girl: I'll be waiting. Love you.

> Me: I love you too.

I stare at the text messages for a few seconds longer before tucking my phone away and attempting to calm my heartbeat. This girl is my own personal version of paradise.

"You look like a blushing bride," Bentley teases, flopping down on the empty seat beside me. He reeks of cinnamon, and I arch a brow.

"If that's a new cologne, you need to toss it."

He pinches the collar of his hoodie and brings it to his nose. "What if I bought it just for you, baby? You're telling me you don't like it?"

"I hate cinnamon."

He nods. "Is that right? Huh, do you wanna tell me the story behind that? I'm bored out of my skull."

"Do you remember the cinnamon challenge?"

"The one where you had to suck back an entire spoonful of pure cinnamon?"

I snort. "Yeah."

He barks a laugh. "You did that, didn't you?"

"Braxton's idea. She thought it was hilarious and posted the video online after. You can probably still find it. I haven't touched the stuff since."

I can still feel the burn of it in my throat and chest. I'm pretty sure I was coughing that shit up for months.

"Seems like you and Braxton have a lifetime of memories together, huh?"

I roll my eyes at his attempt at being slick. "Ask what you want to know, B."

Nodding, he folds his arms over his chest and settles into the seat. I watch the gold hoop in his earlobe shake as he repositions himself and find myself wondering if I could pull off an earring as well as he can.

"I want to know what's really going on. Not the story you're still feeding to the press and the rest of the team. I'm your friend, Madman. And probably the only one here who can handle you even when you sit and pout for nearly an entire plane ride home. I'm here for you, yeah?"

I chew on the inside of my cheek, contemplating what to do. Braxton told Anna the truth about our relationship a couple of nights ago after explaining to me how much she didn't like lying to her, and I agreed wholeheartedly.

If it were up to me, I would make sure everyone knew that Braxton and I are the farthest thing from fake now, but it's not up to me. Fuck, I hate giving people power over me, and I've let an entire team of people dangle my career in front of me over something that wasn't entirely my fault in the first place.

"You have my word, man. Shit, I already know something is up. Things have changed since that day at the clinic," Bentley adds and then leans over his seat and looks around the plane. "Anyone close enough to hear is passed out. This stays between us."

I scratch at my thigh before blurting out, "Obviously it started off fake. But it's the furthest thing from that now. Alexander's plan is working, I think. But Braxton and I . . . *fuck*. We were fake for about two days. We're too real to be anything else. You were right when you said I was in love with her. I've always been in love with her. This entire sham just forced us to come to terms with everything that happened and move on."

"So, now what? I'm happy for you, man, but Alexander is still going to want you to pull through. Are you and Braxton just going to keep up appearances and let everything fizzle out?"

"I think so? The only thing I'm sure of right now is her. Everything else is a giant question mark. She signed an NDA before we started this entire thing, and we're supposed to keep playing by Alexander's rules until after the adoption day she's hosting and the playoffs are done. After that, I'm hoping we can just be normal. You know?"

There's a pang in my gut, but I ignore it.

He hums, nodding. "And what about your contract? You not

being signed with us for next season doesn't sit right with me. This isn't normal."

It doesn't sit right with me either. But there isn't much I can do. It isn't up to me.

"That's supposed to come after everything has died down too," I say, words tight, my worry obvious.

He clenches his jaw. "If I were you, I would have Dougie start to shop you around, even in secret. Test free agency and see if anyone bites. You can't put all your eggs in this basket, man. Not when they're holding your future captive. It's kind of fucked up, actually. You're the best player in this league, and that's not me being biased. Regardless of what's happening in the press, your talent shouldn't be up for debate. You should have been offered a contract months ago."

I groan, a prickly sensation worming up my spine. He's saying everything I've been feeling since I was called into Alex's office. I've played my ass off for this team, and they're going to let a completely bogus story keep us from continuing this journey together? This fake relationship agreement feels a whole lot like blackmail the longer I think about it.

"You're right," I agree. "Braxton's dad soiled my name in the league when I was eighteen, and Vancouver saved me. When I turned down Florida's entry contract, it made a statement. A bad one. They were upset, obviously, and it took my dad and his connections in the league to help turn my decision back around on Roy where it *should* have been. Most teams were still on the fence about me when I re-entered the draft, but it didn't matter. My dad convinced Alexander that they needed me, and they traded a stack of players to get into the position to draft me. I owe them. And they know it."

I drop my head in my hands and grip my hair. "If Vancouver hadn't drafted me, I wouldn't be where I am. I would have been on a team that didn't care for me and let me rot away on a bench. Now, Alexander says jump, and I ask how high. I don't have an option here. My dad would hate me if I turned my back on Vancouver after everything he had to do to get me here."

Silence. Bentley is rigid beside me.

He's the first person I've told all of this to, and I can't say that I feel any more relaxed than I did five minutes ago. Now, there's just another person who knows how fucked I am.

"You've been in the league for seven years. What happened when you were a teenager is in the past. I think you're being too hard on yourself. If you put yourself out there—"

"I can't," I snap, frustrated with myself. "I just can't. Loyalty is everything, and I can't turn away from Vancouver or my dad."

Bentley gently bumps my shoulder with his. "Okay, Madman. I'm sorry I pushed."

"It's okay. I shouldn't have snapped at you."

"You miss your girl. I get it." He winks.

I laugh hoarsely. "Yeah, I do. What about you? You got a girl at home?"

"Not me. I'm loving the bachelor life right now."

"Doesn't it get tiring being with so many different women all the time?" I ask with genuine curiosity.

Most of the guys on the team are either married or are like Bentley and accept the female attention that comes with the job with open arms. Either way, it's never bothered me what they choose to do. Not as long as they still show up at the rink every day with a clear head and a hunger to win.

He shrugs. "Not really. Sometimes, I guess. But I'm having too much fun to really care. I'll know when the girl comes around, right?"

"Yeah, you'll know. When she's the one, the world shifts and becomes brighter. It's like peeling away a film that's been over your eyes for your entire life. Suddenly, everything is so much clearer."

"I can't fucking wait for that."

I rub my palm over my chest and stare out the small window at the black sky. "When you meet her, don't let her go. Keep her forever. Put her at the centre of your universe, and do everything you can to keep her there because I can promise you that you'll hate yourself if you lose her."

"Find the girl and keep the girl. Got it."

I shake my head, my lips tugging up at the corners. "Exactly."

"You should start a love blog or something. I think a lot of guys would take notes."

"I can't tell if you're being sarcastic or not."

"Nah, I'm serious. I respect you for being so down for one girl. I guess it makes sense now why I've never really seen you with anyone else. Rory was the only girl you've dated, and that wasn't anything special. No offense."

I stifle a laugh. "None taken. I know what you mean."

"But hey, like you said. When you know, you know. I expect to be invited to the wedding."

I don't bother telling him to back up because there's no doubt in my mind I'm going to marry this girl.

"Bring a good plus one, yeah?"

He grins. "Only the best for you, baby."

32

Braxton

"To Maddox, the Warriors, and their second-round victory!" Cooper cheers, lifting his beer bottle above the empty serving plates on the table. I tap the bottle with the belly of my wine glass before Maddox clinks it with his can of diet Coke.

"To my man taking home the Stanley Cup this year," I say, looking over at him beside me. Our eyes meet, and his grin makes my heart skip.

Our chairs couldn't be any closer together, but as he uses the arm he's planted on my shoulders to give me a soft squeeze, I wish they could.

"Don't get ahead of yourself, Curly. There's still a lot of work left to do," he says, but I know he's just as excited about his second-round win as I am.

Cooper sets his beer down on the table and pats his stomach. The baby blue button-down he's wearing is still as loose as ever over his slim figure, but the action makes me giggle regardless.

"It's work you're ready and willing to put in, Maddox. Celebrate a little. I promise it won't kill you." He drags the back of his fork over the rest of the mashed potatoes on his plate before licking it off. "You keep playing how you're playing, and I'll keep coming over and eating Braxton's cooking to celebrate."

"You can come over anytime. Celebrating or not," Maddox replies.

"Yes. Please. I missed this," I add.

Maddox flexes his fingers on my bare arm, and I lean into him. "When's the last time we were all together like this?"

"Not since before the two of you graduated high school. Probably in the treehouse," Cooper says.

I blow out a long breath. "That feels like a lifetime ago."

"It's been almost a decade." Cooper takes a long drink of his beer and groans, "I feel really old now."

"We're getting there," I note. "At least, that's how it feels."

"Being around Adalyn makes me feel ancient," Maddox grunts. "How am I old enough to have an eighteen-year-old sister?"

I push out my bottom lip. "Oh, you poor baby."

His eyes twinkle with amusement as he reaches over to flick me in the nose. "Keep teasing, sweetheart. Let's see if you can keep it up when I have you bent over this tab—"

Cooper makes a loud choking noise, drawing our attention. I glance at him and notice his wide eyes, my cheeks heating.

"You know, one would think you'd have prepared yourself for this by now, Coop," Maddox teases and then plants a big sloppy kiss on my hot cheek.

Cooper takes a long swig of his beer, finishing it off. "I don't think anything could prepare me for hearing your god-awful dirty talk."

"Terrible?" he asks with mock offense.

Cooper offers me a sympathetic smile. "I feel for poor Braxton."

I giggle, the empty bottle of wine on the table suddenly catching my attention. *Did I drink all of that?*

"Don't. It's not *that* bad." I wink at Maddox, but I might have closed both my eyes. The following deep laugh that kisses my shoulder makes me believe I did.

"Blink twice if he's forcing you to say that," Cooper whispers, his hands cupped around his mouth.

I make a show of not blinking.

Dox points at me and then at Cooper. "See? Don't be jealous."

"Jealous isn't the word I would use."

"Liar."

"You're ridiculous."

"And you need a girlfriend. Maybe she could help teach you the art of dirty talk. For an artist, I expected you to be good at all art forms. Maybe I was wrong."

Cooper narrows his eyes. "You did not just compare real art to dirty talk."

"Oh, I did alright. What are you gonna do about it?"

I cover my mouth with the back of my hand to stifle my laugh. "Maddox, leave him alone."

He looks at me innocently. "I'm just trying to help."

Cooper snorts a laugh. "You just want me to find a woman so you have an excuse to go on double dates."

"You make it sound like you wouldn't enjoy being on a double date with us," Maddox mutters.

This time, I don't hold back my laugh. "You two still sound like an old married couple."

"I'm the husband, right?" Maddox asks.

Cooper shakes his head. "No way. You're definitely the wife."

"Me? Not possible."

"Well, it's not me."

"How is work going, Coop?" I ask, raising my voice so that I'm heard over their bickering. As adorable as it is, if I don't move this conversation along, we'll be here all night.

Cooper looks at me with a grin, his brown eyes bright. "Amazing. My students are incredibly talented. They're excited about their end-of-the-year projects."

Cooper is a high school art teacher, but his end goal is to be a university professor. It's been his dream for as long as I can remember. It makes me happy to know he's happy.

"What do you have them doing?" Maddox asks, tracing the top of his Coke can with his finger.

"My older kids are making ceramic Fabergé eggs, while the younger ones are doing self-portraits."

"That's cool, man."

Cooper chuckles. "It is. They're excited, which is the most important part. I've found that with the older kids, they genuinely want to be there, so it's a lot easier to hold their attention than when I was with the mandatory students last year."

"How long until you think you can start looking at the university route?" I ask.

His eyes burn even brighter at the mention of the next step in his career. "Hopefully, only a couple more years."

"Professor Cooper has a nice ring to it." I grin.

"It makes you sound fucking old," Maddox blurts out and a second later starts to laugh.

Cooper flips him off, but his mouth twitches at the corners. "You're an asshole."

"Look at you talking dirty. Maybe you aren't so bad after all."

Dox softly kisses my jaw and takes a deep breath before slowly pulling away, as if he would rather stay with his face buried in my neck.

I wouldn't mind that, but I think I would prefer it buried somewhere else. Suddenly, all I can think about is Maddox pushing my chair away from the table, dropping to his knees in front of me, and spreading my legs. I swallow, my throat suddenly dry.

"Curly?" I hear faintly.

With a sweaty hand, I palm the back of my neck and look at Maddox. He's watching me curiously, but the ghost of a smirk is there, flirting with me, as if he knows exactly what I've been thinking about.

"You okay, baby?" he asks, voice low, soft.

"Mmhmm."

"You look a bit flushed, B. Do you want a glass of water?"

Cooper asks, already out of his seat and starting to collect the empty plates.

I clear my throat and nod. "That would be great. Let me grab the rest of this, and I'll meet you in the kitchen."

"No, you sit. I'll bring it out to you before I start the dishes."

"Thank you." My smile is soft. Cooper returns it and kisses the top of my head before drifting off to the kitchen.

Maddox threads his fingers in the curls at the base of my skull and gently presses his fingertips into my scalp. My eyes roll back as I let out a soft moan.

"Give me a minute to be alone with you before I go help with the dishes, yeah?" he murmurs.

"Okay."

The sound of water running in the kitchen is the only noise in the penthouse, and despite how awake I was just minutes ago, the soft sounds and wine have me feeling droopy.

His fingers continue to massage my scalp as I rest my head on his shoulder. Lips brush the tip of my ear before working down the length of it. I shiver.

"I want our kids to have your hair," he breathes.

My lips part on a smile. I don't feel any fear or anxiety after hearing his blunt statement, only excitement and something warm and cozy that fills my chest.

"The colour or the curls?" I ask.

"Both. And your eyes."

"And what are they getting from their daddy?"

"Whatever you want them to."

"That's not how it works, honey."

I can feel his grin when he kisses my cheek and hovers there. "That's too damn bad."

"How about they get my hair and eyes but your lips, talent, and heart?"

"Are you saying you think I have nice lips?"

"That would be all you took from that." I laugh softly. "But yes, you have the best lips."

To emphasize my point, I turn my head and press them to mine. The plush feeling of them elicits a whimper from me. My need for him is never-ending. A lifetime wouldn't be near long enough.

He kisses me back with soft caresses of his mouth, keeping it slow. The care he offers me is enough to have my heart thrashing behind my rib cage. If I weren't already sure it was us forever, this would have done it.

I don't know how long we sit here kissing and exploring, but when Maddox finally pulls back, my body is tight with need. My skin is sensitive, every nerve primed and begging.

"I'm going to help Cooper before I take you to bed," he rasps.

I nod shakily. "Go."

Green eyes burn bright as they focus on me, making me feel like the only woman in the world. "I love you," he says.

I fight the urge to rub at the soft spot in my chest as I whisper, "I love you too."

33

Maddox

AGE EIGHTEEN

I'VE BEEN AVOIDING MY DAD FOR A WEEK, BUT AS I COME JOGGING
down the steps outside of the arena after practice and see him leaning
against his truck door with his arms crossed, I know that's no longer an
option.

With my piece-of-shit truck breaking down and leaving me needing
rides from Mom and Brax for the past month while I save for repairs, I
should have been expecting Dad to take matters into his own hands.
Now I just feel like a deer in the headlights, nerves and guilt sparking.

"Good practice?" he asks when I reach him.

"Awful." My shoulder screams at me when I pull down the tailgate
and lift my bag to toss it in the box of the truck. "Got my shit rocked
more than a couple times. I need an ice bath."

With nothing more than a nod, he closes the tailgate and walks to
the driver's side. I watch him go, hopping stiffly into the truck as a bad
feeling manifests deep in my gut.

I quickly slip into the passenger side, cross my seat belt over my
body, and let the soft drone of music smother the silence. It's still
awkward as all hell, but at least it isn't silent.

Dad starts the engine and pulls out of the parking lot. I tap the *window anxiously, debating whether or not to just come out and say it. He would respect that decision more than the alternative to keep quiet, but at this point, I think the respect ship may have already sailed. I've waited too long for that.*

Ten minutes go by with neither of us speaking, and just as I'm about to crawl out of my skin with anticipation, he turns onto the dirt road leading to our house and clears his throat.

"You think we have a good relationship, right? A mutual sense of trust? That was important to your mother and me when we had you and your siblings. I was very close to my mom growing up. Up until she passed away, I considered her one of my best friends. Your mother and I wanted you three kids to have the same kind of relationship with us as you grew up," he says.

I swallow. "Yeah, I think so. You and Mom are amazing. You're great parents." Better than great. The best.

He drums his hands on the steering wheel, looking straight ahead, not risking even a quick look at me. If it weren't for a heavy bob of his throat and quick tensing of his jaw, I wouldn't suspect that he's even the slightest bit bothered right now.

"Okay, I wanted to make sure."

The back of my neck is wet, and it has nothing to do with today's practice. This sneaky attempt to get me to admit I've been hiding something from him is dirty. He's hitting below the belt and succeeding.

"Please just come out and say it, Dad. You don't have to keep up the act," I blurt out.

"What are you talking about?"

"Don't be coy."

"Oh, I see," he hums.

I turn my body as much as I can restricted by a seat belt and huff a groan. "See what? Cut it out."

"You want me to be outright and honest about what I'm trying to get to here? Do you not like being kept in the dark?" he asks, still as calm as ever.

"You can be a petty man. Do you know that?" I groan, staring out the window, watching the back tires kick up gravel from the side mirror.

"That's funny. I hope you don't ever lose your sense of humour. It's one of my favourite parts of your personality."

"Dad."

"Son," he counters.

"How did you find out?" Because there is no way he's doing all of this on a hunch.

"You didn't think I would be told when my son rejects an offer from his draft team and his agent puts out a public statement announcing that you're up for grabs?"

There it is. The anger I was looking for. It leaks out more and more with each word until he's grinding them out, white-knuckling the steering wheel.

"I know you're upset, but it was my decision to make," I say, desperation thick in my voice.

I'm not positive about what I'm desperate for more of. His understanding or forgiveness?

"Of course it was your decision."

"Then why are you so upset? This reaction is why I didn't want to tell you what I did."

For the first time the entire drive, he looks at me. It's just a fleeting glance, but it's chock-full of enough emotion to do more than enough damage.

"It might have been your decision, but you made the wrong one. That's why I'm upset. And you weren't scared to tell me because you thought I would be angry. You didn't want to tell me because you knew I would tell you exactly that and maybe even succeed in convincing you not to do whatever stupid ideas that Roy fucker filled your head with."

"You don't get it. It wasn't just about me."

"Oh, I do get it. I know exactly what you were thinking, and I'm still telling you it was the wrong thing to do." With a quick flick of his hand, he has his ball cap off and thrown into the back seat. Stiff-looking fingers shove through his hair. "Whatever he promised you, it was the wishful thinking of a money-hungry man. Vancouver isn't going to take you this season."

"*How do you know that?*" I wheeze, my chest tight. *The cab of the truck feels so fucking small.*

His jaw pulses. "*I spoke with Alexander this morning.*"

I close my eyes, my head falling forward in my hands. *Whatever hope I had of starting my career with my dream team disappears as fast as it had appeared in Roy's office. I feel itchy, antsy. Like if I don't get out of this truck right now, I'm going to wind up losing my mind.*

"*We're pulling up now,*" Dad says, reading my thoughts. *He pushes a button on the small remote slipped on the visor, and the following beep tells me the gate at the bottom of our driveway has started to open for us.*

Seconds feel like hours as we drive up to the house, and the truck comes to a slow stop. I'm out the door, taking off before Dad has a chance to kill the engine.

Having most likely been watching for us from the living room window, Mom comes rushing out the front door, her lips parting on words I can't hear.

I shake my head at her when she tries to come up to me and pull me into her arms. The last thing I want is a hug right now, but a sharp pang of guilt at rejecting her love has me avoiding her eyes as I storm past her.

"*Maddox!*" Dad shouts, slamming the truck door. "*Don't run away from this conversation. We can't ignore it.*"

"*There isn't anything left to talk about it!*"

God, I want to scream. I want to let the world hear how pissed off I am. How stupid I feel.

My steps falter when Addie appears in front of me, blocking the entrance with her tiny frame. Prepared to just pick her up and deposit her somewhere else, I reach for her middle only to have her punch me clean in the stomach. For a ten-year-old, she has a hard enough swing to wind me. Noah must have taught her some things.

"*What the fuck?*" I cough, stumbling back, clutching my stomach.

"*Why are you acting like a caveman? And don't yell at Dad. Look at how sad Mom is now,*" she scolds me.

I grit my teeth, not needing the reminder. "*Not right now, Addie.*

Get out of my way."

"No. Not until you go apologize."

"I'm not asking."

"I don't care." She juts her chin out and crosses her arms.

"Addie, sweetheart, go inside. We need to talk to your brother alone," Dad asks softly.

One look over my shoulder and I know that he's behind me. He's stopped far enough back not to spook me but close enough I won't be able to run again.

My sister looks unsure but, after a few seconds, shuffles aside. I walk inside, and Mom and Dad follow. The house smells like freshly baked cookies, and my stomach growls.

"Go sit on the couch, Maddox," Dad says.

Gritting my jaw, I do as he says. Moving through the house, past the first of two offices that us kids use for schoolwork and beneath the exposed wooden beams in the living and dining room. There is an array of beads and string all over the coffee table in the living room, and Legally Blonde *is playing on the big screen, the sound muted. The LED lights beneath the TV flash with pink — Addie's favourite colour.*

I sit on the couch and fold my hands in my lap. My swallow is audible in the quiet room.

Mom sits beside me and places her hand over mine, but it's so small it hardly covers my one hand.

"You should have come to us. To your dad. You didn't have to do this alone," she murmurs.

I search the room for Dad and find him standing a few feet away, his arms crossed and hurt tugging at his features. It makes me feel nauseous.

"I'm going to do what I can to fix this for you, but there's only so much I can do," he says.

"Tell me you wouldn't have done it for Mom. Tell me that you wouldn't have done anything you could to not have to leave her," I croak. "I would have been too far away. From you guys, from Braxton."

Dad looks at the ceiling, blinking. "I understand why you did it, Maddox. I do. But that doesn't change the reason why it was even brought up in the first place. You were manipulated and lied to. I should have been there with you. Roy should never have even had access to your future in the first place."

"Florida doesn't even need me. And you have told me yourself how bad their coaching staff is. I thought I was making the right decision. He said Vancouver would—"

Dad's cold laugh cuts me off. "Oh, I know what he said Vancouver would do. And he was dreaming. Roy Heights has no clue how things work in the NHL. No fucking clue. I should never have let you convince me to let that man be your agent. I knew this would happen. Dougie would never have let this happen."

"What if I didn't want to have to use your agent? What if for the first time in my entire life, I wanted to be Maddox Hutton and not Oakley Hutton's son?" I shout, pushing off the couch, fists curled at my sides. "Roy might have fucked me over, but at least this mistake is my own, and I don't have to hear about how it affected my dad."

Dad flinches, his green eyes wounded. I immediately wish I could take my words back, but I don't backtrack.

"Baby," Mom whispers, and I don't know if she's talking to me or Dad before she closes a warm palm over one of my fists.

"You've always been Maddox Hutton to us," Dad says on a breath.

I shake my head. "You have no idea what it's like to be your son and to feel the pressure to live up to you. I know I messed up. But I don't need you to fix it for me. I need to own it and figure out what to do next. On my own."

"I can't do that. Whether you want to be my son or not, that's what you are. And I'm not going to let you lose everything you've worked for because of this. You can hate me for it if you want, but it's my job as your father. I love you, and I won't let this ruin you."

With that, he wipes a hand down his face, blows out a wavering breath, and leaves the room. Mom is as stiff as a statue behind me, but she doesn't speak. I don't think she knows what to say any better than I do.

I made a terrible mistake, and it might have cost me more than just my career.

34

Braxton

THE CUSTOM-MADE, PAW-PRINT DOG TAG CLIPPED TO THE DEEP brown leather collar in my hand swings as I walk, clinking against Hades' rabies tag. There's an obvious skip in my step, and it makes my smile grow into a cheek-pinching grin.

I swagger into the shelter, and a sense of comfort falls on my shoulders when I notice my boy waiting for me in his pen. His tail swings faster and faster the closer I get, and a whine fills the space between us. It's been too long since I've had the time to come see him, and I'm planning to make up for the time apart with a long walk in the warm evening air.

"Hey, baby," I coo, making quick work of unlatching the pen door. He runs at me and stands on his rear legs, placing his front paws on my thighs. "We have so much to catch up on. I freaking missed you."

He pants, his tongue swiping at my chin and cheeks. I dig my fingers into the short hairs around his neck and give him some scratches.

"I got you something. I figured you needed a nice new one. This one is all yours."

He just stares at me as I slip the collar around his neck and fasten it. The brown looks perfect on him, and my eyes burn as I place a kiss on his snout.

He looks like somebody's pet, not the broken fight dog he used to be.

I pinch the dog tag in my fingers and read back over what I had the guy at the shop written on it.

Name: Hades

Allergies: Please no gluten

Special instructions: I don't like small spaces and please no cats.

Owner contact: Heights Animal Clinic, Braxton Heights. 439-555-9099

There was a moment when I wondered if I shouldn't have put my personal cell phone number and included the clinic's number instead, but it was instinct, I guess. There's nobody I trust the same as I do myself. Not when it comes to Hades.

The door opens behind me, and I look over my shoulder, offering Marco a smile. "Hey."

"The collar looks great. Matches the little patches all over his tummy," he notes.

Hades is watching Marco with cautious eyes, but he's much calmer than he was a few weeks ago. The fear is still there, coming out when he feels threatened or surprised, but I think he's started to feel comfortable here. Possibly even safe.

"He seems to like it enough. We were about to go show it off to the neighbourhood." I glance to my side to see Marco wandering closer, hands shoved deep in the pockets of a pair of sunflower-speckled scrub pants. "Do you wanna come? Sapphire over there hasn't gone for her walk yet tonight, and I told Sadie I would get her out before I went home."

He looks at the butt-wiggling German shepherd two pens over. "Hades does okay with her?"

"He does, actually. Sadie usually takes them together."

Grabbing two leashes off the long line of leashes hung on the wall beside the door, he swiftly hands me the black one I've been using for Hades and takes the blue one to Sapphire's pen.

"Sounds like a plan. I haven't hit my steps for the day yet, anyway." He laughs as Sapphire bolts out of her pen and nearly takes him down. "This one's going to be a great addition to someone's home someday. Hopefully a family with a bunch of little kids."

Hades turns his head to look at his wild-child friend, puffing out a breath at her energy.

"I'm hoping they'll all find a home after the adoption day, but I'm trying not to get my hopes up."

We have nine dogs at the shelter right now, and it pains me to leave them here every night. Even taking Hades and Sapphire out for a walk while all of them just sit and watch us leave has my stomach in knots, but knowing they've all already been pampered today helps soothe some of the discomfort.

"They all deserve something better than to spend their days in a pen waiting for the chance to find someone who will love and cherish them. I know we do everything we can to make them feel at home here, but they're still locked in pens. We would never survive being locked up all day, every day," I add, holding Hades a little closer.

Marco leads the big dog over to us and tells her to sit, which she does happily. He scratches her behind the ear, and her tongue flops out of her mouth.

"I get that. Hell, if I could adopt every dog out there that doesn't have a home, I would. You're right. They deserve better."

"I've never wanted to own a shelter," I blurt out as we head out the back door of the shelter and step onto the street. Hades falls to a slow trot beside me. "I briefly worked at a place like this when I was a teenager, and I went home crying nearly every night because I hated leaving the animals there. If it weren't for all of their cute faces, I wouldn't have bought this place."

Marco's eyes go wide for a brief moment. "Do you regret it? Buying this place, I mean?"

I roll my lip, contemplating that. "No, but also . . . maybe a little? I'm doing what I love, and I thought that if I had my own clinic, I would be more successful? Crap, I don't know. I guess I'm just not sure that all of this is what I had pictured when I graduated. I rushed into the decision to run my own place because of my daddy issues. Wanted to try and do the impossible of making him proud, you know?"

He nods, and I push a few curls out of my face, embarrassed at this rant I've dumped on my co-worker.

"You didn't ask for all of that. I'm sorry." My cheeks burn.

His smile is warm, genuine. "I don't mind. That's what friends are for, right? And for the record, if your dad isn't proud of you, it's because he's an idiot. You deserve the praise for all you've accomplished, even if all of this isn't what you expected."

"Thank you, Marco," I mutter, stopping by a lamppost when Hades starts to sniff at it. "Have you ever wanted to run your own clinic?"

Sapphire steps into Hades and pushes her snout against his, sniffing at the scent they've both found. My heart warms at the sight of him at ease with another dog.

"If given the opportunity? I think so. I was exploring my options before I contacted you about working here, but I couldn't find the right place to start on my own."

I nod and give Hades a gentle pull. He rushes back to my side, and we continue walking.

"I think you would be really great at it."

"You're great at it too, you know? I love coming to work every day because of how much I genuinely like the clinic and its staff."

"Sometimes I just think I'm in over my head. Especially recently with how crazy my life has gotten. I just think that I pictured myself having a lot more freedom, not being latched onto such a heavy chain of responsibilities. I always thought I would be one of those vets who works on my own schedule and is able to move all over the place, helping pets in need. Maybe that's stupid."

"Like a travelling vet?"

I shrug. "There might not even be much work down that line."

He guffaws. "Are you kidding? You would be able to work wherever you wanted, for as long as you wanted. There are tons of clinics looking for that kind of work."

I try to ease some of the excitement that follows those words, not wanting to start getting too many crazy ideas just yet.

"I just figured I would come back home after being away so long and feel like this was where I was supposed to be. But it just isn't the same as it was before I left. Home isn't Vancouver anymore. It's—"

"Maddox?" He chuckles when I glance at him, surprised. "Yeah, I figured that one out quick. It's obvious. Have you talked to him about this?"

Not yet. "I should. I'll wait until after the playoffs are over, though. Maybe by then, I'll have my crap more figured out. The last thing I want is to mess anything up. Things are going so good right now."

He bumps his shoulder against mine. "If you were going to pick a partner to support you through the career you're wanting, it would be a man who travels for his own. Sounds pretty perfect if you ask me."

"You're a lot more insightful than I thought," I admit with a loud laugh.

"Well, if you had ever taken me up on any of the dinners I've asked you on over the past few weeks, maybe you would have figured that out."

I look at him, unsure of whether he's truly upset about all the times I've turned him down, but I find him grinning, totally at ease.

"You're not wrong," I say.

"Eh, I won't hold it against you. It's hard to compete with a guy like Maddox Hutton."

My cheeks burn. "It wasn't about him. Not at the beginning."

"I don't need an explanation, Braxton. I'm just bugging you. We're colleagues anyway. Technically, you're my boss. It was the right move."

"Thank you."

A comforting feeling settles in my belly. It's nice to clear the air and actually make a friend. It's been a long time since I've made a new friend.

"Speaking of Maddox. It's game one of the third round tonight, right? The Warriors are doing amazing this year—do you think they'll make it all the way?" he asks as we turn the corner and the clinic comes back into view. I blink at the sign, not expecting to see it so soon.

There's a lot of pressure resting on the team tonight, but they're ready. Maddox is ready. I'm looking forward to tonight's game more than the others I've been to so far for that reason alone. They're going to be amazing.

"Honestly? Yes. The team is hungry."

"They're playing Minnesota now, right?"

Nerves prick the skin at the back of my neck. "Yeah."

"I'm excited. I would love to see the cup back in Vancouver."

"You and me and the rest of Van," I say, coming to a stop outside of the clinic doors, Hades heeling beside me. Marco's phone starts to ring as he opens the door for us, and I hurry inside while he answers it.

Micaela is gone, and the clinic is empty, the floors shining from the much-needed mopping I asked her to do before she left. I take a long look around and exhale.

This is all mine, yet I don't feel any pull toward it. It doesn't feel like I've really accomplished anything, even though I know that is the furthest thing from the truth.

"Sorry about that. Would you like me to help you close up, or are you okay on your own? I hate to take off, but my mom's at my house an hour early with dinner, and she forgot her key," Marco rushes out, his cheeks flushed with the worry I find in his eyes.

"Go. I've closed alone more than enough times. Enjoy your dinner. And thank you for the company."

He smiles warmly and reaches to squeeze my forearm. "Anytime."

I take Sapphire's leash from him and watch as he quickly collects his bag and coat from his office and then rushes out the door, waving at me from inside his car before he peels out of the parking lot. A frustrating pang of jealousy hits me as I think of how that could be my mother and me if my father would just back off and stop trying to control everything.

"Let's go get you both tucked into bed before I get lost in my thoughts," I tell the two dogs before locking the front doors and leading them back through to the shelter.

If I fall into that rabbit hole, I won't be able to climb back out before the game tonight.

I'M RUNNING LATE.

My hair is a mess, and there's still dried drool on my chin—Hades or mine, I'm not sure.

Falling asleep in Hades' pen wasn't part of the plan, but he convinced me to sit with him for a while after I got Sapphire put away and started getting him settled in by giving me those damn pouty eyes, and apparently, I was more tired than I thought. If it weren't for the weird spout of barking a few minutes ago, I probably would have spent the entire night in his pen.

Now, I'm rushing out the door, feeling groggy and a bit out of my body. This feeling is exactly why I try not to take naps. More often than not, they mess you up more than they help.

It's dark outside as I slip out the clinic doors and lock up. My feet carry me slowly through the parking lot as I pick my car key from the very cluttered key chain in my hand and click the button to unlock the doors.

The sound of breaking glass beneath my shoes has me finally looking up. Despite the warm weather, a cold breeze travels down my spine.

The only car in the parking lot is mine, and while I didn't notice it before, there's a puddle of broken glass on the pavement by the driver's door. I swallow my fear and take a couple of steps toward it, finding the front window smashed.

My legs freeze, muscles turning into lead as I use shaky hands to pull out my phone and dial Maddox's number. It rings and rings and rings before his voice fills the night, telling me to leave a message.

I curse myself out for falling asleep, realizing that he's probably already at the rink. *Stay calm*, I tell myself. Blowing out a breath, I start to back away from the car and call Cooper. I blink back tears when he answers right away.

"Hey, love." His voice is so soothing it makes my body shake with relief.

"Can you come to the clinic, please? There's glass all over the place, and I need . . . I need you to come get me."

Why didn't my car alarm go off? Did I have anything important in my car? Where's the person who did this?

"I'm on my way. But what do you mean, there's glass everywhere?" His voice has gone steely, and I clutch the keys in my hands.

I keep moving backward until my heels hit the concrete step in front of my building. I go to step back onto it when a force at my back has me flying forward. A gasp leaves my parted lips as my phone flies from my hands, skittering across the parking lot. I slam my palms to the pavement to catch my fall and hiss at the pain that flares as they scrape and tear open. My head hits the pavement, and I bite down on my cheek to avoid crying out.

I hear a muttered "Shit" as I try to push myself back up, and by the time I look for the asshole who pushed me down, I'm alone. Just like I thought I was in the first place.

35

Braxton

COOPER IS KNEELING ABOVE ME WHEN I WAKE UP FROM ANOTHER unexpected nap, this time with my back against what feels like a brick wall. My eyelids are heavy as I blink, trying to bring his face into focus. There's something wet on my ear, and my head hurts, a pulse thumping away inside of my skull. A burning in my hands has me lifting them in the air. Scraped skin and blood.

"Jesus fucking Christ, Braxton. I thought I was going to have to call an ambulance. How long have you been asleep? You're bleeding," he rushes out, frantic hands moving over me, eyes examining me.

I drop my head to his chest, exhaustion trying to pull me under again. "Let me go back to bed," I slur.

A growl hits my hair before a set of arms is digging beneath my armpits and lifting me onto my feet. I frown, shaking my head.

"We're going to the hospital. You definitely have a concussion."

"No. My car. Did you see anyone when you got here?"

I manage to tie my words together, trying to dig my heels into the ground as he leads us to the SUV parked beside my car.

"No. And now I know you didn't fall on your own. You need to file a police report as soon as you're done at the hospital."

"I don't want to think about that right now." I reach toward my ear and swipe away the warm liquid there. When I see the red on my fingertips, I gulp. "I *am* bleeding."

Cooper maneuvers us so he can pull open the passenger door and help me inside. Once I'm sitting, he goes to the back of the vehicle and comes back a second later with a first aid kit.

"Let me check your head. I don't like the look of you bleeding," he states gruffly.

Knowing better than to refuse, I nod. "I'm going to miss the game tonight."

"Yeah. You are."

His touch is gentle on the side of my head, but I still flinch. Cooper doesn't pay it any attention; he just continues to wipe away the blood on the side of my face and then starts to push through my curls in search of the wound.

"I tried to call him, but he didn't answer, and now he's going to think I bailed on him," I whisper.

"No, he's not. Now, hold this rag here, and let me clean your hands."

I hold the first one out to him, grabbing the rag and applying the same pressure he was on my head, trying not to wince at the first dab of the peroxide-soaked wipe.

"We need to call the police about your car, at least. You need to get your window replaced as soon as possible. Did you have anything valuable that someone could have wanted to steal?"

Anger flares in his eyes each time I flinch or hiss out a breath. When he cleans the deepest cut, I release a whimper, and he grinds his jaw so hard I worry he'll break his teeth.

"No. I don't know why anybody would want to break into it in the first place. It's old. Half the time, it doesn't even start."

"Switch hands," he mutters, waiting for me to grab the rag in the newly cleaned hand and give him the bloody one. "I don't think they cared about the car. It doesn't make sense. You're not wrong about it being unreliable."

"Hey, I'm the only one that gets to insult her."

He rolls his eyes. "Does this place have security cameras?"

"Yes. One that faces the parking lot and another at the back entrance."

I only had them installed last week, and now I'm grateful that I did, despite the extra cost. Maybe we caught the guy.

"Alright, good. When we're done at the hospital, you're going to report the break-in and hand over the security tapes."

I sigh, feeling the full weight of my exhaustion. "I'll do it tomorrow. Not tonight. I'm tired."

Cooper blows out a long breath. "Okay, love. You just scared me. I've never heard you like that before. And then when you stopped answering . . ."

"I'm sorry," I whisper, twisting my mouth.

"You don't have anything to apologize for. I'm so happy you called me."

I nod, not knowing what else to say as he finishes cleaning up my hands, glancing up at me every few seconds to make sure I'm still okay.

A couple of moments later, he's wrapping my hands in white bandages and saying, "Stay awake on the way to the hospital. I'm serious."

I nod, swallowing the worry in my throat. He buckles me in, then throws the first aid kit back in the vehicle and gets in the driver's side. If it weren't for the heavy reality of the situation, I would laugh at the way he blasts the radio and turns the A/C all the way up in an attempt to keep me awake.

He's so worried that even though the music makes my head throb that much more, I don't say anything. I'm lucky he came as quickly as he did. I'm too scared to think of what could have happened to me had he not rushed to get to me.

"You should be able to go home soon, but I do want someone to stay with you tonight through tomorrow to watch for any of the symptoms I mentioned, alright? Are you able to stay with her?"

One of the emergency room doctors at the hospital—a curvy woman with gorgeous flaming-orange hair and a warm smile—places a hand on my wrist and looks between Cooper and me.

Cooper flicks his eyes to me before staring back at the doctor. "It won't be me, but there will be someone with her tonight."

My brows furrow. "Do you have plans or something?"

He laughs, shaking his head. "No, love. But I think—"

"Braxton?" a deep voice shouts outside of the room. "Don't touch me. Just tell me where the fuck she is. Braxton?"

The doctor's lips pull tight in what looks like an attempt to hold her laugh. "That's for you, I assume?"

My heart goes into overdrive. *He's here.* "Yeah. That's for me. Can we open the door?"

"I'll leave it open on my way out. Remember, come back in if you start to feel any symptoms."

"I will."

"Alright. Have a great night, guys."

"Thank you," I say, cautiously touching the bandage on my head.

My stare follows her out of the door and lands on the man rushing toward me, his body draped in hockey gear and pushing through a crowd of hospital staff. My jaw drops as I look at him, at the worry in his eyes and the way his lips part on my name.

My doctor mutters something toward the group, and they separate instantly, making room for Maddox to walk through.

I try to speak, but my words die the moment he reaches us and grabs me where I sit on the exam table, lifting me into his arms and spinning us away from Cooper. He presses my back to the wall, careful of my head, and buries his face in my neck, releasing shuddered breaths on my skin. I wrap my arms around his neck, not liking how his gear keeps us from being closer.

"You're okay, baby. You're okay. *Fuck*," he breathes, his arms wrapped around me nice and tight.

"I'll be outside," Cooper says softly before the door shuts, and it's just Maddox and me.

"How are you here?" I ask, closing my eyes, careful not to put pressure on my palms as I tighten my grip around his neck.

"That doesn't matter. Fuck, how are you feeling? What happened?"

"It does matter. You're supposed to be playing a game right now," I persist.

He pulls me away from the wall and sets me on the edge of the bed. I go to protest at the distance left between us when he quickly eliminates it, stepping between my legs and cupping my face in his hands. His eyes scour my face, the skin damp beneath them, panic pulling at his features when he smooths his thumb up my cheek and touches my hair around the stitch in my scalp. I blink at him, waiting and waiting for words that don't come.

"Maddox," I whisper.

"Tell me who did this to you, baby."

His words seem calm, but they're vibrating with a thick sense of danger that has me fighting back a shiver.

"I don't know. I only noticed that somebody had broken into my car, and I guess they weren't gone yet. All I remember is being shoved forward and falling and then falling asleep. When I woke up, Cooper was there."

His throat bobs. The air pulls tight around us.

"I'll take care of this, I promise. Whoever did this won't get away with it," he swears.

I nod, wishing I could pull his face toward me without hurting my hands. He's fighting some sort of inner battle, and I want to dive into his mind and be included.

"Cooper could have watched me tonight. You didn't have to come. I don't want you to get in trouble," I murmur.

He drops his forehead to mine, rolling it side to side. "I will always choose you. Nothing else matters to me but you. Nothing."

I tuck my lip between my teeth and breathe him in, ignoring the less-than-appealing smell of his gear and focusing on the hint of his body wash.

"I'm so sorry I didn't answer my phone when you called. I was already on the ice for a final practice," he grits out.

"It's okay. How did you find out?"

"Cooper called my dad. Dad called Coach. Coach told me. I left as soon as the words were out of his mouth. If it weren't for Bentley, I would have left with my skates on I was so out of my head."

I laugh softly, bumping our noses. "Thank you for coming."

"Don't thank me, sweetheart. Just please, I never want to have someone tell me you were hurt again."

"I'll try my best," I attempt to joke.

His jaw pulses. "I'm serious. I don't think I've ever been so scared. I can't lose you again, okay? Just seeing you here, like this . . . it's taking everything in me not to go out there and find this guy."

I press my lips to his jaw, on the bushy beard covering it. The one I've grown to love. "I'm okay, Dox. I promise. Can you just take me home, please? All I want is to cuddle and watch TV."

He traces my bottom lip with his knuckle before kissing me softly. It's a cautious kiss, like he's scared he'll break me, and while there's no possible way for that to happen, I accept the gesture with open arms.

"As long as you let me hold you in the shower and wash the blood out of your hair first," he says. I pretend to think about it, and he nips at my bottom lip. "Please. Don't make me get on my knees and beg."

"Oh, see, that's a tempting picture. You made a mistake offering that to me." I waggle my eyebrows.

"At home, baby girl. Cooper could walk in here any minute, and while I owe him my life for getting to you as fast as he did, I'm not about to let him see me on my knees for you," he says, voice dropping into a growly whisper.

"Sounds fine by me, although I'm sure it would make his entire year to find you in that position."

Maddox shakes his head, smiling as if I've said something ridiculous. "He's been waiting our entire lives to see me on the ground at your feet, Braxton. It would make more than just his year to see it. Now, let's go home."

Home.

I don't know whether he means my place or his, and it doesn't seem to matter. Home is wherever he is.

I grin like a fool as he flashes me a dimple and moves to let Cooper in so we can leave.

36

Maddox

THERE HAVE ONLY BEEN A HANDFUL OF TIMES IN MY LIFE WHERE I have been angry enough to lose my temper in public. Unless I'm on the ice, I keep that shit locked down tight. But the minute Coach pulled me off the ice at practice and told me Braxton was in the hospital, it was like someone else took over my body.

Suddenly, I was stripped of everything but anger. A burning rage that whispered in my ear, ordering me to go find who was responsible and show the universe just how little I enjoy it putting my woman in danger.

There was a desperation thrumming deep inside of me that I was unfamiliar with, and it turned me on my ass. It didn't matter where I was, I knew from the second Coach pulled me aside that I was leaving. My vision tunnelled, and then there was only Braxton.

And as we lie in bed hours later, her cheek pressing against my chest, her fingers carefully curled in my T-shirt, I know that being benched next game was worth it. Without a doubt.

A movie I don't remember the title of plays on the flat-screen in front of my bed. Braxton is splayed across my chest, her leg looped over my hips, holding me like a koala would a damn tree. I'm relaxed, at ease with her in my arms and in my bed.

I brush my lips over the top of her head, back and forth, back and forth, while humming a song that filled my bedroom from the movie a handful of minutes ago. It's been easier to keep Braxton awake than I thought it would, but I think the bowl of sour gummy worms I ordered her to eat has her pretty wired up now.

She uncurls her fingers, leaving my shirt wrinkled in their absence, and then reaches into the bowl at my side, digging around until she pinches a blue-and-pink one. I crinkle my nose when she tilts her head to look at me and reaches up to dangle the worm in front of my mouth.

"Are you sure you don't want one?" she asks, a barely there smirk tugging at her lips.

"I would rather eat sand, baby girl. Thanks, though."

She giggles, plopping the candy into her mouth instead. I watch her chew and then lick the sugar granules from her lips, eyes twinkling the entire time.

"You've never liked sour candy. It's weird for you to have an entire shelf designated for bags of the stuff in your pantry if you won't eat it," she notes, smacking her lips together.

"Mm, I don't like it, but you do," I murmur before stealing a kiss, pushing the lingering taste of the candy to the back of my mind. "And I'm hoping you'll be here enough to eat them. Was that wishful thinking?"

"Not at all." Her lips part, tongue pressing into my mouth. I give it a hard suck, fighting a grin when she pushes at my chest. After I release her tongue, she glares playfully at me. "Actually, now that I think about it, it might have been."

I bark a laugh and drop my head back to the pillows piled behind me. "You're too sore for a spanking, Braxton. But keep it up and I might not care."

She wiggles against my side. "Ooh, is that a threat or a promise?"

"It's neither now that I know you'd enjoy both."

"That's rude."

I push my hand down her side and take her ass cheek in my hand, giving it a squeeze through the silk pyjama shorts she packed in her overnight bag earlier.

"Sorry, princess."

"There is one way you can make it up to me." She says it almost shyly, and I'm immediately curious.

"Let me hear it."

Pushing herself up on her forearm, she holds my gaze and says, "I know we haven't talked a lot about the fundraisers or the adoption day yet, but it's already only a month away, and there's still so much to figure out. One idea Sadie and I had would probably do well enough that we wouldn't need to involve as many sponsors this year. I think it would sell amazingly."

"What's the idea? I don't know shit about this stuff, sweetheart. You're gonna have to spell it all out for me so I can do a good job here."

She nods, a smile peeking out. "So, Sadie told me that usually they set up a few fundraising events before the adoption day to grow some publicity and, combined with their usual sponsors, gather the money for the event itself. The adoption day is meant to bring in as many potential families as possible, and the more we prepare beforehand, usually the better the turn out."

"Okay, and what's this idea of yours?"

A flush slithers up her neck and paints her cheeks as she darts her eyes away. I gently pinch her chin and turn her back to me.

"It can't be that bad," I add, hoping to encourage her.

"Do you think you could convince the VW to do a calendar photoshoot with the dogs that are going to be up for adoption?" She says it all in one breath and then sucks in a long one.

It takes everything in me not to start laughing at her nervousness. Not because it's funny that she's nervous, but because she thought for even a second that I could deny her anything she wants.

"I think this is the perfect time to test how badly Alexander wants to fix my image. I'll make it happen."

Her following smile is all I need to know that whatever I have to do to make it happen will be worth it.

"Oh my God. I love you so much," she gushes, covering my face with kisses. I tighten my grip on her ass and lay my other hand over her thigh, pulling it further up my body. "This is going to be amazing. Thank you, Maddox."

I steal her mouth in a longer kiss before she has the chance to pull away again and rub my palm over her leg, feeling the skin become peppered with goosebumps.

"I love you," I whisper against her lips, heaving a breath. "You've been up long enough now if you want to go to sleep."

She hums, dropping her head to my shoulder and brushing her nose up my throat. "But I'm not sleepy anymore."

I swat at her ass, and she jolts, looking at me with wide eyes. Turning her down goes against every fibre of my being, but it's for her own good.

"Sleep. You're not getting fucked again until you can touch me without your hands starting to bleed and your head isn't throbbing."

"You suck." She tosses herself down on my chest again but keeps close. If I were a cat, I'd purr at the feel of her against me.

"I'll suck if it means you're not hurting," I say.

"Fine. I'll sleep if you join me."

"Deal."

"We need to brush our teeth. I have gummy worm teeth."

I chuckle. "Do you want me to carry you to the bathroom?"

She taps her nails on my side, drawing shapes there that make me shiver. "Would you? My head hurts."

"Oh, does it now? Huh. Funny how that works." I grin and slip out from beneath her onto the floor before scooping her up and carrying her to the bathroom.

She gazes up at me with a loopy smile. "Swoon. My own personal knight in shining armour."

"That's right. Don't you forget it."

"How do you use this thing?" Braxton shouts from the kitchen the next morning, a clang following close behind. "And why is everything so dang high?"

I tug my sweatshirt over my head and shrug to get it fitted properly before leaving the bedroom. Following the sounds of her struggle, I find her tucked away in the walk-in pantry, leaning into one of the sets of shelves on her tiptoes, hands flailing above her head. The plastic container I keep my coffee pods in is on the shelf she's reaching for, so I step up behind her, brushing my chest to her back as I grab it for her.

She spins to face me, gasping when she sees how close I am. I hold the container between us and grin.

"Should I keep a stool in here for you from now on?"

Her eyes roll, but the corner of her mouth twitches. "Maybe just move everything down a shelf. Who makes shelves that high, anyway? Seems a bit extreme."

Snatching the container, she slips around me and pads back into the kitchen. It's a different experience having a woman around, moving around my space with such ease. I love it. Truly.

I would love it more if it looked like her space too, but I don't know if she's ready to hear that yet.

Braxton pops a coffee pod into the machine and shouts her success when the black mug she chose starts to fill with a steady stream of brown liquid.

"Have I mentioned how good you look in my kitchen?" is what I choose to say instead.

She looks at me over her shoulder, eyes warm and so damn blue. "Once or twice. It's a nice kitchen. A bit bland for my taste, though."

I slip my eyes over the space and don't bother denying it. It's big, but with white cabinets and white marbled countertops, it looks too clean. Too sterile.

When I bought this place, I didn't care what it looked like. I just knew I had more money than I was ever going to need, and the penthouse seemed like as good a place as any to spend some of it. But after four years, it's more like a rental space than someone's home. It's a far cry from where I grew up.

I rest my back against the countertop and watch her. The strings on her VW hoodie try to dip into her mug when she raises it to her lips and takes a sip of the black coffee. A pair of grey sweatpants fall over her legs and are rolled up twice at her ankles. Messy curls are piled on her head, and her lips are still a bit swollen from the number of kisses I stole this morning, the feeling of waking up with her in my bed too fucking phenomenal not to.

"You're right. This entire place needs some of the colour from your house," I say.

"Is this your attempt at asking me to move in, Maddox? Because this penthouse is not my style."

My eyes go wide for a second, surprise slipping over me before I steel my expression.

"You're right. It's not. So, let's find something that is."

Now it's her turn to look surprised. "Are you being serious?"

"As a heart attack, baby girl."

We're interrupted by a sudden influx of voices in the penthouse, and I'm suddenly on high alert, ready to push her out of the room, when a head of platinum-blonde hair comes barrelling into the kitchen.

"You're alive! Oh, my goodness, you had us so worried!" Addie yells, running right for Braxton.

Braxton barely has time to set her cup down on the counter behind her before my sister has her in a tight hug. My girl meets my eyes over my sister's shoulder, and I shrug, just as surprised as she is.

"Adalyn, don't you be hurting our girl!" Mom warns, and I turn to find her walking in with Dad at her side.

I double blink and lift my hands in the air. "What are you doing here? You can't just show up unannounced. How did you even get in here?"

"Nothing can stop a mom from getting to her babies, Maddox. And we're here to see Braxton, of course. We brought cinnamon rolls because I know how you can't cook," she says, dropping a white paper bag on the counter.

"Oh, okay then. Make yourselves at home." I scoff.

"Thank you, baby," Mom replies before all but pushing my sister away from Braxton and taking a hug of her own. "Cooper is a gossip, I'm afraid. He called Addie, and as soon as she told us, we knew we had to come and see for ourselves that you were okay. We were so worried."

Dad sidles up beside me, his eyes on Mom. "She swore me to secrecy after I tried to warn you. Sorry to cut your morning short."

I shrug, finding it hard to be truly annoyed as my mom and sister start to fuss over Braxton, showing in their own way how much they love her. She deserves the attention and affection they so eagerly want to give her.

"It's good for her to start getting used to them again. I'm not letting her go this time," I state.

Dad laughs softly, patting my back. "Didn't think you would, but I'm glad to hear it. She's family to all of us."

"How soon do you think is too soon?" I blurt out.

"Depends on what you're talking about."

Braxton grins at me through the gap between Addie and Mom, and fuck if I don't want to steal her back and bring her to my side. She looks like she belongs here. With me and with my family. And I know to my very core that she really, *really* does.

Addie leads them out of the kitchen and toward the living room, carrying Braxton's coffee for her. Mom snatches the bag of cinnamon rolls on her way and winks at me.

I look at Dad, my expression open, heart bared.

"I'm talking about everything, Dad. I want it all with her, and the thought of wasting more time makes me feel ill."

"I don't think there is a too soon with you two, Maddox. It's been a long time coming. If you're asking me for approval, you've had it for over a decade. Do what feels right to you and your girl."

"Thank you, Dad." I scrape the words up my throat, the emotion there making it a difficult task.

"For what?"

"For bringing her back to me when I was too scared to do it myself."

37

Braxton

I THINK I'VE DIED AND GONE TO HEAVEN. A HEAVEN FULL OF shirtless, muscular bodies and thigh-hugging black boxer briefs.

I've been in a perpetual state of sweaty since the six Vancouver Warriors players showed up an hour ago for this photoshoot, each player more excited than the last to get started. Their excitement might also have something to do with their third-round win against Minnesota and the fact they've made it to the fourth and final round of the playoffs, but I'll take it regardless.

With a four-day break between now and the start of the fourth round, we're also closing in on adoption day. It's two weeks away, and this photoshoot is the perfect way to finish our preparations.

"Colt Warner! For the love of God, please stop thrusting at Maddox. You're scaring Bernie," Diamond, the photographer Sadie hired, huffs.

She keeps trying to pull Colt's attention back to the dachs-hund who's staring up at him, head tilting side to side beneath his miniature cowboy hat, but the country boy seems to have the attention span of a toddler.

Maddox belts out a laugh and shoves his teammate back over to the dog he was paired with. Bernie sits patiently as he waits for Colt to sit back down and pull him into his arms.

"Smile, Colt. Or I'm going to take away the matching cowboy hats," Diamond threatens, starting to snap some photos with her expensive-looking camera.

The white backdrop set up behind Colt and Bernie takes up most of Diamond's studio, but even with the addition of the massive men, it surprisingly doesn't feel too crowded.

"You look so sexy over here, all in charge and shit," Maddox murmurs, suddenly beside me, mouth at my ear.

I lean into his side, humming at the feel of him all warm and bare brushing against my arm. It's been a test of my self-control to keep from jumping him already, and it's only gotten harder and harder to keep my hands to myself the longer I've had to stare at him half-naked. He's a walking wet dream, all rippling muscles and tattooed skin.

He hasn't had his turn being photographed yet, so I can only assume it's going to get worse the minute I see him posing with a dog. I'm suddenly thankful for my decision to put on a sundress today and not a pair of pants. At least there won't be visible evidence of my arousal with a dress.

"I haven't had to do much so far. Diamond is doing a great job at keeping you guys in line all on her own."

He laughs softly. "I like her. She's got balls. You have to have a pair of steel ones to be able to rein in these guys. They're old enough to know better than to jerk around but crazy enough not to care."

I press my cheek to his bicep and slip my arm around his front, dipping my fingers in the crevices of the muscles there, unable to stop myself. A rumble grows in his chest before he grabs my hand and intertwines our fingers, keeping me from continuing whatever it was I was trying to do.

"Baby, I'm already fighting off a boner at the image of you in this pretty dress. Please, don't make it any worse," he says tightly, almost begging.

"Yeah? You like it?" I glance down at the green dress before flicking my eyes back up to him. "I figured since you agreed to let me wear your jerseys just on game days instead of every day, I would still try to keep to theme."

I've bought more green-coloured clothes in the past month than in my entire life, but it's better than having to wear a heavy jersey in the warm weather.

"You look fucking gorgeous, Curly Fry."

I blush at the compliment, darting my eyes away. "Thank you."

"I love that I can still make you blush after this long," he admits, the weight of his stare heavy on my cheeks.

"I don't think I'll ever not blush at the things you say to me."

He dips his head, and his hot breath hits the tip of my ear. "Good. I like the colour pink on you. On your cheeks and that pretty pussy of yours."

I nearly drop my head back and groan but choose to press my thighs together instead, feeling the damp material of my panties stick to the skin beneath.

"Stop it right now. I'm telling Diamond to put you next so that you can get dressed sooner," I mutter.

Moving to step away from him, I hear his strong laughter and feel a tug on my hand. I have to blink away the lust from my eyes before looking back. He's grinning so wide his dimples are out in both cheeks. *Asshole.*

"I'm sorry. Forgive me?"

I stare at him, expression flat. "No. Now, get ready to pose."

He releases my wrist with another loud burst of laughter, and I leave him standing there, a slickness between my thighs that makes me feel far more annoyed with myself than him.

Diamond is pulling her rainbow-coloured hair up into a bun when I reach her, a slight sheen across her forehead from the heat of the overhead lights. Colt is stretched out on his side in front of us, Bernie lazing against his stomach, both of their cowboy hats tilted back, almost hanging off their heads.

"One more, boys. Give me a smirk, Colt. I know you must have a good one. Yes, great. Now, put your hand on Bernie's back and pull him right against you. Perfect," Diamond instructs, dropping to her knees to snap more photos. "Okay, you're done, Cowboy. Take Bernie back to the other room—he probably needs a break from all that testosterone."

Colt pushes himself up and grabs Bernie in a single hand. His eyes fall back to Diamond as he says, "What are you doing after this? Feel like taking Bernie's spot for a bit?"

"Not at all. But thanks for your good work," she replies before turning to me with a warm smile. "How are you liking everything so far? Do you wanna see some of the shots before we continue?"

I swipe a hand through the air. "Oh, no. I trust you. Everything has been great so far. I was actually wondering if you could do Maddox next? I know Bentley was supposed to go, but—"

"Sure! Who is he with again? I don't think I saw a name beside him when I looked earlier."

"Right. I actually was hoping to try him with Hades, but I might need some of the guys to move out for a bit to see if Hades is up for it. Is that okay?"

The decision to have Hades pose with Maddox wasn't an easy one to make, but it made the most sense. Hades is doing much better, but I don't know if he'll do well with the other guys. Hell, I don't even know if he'll do well with Dox, but I feel less stressed at the idea of Dox being able to be with him in case anything were to go wrong.

Hades needs a family, and this calendar might be the best way to ensure that happens. I don't want him to be excluded.

"For sure. I can get them all to take a quick break while you get them all ready," Diamond says.

"Thank you," I breathe, relieved at her easy acceptance.

She gives me another smile before starting to usher the guys out of the room, her orders clear and precise. They don't put up much of a fight, choosing to start flirting with the poor woman instead.

A tall body wraps around me from behind, and the spicy scent of Maddox's cologne gives him away. He kisses the crown of my head.

"If you wanted to get me alone, you could have just said that," he teases into my hair, body shaking with a silent laugh.

"If I told you that you were with Hades today, would you agree?" I ask, ignoring his flirting.

At my worried tone, he holds my hips and spins me around, brows furrowed. "I trust your judgement, Braxton. Whatever you think is best works for me."

"Okay. I'm going to get him and bring him in here. Just go sit where Colt was and let him come to you," I ramble.

He nods, face still twisted with concern. "Okay. Breathe, sweetheart. It'll be fine."

"Breathe," I echo. "Right. Okay. I'll be right back."

Spinning on my heel, I head out of the open door and toward the small room usually used for dressing changes but today has been transformed into a doggie daycare. I find Hades lying in his crate, on top of the fluffy VW blanket I stole from Maddox's house and brought with us, hoping that the early scent introduction would help. From how cozy he looks snuggled up on it, it looks like he doesn't mind his scent.

Smart dog.

My heart aches at the lack of playing he's doing, but I know he isn't ready to be let loose on his own with the other dogs yet.

I pick his leash and collar up off the ground beside his crate and open the door, quickly slipping them both on as he stands and stretches.

"It's your time to shine, baby. I need you to really work with me here, okay? Maddox is a good guy. I promise," I tell him.

He licks my cheek before I stand, encouraging him to walk out before shutting the crate door. While a bit tense, he doesn't look afraid, and that's a great sign.

When we get back to the main room, my nerves come racing back. Hades is more relaxed than I am now, even when he sees Maddox sitting on the floor, legs outstretched and arms back, keeping himself upright.

"Hey, buddy," Dox says softly, keeping still, his warm green eyes flicking between me and Hades.

Hades slows his walk slightly as we approach him, moving a bit closer to me. I'm holding my breath when he stops right in front of Maddox and stares at him.

"Put your hand out in front of you but not too close to him. Just give him the option to come sniff you," I say.

He does exactly that, and Hades creeps closer, butting Maddox's hand with his nose. I blow out a breath and crouch at Maddox's side, stroking Hades' back.

"Good boy," I praise before sitting beside Maddox with my legs tucked beneath me, leaning into his side. "You can pet him now. Right where I am."

His fingers brush mine as he pets his back. "Does this mean he doesn't hate me?"

"Yeah, I think he might actually like you. That's a really good sign."

"I think he likes us together. He didn't seem to be a fan of me the first time we met."

"He's made so much progress since then. Plus, it wasn't like any of us had a good energy that day. It wasn't a happy meeting," I say.

Maddox makes a low noise in his throat. "Do you think he'll get adopted?"

"I hope so. He deserves a loving home. Someone just has to give him a chance."

As if he knows we're talking about him, Hades pushes closer, demanding more attention. Maddox chuckles while I let out a wet laugh. When it comes to this dog, I can't seem to stop crying.

"Have you thought about adopting him yourself?" he asks, swiping the wet from beneath my eyes.

"I have. But I'm not sure if I'm the right person for him."

"What? You're the perfect person for him. Nobody is going to love him as much as you do."

Hades pushes his face into my chest, and I kiss the top of his head, breathing in the lingering coconut smell from his bath yesterday. It scares me how clearly I can see us together—Hades and me. Maddox too. We'd play fetch all day in a spacious back-yard with a big red doghouse by the fence for Hades like Snoopy has in the Charlie Brown cartoons and then spend the night in front of a brick fireplace. It's a dream that I'm scared I could never make a reality.

"My life is so hectic—what if I couldn't give him the time he deserves? Someone else could. Someone who wouldn't have known about him without this calendar we're shooting for today. It has to be perfect," I say.

Maddox holds my waist and kisses my cheek, nodding. "There's no rush. Let's call Diamond back in here and finish this up. We can go from there, yeah?"

A knock on the open door comes at the perfect time, and all three of us turn to see our lovely photographer peering in at us. Her smile is contagious, and I find myself smiling back, waving her in.

"Hey. We're good to go. Hades should let Maddox move him around well enough for the photos, but if everyone could stay a bit back just in case, that would be great," I tell her, noticing the guys starting to fill the space behind her.

She walks toward us, eyes bright and a finger tapping on the top of her camera. "Actually, why don't you stay for these ones? Hades is calmest with you, right? Plus, the three of you look really great together. Like a family."

My stomach does a weird twirling thing.

"Hear that, baby girl? A family," Maddox whispers in my ear.

"Are you sure? I don't want to ruin the whole vibe. Maddox doesn't even have clothes on," I ramble, fighting back the urge to run and hide.

"Can one of you do something useful and go get Maddox his clothes, please?" Diamond yells at the guys, and it's Bentley that rushes out the door a second later. She shoots me a wink. "There. This will be perfect for the whole family thing you're trying to bring into the adoption day."

She's right, so I don't fight her on it.

A minute later, Bentley is back and handing Maddox his clothes. My side is cold when he stands to get dressed, but it's not long before I'm burning up again, the sight of him in all of his glory stealing my breath. It's still hard to believe that this man wants me and continues to do everything he can to cherish me.

I feel like the luckiest girl in the world.

A beat later, he's dressed in a pair of light blue jeans with a small rip over the knee and a black T-shirt that hugs his biceps in the most delicious way. His feet are bare, and it fits the look perfectly.

With hearts in my eyes, I blink up at him and smile. Hades is turned away from me but flush to my body, waiting for Maddox to join us again. As soon as he does, any previous tension and anxiety at the idea of being photographed slips away, replaced with an almost giddy feeling of excitement.

"I'm going to steal these photos and plaster them all over my house," Maddox says confidently.

I scoot closer as he drops an arm over my shoulders and pecks my cheek, interlocking the fingers I have buried in Hades' fur with his.

"I like that idea," I murmur.

"Stay just like that!" Diamond shrieks before rushing around and dropping to her knees again a few feet in front of us, camera lifted and pointed directly at us. "Just like I said! A family."

Yeah. We are a family.

The term replays in my mind over and over again, growing more perfect each time. I soak up this moment, praying that I get to experience this feeling of pure bliss every single day for the rest of my life.

38

Braxton

It's late into the evening by the time we get home from the shoot, the setting sun casting a pretty pink glow through the windows of the penthouse when we enter. The A/C drones on to try and beat the June heat, but the place is otherwise silent, calm.

My bare feet pad across the cool wood floors and into the kitchen. Turning on the light, I spot my coffee cup in the sink beside the shaker cup Maddox used for his pre-workout this morning and a rainbow-decorated scrub top that's hanging from the back of a bar stool at the island.

Ever since our first night together a few weeks ago, my stuff has started to fill this place—a pair of slippers here and my favourite silk pillowcase there. I've been watching it happen with both eyes open, and I haven't made any move to slow down my roll. I'm pretty sure Dox has been slipping things into his overnight bag on the nights he stays at my place and depositing them here when I'm at work, and it makes me feel all fuzzy inside. Not scared or nervous like I thought it would.

Our lives are becoming intertwined so effortlessly. That's a good sign, right? Because it sure feels like one.

"Are you hungry? I can order in if you want to take a bath.

There are those fancy bath bombs you like in a jar beside the tub," Maddox says, setting my purse on the slim table by the front door. Keys clatter into the ceramic bowl beside it as he kicks off his shoes.

Dropping an elbow to the island, I rest my cheek in my palm and watch as he follows me, lips lifted in a natural smile, one that always seems to be there lately. My stomach swoops when he bends down to kiss me, one hand on my waist and the other softly cupping my jaw.

Hours spent watching my man strut around in nothing but a pair of underwear and posing with my favourite dog in the entire world have made me more wound up than I've ever been. One innocent kiss is enough to send me right over the edge, desperate to be touched the way only he can touch me.

"What if I said I wasn't hungry?" I whisper, leaning back against the counter, my hands starting to wander over his chest, nails scratching at his T-shirt.

"I'd say you're lying because we haven't eaten since breakfast."

"Okay . . ." I tip his head to the side with my nose and press my lips to his jaw, kissing the underside before working my way down over the steady thump in his throat. "What if I just want to do something entirely different first? I've been wet for hours, Dox. *So* wet."

A pained sound escapes him when I push the hand he has on my waist over my stomach and down to the space between my thighs. The veins that protrude along the back of his hand flex against my palm, and suddenly, nothing has ever been sexier than a veiny hand.

"Have you spent all day with slick thighs, sweetheart?"

He takes control of his hand now, using his fingers to push my dress up until a cool breeze hits my inner thighs and the centre of my wet panties. His eyes trace my features, watching my expression the further my dress climbs. The moment the tip of his finger brushes my pussy, I'm slouching forward, dropping my head to his shoulder as the single touch sends a zap up my middle.

"*Fuck*. I'm sorry," he groans, moving his finger in a circle over the satin, avoiding my clit.

My hips push forward, seeking more than just the hint of a touch. His pupils are so big as he watches me that the green is nearly washed out.

"For what?" I gasp.

One long finger slips under the side of my panties and pushes them to the side before dipping between the folds of my pussy. He rubs his finger up and down, inching closer to my clit with each upstroke. I spread my legs as much as possible while standing, but annoyance nips at me when he still doesn't give me what I want.

"I should have taken care of this earlier. Should have taken you to a dark room and eaten this pretty cunt until you begged me to take you home and fill you up. I'll make it up to you, though, baby. I promise."

My eyes roll back at the dirty promise. "Please. I need you right now."

He pushes his finger deep inside of me, and I buck up, hands grabbing at his shirt, using his body as an anchor. Another finger joins the first as he starts to fuck me with them, scissoring them inside of me until my knees are threatening to buckle, and my grip on him is the only thing keeping me on my feet.

"Maddox," I beg, not sure what I'm even asking for at this point. Desperation thrums in my veins, turning my head fuzzy and my lips loose. "Just fuck me. *Right now*."

"That's it, sweet girl. Tell me what you want."

His other hand drops to the front of his jeans as he pops open the button and pushes down the zipper. The tip of his cock is pushing against the waistband of his briefs, wet with precum. My mouth waters, desperate to have him in my mouth.

"You want my cock, Braxton?" he asks, shoving both his jeans and underwear down.

I nod, eyes glazing over as he grips it in a tight fist, giving it two slow pumps before collecting the precum on his thumb and lifting it to my lips. They part instantly, and he pushes his thumb inside.

"Suck," he orders, nostrils flaring when I do as he says without hesitation, his taste making my thighs rub together.

There's something oh so satisfying about seeing the man you love turn feral with desire for you, and watching Maddox lose his grip on control has me on the brink of orgasm before we've even really started.

He pulls his thumb from between my lips, and I let it go with a loud pop. There's a beat of silence where neither of us moves before he's lifting me by the hips and setting me on the island.

His throat moves with a swallow before he says, "Tell me you're mine, Braxton. Tell me you're never leaving me again, and I'll slide in deep and fuck you until you can't walk tomorrow without feeling me inside of you."

"Never again, Dox. I'm yours," I breathe, holding his stare, meeting the intensity of it with one of my own. The fire in his eyes spreads to my core, and I shudder, pressing my thighs around his hips, drawing him between them.

I watch the space between us when he lines his cock up with my pussy and starts to slip it back and forth over my entrance, coating himself in my arousal. I'm dripping for him, so greedy to feel the stretch and burn that follows the first thrust.

A calloused palm grips my ass cheek, massaging it roughly. "I've been thinking of spanking your ass for weeks. Fucking months, actually. Ever since the first time I saw you again."

My heartbeat kicks up. "So why haven't you?"

I'm playing with fire, and when the corner of his mouth lifts in a dark smile, I know I'm about to get burned in the best way.

"Are you asking me to paint your ass red, sweetheart?"

I shake my head. "No. I'm begging you to."

The air held in my lungs is pushed out all at once when he pulls me from the counter, spins me around, and, with a hand flat on my lower back, bends me over the edge of the island. He flips up the back of my dress and then reaches around me, pulling my breasts from the top before cupping my left one in his hand and squeezing softly.

His beard scrapes the sensitive skin of my neck as he leans in and nips at my earlobe. "I've never seen a more perfect body. You're a fucking masterpiece, Braxton."

"I love you," I croak.

"I love you, baby. I love these hard nipples—" He pinches one between cold fingers before twisting it, sending ripples of pleasure between my thighs. "I love this round ass and how it feels in my hands."

I'm aching, my clit throbbing, and when I try to press my legs together, he steps between them, pushing them open further.

"Maddox," I whimper, pushing my ass back to try and brush his cock.

"Braxton," he coos, drawing a line with his fingers from my breast to my stomach and then lower to the inside of my thigh, where it's slick with my arousal. "I love these thighs . . . the way they press to my ears when I'm lapping at your pretty cunt. And fuck, do I ever love how they feel wrapped tight around my waist as I slip my cock deep inside of you."

A strangled noise claws its way up my throat. "Please."

"Please what?"

He tugs on my nipple, and I press my cheek to the island, seeking the cool feel of it against my flaming skin.

"Spank me. Touch me. Fuck me. Just do *something*. Please," I cry out, looking at him over my shoulder.

The first touch of his palm to my ass makes me jump in surprise, my body curling away from the island and against the body suddenly so close behind me. It's a gentle slap, something to test me, and while I'm thankful for the thought, I need something more.

"Harder," I mutter, wiggling my hips. A shot of excitement

bursts through me when I feel the tip of his cock brush my core. *So close.*

The next hit brings a sting that has arousal leaking from my pussy and dripping down my thighs. I bury my teeth into my bottom lip and moan, dropping my forehead to my wrist.

"Harder?" he grunts, dropping to his haunches behind me and pressing his lips to my burning ass cheek. Shifting slightly, he drags his mouth to the underside of the other cheek, taking the skin between his teeth and biting softly.

"A little." I puff out a breath.

He reaches between my legs and parts my pussy, sinking a finger deep and stroking me as he bites down again.

"Just one more time. I need to be inside of you."

I nod rapidly, holding my breath in preparation. The final smack comes at the same time he slips his finger out and replaces it with his cock, slamming home, making me cry a strangled version of his name.

"That's it, you dirty girl. Fuck, you feel perfect," he grunts, wrapping my hair in his fist and pulling my head back and to the side, just enough that our eyes clash, the air tight between us.

I curl my fingers tight, nails pressing into my palms on the island. My arms are outstretched, every muscle tight. Maddox fucks me hard, each thrust sending me lurching forward, our skin slapping and echoing through the penthouse.

My lungs are burning from a lack of oxygen as I struggle to breathe, too caught up in the bursts of pleasure sparking through my body, building toward a high that I'm so close to reaching.

Maddox grips my hip and yanks me an inch from the edge of the counter, just far enough he can slip a hand between my legs and touch my clit. He rolls it in quick circles, and I moan, pushing back to meet his thrusts.

"So close," I whine.

"Me too, baby. Want you to come with me. Want this pussy milking me dry as I fill you up."

I clench around him, and he picks up speed, fingers pressing deep into my hip.

"You want that? Want me to fill you up and put a baby in you?"

The shock of his question only lasts a beat before I'm coming, my calves cramping and a broken cry tearing up my throat. Maddox folds his body over my back and covers my throat with his hand as I tumble through my orgasm, spasms making me lurch against his chest.

"*Fuck.* So good, baby. So good. I'm right behind you," he groans before his hips stutter and warmth fills me.

My eyes flutter shut as I sag against the counter, my muscles sore as they start to relax. The pressure on my throat is removed as he strokes it gently instead, pressing kisses to my upper back and then down my spine.

He abandons my clit and moves his hand to my stomach instead, his fingers tracing my belly button.

"One day, I really do want to get you pregnant. Is that something that doesn't just turn you on, but you think that you could want?" he murmurs, pulling out and moving back as he continues to kiss down my spine.

I whimper at the loss of his warmth but swallow back my beg for him to come back. His lingering kisses and soft touches feel so good after what just happened. Like the best form of aftercare.

"I want everything with you. Babies and white picket fences and a tree house in the backyard," I reply, twisting my body so that we're facing each other. His eyes are warm on my face as he smiles lazily. "Do you want everything with me?"

He pushes to a stand, tucks himself back into his jeans, and then closes the gap between us, pulling me into his arms.

"Babies, a white picket fence, a tree house in the backyard, and a big diamond ring on your left hand. Everything with you isn't nearly enough."

39

Maddox

In my seven-year career in the NHL, I've been to the final round of the playoffs twice. The first time came during my second season with the Warriors when we lost in game six against Carolina. The second time was two years ago, and while we lost again, we played our asses off and pushed Florida to game seven.

Today, we have our final practice before I get my third chance at the cup tomorrow. And third time's the charm, right?

The first two times I was in this spot, I thought I had something to prove. Like if the team failed, that meant I failed. There was a near-suffocating pressure on me back then, and I'm relieved to know that whatever was causing that pressure is long gone.

Now I'm hungry. Goddamn starving to hold that beautiful silver cup in my hands and give it a sloppy kiss.

The sun has risen already, and I'm too scared to look at my phone to see how little time I have left with Braxton this morning. The past couple of days have been something out of a movie, and even though Braxton's mattress is a far cry from the one in the penthouse, I've been here for the past two nights, a sore back and happy everything else.

A soft sound slips from Braxton's mouth as she stretches her leg over both of mine before flopping to her back. A smile curls my lips as I drop my gaze to her sleepy eyes as they blink at me. She yawns and pulls the heavy reddish-pink blanket up to her chin.

"How long have you been awake?" she asks, voice scratchy with sleep.

"Not long. I feel like a kid on Christmas morning. I'm too ramped up to sleep."

"I'm excited to see you play tomorrow. I'm flying with your family, right? I think that's what your mom said on the phone yesterday."

I roll to my side and stroke my knuckle over her cheek. "That's right. I fly out tonight, and your flight is tomorrow morning."

"Are you going to be able to last a night all by yourself?" she teases.

"Probably not."

She giggles, turning her head to kiss my knuckle. "One game, and then we're back home."

"Hopefully with a win."

"Definitely a win. The Warriors look amazing," she says proudly, chin jutting up.

I pinch it and bring her in for a quick kiss, knowing how much she dislikes kissing too much before brushing her teeth. When I pull away, I bump her nose with mine.

"Thanks, baby girl." I roll to my other side and grab my phone from the nightstand as she does the same. We fall back to the bed at the same time, but Braxton is a whole lot tenser than she was a second ago.

"Something's wrong," she blurts out, fingers tapping quickly on her phone screen.

I turn off the do-not-disturb mode on my own and stiffen at the surge of messages and missed calls that fills the screen. Bits and pieces of each message is all I catch before Dougie's calling.

Answering instantly, I put my phone to my ear. "What happened?" I ask, skipping a hello.

"You need to get to the arena. Now. Bring Braxton with you," he orders. There's a nervous wobble in his voice that I have never *ever* heard before.

My eyes fly to Braxton as she jumps out of bed and hastily gets dressed. Her phone is against her ear, but her words are muttered, quiet.

"Don't blindside me, Dougie. Tell me what's going on, and we'll head there right now," I say.

"I need you to bring everything you have about the break-in with Braxton's car and any proof you have that she's filed a police report. The car window has been repaired, right? Drive it here."

"Slow down, man. Yes, it has—we got it repaired the next day—but what does her car have anything to do with needing to be at the arena? You're freaking me out right now."

There's a shuffle, and then my dad's voice replaces Dougie's. "Hey, Dox. I need you to listen to me right now and not lose your cool once I've finished speaking. You're with Braxton right now, right? Your mom is on the phone with her right now, but you can't freak out and scare her any more than she most likely already is."

I gulp, nodding, even though he can't see me. "Okay," I breathe.

"Have you spoken about the fake relationship agreement recently? Maybe in her car sometime after it was broken into?"

"Uh . . . maybe? We've talked about it lots, Dad. Recently and not so recently."

"Okay. Well, there was another article written on Sports Weekly this morning, and there's a recording of Braxton talking about the agreement, confirming that it was fake and in turn breaking her NDA. They're claiming they recorded a conversation with her after she requested to give an interview with them. It's been picked up on bigger platforms since it was posted and is circulating all over social media now. The VW are pissed, Dox. Really, really pissed. Alexander wants you both in his office as soon as possible."

A cold flush slips from my head to my toes. Panic digs into my gut.

"What do you mean there's a recording of her?"

Dad blows out a heavy exhale. "Dougie and I think there's a bug in her car. We have to look to be sure."

"There is one. She wouldn't have met with a news outlet," I state harshly.

"We know, son."

"She was hurt. She was pushed and hit her head when they planted that bug. She could have—"

"Maddox. Calm down."

"Calm down?" I bark, shoving myself out of bed, fists curled at my sides as I stride out of the room, too scared to look at Braxton on my way out. "Who posted the article? Tell me the name of this guy so I can teach him not to fuck with my family. I wonder how he would like getting shoved onto the concrete."

"Rose Carpenter."

I freeze.

"Fuck!" I shout, squeezing my eyes shut. That fucking snake. "What are they saying about my girl, Dad? Why is Mom on the phone with her?"

"She's just telling her exactly what I'm telling you because we knew you would be too upset to do it. It will be okay. We'll get this figured out," he attempts to reassure me.

"Alexander needs to watch his mouth around her. The minute he tries to pin this on her, I'm done."

"We're going to be with you to make sure that doesn't happen, and then we'll figure everything else out together."

"The cops said it was just an attempted carjacking. That she interrupted the guy and he pushed her to get away. They pulled the security footage from the clinic, but the guy wore a mask. Nothing came from it. It won't prove anything to Alex."

"Worth a shot. A broken NDA is serious. We need anything that could help take the heat off of her. As far as your contract goes . . ."

"You don't think there will be one. Yeah, I figured as much."

"Dox," Braxton calls. I whip my head around to see her standing a couple of feet away, eyes brimming with tears.

"We'll be there as soon as we can," I mutter, lifting my arm and ushering her toward me.

She rushes over and burrows her face in my naked chest as I wrap my arm around her and rub her back.

"I love you, Maddox. It'll be okay," Dad says.

I steal some of his confidence for myself, filling my depleted tank. "I love you too, Dad. Thank you."

"You're welcome."

We hang up, and the next second, I'm pulling Braxton closer, dropping my chin to her head. She smells like me mixed with her shampoo, and I sniff her like a fucking dog, trying to calm myself.

"I'm sorry," she whispers.

"This isn't your fault."

"It's my voice out there. It was my car that was broken into. Hell, it was most likely my dad that orchestrated this entire thing."

"The actions of that man are not on you, and the actions of a low-life who broke into your car and *hurt* you sure as shit aren't either. I don't blame you for this, and I don't want you to blame yourself for it either."

"This was supposed to fix everything."

Frustrated that she doesn't understand how deeply I care for her, I rest my hands on her arms and move her away from my chest, staring down at her with my heart on my sleeve.

"This agreement might not have fixed my career, but it fixed the most important thing to me. You're here, baby. You're in my arms and in my fucking life, just like you should have always been. My greatest mistake in life is letting you run from me, and

I would give up my career in a heartbeat if it meant that I don't ever have to lose you again. Fuck the VW, and fuck this Rose woman. I can't live without you again. I won't."

"I won't stand between you and your future, Maddox. I did that once, and while you've forgiven me for it, I don't know if I'll ever forgive myself. I regret a lot of things from my past, but my greatest mistake is letting my own selfish wants almost ruin your future.

"It killed me to leave you. But look at what happened after. You're a four-time Art Ross trophy winner and are about to play in the Stanley Cup finals for the third time in seven years. I don't know if those things would have happened if I had stayed, but I do know that we're on the cusp of reliving our past, and I refuse to be an obstacle you have to overcome again."

I shake my head, cupping her cheeks. "No. You're not doing this again. I'm not letting you back out. We're going to wipe away these tears and go to the arena and deal with this together. Nobody is sacrificing anything this time. Do you understand me?"

She drops her eyes, tears leaking from the corners. I brush them away with my thumbs.

"This is not the same as last time. I'm not a lost cause without Vancouver. It isn't Vancouver or nothing. I just need you to put your faith in me here, Curly. Please, let me take care of this," I beg.

"Can you promise that you aren't going to resent me for this?"

My answer is instant. There isn't an ounce of hesitation or doubt in my mind. I've never been surer of anything besides my complete devotion to her.

"I promise."

Her eyes search mine for a long, silent piece of time. Nerves fill my chest.

"Okay." She breathes in and out slowly. "Okay. You should get dressed before we leave."

I furrow my brows and tilt her face up when she continues to stare at the ground. "Hey. I love you, Braxton. This is a forever-type thing. Got it?"

She nods, trying to smile, but it's weak. Completely unconvincing.

"I know. I'm just . . . I'm trying to get a grasp on this situation. I didn't think my dad would go this far to get what he wants. I was hurt, Dox. I was actually physically hurt because of this. Yeah, he might not have thought the guy would end up shoving me, but he did. What am I supposed to do here?"

"We talk to everyone and go from there. Once we have all of the details, we can make a plan. I'll be here for you no matter what you choose to do, okay?"

Her shoulders deflate as she moves back into my arms. "Okay, Dox. I trust you."

I hold her tight, letting her trust in me sink into my mind. As much as I wish I could fix this with pretty words and promises, I have to prove to her that we can get through this. That starts with getting this sorted out before anything else can fall into our laps. I just hope I'm ready for the consequences of whatever choice I'm going to have to make.

40

Maddox

THE ARENA IS FREEZING WHEN WE ENTER, HEADING STRAIGHT FOR Alexander's office. Braxton's fingers are squeezing mine tight, and I hate how terrified she looks right now. Seeing her so afraid only pisses me off more, and that's not a great way to start a conversation with my boss.

Although, at this point, I'm not sure he even counts as my boss anymore. Not after we're finished with this conversation, at least.

The realization is daunting. It's one that's been bouncing around in my skull since we left the penthouse, and still, I can't get a good grasp of it. Of what it means or what will come next for me in this league.

We turn the corner, and the closed office door comes into view. Braxton sucks in a tight breath, and I squeeze her hand, stroking the back of it with my thumb when we come to a stop. A rock lodges in my throat when she pushes her shoulders back and looks up at me with a completely fake smile.

"Not for me, sweetheart. You don't need to wear a mask for me," I tell her softly.

She blinks, and her lips roll. "I know. This is for me. I can't walk in there looking like a wounded deer, or I'm going to get eaten alive."

"I'm proud of you."

The hint of a real smile. "Good."

"We're walking out of here together, better than we were when we walked in," I remind her.

"Okay," she breathes.

I tap a finger beneath her chin and then lift it, bending to kiss her softly. She pushes up on her tiptoes and returns the gesture, lips parting with mine, our breath curling together.

"Okay, let's get this over with," she whispers.

Drifting my thumb across her bottom lip, I nod and take a step back.

As we cover the last of the distance between us and the office door, I clear my throat. "Nobody is going to let anything happen to you."

"I know," she says, confident.

After taking another look at her, I rap my knuckles against the door and slip on my own mask just as it's pulled open. The scowl on the face of the man who opened it makes me step inside first, shifting Braxton behind me slightly as we enter.

"Maddox," Alex says, voice gritty. "Braxton."

"Alexander."

"Hi," Braxton whispers.

He shuts the door, and I lead Braxton toward where my dad and Dougie are sitting on the long leather couch. Dad gives her a brief smile as she sits beside him, leaving enough room at the end of the couch for me to sandwich her in. Dougie's stare grips mine when I glance in his direction, and the barely restrained rage in them is enough to give away just how terrible their conversation prior to our arrival has gone.

I sit beside Braxton and drop my hand to her thigh in both a reassuring and protective gesture.

"Now that we're all here, why don't you continue what you were saying, Alex? I don't particularly want to sit here on this couch like a scolded child for longer than necessary," Dougie says through clenched teeth.

I have to hide my surprise, not used to him taking that tone with anyone.

Alexander's eyes narrow on him. "I'm only going to remind you once where you are right now."

"We haven't forgotten," Dad puts in, jaw ticking.

"Excellent." Alex looks at me then, a coldness to him that I was expecting. "You've made a mess. One that makes us look like shit. I'm not going to beat around the bush with this. You need to make some hard choices here."

"What are these choices?" I ask.

"I'm assuming you've already been filled in on what's happened, but I would like to recap. Sports Weekly has not only uploaded an article claiming we set up this relationship to cover our asses, but they have audio confirmation that proves them right. Douglas and your father have told me that this audio was collected illegally, but if I'm to be blunt, it doesn't change anything.

"There isn't a single person out there who believes our narrative now, and it's put this organization in quite the predicament. Every main sports page has posted about this situation, and it has spread like a wildfire. The fans aren't happy. Both ours and yours."

"If their proof is proven false, you're really telling me it doesn't change anything? It's not our fault someone went to such extremes to ruin all of us. Not just me," I grit out.

His eyes blaze. "While it might not be your fault that someone went to those lengths, it is your fault that we had to build this story in the first place. You and that deadbeat brother of yours were the cause of this mess. I only did what I could to fix your mess."

Silence. Edgy, tense silence. And then, "What did you call my son?"

One look at my father's face has me standing and moving in

front of him, blocking his view of Alex. "Dad," I mutter in warning.

"For fuck's sake, Oakley. Noah was the cause of all of this, and you still won't do anything about him. I may be your friend, but I won't hold my tongue when it comes to that boy," Alex growls, clearly not caring that Dad is about to send him through a goddamn wall.

Even as my head fills with questions as to why Alex even cares about Noah or my family at all for that matter right now, I stay where I am, refusing to let my dad join this fight.

"Noah isn't a part of this right now. This is about me and my own mistakes. I'm not denying that I fucked up. But this right here? This isn't my fault. So, tell me what you need me to do to fix it," I say.

He pins me with a withering glare. "You're noble, Maddox. You always have been. I'll give you that."

"What does that mean?"

"If you want to point the finger away from your brother, it should be on the woman behind you. We all know that for the most part, you were a victim of circumstance."

"A victim of circumstance?" I sputter. "The woman has a name, and she isn't the cause of this. You're the one who brought Braxton into this. You could have left her be, but you wanted to throw shit in Roy Heights' face, and she was the easiest way for you to do it."

His tongue pokes at the inside of his cheek as he sniffs. "You asked what your choices were going forward. And now I'm telling you, it's her or us. Either put the blame on her publicly for this entire thing, or you're done here. Keep in mind that at the end of the day, we also have a broken NDA on our hands."

"Are you blackmailing him? Fuck, Alex. We're not going down this NDA route. You know that's a far-fetched plan if we can find evidence that she didn't break it, which I'm positive we will the minute we start ripping her car apart," Dougie cuts in.

Alex laughs, but it's bitter. "If Maddox wants a contract

with the Warriors next season, he's going to do exactly as I ask. There's no other way to fix this for us. The Warriors organization comes first here, not the feelings of a woman or a player who's lucky to still even be here in the first place."

"You've been dragging your feet on this contract for months. I want to know the truth before we even continue this conversation," Dad says.

"I want more than the truth. I want a contract in front of me right the fuck now," Dougie adds.

I rear back. "Are you kidding me? I don't need to see a contract because I'm not going to say shit about Braxton. I'm not going there."

"What would he need to say?" Braxton asks, and four sets of eyes fly toward her. She doesn't shrink under the pressure of it all, and I want to shout how proud I am of her while also shaking some sense into her.

Alex sidesteps me and focuses on her. "He needs to say that this was real for him, but you were playing him the entire time. Everyone needs to think that you were simply playing a hand for your father. You lied to Rose Carpenter about the fake dating arrangement to make Maddox look bad. Like father, like daughter."

"You want me to be your scapegoat," she says.

He nods. "Exactly."

"Braxton," Dad mutters, shaking his head at her. "Let us take care of this."

My girl gives him a soft smile before slipping her eyes over me—an apology glistening in the deep blue—and finding Alex again.

"And if he does this, he'll still be a Warrior next season?"

"I don't need a contract from you, Alex. You know damn fucking well that I don't need you anymore. I'm not doing this," I interrupt, taking a step forward only to have Dad hold me back this time, a hand clamped around my wrist.

Alex ignores me and walks to his desk, grabbing a thin stack of paper and bringing it to Dougie.

"Yes. If he does this, he'll be a Warrior for the next eight years. I've already had the GM draw up the contract. Eight seasons, twelve million dollars a year."

Braxton gasps at the high number, and I stiffen further, my muscles burning.

"So, I'll have a contract, a fat bank account, and be miserable every single day because of what it ended up costing me? No, thanks. I'll take my chances at free agency," I say, spinning to face Braxton. Her eyes are wide, cheeks flushed. "We're leaving."

"Maddox," she starts softly, but I shake my head.

"I'm assuming you still want me at practice today, or are you going to risk the Stanley Cup finals without me?" I ask Alex, still staring at my girl.

"Be at practice," he grinds out, anger vibrating in the words.

I nod. "Then we're leaving. You can talk to Dougie on my behalf from now on. There's nothing else I have to say."

I'm grateful when Braxton stands, moving toward me. As soon as she's within arm's distance, I'm pulling her into me, breathing her in to try and calm down.

I glance at Dad over Braxton's head and watch as he nods at me, a heavy sense of understanding in his stare.

"The offer won't be around for long, Maddox. I would think carefully about what you could be giving up," Alex says as I start to lead Braxton out of the office. If I didn't know better, I would think there's a hint of desperation in the words.

"I already have, and I'm not losing her again," I say before walking out of the room, wanting nothing more than to just toss Braxton over my shoulder and run away from this place. From all of this.

Neither of us speaks on the way to the parking garage, and I think that's because we don't know what to say. If I'm still reeling from everything that was said back there, I can't imagine what's going on in her head right now.

I would be lying if I said that didn't scare me.

Her car is in the spot we left it, tucked between Dad's truck and the concrete wall with a Reserved parking sign hung from it.

The ride here was spent in silence, not because we were both too nervous to speak, but because we still weren't sure if there was a bug, and now that we're here again, I'm not reliving that experience.

I'm finding this fucking bug.

"Unlock the doors for me, baby girl," I mutter, a hand on the driver's door.

She does, and I tear open the door. I'm frantic as I dig through the car, blood pumping in my ears. I root through the things in every compartment there is, every crevice and dip, and still come up empty. It's not until I slide my hand along the underside of the passenger seat that I feel it.

A curse claws its way up my throat as I rip it out and push out of the car. The small black device that caused so much trouble feels so breakable in my hand, and after taking a picture of it to send to my dad and Dougie, I shove it in my jean pocket.

"Fuck," I mutter.

"You were right," Braxton whispers. "I think I feel more creeped out than angry."

"I'm sorry. Shit, this is all my fault." I dig my fingers into my hair and pull.

She grabs my forearms, and I let go of my hair.

"No. It's not. You didn't hire someone to break into my car and put a listening device inside. But I know who did, and I need to go talk to him."

My eyes fly up. "Let me come."

"No. I need to do this on my own. He's my dad, even if he's an awful one."

"Are you sure?"

She nods. "I can't keep doing this with him. Even if he doesn't listen to me, I have to talk to him. And you need to talk to your dad. There's a lot on the line here, Maddox. You can't be hotheaded."

My lungs tighten. "I don't like your tone, Curly. We're going to get this cleaned up and then get back to where we were this morning."

I don't know who I'm trying to convince. Her or me.

She offers me a smile. "I know. But it's going to take some time."

"Not a lot of it."

Her hands link behind my head as she pulls me down and kisses me fiercely, like she's scared it's the last one she'll ever get. I slip my arms up her back and kiss her just as eagerly, pushing her up against the car. Fitting myself against her, I hold her hips in my palms and squeeze.

"Go talk to your dad and then come right back to me, okay? Practice will probably run until five, but then I'm all yours," I murmur against her lips.

She moans softly, burying her face in my neck. "I love you."

"I love you too, Curly Fry. Forever and always."

41

Braxton

THERE'S A HOLLOW FEELING IN MY CHEST AS I WALK UP MY PARENTS' driveway. Like I've already tucked my heart away in a protective case in preparation for this inevitable conversation. Maybe his words won't hurt as much now . . . or maybe they'll hurt just as bad.

My mind is a jumbled mess of skittish thoughts and terrifying probabilities. How can things go so wrong so quickly? One second, you're floating on cloud nine, and the next, you're an ant crushed beneath a steel-toed boot. Or in my case, a victim of a vengeful father who cares more about his career than his family.

I swallow past the rock in my throat and test the door to see if it's locked, surprised to find it's not. That's not the most surprising thing, though, because as soon as I walk inside, I'm met with dozens of moving boxes in the doorway, each with elegant handwriting on the side labelling which room each box should go to.

"Mom?" I call, shutting the door softly and moving through the maze of boxes. Pulling open the flaps of the smaller one on the entry table, I freeze with my finger on an old photo frame.

These are baby photos. Anna's and mine.

The photo at the top is of the two of us in the sandbox we

used to have in the backyard. It was one of those plastic ones you could buy in different colours and shapes. Ours was a green turtle.

Anna has to be no more than three in the photo, which would have made me seven or so. She's sitting in front of me, a tiny pink shovel in one hand as she fills a matching bucket with sand. I'm dropping sand into her hair, grinning like an absolute fool.

My chest squeezes as I step away from that box and start to open others. One after another, I tear open the flaps, my heart rate increasing with each open box.

Mom's clothes, her shoes, my great-grandmother's fancy dishes we've only ever used for Christmas dinner. I suck in a tight breath and rub at my chest.

"Your mother isn't here."

I whip around to find Dad standing at the bottom of the staircase, fingers tight around the railing. He looks almost unfamiliar, like a ghost of a past I don't want to revisit. His dark eyes hold little to no emotion as he watches me stand frozen, confused.

"Where is she?"

"Probably with your aunt. The moving truck she hired to move her things should be here in an hour, if you wanted to wait for her."

I pinch my brows. "I didn't know she was moving out."

"We signed the divorce papers this morning."

Shock nearly renders me speechless. "You what?" I whisper.

"Don't act surprised. It's not shocking. She's been seeing someone else for months. The only surprising thing here is that she thought I didn't know."

"What?" I wheeze. My lungs pinch, making it hard to breathe.

Dad darts his eyes away before I can determine whether or not he's the slightest upset about this. I know they weren't happy . . . but he really doesn't feel anything? He's that cold?

"His name is Ritchie. He's an accountant for a large firm

downtown. No children. Widowed," he says, listing these off as if they're as casual as items on a grocery list.

"Why wouldn't she have told me she was seeing someone?"

His gaze settles on me again, but I force myself not to buy into the slight spark of emotion in them. "You have a soft heart, Braxton. Knowing she was staying with me for the sake of you and your sister would have crushed you."

"I already knew that. Were you under the impression that me or Anna thought she was with you because she loved you? It's been obvious you haven't loved each other for years."

"Oh."

"Oh?" I repeat, in awe. "Do you think that because we knew you weren't happy together that that somehow makes it okay? Anna doesn't ever want to get married one day because of you. Doesn't that bug you at all?"

"That's her choice. Marriage isn't for everyone."

I let out a bitter laugh. "It wasn't her choice, though. Not really. You and Mom did that to her. You would have done it to me, too, had it not been for the Huttons."

A dark cast slips over his face as he curls his lip. "You're not a Hutton, Braxton. You're a Heights. It's time you started to remember that."

"Not yet," I retort, snapping my spine straight.

"Not yet?" he repeats slowly.

"You said I'm not a Hutton. You're right. I'm not a Hutton *yet*. But I will be."

His knuckles turn as white as snow on the railing as he grips it tighter and grinds his jaw hard. I wait to hear a crack, but it never comes.

"You deserve better," he spits.

"You have no idea *what* I deserve! You don't care about anybody but yourself. You never have. It's been all about you for decades!" I shout, hands curled into fists at my sides.

"I've done what I've done for our family!"

"What family? Do you see one here? Because I don't. You

don't have a family because there isn't a single one of us who can stand to be around you. You hired someone to break into my car and didn't even call when that person sent me to the hospital!"

A rush of cool air hits my cheek, and I realize it's wet, stained with tears. My anger grows, both at him and myself for not being stronger.

"I never hired that guy. And I didn't know you were hurt. Nobody told me," he mutters. His eyes soften slightly, and I nearly flinch. "Are you okay?"

I ignore his concern, not buying it. "You expect me to believe you didn't have anything to do with what's just happened? The article that calls me desperate and naïve and calls Maddox a money-hungry fraud?"

I might have looked over the article as I sat on the driveway outside before collecting the nerve to get out of the car. It doesn't paint me in a good light, despite its false narrative as an interview I had willingly given, and it paints Maddox even worse. The audio she had of me is obviously not from a real interview. It sounds like it was recorded from inside a backpack.

"I never denied that I was involved in the article, just in the hiring of that man. I would never put you in harm's way. I distinctly told Rose to bug Maddox's vehicle. Not yours. It's not my fault she decided to do whatever she wanted."

"Is that how you get yourself to fall asleep at night? By convincing yourself of things that aren't true? Does the guilt ever get too much? Too heavy?" I ask, wiping at the tracks of tears on my cheeks.

"What do you want me to say, Braxton? You won't accept any apology I give you, so I'm not going to bother."

I shake my head, dread heavy in my chest. "You're right. I don't want you to apologize because I know you won't mean it. I want you to own up to what you've done. To accept that it was wrong and evil. I want you to tell me that you'll stop and leave this alone. I want you to be a real father and put my happiness above your own, because Maddox Hutton makes me happy, and no matter what you try to do to tear him down and make him pay for your mistakes, you will never win. The only thing you'll continue to win at is being alone and miserable."

The silence echoes in the empty, cold house. Roy stares at the floor and scratches at his jaw, grip loosening on the railing.

At one time in my life, this man was my hero. The protector of my kingdom. But that time has passed, and I've learned that not every hero deserves his happily ever after. Sometimes, the hero is just a villain in disguise.

"I want you to tell me that you love me and that that is enough to break this hideous cycle, because if you continue to hurt the people I love, you will never see me again," I finish, heart in my stomach.

I stand and wait for a reply, but when one never comes, I wipe at my eyes one final time and then turn around. There's nothing impressive about the way I steel my spine and lift my chin as I start to walk out, because it's all an act. A way to pretend that I'm not hurting inside because a man who was supposed to love me no matter what, every single day for forever, has chosen revenge instead, knowing just how badly that would hurt me.

My nose burns as I weave through the mess of boxes and set my hand on the doorknob. I nearly jump out of my skin when footsteps sound behind me before coming to an abrupt stop.

"What would you need me to do, Braxton?" he croaks.

My shoulders fall, a wobbly breath escaping me as I hang my head, knowing full well Maddox is going to hate this.

"Get me an interview with Rose Carpenter."

Maddox

"HUTTON! Where the fuck is your head?" Coach yells from the boards.

I can feel his glare boring holes in my back as I miss another pass from Bentley and narrowly avoid the urge to toss my stick across the ice.

Practice has been a nightmare. I don't want to be here. My head isn't in it. I haven't stopped thinking about Braxton since the moment I watched her drive off, and this bad feeling in my gut won't lay off.

"Set up again! Nobody is leaving here until Hutton makes a fucking shot."

My forwards offer me sympathetic smiles as we set up again, and Bentley starts skating to the net, grabbing a puck along the way. I take a deep breath and move along my side of the ice, prepping for the pass. Sliding into the slot, I prepare for the pass, but as soon as I get the puck, I shoot it off and completely miss the net. It tings off the crossbar, and I lose it.

My stick comes down on the boards, and the crack that follows tells me I've broken it. I drop it on the ice and rip off my gloves next, tucking them beneath my arm as I throw my body over the boards and take off down the hallway.

"Maddox! Enough of the tantrums! Bring your ass back here right now before I bench you for the next game," Coach threatens, but I keep walking.

This team means nothing to me anymore. Not after what happened earlier.

I come thundering into the locker room and start shredding off my gear. The Hutton on the back of my jersey doesn't give me the same thrill it did a year ago. Back then, it was everything. Now? Now it's just a name on a jersey.

It only takes me five minutes to get dressed in normal clothes again, but it's five minutes that Alex has had to come fucking find me, most likely having been at our practice. Or more specifically, me.

"Get back out there, Maddox. Now. You're a grown man, not a child who throws tantrums when he's playing like a rookie," he snaps, and I find him blocking the door with his arms crossed.

"No," I say, tossing my bag over my shoulder.

"No? If you want to see the game tomorrow, you sure as shit are going to get back out there and finish that practice."

"I don't want to play tomorrow. I'm done, Alex. Now, get out of my way."

He drops his arm and takes a step toward me. "You're not done. You're still under contract."

"So don't pay me for the next seven games."

I try to move around him, but he follows. "Maddox, I've known you since you were a boy. Don't do this. Don't throw your career away for that girl a second time. It'll be a mistake you might never recover from again."

I huff a laugh. "You keep saying that, but choosing Braxton is the easiest decision I have ever made. Even if I never stepped foot on NHL ice again, I would absolutely, without a doubt, make this decision again. So, please, take your offer and your pleas, and shove them up your ass."

His jaw falls open, and I use his surprise to shove past him, my shoulder smashing into his.

"Oh, and if I find out you're planning anything against Braxton, I will make your life a living hell. And I mean that with every fibre of my being."

And then I leave the Vancouver Warriors locker room for the very last time.

42

Oakley

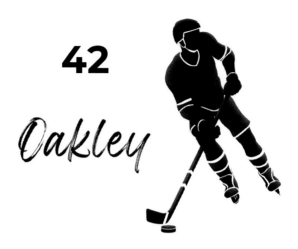

THE DOORBELL RINGS, AND AVA'S ALREADY AT THE DOOR, USHERING Alex inside our home before shooting me a soft, encouraging smile and heading back to the patio where she left Adalyn. She's putting on a strong front, but I know how hard this has all been on her, watching Maddox and Braxton struggle like this without having a solution at the ready to fix it all.

I'm tense on the living room couch, one of my wife's favourite movies droning on in the background. My nerves are frayed, betrayal thick in my veins, and as much as I want to skip this meeting altogether, I know that I can't. It needs to happen.

"Oakley," Alex says gruffly, about as impressed to be summoned here as I am to have asked him to come.

His usual pristine attire has been wrinkled, a button loose on his dress shirt and a cufflink missing on the sleeve. Short grey hairs stick up in all directions, as if he's been yanking on them for a while.

Having known Alexander since his father was the owner of the Warriors, I would have called us good friends. He's been there for my family for over two decades, and while we weren't the Friday dinners at six every week and Christmas gift-giving type of close, I thought we had a better relationship than I've come to see over the past couple of months.

He was there for me when I retired after my final shoulder injury, was there for Maddox's first U6 hockey game, and was even one of our visitors at the hospital after Ava's emergency C-section with Adalyn.

His betrayal hurts more now than it would have years ago. Maybe because I really didn't see it coming. I was blindsided. My entire family was.

"Alex." I don't stand and greet him, choosing to let him come to me instead.

"I cancelled a meeting for this." He sits beside me, his body stiff. The energy around him screams *fuck off*, and I'm sure mine is pretty close to the same.

"You're lucky that's all you've had to do, Alex. What is going on?"

"An hour ago, your son told me that he's done playing for me. Did you know he was going to do that?"

"Would it matter if I did? I didn't know we were still being open with one another."

Maddox didn't tell me he was going to walk out today, but I can't say that I blame him for it. If he *were* to have given me a heads-up, I would have told him to do whatever felt right. Clearly, that's exactly what he did.

I'm proud of him. *So damn proud.* All I've ever wanted is for my children to be happy, and knowing that my boy is chasing his happiness makes me feel like I've done something right.

Happiness doesn't have to come from success or popularity. My wife and children are my happiness. They always have been. Everything else has been an added bonus, and Maddox sees things the exact same way.

What isn't there to be proud of?

"You should have warned me. Should have talked to me about it. I would have tried to talk him off the ledge. What am I supposed to do now? The team is in shambles. There's no way we'll make it past the fourth game," he spits.

"What did you think was going to happen? You might not have been close to my children while they were growing up, Alex, but you were still around. There's no way you didn't know better than to tell my son to choose you and your team over Braxton. If you thought for even a second that he would choose you, you're dumber than I thought you were."

"I did what I thought would save this team, Oakley. I saw a possible fix for the mess your sons caused and tried to make it work. Clearly, I should have thought of something else, but it's too late for that now."

"I need you to be honest with me, Alex," I mutter, narrowing my eyes on him. "I want to know your relationship with Rose Carpenter, and I want to know your relationship with Roy Heights. I need answers here."

His face pales as he exhales slowly. Whether he's decided enough is enough or he just doesn't care anymore, he doesn't hold back any longer.

"Alright. I didn't know she was going to write that article about Maddox and Noah, and I didn't know that she had Braxton's car bugged. When I met her, I didn't even know she was a reporter, let alone one for that rag tabloid."

Surprise shackles me. "You're sleeping with her, aren't you?"

"I was. I cut things off with her after she wrote that first article. I think the bug and the most recent story was a mix of retaliation for the breakup and an opportunity to make a name for herself. The messages I got before and after the latest story ran helped fit the pieces together. I've had a PI watching her for the past couple of weeks," he admits, face flaming with shame.

"You've what? What messages?" I grit out, fingers itching to curl into fists.

"I've had a private investigator watching her, trying to find something I could use to get her to shut up. We've found out a lot about her, stuff that could help. And her messages are what you would expect from a crazy woman. Ones that said I would regret leaving her and that I deserved what was coming. She thinks me breaking up with her is some sort of punishable crime."

"So, this was never about my son? Or Braxton? This was all about you and your dick?" I ask, growing more livid with each second that passes. "You blamed my son, withheld a contract from him, and blackmailed him . . . all because you got involved with the wrong woman?"

He pushes his shoulders back, going on the defensive. "Slow down. This wouldn't have even happened if Maddox hadn't gotten involved in Noah's drama. The whole addict narrative Rose played at? That's all on your youngest son."

"You know, I'm getting really sick of you throwing Noah back at me. Are you really holding on to some grudge against a twenty-year-old because of an article the woman you were sleeping with wrote?" I shake my head, laughing incredulously. "Unbelievable."

"The VW are my legacy! You can't possibly understand what it's like to be me right now," he snaps.

"You're right. And you can't understand what it's like to be me right now, a father watching his son be torn apart by the public because of a man twice his age who cares more about himself than anyone else."

"You know that isn't true," he says.

"No? Fine. Tell me how Roy ties into this. Is it really coincidence that he's hip and hip with Rose? Or do you have more involvement than you're telling me."

He flinches. "You really think I would have allowed Roy to say such awful things about Maddox? About my organization?"

"So, that's a no? You're not involved with him?"

"No. Believe it or not, but his relationship with the woman I was sleeping with is coincidental. I think he just wanted to find someone desperate and with something to prove, and that just happened to be her."

I push out a breath, rubbing at my jaw. "You understand how it's hard to believe you."

"I do. But I'm asking you to try. I've been your friend for a long time. Back when it was my dad running the show. I might have done a lot of shit that I wish I could take back, but I would never sabotage your family."

He seems honest, but my protective nature makes it hard to believe a damn thing he's saying. It's not as easy as reminding myself of our friendship and letting it go. This is my family on the line here.

"Why the wait for Maddox's contract? Why not offer it to him sooner, before this all happened?"

He huffs a rough laugh. "I was trying to find the money. The new GM is a disappointment. He offered too much to too many guys last season, and I needed to figure out a way to make it work."

A small tinge of guilt settles in my stomach, but I ignore it, nodding tightly.

"You need to let Maddox make his own choices, Alex. Without judgment or your petty threats. Own up to your part in this, and stop blaming everyone else. He's not going to change his mind on this, and pushing him even harder is only going to make things worse," I say shortly.

His jaw pulses, eyes drifting shut for a moment before opening again. "You're asking me to let my best player skip out on the final round of the playoffs and potentially cost the VW a shot at the cup."

I shake my head. "No. I'm asking you to leave my family alone. As a friend. And to help me get rid of Rose Carpenter."

Braxton

THE SPORTS WEEKLY office is small, tucked between a pet store and a seemingly empty hole-in-the-wall diner. Only a handful of cars are parked in the joint lot.

All it took was a quick phone call from my father to get an interview arranged for this afternoon. Rose Carpenter is a snake in high grass—impossible to see coming until it's too late. But I'm ready, and I refuse to be taken by surprise again.

If a story is what she wants, then that's what she'll get. I'd do anything for Maddox, and if this will save his career, I'm going to risk the fallback. I will never let him suffer at my expense again.

My phone vibrates in the pocket of my jeans again, and I ignore it. Just like I have the past three times it started to vibrate.

I step inside the office and take in the strong smell of coffee and concerning number of potted plants. There's a young woman at the front desk, spinning the desk chair in circles and blowing bubbles in bright pink gum. As soon as she spots me, she lurches in the chair and pops the bubble between her lips, sucking it back into her mouth.

"Hello! Oh my God, I am so sorry about that," she rushes out.

I stifle a laugh. "It's fine. I'm here to see Rose? We have a meeting at four thirty."

She nods, dipping her head toward the computer and beginning to type. A second later, she's bringing the corded phone to her ear and making a call to her boss.

"Mhm. Okay. I'll send her back," she says before setting the phone down. Clearing her throat, she glances up at me, smiling timidly. "You can head back. First door on the right."

I'm not sure why I expected Rose to come rushing out to lead me to her office herself, but I'm a bit surprised she didn't. For someone as hungry for a story as she is, I was ready for a bit more . . . excitement.

"Thank you," I tell the receptionist before brushing past the desk.

There are only two other offices across from Rose's—one door open and the other closed—and a staff room at the end of the hall. A few frames line the walls with small snippets of articles and a signed photo of the Warriors in their retro jerseys from last year.

Suddenly, the door to Rose's office flies open and she steps out, wearing a navy pantsuit and heels so high they should come with a safety warning. Her thick black hair is tied in a pretty bun at the base of her head, and her makeup is applied flawlessly.

If she weren't out to get me and my man, I might have asked her for some tips.

"Braxton Heights," she greets me, painting a sly smile on her glossy lips. "I'm so happy you decided to come in. I've been wanting to talk to you for a while now."

She shifts to clear the doorway, and I walk past her, trying to bite my tongue but failing.

"Oh, but I thought we already had an interview?"

Sitting on one of the dusty pink chairs in front of her desk, I watch her fumble slightly from my peripheral vision as she walks past me and then sits in her desk chair.

"Your father told me about your quick comebacks. I should have been better prepared."

I hum. "I heard my father also told you not to bug my car, but you did that anyway."

If it weren't for the heavy bob of her throat, she wouldn't have given her discomfort away. Her face stays blank as I stare at her, accusation heavy in my eyes.

"I don't know what you're talking about, but I did hear about your head. I hope you're doing okay."

"You can drop the act, Rose. I might be here to talk, but I'm not going to give you anything you can use unless you give me some answers. Let's be honest with each other here."

She blinks, her lips twisting as she pushes forward in her chair and folds her hands on her desk.

"And here I was hoping this would be a civil conversation," she says bitterly.

"Oh, it can be. Are you ready to answer my questions?"

"What questions do you want answered?"

"Let's start with your relationship with my father. How did you meet?"

"He came in after Maddox was seen outside of that bar. He said he had a story that would help put me on the map, one that would help guarantee me a spot at a bigger, better news outlet."

None of that is surprising to me.

"And you just took his words and ran with them? You didn't think to verify any of the claims?" I throw back.

She laughs, staring at me as if I'm completely clueless.

"Are you kidding? No. I took the story and ran with it. I'm a journalist writing for a tabloid, Braxton. I take what I get and hope that the story blows up. And that's exactly what it did."

"And journalists usually hire people to break into vehicles and bug them? You are aware that that's a criminal offense, right?" I ask through gritted teeth.

"Are you saying you have proof of those claims?"

My lips part, a quick retort at the ready when I swallow it down, a commotion outside of the office stealing our attention.

"You can't go back there, sir. She's in a meeting!" the pretty receptionist shouts over the scuffle of feet on the floor.

"I know. And I'm about to be involved in that meeting," Oakley snaps.

I spin around in the chair, my eyes widening when I see Maddox's dad storm into the office, a dirty glare on his face. He steps up behind my chair and sets a hand on my shoulder, staring above me at Rose.

"Whatever it is you thought you were getting from Braxton

today isn't happening. You're going to sit there and listen to what I have to say, and then you will never speak my son's name or my daughter-in-law's name again," he states, confidence dripping from every word.

I don't even have time to digest the label he just gave me before Rose is laughing, the sound grating.

"That's a pretty big claim. It's nice to meet you, Oakley Hutton."

He snorts a laugh. "I bet it is."

Rose's face sours. "You are aware that you can't just bust into other people's interviews, correct?"

"Was there an interview? Or were you just talking out of your ass?"

I bite the inside of my cheek to keep from laughing, and Oakley gently squeezes my shoulder as if he knows.

"Right. Well, if you came here to insult me, I would appreciate it if you left," Rose says.

"Have you checked your email in the past few minutes?" Oakley asks her casually, and hell if that cold tone of voice wouldn't have intimidated me if I were in her shoes.

She blinks, once, twice, and then her eyes are flying toward her screen, fingers tapping on the keyboard. It's like watching the main character in a horror film peek out of the door to scan their surroundings, only to find the axed murderer waiting a few feet away. Her entire face goes alight with fear.

"Where did you get this? Who took these photos?" she breathes, wide eyes looking forward at the screen.

"Never underestimate the power of money, Rose. Threatening two very wealthy men while you have nothing might have been the biggest mistake you've ever made. Now, are you ready to talk about what happens next? Because I sure am."

"I never threatened you!" she squeaks.

"You threatened my family. The people I love and care about. You would have been better off threatening my money or reputation," he growls.

I swallow heavily, questions running through my head that I know I won't have answers to until Oakley and I walk out of here. A near-crippling feeling of appreciation throttles me, and I have to blink back the emotion it brings with it.

"What happens next?" she asks, suddenly timid.

"You're going to retract your latest story and create another, one that portrays my son as the person he is, not the one you've made him out to be. I want Braxton's animal adoption day to be highlighted, along with information about when and where it is. And then, I want you to forget that my family exists. You won't write about them again. Hell, don't even think about them again.

"If you fail to do that, everyone will know that one of the most popular up-and-coming sports journalists—the one who had the balls to come at the Hutton family—actually has a heavy gambling problem and has been stealing money from Alexander Torrello's bank account as payback for him breaking up with her to fund said problem. He might be rich, Rose, but all it takes is one close look to find out what's really been happening. You have confidence, though. I can't think of a person off the top of my head who would stoop as low as to steal the bank information of a man who spent his nights sharing her bed. I'll give you that."

My jaw slacks. She was dating Alexander? And gambling? Really? She doesn't look like a gambler, but I guess I don't really know what that does look like.

"Oh my God," she rushes out. "Yes. Fine. And this information . . . these pictures of me . . ."

"The pictures of you gambling that Alex's PI took? The one he has had watching you for weeks now?" Oakley asks.

She flushes a deep red all the way down her neck and below the neckline of her shirt.

"Yes. They'll disappear?"

"They'll remain unseen but not gone."

She nods slowly, shoulders sagging. "Okay, then you have a deal."

"One more thing," I add tightly. "The guy you hired to break into my car. Who was it?"

"I don't know his name. I asked some random guy outside of one of the casinos I go to often. He wasn't much older than twenty, I don't think. I offered him two hundred dollars to slip the bug inside. I didn't tell him your name, just where to find the car," she replies, a hint of shame in her tone.

"You didn't tell him to hurt me?"

She shakes her head quickly. "No. My guess is that you scared him and he acted out of impulse. I don't think it was premeditated."

I stand then, and it's Oakley that says, "If I find out a different side to that story, there isn't a damn thing that will stop me from destroying you. Is that clear?"

She swallows. "Crystal."

43

Maddox

I'M RUSHING OUT THE DOOR OF MY PARENTS' HOUSE THE MINUTE I see Braxton's car pull into the driveway, my dad's truck following close behind. Mom brushes a hand down my back as I sidestep her and duck out the doorway.

I left practice two hours ago, coming straight here after reaching Braxton's voicemail back to back to back. Mom didn't lie to me when I asked where Dad was—I'm not sure if she even knows how to lie, actually—and while I didn't have proof that Braxton was also in Rose Carpenter's office, my gut was screaming at me that that's where she was.

My beautiful, thoughtful, self-sacrificing woman was out there doing just that. Sacrificing herself for me.

It took everything in me not to tear through the Vancouver streets to get to her and stop her from making a mistake. From throwing away her reputation for me and for the shitty people in our lives that have never deserved us in the first place.

I know deep down that no matter what she did or said to Rose that nothing will change the way the fans see things. Everything is black and white to them. Every decision I make, every game I play—good or embarrassingly awful. They don't care about the details or the excuses, and it's not their job to.

But Braxton doesn't see things like that. She never has. She sees things in beautiful, vibrant colours. There's always a reason behind an action or a decision, and when others don't understand that, it's a question as to why and how.

Her outlook on life is one of the things I love most about her. It makes Braxton, Braxton. But at times like this? I wish I could convince her to see things through the eyes of others.

And while I may want to shake some sense into her, I also want to run to her and toss her over my shoulder and kiss the hell out of her until we're both blue in the face.

I need to tell her how grateful I am for her. For her love and unwavering support. There will never be a way to properly thank her for what she's risked for me today, and I just hope that Dad was able to stop her and bring her back to me—clear and free of the mistakes I fear she could have made.

Her car comes to a jerking stop a handful of feet in front of me, and I plant a hand on the hood before rushing to the driver's-side door. She's already pulling her keys out of the ignition and opening the door when I swing it the rest of the way and dip toward her. With a hand across her front, I undo her seat belt and haul her out of the car.

"Maddox!" she squeals, surprise flickering in her blue eyes.

I grumble something unintelligible and grab her beneath her thighs, using my grip to pick her up and push her back against the side of the car. She hooks her legs around my back, pulling me close.

"You don't get to do that," I huff against her mouth. "You don't get to just disappear again." My fingers tingle as I press them deeper into her thighs. "You don't get to throw away your reputation for me."

Her hands fold behind my neck, elbows brushing my shoulders. As if it's possible, she pulls me closer with her legs around my middle.

"You don't get to tell me what I do and don't get to do, Dox. When I told you I loved you, I meant it. And me making sacrifices for you—whether you agree with them or not—is just one of the ways I'm willing to show that love. You would have done the exact same thing for me."

My eyes drift over her face, soaking her in. And fuck me, every time I look at her, she becomes more and more beautiful. How am I supposed to last the rest of forever? I'm already popping a boner at a mere glimpse or thought of her.

"I'm trying to be mad at you," I murmur, skimming my lips over hers, tasting what's left of the fruity lip balm she always uses.

"Don't be mad. It's over."

My heart skips in my chest. "It is? I'm so fucking antsy to know what happened, sweetheart. I don't know how long I can wait to find out, but I also want to bring you to my old bedroom and ravish you on my bed before you tell me all about it."

Braxton flushes, eyes drifting down to where my mouth is teasing hers. "I always wondered what it would be like to be ravished by you in your bedroom. I used to dream about it, you know?"

Decided, I nip at her lips and hike her up against my front. "Let's make some dreams come true, then, yeah?"

"Ew! Have you ever heard of PDA, Dox? Because I think you need a lesson on how to calm it down," Adalyn yells from somewhere behind me.

I swallow a curse and look over my shoulder, spotting her staring at us from the doorway with a finger pointed into her open mouth. Mom and Dad are trying to usher her inside, and by the small, knowing smile on my dad's face, he was already expecting this reaction from me.

Maybe I should be more embarrassed that my family knows how wild I am for Braxton, but that ship sailed long ago. Shit, when I was sixteen, I got drunk and told my mom that I was planning on staying a virgin for Braxton, and when Cooper's dad overheard our conversation, he played it off as something entirely different, not wanting everyone to tease me about it. It's been me and Curly Fry since the moment we met in that kindergarten parking lot twenty-one years ago.

I've waited for this too long to fear the judgment of others when it comes to her.

"Has your sister ever dated anyone?" Braxton asks softly, clinging to me and pressing her cheek to my chest as I move up the driveway.

"No. And she never will."

She shakes with a laugh. "You can't keep her as a little girl forever."

"I can and I will. God help the first guy she brings home because he might just disappear off the face of the earth one day," I growl into her hair as we step under the threshold and walk inside.

"Mmhmm. Maybe you'll actually like him."

Moving my lips to her, I say, "Fat chance. Now, stop talking about my sister and her potential boyfriend before my cock shrivels up to nothing. I have plans for you that very much involve being hard as a rock."

"After. We really need to talk about what happened today first, okay? Then you can bring me home and have your wicked, wicked way with me."

"For you, baby? Anything."

Let's get this over with.

DAD LAYS it all out for me, and I sit between Braxton and Mom on the outdoor couch on the back deck, stunned. The air ripples with my anger, even as I try to reel it in. Disbelief is a nip in my side, but it's the pain of betrayal that hits the hardest.

"So, she's changing the article?" I ask slowly.

Dad nods. "And retracting the first one. As long as she keeps up her end of the bargain, nobody will see the photos or learn about the things she does in her free time."

"And Alex willingly gave you that information? The PI photos and everything? Without something in return?"

"It was the *least* he could do," Mom snips, patting my knee.

"And the guy that bugged Braxton's car? He just gets to get off with no repercussions?" I curl the fingers I have on Braxton's thigh into the rough material of her jeans.

Dad frowns, looking as displeased by that as I feel. "Rose said she didn't have a name, and I believe her. I don't think that if this guy meant to hurt her that he would have just pushed her out of the way."

A cold sensation slithers through my chest at the idea of what could have happened had the person who broke into her car been intent on really hurting her.

My thigh warms beneath Braxton's palm, and I turn to her, letting her presence calm me.

"Are you okay with not knowing? Because this is about you, not me or Rose or anyone. I'll do whatever is necessary to find this guy if that's what you want," I say softly.

She smiles at me, head shaking slightly. "I want to forget about it and move on, not drag this out any longer. I believe Rose, and I don't think I'm in any danger."

"Okay." I steal a quick kiss and wrap my arm over her shoulder, pulling her into my side until she's all but sitting in my lap.

"Now, you need to decide what you want to do next, son. The ball is in your court. Dougie is waiting on your call," Dad says.

"Tell him that I'll call him tonight. This is something I have to discuss with Braxton first," I tell him.

A glimmer of approval lights up Dad's eyes. "We'll leave you to it, then. You're both welcome to stay for dinner too."

"That would be great," Braxton replies, and Dad stands, grinning at her.

Mom releases a wobbly breath, squeezing my knee. "I'm

proud of you," she whispers before kissing my cheek and step-ping into Dad's arms as he leads them back into the house, leaving Braxton and me alone.

"Will you come somewhere with me?" I ask her, collecting both of her hands in mine and bringing her knuckles to my lips.

"Anywhere, Dox," she answers, eyes so soft and warm.

I swiftly pull her up and, with her hands still in mine, tug her down the patio stairs and across the yard. The grass is short, freshly mowed, and the smell of fresh air sparks old memories of days and nights spent out here, just her and me.

Our tree house is tucked off to the side of the yard, in between the side of the house and another massive oak tree that has been here since I was a boy. A tire swing hangs from one of its thick branches, and I'm sure it hasn't held the weight of a person in years. Not since Adalyn was young enough to hide out in here.

The tree house is more worn than it was the last time I wandered off this way, but it's still the same. The six red-painted pegs are in the truck of the tree leading up to the opening in the house's base that's still shut, keeping the animals out that used to try to make the place their own.

Braxton keeps quiet as I lead us to the stepping pegs we used instead of a ladder. My eyes are drawn to the design in the bark of the tree, the one I have tattooed on my chest.

With a warmth settling behind my ribs, I step on the bottom peg, testing whether or not it can still hold my weight. When it does, I move up to the next one and the next before pushing at the door and letting it flop open with a loud creaking noise, dust flying everywhere.

I push my body through the hole in the floor and move inside, looking around the place to make sure there aren't any surprises before calling down to Braxton to let her know it's safe to follow me up.

"Are you sure it isn't going to collapse with us both inside?"

she asks, peeking her head inside, inspecting the tree house with a look of pure awe.

"We used to fit six people in here when we were younger, baby girl. I think it can handle it."

"Okay," she mutters before setting her palms on the wood and climbing inside.

"Everything is exactly how we left it," I say, brushing my fingers over the Warriors logo sewn into the blanket covering the window, held up by two nails, one in each corner.

Two beanbag chairs rest beneath the window, one blue and one purple. A shelf of old books is on the wall opposite, decorated with a ceramic bowl of old guitar picks, a stack of chipped hockey pucks, a dirty paint pallet, and a couple of old vinyls.

"How did none of this stuff get ruined?" Braxton mutters.

"Dad must have closed the shutters every winter."

I avoided this place for years. I never would have noticed if the shutters outside of the window had been left open or closed.

"I didn't think I would get to see this place again."

"I didn't think that I would ever want to," I reply.

I turn to her, finding her closer than I thought. She moves toward me without saying a word and wraps her arms around me.

"Sit with me," I whisper, smoothing a hand over her hair.

She nods, and as soon as my ass hits the wood, I pull her onto my lap, biting my tongue at the pleasure that sparks as her centre brushes my cock. Her palms find my chest, and her thumbs make slow, soothing circles there. She smells so good, like a mix of all my favourite things.

"Are you going to enter free agency?" she asks, eyes trapping mine, as if I would dare look away.

I stroke my hand up and down her back. "I think so. It's time I moved on from the VW."

She takes in my words, chewing on the inside of her lip as she contemplates them before asking, "Do you remember when we were seventeen and I told you that I couldn't chase you?"

An overwhelming sense of nostalgia comes over me, along with a mix of bad and good memories. "Yes."

"Well, I think that things have changed. And while I don't want to chase you, because I really hate that term, I do want to follow you. Wherever you go, I want to be with you, by your side."

"What?" I force past the emotion in my throat.

A soft smile tugs at her mouth, and she raises a hand to my face, stroking the line of my jaw. I press into her hold, taking as much from her as I can.

"I want to try something new. I've been thinking of attempting a career as a travel vet instead of being hunkered down in one place. Running my own business isn't what I thought it would be, and I know it might seem like I'm just scared of you leaving again, but that's not it. I mean, that does play some part, but I've been thinking about this for a while, and I know I won't be able to follow you everywhere you go, but we'll still get to travel all over together and—"

"Baby, why didn't you tell me earlier? Shit, the answer is yes, whatever it is you want to ask me or tell me. It's yes. Let's do this," I interrupt her rambling, my pulse racing.

Her eyelashes flutter over wide eyes. "Really? That's something you would want? You don't think it's too much?"

"Fuck no. If that's something that will make you happy and that you're positive about, then absolutely, because nothing would make me happier."

"Nothing?" She toys with the bottom hem of my shirt, slipping her fingers underneath, above the waistband of my pants. Her smile is coy and fucking sexy as hell, and I resist the urge to suck it right off.

I fit my hands to her waist and slide her up my lap, seating her right on top of my cock as it hardens beneath her. Grinning as she moans, I lean my head against the wall of the tree house and say, "Nothing. Everything else is just icing on the goddamn cake."

Bringing our foreheads together, she rubs her nose along the side of mine and whispers, "You know, the last time we were sitting here together, I wanted nothing more than to kiss you."

"Is that right?"

She hums, ghosting her lips over mine. "What do you say we do more than just kiss?"

"I say fuck yes." And then I kiss her and make another memory in this tree house that I don't ever plan on forgetting.

44

Braxton

I LEAVE A YOUNG FAMILY BESIDE SAPPHIRE'S PEN, FEELING A SEARING hope build inside me that I pray isn't too obvious in my grin. The last thing I want is to scare them off, but as soon as I saw their toddler rush toward her earlier, smile beaming, I just had this feeling that we might have just found our sweet girl a home.

The adoption day has only been in full swing for a few hours, but the attendance has been startling. Sadie has mentioned more than once that they've never had such a big turnout, and I might have had to sneak out a few times to collect myself before I broke into tears in front of everyone.

Between the help from the Warriors and their calendar, our own promotional work, and Rose's new and improved article, the parking lot in front of the clinic is packed. We've already sold out of all the calendars we had and are taking pre-orders for another print run.

"This is amazing, Braxton. You're really going out with a bang," Marco says, coming up beside me.

I knock his shoulder. "I'm happy that I know I'm leaving this place in good hands. It makes it easier."

"Good. I still can't tell you how grateful I am that you offered this place to me. It's perfect."

"It sure is. Just promise me that whenever I find my way back here for a few weeks that you'll have a spot open for me."

He laughs, knocking my shoulder back. "Anytime. You have my word."

I nod, and a comfortable silence settles between us, both of us looking out over the parking lot and smiling at the happy faces. While the paperwork only dried on the sale of the clinic yesterday, it's a relief to see how excited Marco is to take over. It's not surprising, though. Not when he immediately said yes when I asked if he would be interested in buying it from me. It's been an easy, quick process, and it's made all of the upcoming changes in my life easier to grasp.

Flutters build in my belly when I think of the man who's at the centre of all those plans. Maddox announced his decision to enter free agency shortly after our magical moment in the tree house—the same day I asked Marco about the clinic, actually—and everything has been moving so fast since then.

Dougie has been a busy man sorting through all of Dox's potential offers, and while my man wants to stay in Canada, it hasn't deterred the other teams from trying to snatch him up anyway. It's been a little overwhelming, but he knows that wherever he chooses to go, I'll be right there with him.

He's been a total trooper while he watches his old team try to keep themselves in the Stanley Cup race, but they're down by three games, and it isn't looking good for them. While he might blame himself for his part in their approaching loss, playing without his heart in the game might have done more harm than good, anyway.

Speaking of Maddox, his sister calls my name from across the parking lot, and I search through the crowds until I find her at the edge beside her parents, hand flying through the air. I don't spot Maddox with them, and I have to fight to keep from frowning.

Where is he?

Marco chuckles, following my gaze. "Looks like you're wanted. I'll catch you later, yeah?"

"Of course. Find me before you leave. Have fun," I rush out, shooting him a smile before beelining it for the Huttons.

It's a task maneuvering my way through the crowds, but I wouldn't change how busy it is for anything. The only thing I wish I could change is Hades being out here with the other dogs. But I knew it would only overwhelm and possibly scare him, so he's inside, in his own special spot in the clinic reception, still there waiting for a family.

"My beautiful Braxton," Ava says, pulling me in for a bear hug when I finally reach them. I blink away the tears gathering in my eyes at the thought of Hades and soak up her love.

"This is an amazing turnout. Everything looks great," Oakley notes, rubbing the portion of my back exposed between his wife's arms.

"Thank you," I murmur, stepping back when Ava releases me.

"I bought like ten of those calendars online, and holy shit, I have no idea how you handled being around all of those hot bods," Addie says in awe, fanning herself.

I stifle a laugh at the way Oakley's scowling at her. Ava simply grabs her hand and then reaches for mine.

"My favourite part of the calendar is the photo they used for September. I asked Maddox to order me that photo by itself so that I could frame it. You two are so beautiful together," Ava says softly.

I flush all the way to my toes. "I might have done the same thing. It is beautiful."

The first time I saw the photo of us that they chose for the calendar, I cried. With Maddox's body at my side, turned toward me as much as possible—a detail I didn't notice at the time—and our eyes meeting over Hades as he sits pretty between us, we look like a family. Even on paper, it's impossible not to feel the adoration and love that lives between us.

"Maddox told us that the dog between you is your favourite," Oakley says.

My heart swells at the fact they've talked about Hades.

"Yeah, he is. Hades is special. He's been through so much." I squeeze Ava's hand, using my grip on her fingers and the cool feel of her wedding band as a way to keep from letting my thoughts wander off to what will happen if he doesn't get adopted today. "Where is Maddox, anyway? He said he was coming with you guys."

"He did! I think he wanted to say hi to Hades first," Addie tells me.

"Oh." My smile is instant as my worry evaporates.

"Do you think we could meet Hades too? I've never been a big pet person, but if he's important to you, then I would like to meet him." Ava smiles, eyes glittering as she waits for my answer.

"Of course. He's just inside the clinic. His past is tragic, and he isn't big on new people, though. Just a warning."

Addie has already started pulling Ava toward the clinic before I've finished speaking, in turn pulling me behind them. A laugh slips from my mouth as Oakley follows and mutters something under his breath that sounds like, *calm down, speed racer.*

The crowds start to slim out the further we get from the animal pens in the parking lot and the closer we get to the clinic entrance. Actually, there isn't a single person standing anywhere close to the entrance.

My brows tug together as Addie whips open the door, and Cooper appears on the other side, wearing a cheek-splitting grin.

"Cooper?" I mutter, suspicion thick in the single word.

"Hello, love." He winks at me and then focuses on the other three bodies. "Hutton family."

Addie cocks her head. "Braxton gets an adorable pet name, and I get a group greeting? You wound me, Cooper."

"What would you have preferred I call you?" he asks, staring down at her with a wry smile as Ava giggles.

"Adalyn or Addie. You do still remember my name, right? Or has old age finally caught up to you?"

Something along the lines of amusement flares in his eyes before he's blinking it away, stepping to the side to make room for us to walk inside.

"My apologies, Adalyn," he says slyly as she slips by him.

I follow the two women inside but pause beside Cooper, narrowing my eyes at him. "What have you been doing in the clinic?"

"Me? Nothing."

"I don't believe you."

"It's a good thing it doesn't matter, then," he tosses back and then lifts his gaze to the older man behind me. "Please tell her to stop bugging me."

Oakley laughs, and I roll my eyes at Cooper's tattling. "You're going to let bugs inside, Braxton. In you go."

"You're far too old to be asking a grown-up for help, Cooper-oni," I mutter before sidestepping him and walking into the clinic.

He starts to laugh, but it fades into the background when I take in the picture in front of me.

My stomach swoops as I focus my eyes on Maddox. He's standing in front of Hades' pen, affection heavy on his features as he stares at me, our eyes locking. The air tightens around us as neither one of us says anything for a few moments, my tongue tied simply from the way he's looking at me. Like he wants to whisk me away and seal us in my office for hours on end but also wants to drop to his knees right here in front of me and profess his love for everyone to hear.

It's not until I catch the movement of him shifting something in his hands that I'm able to look away, down at the leash in his grasp. I follow it down to where it's connected to a familiar collar, the one I bought Hades only a couple of weeks ago.

My sweet boy stares up at me, his body language a mix of calm, excited, and a bit nervous. I smile at him, anxious to rush over and give him some pets but far too curious as to why he's leashed up.

Looking away from Hades, I find other people in the room, surprising faces that have me gasping. My mom and sister are off to the side, both wearing such encouraging, soft expressions. Anna wiggles her fingers in a wave, and I puff out a laugh.

Noah and a beautiful, tall brunette with caramel-brown eyes that belong to none other than Tinsley Lowry stand beside Addie, Oakley, and Ava. Despite the cold look on Noah's face as he watches me and keeps a close eye on Tinsley at the same time, I'm happy that he's back in Vancouver.

"You're gorgeous even when you're surprised," Maddox murmurs, drawing my attention back to him.

"And you're handsome even when you're confusing me," I reply, and quiet laughter fills the room.

He takes a confident couple of steps toward me before stopping and dropping to his haunches, pressing a kiss to Hades' head and letting the leash fall to the ground.

"Go get her, buddy," he mutters.

Hades rushes toward me, butting his head against my knees before I drop to his level and finally give in to the urge to shower him with pets. Something cold brushes my fingers when I scratch beneath his collar, and as I push his dog tag out of the way, I feel something else dangling beside it. Something I didn't put there.

A hand flies to my mouth when I find a new silver tag beside his original one, the words *Will You Marry Me* written across it.

"Dox," I whisper, looking up to find him right in front of me, on one knee with a small black box in his hand.

He's staring right at me, eyes clear, his heart and soul bared for me. I blow out a shaky breath and pinch that silver tag, staying crouched, not trusting myself to stand out of fear of collapsing.

"Baby girl, I've loved you since the moment our eyes met, and I knew I wanted to marry you just moments later. It's been two decades since then, and while I spent eight years without you, I don't think you were ever fully gone." He covers his chest with his hand, throat bobbing heavily. "You were here the entire time because I refused to let you go.

"You are my soulmate, Braxton. I believe that wholeheartedly, and I know you do too. We were meant to meet that day, and we were meant to meet again. Fate brought us back together because we weren't finished yet. Fuck, I don't think we'll ever be finished. In this life or the next. I'm never letting you go again, not now or ever. So, Curly Fry, what do you say? Will you marry me?"

I release a mangled sob and throw myself over Hades, looping my arms around Maddox's neck and nodding frantically.

"I would have married you when I was five, Dox. Yes. Without a doubt, yes," I cry, burying my face in the crook of his shoulder and slicking his skin with my tears.

Our friends and family start to shout their congratulations, but the only thing I focus on is the man nudging Hades out from between us and pulling me close, taking me into his arms.

"Hades is ours, baby girl. If you'll have him."

I peel back enough to meet his eyes, and the sight of his tears sends me into another fit of sobs. He cups my cheeks and presses our foreheads together, rolling them back and forth.

"He's ours? You adopted him?"

"We did. There's no better family out there for him than ours. You and me."

I sniffle, overwhelmed but so, so happy. "I don't even know what to say other than thank you."

"Don't thank me. I love you so much," he breathes.

"I love you too, Dox. Forever."

"And always," he finishes, finally closing the distance and kissing me.

EPILOGUE 1

Maddox

TWO MONTHS LATER

There are moments in your life that you never forget. I have a bucketload of those memories, and most of them feature my best friend.

From our first meeting outside of a busy kindergarten to the time I found her struggling to paint the nails on her right hand in the yard at recess and offered to help regardless of how it might damage my badass, eleven-year-old reputation, Braxton is a living entity in my mind. She's in my past, present, and sure as hell my future. Everything that I am today, she's played a part in moulding.

And as I watch that short, frizzy-haired little girl with the electric-blue eyes from my memories become my wife fifteen years later, I know that I'm exactly where I'm supposed to be. Every wrong path I took, every mistake along the way, all led me right back here. To my other half.

To my soulmate.

I dreamed of seeing her in a white dress and veil someday, but Braxton is beyond dreaming. She's a goddess, and somehow, I'm lucky enough to call her mine. My wife.

A white silk dress hugs her curves and spills at her feet. It trails behind her on the deep blue carpet in the aisle of the chairs and over the grass in my parents' backyard. Sparkling, sheer sleeves cover her arms, and the material carries over to the dipped neckline, hiding the swell of her breasts. Her waist is cinched, and I want nothing more than to place my hands on her hips and pull her the rest of the way.

A veil is clipped to the back of an intricate-looking updo, and it shines the way her sleeves and chest do. There are daisies in her hair, matching the bouquets tied to the backs of the guests' chairs and hung by the aisles and from the tree house behind me. I swallow when my eyes finally reach hers, and I find them waiting, so warm and familiar.

Her eyelashes are long and thick and make the blue in her eyes sharper, more defined. With each step she takes, the sheen across them becomes clearer, and I know she can tell the same about mine because I can feel the tears on my cheeks, and I don't care to wipe them away just yet.

She's so beautiful it hurts, and when she smiles at me, my heart skips a beat—or five. My lungs fold in on themselves, and I force a breath out, grinning at her and fighting back the urge to steal her from my dad and pull her close.

Speaking of the old man, I watch as he places a hand over the arm she has threaded through his and gives it a squeeze. It's a touch that says a million words, and when he looks at me and dips his chin, I know what he's trying to say.

I love you both. I'm so proud of you.

A ball lodges in my throat as I nod back, swiping a hand across my cheeks.

When Braxton reaches me, the minister says a few words that I don't register before Dad is placing her hand in mine and patting me on the shoulder before moving to his seat beside Mom.

My next inhale is shaky as I bring our joined hands to my lips and grab her other one, moving it to rest against my chest and the thundering beat inside of it. I want to kiss her already, want to sweep her up and take her away from here, but I focus on the zaps where we touch and remind myself that she's not going anywhere. There isn't any need to rush.

"You are breathtaking," I whisper, lowering our hands to rest between us while gliding my thumbs over her knuckles.

"So are you."

And I believe her, because when she trails her eyes over my face and down the front of my suit, she looks as taken by me as I imagine I do as I stare at her.

The minister starts to welcome everyone, but his voice is nothing more than a whisper as I stare at Braxton. At her wobbly chin, the loose curls left out of her updo to frame her face, and the frantic fluttering of her eyelashes as she tries not to cry. The crowd fades, and she becomes my focus, like she has been for my entire life.

Time moves fast, the ceremony speeding by, and I don't take my eyes off my bride once. Not as I recite my vows and not as she speaks hers. Even as Noah hands me our rings and I slide the band onto her finger, my eyes don't waver. It's not until she pushes a silver band up my finger and over my knuckle that I drop my gaze to our hands.

Fuck, I already love wearing this ring. I make a promise to myself right here and now that I will never take it off. It will become a part of me.

As soon as the words "kiss the bride" fall from the minister's mouth, I'm diving toward my wife. With her cheeks in my hands, I press my thumbs to her chin and press our lips together. She meets my kiss with the same urgency, and it takes everything in me not to groan in approval.

The crowd hollers, and someone claps me on the back, but as I drop a hand to Braxton's waist and pull her into me, I don't give a shit who's around. I continue to kiss my wife until she pushes away, a furious type of love in her eyes.

"Save some for later, husband," she teases.

I squeeze her hip and bump her nose with mine. "Be careful what you ask for, wife."

And fucking hell, if finally calling her my wife doesn't sound like the most beautiful thing on this earth.

Braxton

"I don't think I'll ever get used to calling you my sister-in-law!" Addie squeals, carefully brushing a few hairs out of my face.

We're taking a minute to hide in one of the bathrooms in Oakley and Ava's house after the past few hours of absolute insanity that is a big wedding. She's helped me change out of my wedding dress and into a looser, knee-length white dress with thin straps and a modest neckline. For the first time since this morning, I can take a full breath without the corset crushing my lungs.

"I know. I don't think it's fully hit me yet," I breathe, glancing down at the wedding ring on my left hand. Flutters fill my stomach as I twirl the band.

"How does it feel to be Mrs. Braxton Hutton?"

My cheeks warm. "Like it was meant to be?"

"God, you two are adorable," she sighs.

I smooth my hands down my sides and lean over the counter, taking in my red cheeks and slightly swollen lips in the bathroom mirror. There's a red mark on the side of my throat, and I think my cheeks flush an even deeper shade of red as I remember how that mark got there.

"I just feel really lucky, you know?"

"I can. But remember that he's lucky too. Dox might be my brother, but you're amazing too. You deserve the best kind of love, and I'm so glad that you've found that with my brother."

I look at Addie and smile, pulling her into my arms. "For someone so young, you're incredibly wise."

She laughs. "I think that's because I had all of you guys to watch growing up. I always wanted to be one of you, and I think that made me grow up a bit faster."

"You were always perfect the way you were, Addie. And you're perfect now."

"Thank you," she says softly, squeezing me once before letting go. "How do you feel now? Ready to go back out there? I know we can be a little crazy and overwhelming."

"I'll take a little crazy over whatever the hell is going on with my family," I say, bitterness burning my tongue.

Addie scowls, and it looks wrong. Her soft features and bubble-gum-pink lips aren't meant to twist that way.

"Have you spoken to your dad yet today? I was surprised when I saw him in the crowd at the ceremony," she says.

I turn my back to the mirror and fiddle with the dainty tennis bracelet on my wrist. A gift from the Hutton family for my wedding day.

"He caught Dox and me right after the ceremony finished. Wished us a rushed congratulations and then left. I don't know whether I should be grateful that he showed up or annoyed that he couldn't get past his issues with your family to stay for the entire thing," I admit.

My relationship with my father hasn't changed all that much in the past couple of months besides him not being out to get my husband. He seemed to take my threat seriously the day I told him to leave his past with Maddox alone, and while he hasn't made much of an effort to build on the weak foundation of a relationship that we have, he hasn't broken it further.

It's really the bare minimum, but as long as he leaves my family alone, I'll continue to try and encourage a relationship with him. He is still my father at the end of the day, even if he's not the greatest one.

My mother, on the other hand, she's flourishing. Her boyfriend is here with her today, and while our initial meeting was fifty shades of awkward, he seems like a nice guy. He treats my mother well, and as far as I'm concerned, that's all that matters. How and when they met doesn't change anything in my eyes. We're closer than we were months ago, and when Maddox and I decided to get married before moving to Ottawa for his first preseason on his new team, Mom was so excited to be included in the planning. I'm so, so happy to be able to see her smile again.

"I think you're allowed to be both. Happy that he showed up and annoyed that he couldn't put you first again and stay," Addie says.

"Either way, I refuse to let it affect my day. Today has been perfect."

More than, actually, but I'm not sure how to put it all into words.

I jump when a knock sounds on the door, and Addie flies toward it, slowly peeling it open to peek at who's on the other side.

"Stop hogging my wife, Adalyn," Maddox orders, voice gruff and commanding.

I fight back a shiver in anticipation of seeing him again and move behind her. She rolls her eyes at her brother before giving me a quick side hug and a knowing grin and slipping out. As soon as she's gone, Maddox is pushing his way inside, eyes nearly glowing as he takes me in and locks the door.

"Fucking hell, baby girl. You expect me to keep my hands to myself tonight when you look like this?"

His actions contradict his words because in the next breath, he's palming my waist and lifting me, sitting me on the counter. My legs part for him as he steps between them and threads his fingers into the hairs at the back of my head, releasing a deep groan. I bite my lip, convinced I made the right choice by having Addie take my hair down.

He pushes his face into my neck, inhaling deeply while pressing frantic kisses all over my skin. "I'm barely holding on here. All I want is to take you home and make love to you over and over . . ." He nips at my earlobe. "And over again."

"Maddox," I sigh, letting my head hang to give him full access to my neck. His prickly jaw scrapes at the sensitive skin, but I've grown to love the feeling. Plus, it's not like it wasn't already red. "We're in your parents' bathroom."

"Can't you be quiet, sweetheart? Besides, nobody uses this one."

One of his hands travels from my waist to my thigh before sliding up over my garter and then cupping my pussy. I grip his suit jacket and let the immediate pleasure of his touch wash over me.

"Not enough time," I gasp when he pushes my panties to the side and parts my wet flesh with one finger.

"You're so wet, you filthy girl. I can just slide right in. Hmm?"

I buck up when he slips that finger inside of me and twirls his thumb over my clit. A broken cry breaches my lips before he's taking my mouth in a hard kiss and pulling my bottom lip between his teeth, biting down on it.

"Unbuckle my belt for me. I'm not letting you out of here without knowing I've taken care of this wet, needy pussy," he grunts, adding a second finger to the first and starting to slide them in and out of me. The wet sound that follows fills the room, and I start to nod, too far gone to turn him down.

My fingers move quickly as I pull the leather from the heavy black buckle and all but rip the button of his slacks open. My throat bobs when I find his cock hard, straining against his briefs, tip peeking above the band and glistening with precum.

In one shove, I bring his pants to his thighs and wrap my hand around his erection, feeling the hard warmth of it in my palm. Stroking up, I swipe the glistening bead of cum from his tip with my thumb then and spread it along the shaft as I bring my hand back down.

He hisses out a breath, slamming a hand to the counter beside my thigh. "Put it inside of you, Braxton."

I scoot to the edge of the counter and shake my head. "Not like this."

His eyes widen slightly as he frowns. "What's wrong?"

"Nothing. I just want you to take me from behind. I want to watch in the mirror," I admit, not the least bit embarrassed by my suggestion.

Maddox makes me confident. I love who I am with him and who I am when he can't be beside me. I just love me, period.

Desire flashes in his eyes before I'm being set on my feet and spun around, the edge of the counter biting into my hips as he flips my dress up, exposing my ass. I rest my hands on the round edge of the sink and look over my shoulder at the man behind me, so completely in love with him.

"You're a goddess. A goddamn vision. Now and always. I can't wait to spend the rest of my life with you," he mutters, shaking his head while he stares at me, as if he can't believe I'm here and that this is real life. Most of the time, I wonder the same thing.

I push back against him, feeling his cock press against the seam of my ass. My eyelids begin to drop as pleasure zips through me, the anticipation killing me.

"This is real, Maddox. Today is the start of our forever."

He bends over the curve of my back and kisses my head, my neck, and then my back, starting at the top and slowly moving down along my spine. Each touch of his lips to my skin is a silent promise, and I swallow the ball of emotion that builds in my throat.

"I love you, Curly," he whispers, cock teasing my entrance.

"I love you, Dox," I cry as he enters me, filling me to the hilt with a single thrust.

A carnal noise escapes him, and I let my head fall forward, arms already shaking. His hands are everywhere as he starts to move inside of me, a rush of quick, desperate touches. He pulls at my nipples, and I bite down on my lip to keep from screaming at how good it feels.

Suddenly, his fingers are in my hair, and he's gripping it, using it to pull my head back. Our eyes meet in the mirror, and the fire in my belly grows at the wild look in his. At the pure possession and obsession turning them a deep, dark shade of green, almost brown.

"You said you wanted to watch, Braxton. So, watch."

I do, fighting back the impulse to let my eyes roll back into my head. His jaw pulses with each thrust, and his cheeks are a similar shade of pink as mine, but he never looks away. Not as I clench around him, trying to keep him deep as my orgasm comes barrelling toward me, and not when he buries his face in my throat and curses his pleasure against my skin, warmth filling me.

Only once he's peppered adoring kisses all over the side of my face does he pull back and slip soft touches over my body. I hum low in my throat, letting him run a soft towel between my legs and press his lips to my butt cheek before he stands.

"Are you sated now, husband?" I ask teasingly, spinning around and giving him a lazy smile.

He grins wickedly. "And then some. Are you, wife?"

"Perfectly sated. Enough to last the rest of the reception, anyway."

"My dirty girl." He winks. "Are you ready to go back out, or do you want a few more minutes alone?"

I shake my head. "I'm ready. I still have to throw my bouquet. Any guesses on who will catch it?"

He lowers his head and kisses my forehead. "As long as it isn't Adalyn, I don't care who catches it."

Giggling, I step into his body and press my cheek to his chest, not caring about leaving a foundation stain on the expensive shirt. And when he wraps his arms around my back and pulls me close, I know that he doesn't care either.

I've learned that not much matters when we're in each other's arms, and for that, I feel like the luckiest woman in the world.

And when Adalyn makes Maddox's nightmare come true by catching my bouquet an hour later in their parents' backyard, I know that she's one step closer to getting a chance to experience this type of all-consuming love too.

EPILOGUE 2

Braxton

TEN MONTHS AFTER THAT

MY EARS RING AS THE OTTAWA BEAVERTAILS LOSE THE GOAL THEY just scored, and the home crowd goes up in arms. The referee ignores them, but when Maddox skates up to him and leans in close, throwing his hand angrily into the air, he has no choice but to listen to him.

Oakley is standing beside Ava at the end of our row in the stands, a similar look of rage tugging at his features while he shouts at the ref as if he can hear him over the crowd. My neck is slick with sweat despite how close we're sitting to the ice, and my heart is in my throat.

Goalie interference is the call on the ice, but as a replay of the goal hits the jumbotron, it's obvious Dallas' goalie had more than enough time to collect himself and make the save after he was knocked down by one of our players. With only five minutes left in regulation time and a now even score of two to two in the Stanley Cup final game, this is the worst possible scenario for Ottawa.

"They're calling Toronto," Oakley grunts, watching the referees head to the side of the rink with laser focus.

"What does that mean?" Addie asks from her spot on my right.

Cooper answers her from her other side. "They're getting a second opinion from the review team in Toronto."

"How hard would that have been to say, Dad?" she scolds. Oakley sends her a quick, apologetic smile before turning back.

If it weren't for the tense atmosphere, I might have giggled at her frustration. Even after all of these years watching her dad in the league and then her oldest brother, she still hasn't figured out the nitty-gritty details of the game. It's adorable.

I figured they would call for another review of the play from the guys in Toronto, especially with this game being so do or die, but hearing it out loud makes my stomach twist into one giant knot of worry.

My eyes are drawn to Maddox as he stands by the boards, his new team behind him. Their coach is livid, his face the shade of a tomato. The C on my husband's red-and-black jersey is new, only having been placed there a handful of months ago, but it looks right. Like it belongs there. I never thought I would see a time when he wasn't in green, but the red fits him just fine.

Free agency was an overwhelming process, but after weaning through a dozen offers over the course of only a few days, Maddox signed a seven-year contract with Ottawa. And once we got married in August, we moved to Ottawa.

I've been working as a travelling veterinarian since we got settled in our new home, and it's been amazing. I feel like I've found what I'm meant to do, and the fact I get to travel with my husband? That's the cherry on top of it all.

In all honesty, life has never been better.

Even with our families back home in Vancouver, we nearly see them just as often as we did before. It's easy to make time for the people you love, and it's a great feeling knowing that they think the same way.

"He deserves this win," Ava breathes, nervously flexing the fingers she has intertwined with mine.

"He'll get it. There's nobody else who could pull this off like Maddox. Goal or no goal," I say.

"If he doesn't, I'm sorry for the grumpy man you're going to be going home with later, Brax," Addie says, patting my lap sympathetically.

This time, a smile does crack through my tight facial muscles. What I have planned for tonight will put a smile on his face, regardless of if they do lose.

"I'm sure a few kisses from Hades will help. That sweet boy can heal all wounds," Ava adds.

The Huttons love Hades and have all but adopted him into their family. He has a bigger family now than he could have ever dreamed of, and he's doing so much better. The broken dog with a lifetime of scars has found happiness again, and I'm honoured to have a part in his journey.

"They made a decision," Oakley says, and we all glance at the refs as they drop their tablet and headphones back behind the boards and skate back to centre ice.

The ref who originally made the no-goal call stares out at the crowd as he starts to speak into the small mic he's wearing. "After review, the call on the ice stands. We have a no goal."

The crowd starts to boo as his arms come out to his sides, forming a straight line across his body.

I find Maddox again, but this time, he's already staring at me, his shoulders the slightest bit slouched, yet his mouth is turned up in a small smile. It's a smile that says a thousand words—a way for him to show that win or lose, he's leaving this arena happy. With a sense of accomplishment.

Tears of both pride and love burn my eyes when he pulls his glove off and touches his palm to his chest before bringing it out and pointing at me. Without hesitation, I kiss my fingers and point back.

"I love you," he mouths.

"I love you more," I mouth back.

A beaming grin, and then he's putting his head back in the game, setting up on the Dallas blue line for a faceoff.

Two minutes later, he receives a quick pass from one of his teammates, finds an opening, and scores a goal no ref could possibly call off.

Then . . . then he wins his first Stanley Cup.

OUR NEW HOME is full of happy faces and a buzz in the air that I want to bottle up and keep forever.

The amazing family I married into chats among themselves in our living room, glasses of wine and beer bottles clinking as they give another congratulatory toast to my husband, and I join in with my non-alcoholic spritzer. The chest at my back is warm and inviting, and as I snuggle further into Maddox's lap on my favourite cushy armchair, I let a sense of contentment wash over me.

The Bateman family is here too, and Jamieson and Oliver haven't stopped teasing Maddox about the way he seems to track me wherever I go when I'm not with him. I think Maddox likes it, though, because he takes it on the chin every time, flashing smug grin after smug grin.

Even after Rose's initial story about Maddox and me faking our relationship, we didn't have many questions to answer from his family. We admitted that, at first, it was an agreement to help his image, but there wasn't much convincing needed when it came to telling them that we were then very much real. According to his aunt Gracie, it was obvious from the start that agreement or not, it was absolutely real.

She's always been a smart woman. Not much slips past her.

"Stop being so growly," Tinsley scolds from the loveseat across from Dox and me, her words pointed at Noah.

I fight to keep the shock off my face at the total ease in her movements as she flicks him in the cheek and scowls at him. But it's when he lays those dark eyes on her and bluntly apologizes that I lose that ability, my surprise obvious.

Maddox's chest shakes with a silent laugh before he leans in and places his mouth at the shell of my ear.

"I know. It takes some getting used to seeing him like that."

"I don't think I've ever heard him apologize to anyone," I mutter.

Noah plants an inked arm on the back of the couch behind Tinsley, but he never so much as brushes a finger against her. The skull tattooed on his throat pulls as he swallows, and his eyes remain on the side of her face even after she's turned back to the conversations around her.

"Is he really moving to Toronto?" I whisper, asking the question I've been rolling around in my head since I originally heard the news a few weeks back.

"Mmhmm. Took longer than we all thought it would. Her lease is up at the end of August, and they're renting a place together. Poor girl has no idea what she's signing up for."

"Maybe she does. They seem very close."

"As close as us, I think. Best friends to the very end."

I chew on the inside of my cheek as I watch Noah shift his body around Tiny with every slight movement of hers, like he's connected to her in some molecular way.

"Just best friends?" I ask, eyes darting away when Noah catches me staring and cocks a brow.

"Best friends in her mind, anyway. I think if Tinsley asked him to kneel for her, he would drop to the floor right now," Dox states, drifting his lips across my ear.

Suddenly, images of Maddox on the floor in front of me flood my thoughts, and before I can stop myself, I ask, "And you? If I asked you to kneel for me, would you?"

The arms he has wrapped around my front tighten ever so

slightly. I lean my head back against his chest, and he rests his chin on my shoulder.

"Always, baby girl," he murmurs.

I lift my drink to my lips and smile into it before taking a slow sip. The nausea that hit me on the way home from the game is gone, but I'm still nervous to drink too fast in case it comes back.

"If I asked you why you chose a non-alcoholic drink tonight, would you tell me the truth?" Maddox asks after a beat.

I force myself not to freeze up. "Maybe I just didn't want to drink tonight. It should be you that's celebrating, anyway, you know, Mr. Diet Coke."

"I found the sticks in the bathroom drawer before the game, sweetheart," he whispers, fingers drifting over my stomach, moving in soothing circles. "Knowing you might be pregnant is what kept me from throwing that referee down on the ice. All I wanted was to finish the game and come home to you, win or no win. The entire time I held that cup, all I could think about was you."

My heart thrashes in my chest. I spin in his arms, uncaring about everyone around us, and thread my hands behind his neck. His hands find my waist as he holds me in place, thumbs stroking my hips.

"Tell me it's real," he begs softly.

"It's real."

Bewilderment floods his face before he stands with me in his arms and spins us around the room, my face falling to his throat and legs wrapping around his waist.

"I'm going to be a fucking dad!" he shouts, and gasps and cries from our family follow his announcement. I hold him tight as he continues to spin, like I'm scared he could disappear into thin air at any moment.

"Are you kidding?" Adalyn squeals, and then Maddox is setting me down on my feet, still keeping me tucked in to his body even as his sister pulls me in and squishes me.

I release a watery laugh as I hug her back. "No joking here."

"I'm going to be the godfather, right?" Cooper asks, sweeping me into his familiar arms the second Addie releases me.

"We'll see," Maddox teases from behind me.

"And obviously, I'm going to be the godmother," Addie states.

Cooper kisses the top of my head and releases me. He pinches the back of Addie's bicep and chuckles when she screeches and swats at him.

"You're a little young to be a godmother, Adalyn."

She narrows her eyes at him. "And you're a little old to be a godfather. How's your hearing? Need a hearing aid yet?"

Cooper grins, eyes twinkling. "What did you say?"

"Funny."

"Huh?" he asks, pulling at his earlobe.

Addie turns to her brother and me now, exasperated. "This is exactly why I vote for Jamieson to be godfather."

"Jamieson?" Cooper sputters. "He's never even held a baby! I have a little sister!"

"Hey, asshole! I've held a baby before plenty of times," Jamieson shouts from somewhere in the living room.

Cooper snorts a laugh. "A baby doll doesn't count."

"At this rate, none of you will be godparents," Oakley says, working his way through the crowd of loved ones and smiling softly at me.

He opens his arms, and I barrel into him at the sight of his wet under eyes, a sob wrenching from my chest. His arms are strong around me, keeping me from collapsing at the onslaught of emotions that are threatening to buckle my knees.

"I'm so happy for you," he says, squeezing me tight.

I turn my cheek to his chest and find Ava watching us, her chin wobbling and hand over her chest. She smiles softly at me, and I smile back, blinking through my tears.

A few steps and she's closed the distance between us, pulling

Maddox with her toward Oakley and me, creating one big family hug. I push out a rasped breath when Maddox wraps my hand in his and squeezes, running a finger over my wedding rings as if he's reminding himself that this is real.

And it is, because like I said . . . life has never been better.

THE END

Thank you for reading Her Greatest Mistake! If you enjoyed it, please leave a review on Amazon and Goodreads.

To be kept up to date on all my releases, check out my website! www.hannahcowanauthor.com

The Greatest Love series continues with Cooper and Adalyn.

Her Greatest Adventure, a forbidden, brother's best friend romance – Adalyn Hutton and Cooper White (April-May)

His Greatest Muse, a dark themed romance – Noah Hutton and Tinsley Lowry (TBA)

Book 4 – Oliver Bateman and ? (TBA)

Book 5 – Jamieson Bateman and ? (TBA)

Curious where to go next?

Meet Oakley and Ava in the story that started it all, Lucky Hit, then follow the reading order!

Between Periods – Swift Hat-Trick #1.5 (5 POV Novella)

Blissful Hook – Swift Hat-Trick #2 (Tyler + Gracie)

Craving The Player –Amateurs In Love #1 (Braden + Sierra)

Taming The Player – Amateurs In Love #2 (Braden + Sierra)

Vital Blindside – Swift Hat-Trick #3 (Adam + Scarlett)

Keep reading for the first chapter of Lucky Hit

1

Oakley

I need a shower. Desperately. Before I pass out from a mix of overexertion and dehydration and end up needing my ass carried to the dressing room.

But right now, that's the last thing I want to do.

Instead of ridding myself of the stench that's wafting up from beneath my gear when I should have, I hung back to do another lap around the ice. A victory lap, if you will.

For most of my teammates, this is just the end of another winning season. For me, this is the last time I will ever skate in this arena, as not only a player but the captain of my hometown team, the Penticton Storm. I'm allowed to feel a little nostalgic. This arena has been my second home for the past three years.

The familiar cold of the ice nips at my skin through my jersey as I stare at the empty stadium like a wounded puppy. This old, outdated arena helped me rediscover my passion for hockey when the last thing I wanted was to slip on a pair of skates.

It's where I watched my mom and sister scream at the top of their lungs, waving around their cheesy signs at every game.

And where I realized I could be a leader—a genuine force to be reckoned with.

Lines of fluffy snow trail behind me as I skate slowly around the rink, my breaths ragged as I push myself along the boards. It's peaceful. The silence is unusual compared to the screaming crowds during a game or Coach's colourful words after a loss.

By the time I haul myself off the ice and down the hallway leading to the locker room, my chest is tight, tense with nerves and a sense of loss that I wish I wasn't already familiar with.

With a hard yank, the locker room door rips open, and I narrowly avoid smacking chests with my best friend.

The walking brick wall otherwise known as Andre Spetza flashes me a wide grin and clasps a hand over my shoulder. "I was starting to think I needed to go out there and pull you off the ice."

"Any longer and you would have."

He adjusts his grip on his hockey bag before simply tossing it to the side of the room and following me to my cubby. I arch a brow but don't say anything. Collapsing on a bench, I start untying my skates.

"What? I'm going to wait with you. I need as much time in your superstar presence as I can get."

"You make it sound like you'll never see me again. This isn't a breakup." Despite my attempted joke, the hurt in his auburn-coloured eyes is obvious. He isn't the only one hurting. "You guys can carry your own. With or without me."

He forces a laugh. "Humility looks good on you."

"Soak it up, big boy. Maybe you could learn a thing or two."

This time, his laugh is genuine. "Nah. Me and humility aren't meant to be."

"You'll have to force it, then, if you want to take my spot next season."

His eyes widen. "Not happening."

"I've nearly convinced Coach." I shrug. "The team is going to need a new captain, and you're the only one I trust to step up." If he can manage to keep his dick in his pants long enough to actually focus on something other than sex.

He sits stiffly beside me. "I told you not to do that. The only thing I'm good at is throwing my fists around and snapping at the other D-men to focus. I can't lead an entire team."

"Just think about it, man. That's all."

"Yeah, okay. I'll think about it. But no promises."

I nod. "No promises."

The silence is heavy as I finish untying my skates and grab my bag from my cubby, stuffing them inside. I remove my jersey and gear, putting everything away before throwing on a T-shirt and sweatpants.

By the time I have my bag over my shoulder, Andre is typing away on his phone, a scrunch between his brows.

"You good?" I ask.

His eyes snap to mine. "Yeah. Just last-minute party prep. Friday night, remember? If you stand me up at your own going-away party, I'll never forgive you."

I swallow a groan. "I'll be there." Even if going to a party is the last way I want to spend my final night in town.

"I wouldn't dream of it. You know how much I love to party."

"Your sarcasm is unbecoming," he scolds.

I laugh. "Just try to keep the invites to a minimum. I'm not going to be in much of a party mood."

There's a devious look in his eye that has me fighting back a scowl. If it weren't for the fact I know he just wants me to have a good time before I leave, I would have told him to call the entire thing off. But if it makes everyone else happy to get drunk in my name, I'll suck it up and drag my ass to a house party for a couple of hours.

He stands and clasps his hands together. "That's nothing a platter of Jell-O shots can't fix, Lee. But you have my word I'll be stingy with the invites. Now, let me walk you out of here for the final time. Wouldn't want you to get lost."

"Unlikely. You just don't want to say goodbye," I tease, standing and bumping his shoulder with mine.

"Damn right I don't." He shakes his head and collects his bag from the corner of the room before following me out the door.

The lights in the arena have already been dimmed, and our shoes echo through the halls as we walk. Silently, we pass the equipment room and the wall of team photos, from the first Storm team to ours this season, before coming up to Coach's office. My feet falter, and Andre pats my back.

"You want to talk to Coach?" he asks.

I exhale a loud breath and debate walking through the door. It should be an easy decision. I should go in and say goodbye. But it won't be that easy. There's a lot more I owe that man besides a simple goodbye.

"What are you two talking about out there? Spetza, you better not be here to tell me you're leaving too!"

Andre and I spin on each other, our eyes wide before Coach's brash laugh fills the hallway. I swallow and steel my spine. "Go home, Dre. I gotta do this. Friday night. I'll be there."

He nods, and we throw our arms around each other in a tight hug. After a minute, I pat his back, and we break apart.

"Text me later. See ya Friday." With that, he walks away, leaving me alone.

It takes me four steps to reach Coach's office. Banner Yaras is sitting behind a large mahogany desk with one hand around a massive cup of coffee—regardless of the time—while the other scratches his overgrown salt-and-pepper beard. He grins when he spots me in the doorway.

"Hey, Coach."

He motions toward the grey two-seater couch resting against the opposing wall and relaxes in his chair. "I was beginning to wonder if you snuck out of here without saying goodbye."

I flop down on the couch and lace my fingers behind my head, kicking my legs out. "I was debating it. Goodbye doesn't seem fitting. Not after everything you've done for me and my family."

"That was all you, kid. I just lit the fire under your ass that got you out of a slump."

"It was more than a slump, and you know it. But thank you. You have no idea how much it means to us. My mom especially. I owe you."

He swipes a hand through the air. "You can thank me by kicking ass in Vancouver. They need the help."

"Not you too. Please don't give me the 'why are you doing this' speech. My mom has laid into me enough for it."

Nobody is happy with my decision to join the Vancouver Saints and not the Ontario Rebels like I was expected to. They don't understand why I would turn down an offer to play for a more successful WHL team instead, but I don't need them to. Ontario is too far from my mother and sister, and that's that. No discussion needed on the matter.

Vancouver is going to be my home until I get drafted into the NHL. It would be easier if everyone just accepted that now instead of trying to change my mind.

"Your mom wants you to have the best chance possible. She doesn't think that's the Saints."

I narrow my eyes. "She doesn't, or you don't?"

Coach meets my stare with one of similar intensity. He's the closest thing to a father figure I've had since I was young, and I know his heart is in the right place, but that only makes his doubt more hurtful.

He releases a tight breath. "You just turned nineteen. It's this year or nothing. You wanted to wait to enter the draft until you were sure your mother could handle it, and I've always supported that idea. But we're past that now. The teams know you're eligible this draft, and I'm scared you could be throwing away your shot at the NHL with this team because you don't want to leave your family."

My stomach sinks and twists. "You're not telling me anything I don't already know. But I'm not changing my mind. I need your support here, Banner." I push a hand through my hair. "Please."

He rolls his lips, looking torn. This is a man I've had shout at me for messing up my footing during drills but also bring left-overs his wife had wrapped in tinfoil containers to my house on nights my mom had had to work late. Sure, it helped that his wife is good friends with my mom, but they didn't have to do half of the shit they've done for my family over the years.

Disappointing Banner is almost as bad as disappointing Mom.

After a few long moments, he relents. "I will always support you, Oakley. Always."

A weight lifts from my shoulders. Suddenly, I can breathe again.

The sun has just about set by the time I park outside our small two-story home in my dad's old, beat-up white Ford.

My childhood home is not grand by any means, but it's home. A small porch with scuffed wooden steps sits in the centre, in front of a bright red door that Mom painted with Dad shortly after buying the home. It's chipped and peeling now, but Mom refuses to repaint it.

A bay window sits on the right side of the house, in the middle of the living room, along with a wooden flower box that lies underneath, filled with yellow daisies.

Tilting my head back, I stare at the water pelting down from the grey, puff-filled sky and groan. It has been pouring rain ever since I left the arena, which isn't that much of a surprise. April in British Columbia is nothing but goddamn rain.

I grab my hockey bag from the passenger seat, throw it over my shoulder, and run inside. "I'm home, Ma!"

I kick my shoes off and haul ass upstairs to deposit my bag in my room before Mom catches a whiff of the smell.

After I've disposed of it, I shut my door and plop myself down on my twin bed, sinking into the worn-in shape of my body on the mattress. My long frame makes it nearly impossible to keep my feet on the narrow bed as they dangle almost comically off the edge.

I look up at my open door when my mom knocks, catching her as she leans against the frame, her arms folded and her lips tugged up.

"Hey, sweetheart. How was your day?"

My mom looks exceptionally young for her age. Maybe it has something to do with how she always has her short blonde hair done up or how her crystal-blue eyes haven't lost their sparkle over the years.

I got most of my features from my dad. Dark brown hair that swoops at the back of my neck, evergreen-coloured eyes, and long legs.

"It was alright. Hard to say goodbye, but I'll be okay."

"I would be worried if you weren't the least bit sad, honey. Goodbyes are never easy." Her eyes shine with tears before she blinks them away. "But you should also let yourself be excited. You're so close to your dreams."

She sits down on the edge of my bed and gives me one of her famous Anne Hutton smiles, her blue eyes bright. "I am so proud of you. I know your father would be too."

Mom always has a way of smiling and lifting people's spirits. Dad always called it her superpower. I didn't understand how a smile could be someone's superpower until after the crash.

Her smile was one of the few things that got me through it all. So, in my eyes, that does make her a damn superhero.

I sit up to look at her properly. "I am excited. What about you? Will you be okay? I'll try to come home as often as I can."

My promise is clear in my words, and I'll do everything in my power to keep it. My new schedule is going to be crazy, but I would do anything for my family. Even driving four hours each way just to see that damn smile on my mom's face.

She clucks her tongue against the roof of her mouth and shakes her head. "You need to stop worrying about your sister and me. You're going to get grey hairs before you make it to your twentieth birthday. We will be fine. I promise."

I frown. "Gracie is going to push you without me here. Have you seen the piece-of-shit car that's been bringing her to and from school lately? It looks like it could catch on fire if the air conditioning and the radio are on at the same time."

Mom just laughs. "It's not that bad."

"Not that bad? Mom, the exhaust is black."

She stifles her laugh behind her hand, and her eyes crinkle at the corners. "Yes, I suppose that could be an issue. Maybe you should talk to her about it."

I snort a laugh. "Right. She won't listen to me. That's a guys car. Have you noticed the tinted front windows? It screams troubled teen. Is she dating this guy? You're not going to let that happen, right? There's no way my baby sister is going to be dating a guy who can't even take care of his own car. Actually, there's no way she's ever dating. Period."

"Oakley, relax, sweetheart. You're going to blow a blood vessel. Your sister is a teenage girl who's spent her entire life under your protective wing. Let her breathe while you're gone. I promise she'll be okay. I might be small, but I'm mighty when it comes to my babies."

Some of the anger leaches from my veins, and I nod. "I'll try. But no promises. I would appreciate weekly updates regarding that boy and his . . . car. I don't think it's safe for her to be on the road in that thing."

She smiles sadly and places a hand on my forearm, squeezing it. "I will. I'll get it figured out. You're right, she shouldn't be on the road in a dangerous vehicle."

I cover her hand with mine, not liking how cold it feels. "I love you, Mom. You know that, yeah?"

"I know. There are leftover burgers in the fridge if you're hungry. I'll leave you to relax. Good night, I love you." She gives me one final squeeze before standing and heading for the door.

"Night, Mom," I mumble as she leaves.

Acknowledgements

Writing The End has never felt so bittersweet. Maddox and Braxton pushed me out of my comfort story with his one, but I am so happy with how it turned out.

Maddox is every bit Oakley's son as he is Ava's, and to everyone who has read Lucky Hit, I hope I did him justice. Writing this second-generation series has been something that I've wanted to do ever since I first wrote Lucky Hit in 2020, and the fact I am getting the chance to do so, is the best gift.

My thank you's with each book get longer and longer, so here it goes.

To my Alpha reader team, you make my life so much better. My appreciation for you is incomprehensible. Without you and your feedback and ideas, this book would be half of what it is today. Hayley, Becci, Megan, I love and adore you.

A massive thank you goes to my beta and ARC team's as well. Not only do you give me much needed feedback, but you are my biggest cheerleaders. Thank you.

To my editor, Sandra, I am blowing you kisses right now. Thank you for everything that you do.

To Jordan, my beautiful graphics guru, thank you for the gorgeous images for this book. You never fail to turn my vision into something real.

And to the Booksandmoods team, you nailed these book covers. Muah!

About The Author

Hannah is a twenty-something-year-old indie author, mom, and wife from Western Canada. Obsessed with swoon-worthy romance, she decided to take a leap and try her hand at creating stories that will have you fanning your face and giggling in the most embarrassing way possible. Hopefully, that's exactly what her stories have done!

Hannah loves to hear from her readers and can be reached on any of her social media accounts.

Instagram: @hannahcowanauthor
Twitter: @hcowanauthor
Facebook: @hannahdcowan
Facebook Group : Hannah's Hotties
Website: www.hannahcowanauthor.com

Made in United States
North Haven, CT
30 January 2023

31834737R00228